STEPHEN CHEEK was born in Kosciusko, Mississippi, in 1950.

He is a registered Landscape Architect. *Cane and Able* is his first novel.

Cane

and

Able

A Novel

Stephen Cheek

This book is fiction. Names, characters, places, and incidents are either the product of the author's imagination or used fictitiously, and resemblance to actual persons, living or died, business establishments, events, or locales is entirely coincidental.

Library of Congress Control Number

2008910663

Printed in the United States of America

Acknowledgements

My wife, Sherrie, the English teacher, is the best wife a writer could ask for. As I wrote my first drafts years ago, she was there for me supporting, even though I had horrible writing skills. To this day, she continues to critic and edits my stories with love in her heart. I accept that I will never be error free, maybe better, but never free. She knows she married someone with imagination and has accepted that. Somehow, she has found the time to allow me to continue doing something that I love.

To my three children, Corey, Megan, and Logan, who persuaded me to continue telling stories night after night, I can't thank you enough. I know now those nights were the start of this crazy writing adventure.

A special thanks to Amanda Avutu, at Wordsmith, for making me sound like a better writer than I am.

Never can I say enough about my dear high school English teacher, Sue Powers for the mountains of encouragement and painstaking time she afforded me as an advance reader and editor of *Cane and Able*.

And how can I leave out my great friend Bubba Pettit, who read *Cane and Able* in its infant stage. He fought his way through it and gave me some great advice and encouraged me to keep writing.

Cane and Able

Written by: Stephen Cheek ©2008

Some people called them Cane and Able, but to Justin, they were known as Dad and Abe. Either way, they were the two greatest men in his world and this is why.

* * * * *

One

The Hay Fields

THE END OF July was nearing in the summer of 1959 and it was hotter than a frog sitting on an asphalt parking lot. The sun was straight up and pouring every stinging ray it could muster out on to the farm below. Over in the hay fields, the field hands, some men and some high school boys were lifting hay bales that weighed sixty pounds or more and tossing them onto a slow-moving flatbed truck. The sweat was pouring down their faces, stinging their eyes and dampening their bellies. Hauling hay was a dirty job, but it was a job that had to be done. Some of the younger boys hung onto the truck's bed rail and let the truck pull them along from bale to bale. Daydreaming helped somewhat, but the monotony of what they were doing was like a death march. The old men and boys seemed to stagger along like drunks on Sunday morning but the slowness gave each time to carefully consider what they were going to do at the end of the day. The options were simple: clean up and head to the local hangout and meet girls or relax in the cool summer night on a quiet front porch swing.

Today was no different from any other day though, because the chatter of dirty talk was rolling with every bale tossed. That's how most of the younger boys learned about girl things. Somebody was always cracking a joke or saying something about a girl. All that kind of talk helped make the job bearable. And that's where Justin learned his first bad words. He said it kinda stuck to him like dirt. No doubt about it, he was learning a lot in the hay fields this summer.

Curiously, he always wondered why his dad didn't just buy the hay rather than go to all the trouble of growing and cutting that crazy grass. Justin allowed himself to imagine his father had simply plotted to ruin his summer. It was a sucking way to grow up he thought. He would much rather be swimming in a pool or fishing on a cool riverbank somewhere. Each night all he could do was daydream about a summer not ruined.

Overseeing the day-to-day operations of the farm was Able, standing 6'6," weighing about 250 pounds, and black as the ace of spades. He was as big as an oak tree. It was a sight to behold to see Able pick up and throw hay bales almost clean over the hay truck. He was the strongest man Justin knew and when Able got hot and unbuttoned his shirt, everybody could really see the same thing. Justin didn't think Goliath could have been any bigger than Able. Able also knew the Good Book. Justin didn't think he was a Sunday schoolteacher or anything like that, but Able sure could quote the Bible. Once in a while, Justin thought maybe Able made up his own scripture, but if Able said the Good Book said it, everyone believed him. Justin didn't guess he ever heard anybody disagree with Able's sayings. Of course, he figured if they did, they wouldn't live to know the difference.

Nobody ever messed with Able. The townspeople say he whipped five colored men one day when one of them whistled at a white girl. Made every one of them go apologize. The girl never knew why. That's what kind of man he was. In Justin's book, Able was everything right, just like Justin's dad.

Able had been working on the farm sixteen years. He loved his job. He said he owed everything he ever got in life to Mr. Cane. He said Mr. Cane was a good man and a tough man, a man of grit. Mr. Cane seemed to understand what it was like to be the underdog, a colored man with little education living in the South. Mr. Cane was the fairest man he had ever known. He said Mr. Cane always gave him what he needed when he went to him, no questions asked.

Able was quick to warn most of the men working on the farm that Mr. Cane could see right into their heads. He said there was no way to fool him none. "Sho' can't," he said. He said Mr. Cane was ahead of you all the time, "kinda like the Lord is." Mr. Cane seemed to know where you were going and what was on your mind before you asked. He said," you better not ever be trying to pull nothing over on Mr. Cane because he gonna catch you."

Justin called Able "Abe" and Able called him "Jussin" instead of "Justin." Justin guessed it was just easier for Able to say "Jussin." Either way, it didn't bother him none. In fact, to Justin, it was always funny listening to how Able made words come out. Of course, Justin's whole name was Justin Cane, youngest of the Cane boys.

Justin's job in the hay field was to drive the hay truck and keep it moving ever so slowly into the middle of the hay rows while everybody else tossed the hay onto the truck. He was the driver because he was only twelve and therefore too little to do anything else. The hardest part of his job was to stay awake. This was his first year to drive. In his family, a hay truck was usually the first step in learning how to drive. All his brothers learned the same way. A day didn't go by that he didn't have to listen to each one of them telling him this and telling him that. Able told him not to pay attention to his brothers. Able said Justin's brothers had a lot to learn yet themselves.

When the last bales were on the truck, Able would say, "All right boys, she's loaded. Take her to the barn, Jussin." That was Justin's signal to start turning the hay truck as gently as he could toward the pasture gate. Then Able would mount the running board and tell Justin to relax and take it easy. When time came for shifting gears, Able was right there, telling

8

Justin how to push the clutch in and where to go for the next gear. Able was a good teacher, and there was always a "keep her straight and watch the fence," as they came out of the field. A necessary warning because on the third trip to the barn today, as Justin came through the gate, he heard a big ole screech and immediately heard one of the hands holler, "Whoa now... Whoa now! Whoa now! Justin, stop! You're tearing down the gate post, boy!"

Justin was panic-stricken when he looked in the mirror and saw that he had gotten too far to one side. When he turned sharper to the right, his foot slipped off the clutch. The truck started lunging forward. It was then that he felt the truck begin to lean.

"Whoa now!" somebody shouted from the back as the first bale fell off followed by another and another. Justin looked again at the side mirror and saw that the rest of the hay was starting to shift. He knew that meant real trouble.

"Get out of the way, boys. She's coming down!" one of the hands shouted.

Justin felt that his worst fears as a new truck driver were coming true. The entire load of hay was falling off and it was his fault.

The truck sputtered a little. A puff of smoke came out from under the hood as the front end of the truck dropped into a hole. The engine died. No one said a word. Everyone just walked around looking at the hay all over the ground and the big hole that the front wheel was stuck in.

Justin wiped the sweat off his face. His hands were trembling. He couldn't control them and couldn't hold the tears back anymore either. His stomach was beginning to knot as Able came around the corner of the cab of the truck and looked in.

"Can I just go back to the house, Abe? Everybody's thinking I ain't no good."

"Hold them tears back, Jussin. It'll be all right. Anyway, we's on the homestretch to the barn now. Only a few bales fell off anyway. We'll just pick that little bit up when we come back into the field. Slide on over and let me getcha out this here sink hole."

As Able stepped up on the sideboard and grabbed for the steering wheel, the frame of the truck seemed to bend trying to carry his added weight as he pulled himself in. Justin stared in awe as the muscles in Able's arm contorted to support his weight. He gazed then fell to his own pale, thin arm and he wondered if he would ever to be that strong.

"Okay, boys, y'all push when I says to."

Able turned the key, and the motor cranked again with no problem. Then he revved the motor up one or two times on the ole truck and hollered. "Now push, everybody!"

Justin was hanging out the passenger window, praying the truck would come out before his dad saw it. Then everyone started pushing and grunting. The truck started to move a little and then a little more. Slowly she rolled out of the hole and out onto the gravel road. Able looked over at Justin who was smiling and wiping his forehead with relief.

"Man, now we can all breathe a little easier," Able said.

"Sure glad Dad didn't see that, Abe."

"Oh, it'll be all right, Jussin. That old gate is wore out anyway. You just done it a favor by putting it out of its misery. Your brothers done hit that thing a hundred times."

Justin sat a little taller in his seat again feeling satisfied his so-called mistake was not as bad as it seemed. As they drove off, the field hands pulled the broken gate aside and leaned it up against the fence. Able got out and looked back at the fence and said, "Jussin, you get back under the wheel now. You'll be alright."

Justin didn't want to, but he slipped back under the wheel. The truck never stopped moving. Justin looked again in the mirror and could see the others gesturing with their hands how the hay was hanging on the truck. He heard one of the hands say, "There ain't twenty bales left on the truck. Why we going to the barn?" After that, Justin saw Able go back to the rear of the truck pointing his finger. He couldn't hear what he was saying but his face got all screwed up and them men were quiet from there to the barn.

As they approached the hay barn, Able told Justin to turn and back the truck in. Justin wondered why his Dad hadn't built a barn that they could just drive straight through. All that backing up was for the birds. Somebody wasn't thinking, he guessed.

"Darn it! Sh....! Crap! I can't ever make it the first time," Justin mumbled.

After several tries and a lot of hooting from his brothers, Justin managed to get the truck backed in the right direction. No doubt about it, this was the second hardest part of driving the hay truck. After the truck finally got situated, Able told the men to unload the truck.

"That's it. Unload 'em, boys. Jussin, run down there by the tree and get you some water and cool off."

There was a water hydrant sticking out of the ground right under a big oak tree right beside the old farm tenant house where everybody stopped and drank from between loads. The old three-room house, with a long front porch across the front, was only used to store fencing materials and seed now. Able's granddaddy, Jake Johnson, lived and raised his family there while working the cotton fields for Mr. Cane's daddy, Dewey Cane. Jake Johnson worked for Mr. Dewy Cane until he had a sudden heart attack and died when he was just twenty-nine years old. Mr. Dewy Cane continued letting the family live on the farm until Jake's wife, who no one knew was with child, unexpectedly up and decided to move to Belzoni to be closer to her kin. Mr. Dewey continued to check on them from time to time and even played a big part in helping Pearl, the oldest of Jake's three girls, get her college education. He would have done the same for the other two, Dorothy and Candy, if they had wanted to, but they married early and didn't go. Some say Mr. Dewey Cane watched out for Jake's family as much as he did is own.

* * * * *

12

Two

The Accident

ABLE LOWERED HIS head, pursed his lips and said, "Don't want you burning out on me, Jussin. And you need to wash your mouth out too. Think I heard something back there I didn't like hearing." Justin knew what Able was talking about but also knew Able was watching out for him. His dad's last words every morning were, "Able, don't let Justin get hot, now."

Able would always reply, "Oh, no, sir, Mr. Cane, I won't. He'll be all right with me."

That's why Justin liked Able so much. He knew he'd kept his promises.

Now, in every group of working men, there is always one sorry old soul who you wondered how he even made it to work each day. Old Pete was the sorry soul here. Justin didn't know why his dad hired him or kept him around. He didn't even call his dad "Mr. Cane," like the other men, just called him "Cane" for some reason. Able told Justin he just wouldn't understand, but Pete used to be a real decent man and still was down deep. In fact, he said Pete was smarter than most men knew. The problem was that he had been down on his luck for a long time. Justin never had the courage to ask Pete where he was from or what happened to make him be so sorry, but he surely wanted to ask.

Pete didn't speak much to anybody. He kind of kept to himself and passed his time whittling. To Justin, it was hard to speak to somebody who wouldn't speak back, and ole Pete had a habit of doing just that. He also had a habit of drinking, too. Some of the men talked about the fact that he had something heavy on his mind, but nobody could really say for sure what that something was. All Justin knew about Pete was that when Able left work, Pete was with him and when he came back to work the next day, Pete was with him too. Another thing Justin noticed about ole Pete was that for lunch each day he always brought a pork chop sandwich in a brown paper bag, which wasn't so weird. What *was* weird was that he never drank anything until he'd finished eating. That drove Justin crazy. An old pork chop sandwich smelled good, he supposed, but he couldn't understand how somebody could eat a pork chop sandwich and not break every tooth in his head. Justin got up the nerve and asked him about it one time. And boy did it burn him when Pete didn't say anything.

As strange as Pete was, one thing about him was that he knew snakes. One time he saw a snake and told Justin that a snake could tell him whether it would rain or not. Justin didn't believe him at first. But after Pete stared hard at the snake for a minute, said a few words and then poked it a little, the snake got good and mad, slithering off really fast. Pete explained to Justin that the direction the snake went told him what the weather was going to do. Justin couldn't ever figure that out. He guessed Pete was telling the truth because one day he saw two chicken snakes running the same way, and Pete said it was going to rain for two days.

"Why's that, Pete?" Justin asked.

"Because s-s- snakes they are running back to back. If they runs back to back, it means it's gonna rain back to back for t-t-two days." Pete muttered to no one in particular.

It did, too, just like Pete said and Justin loved it! Rain to a hay hand means no work that day. Rain days were special. Most of the time the summer rain just blew in quickly with little or no warning. Sometimes it went right around them. Other times the rain stopped across the road. Justin hadn't figured that one out yet, but figured Pete knew the answer if he could just get him to talk. One thing about those rains though, it was sure a letdown when they did stop at the road.

One morning when they had made it to the barn, Pete saw a chicken snake coiled on a bale of hay. Pete was poking it when all of a sudden he ran out of the barn rambling on about how something bad was going to happen. He said the snake looked him in the eyes and spoke to him. Justin had never seen a colored man turn so white as Pete did that day. The next morning Able said he had some bad news to tell all the hands. Pete's boy had been hit by a train in Detroit and killed. Word was that the boy was apparently crossing the track and somehow hung his foot between the rails.

Justin didn't know what to think, but the old colored men insisted that it all sounded like a curse of "Voodoo." Of course, they were all superstitious to start with. Anyway, to Justin, it was spooky hearing them talk about crazy things like sticking pins in dolls, spells and victims' eyes turning red as fire coals.

That afternoon after work, Justin saw Pete talking to his dad on their front porch. Justin had never seen Pete's mouth working so quickly. Justin figured Pete must have been asking his dad for money because he heard him tell Pete that he would lend him whatever he needed for the trip to Detroit. His dad asked Pete when he wanted to leave, and Pete said that the next day would probably be best. As the two casually stood on the porch talking, the orange sun fell behind the trees until darkness consumed the air. Mr. Cane patted Pete on the shoulder as he turned and walked back to the truck where Able was watching fireflies begin lighting up the twilight. As the half-moon took the place of the sun, they drove off with the crackle of gravel echoing across the pasture.

Cane and Able

The next morning the "Big Eye," as Able called it, came up and started shining through Justin's bedroom window warming his sheets and hitting him directly in the eyes. Justin pulled the covers over his head, trying to block out not only the sun, but the thought of working. He was wishing he could be anywhere besides the blistering hay field that day. He so much wanted to get away to a friend's house, maybe hang out on their bikes all day and go to the picture show or something. Anything would be better than another day of work on the farm.

It wasn't long until Justin heard the familiar footsteps of his dad and the sound of his knuckles rapping on the door to tell him to get up. That tapping noise drove Justin crazy. His dad usually wouldn't stop until Justin spoke back to him, indicating that he was awake. After his dad left his door he would go down the hall and rap on the William's door and then Bud's. Justin could hear each brother holler back to his dad to go on, that they were awake. After putting his pants on, Justin struggled down the stairs to the kitchen, found his seat around the breakfast table with his brothers, and started eating a big Southern breakfast of scrambled eggs, country ham, red-eye gravy and biscuits. Very few words were ever said between the brothers because everyone was still half a sleep. Hair sticking straight up, T-shirts on backward, and belts undone were a common sight. School would be a relief some mornings, Justin figured.

This morning was different in that Justin was thinking hard on how he could get out of work when he heard the sound of tires on the gravel road, a sign that Able and Pete were getting to work.

After the Cane boys finished eating, they all filed out the front door, walking towards the barn, the "meeting-up-place" for announcements of the day's duties.   All of a sudden, for no apparent reason, Justin started running to be the first one there.

" Bud, you and William go on and start back to raking and baling from where you had left off yesterday," Able said, pulling a pair of worn leather gloves from his back pocket and pulling the first one on. "Mr. Cane will be here in a minute now, so get to hustling everybody." Then he told the rest of the hands they needed to finish unloading the last load from the day before. In about ten minutes, Mr. Cane drove up and called Able to the side, but he first waited for the other hands to clear away.

Able, "I need you to carry Pete to the train station in Yazoo City." Able looked over at Justin peeping around the corner of the barn. Justin had already told Able that he had heard his dad and Pete talking about Detroit. If Able was going, Justin wanted to go too. He was just waiting on Able to bring the thought to his dad.

"Mr. Cane, reck'in it will be okay if little Jussin goes with me?" Able asked, knowing the answer would eventually be 'yes.' He rubbed his eye as if something small and bothersome had gotten stuck in it. Then, he glanced quickly over at Justin as if to say, *get ready*.

"I don't know, Able," Mr. Cane said. "Justin's got a lot to do around here. He's still learning, you know. We're not through with the hay yet, and anyway, he's liable to get in your way."

"Oh no, Mr. Cane, he sho' won't be in the way now." Able motioned with his eyes for Justin to hurry up and get out there. "In fact, he'll keep me company coming back."

"Can I go, Dad?" Justin blurted out, giving away his hiding spot.

"What about your work, Justin?" Mr. Cane asked. His eyebrow raised letting Justin know that he'd noticed the boy had been eaves dropping but that he was letting it slide.

"It'll be here when we get back. I promise it ain't going nowhere, Dad."

Mr. Cane looked at Able and laughed, "I guess you're right about that. Oh, I guess it'll be okay, but don't you be getting in Able's way now, Justin."

No hay field today! he thought, his mind racing with thoughts of all the adventure the day might have in store for him.

"I won't, Dad, I promise."

"Oh, no, sir, Mr. Cane. Jussin ain't going be in my way at all." Then Able paused and looked at the ground. "Huh, now how's we goin', Mr. Cane? You done figured that out?" Able glanced sheepishly at Mr. Cane's new blue Ford pickup truck parked in the drive.

"We can take the new Ford truck, Abe," Justin offered.

"Oh . . . now wait a minute," said Mr. Cane. "That's my new truck, and I don't need y'all messing it up for me before I get a chance to break it in good."

"Now think about it, Mr. Cane, we sho' don't need to get stuck on the side of the road somewhere, broke down in Ole Red, especially with little Jussin with us. That pickup just ain't what she used to be," Able said glancing upward at Mr. Cane.

Mr. Cane glanced down the driveway past his crops to where the sun was pulling itself up over the road. "I swear this is a setup. You two are going to put me in my grave. Okay, then y'all take it, but, Able, if you so much as put one little scratch on that truck, you might as well not come back."

"Oh now, Mr. Cane," Able said, walking over to the truck hood. " It'll be just as shiny and new as it is now...we just going to break it in a little," with that, he stretched his hand out in slow motion as if he were polishing the hood gently. "I promise. We gonna go right there and right back. We be back here before you miss us good."

"I'm more worried about the breaking-in part. No more than fifty miles per hour for the first three hundred miles is what the dealer told me. So you keep it under that. Do you understand?"

Able walked to the new pickup and peeped in to see if the keys where there. He turned around and saw Mr. Cane holding the keys in his hand. Reluctantly, Mr. Cane handed the keys to him and began again. "Now, Able . . ."

Laughing, Able gently cut him off holding up his palms in mock defeat.

"I know Mr. Cane, one scratch, fifty miles per hour," Able finished for him. Able spotted Pete off in the distance. He held up his arm and shook the truck keys. Pete got the message and walked briskly towards the truck. It was understood all around, a ride in the new truck would be a mighty fine ride. None of them wanted to risk spending another moment hanging around, giving Mr. Cane a chance to change his mind.

"Justin, you go give your mom a good hug before you go," his dad told him.

As Justin ran towards the front steps, Able said, "Tell Mrs. Kate I's gonna take care of you now, Jussin."

"I will."

With those words Mr. Cane realized he was watching his youngest son depart the farm for the first time without the supervision of his mother or father. The last of his boys was growing up right before his eyes.

Justin jumped up the steps onto the front porch and ran through the house, hollering and looking for his mom. The first thing she said when she saw him was that he should tie his laces before he broke his neck. Justin gave her a quick peck on the cheek, promised her he'd tie them in the truck and took off. In no time, he was back with his baseball cap perched on his head ready to go.

"That was fast, Jussin," Able said.

"Don't take me long. I'm ready," Justin was panting from running so hard.

Able opened the door on the driver's side, giving Justin time to scramble under his arm and slide over to the other side. They both caught the smell of the new seats. It had been a while since that smell had been around the Cane farm.

Pete walked slowly around the truck, looking at it carefully. Then he opened the door and started to get in. Justin turned around when the passenger door opened. He couldn't believe his eyes. Ole Pete was dressed up like a preacher. He never knew Pete could look so respectful. He had even shaved. Then Justin realized he had on one of his dad's Sunday ties with his dad's coat over his arm. Even the suitcase looked familiar.

Pete gently set the suitcase in the back. Justin nearly said something about the suitcase but stopped himself short. He didn't want to embarrass Pete.

Mr. Cane pulled out his billfold and handed Able ten dollars, telling him once more to be careful and that he'd better take care of that truck. "Y'all don't mess around getting over there now," he said. "And one more thing, Able. Did you get that tag on good?"

"Oh, yes, sir," Able answered.

"Now you know that the train leaves at 12:00 noon, Able," Mr. Cane looked Able right in the eyes. "Don't miss it," he said.

They backed out of the drive, Justin sandwiched between Able and Pete. Pete took the window because he smoked those "roll your own" cigarettes. Justin hated those things. Justin didn't know whether Pete could drive or not. He thought, if he could, nobody would want to ride with him because he drank a lot. Justin could smell it on his breath every day. Able said the drinking had something to do with that snake speaking to him.

As the threesome drove away, Mr. Cane put his arm around his wife's slim waist. They watched from the front porch, waving 'bye. Mrs. Kate, twitching and holding on to the ties on her apron, was wondering if she would ever see her baby again; Mr. Cane was wondering if he would ever see his new truck again.

* * * * *

Three

Last Night Out

IT WAS MAY just after graduation in 1959 and standing outside Moffet's Country Store, Jeanna waited for her friend, Rob, to come out. She was a striking girl with sharp facial features, a sure sign of white genes emerging from her roots. Simply put, she was pretty and she knew it. She could get just about anything she wanted if she asked for it. As is the curse of a pretty girl who knows it, other girls didn't like her too much. Jeanna wasn't a bad girl, she was good hearted but she did have one or two little mischievous streaks in her bones and she got those honestly. Pretty much she toyed with the boys so as far as it got her what she wanted and in the end told them where to get off the boat. Her girlfriends knew she was playing with the boys and that she would never cross the line. All-in-all it was Jeanna's way of having fun. She always made Rob carry her books as they walked to and from school each day but those days were over now and Rob was trying to earn money to go to college. Jeanna, on the other hand wanted a break from school. She told her Aunt that she needed a break from the books and wanted to work a spell before she took on the role of a college girl. Rob was more willing to accept the reality of life and was eager to get all the schooling he could before his time ran out. Education was most important to him and he tried to persuade Jeanna that she should go on to college too, but Jeanna would have no part of that. For right now, Jeanna was just wanting to be on her own, do some things her way and have time to sort some things out. At least that was what she told Aunt Pearl. Aunt Pearl and Able hoped she knew what she was doing. Today, however, Jeanna was going to try one more time to twist Rob's little ear until she got what she wanted.

"Jeanna, what are you doing here? I thought you were gone to the big city for fame and fortune?" Rob said jokingly.

"Shut up, Rob, that's not funny at all. You know I can't go without money. I've been promised a job in New Orleans, but I can't get there without a ticket. I can't get any kind of a decent job around here in this dirt blown God-forsaken town. I should have been a boy!" Jeanna faked a sniffle.

Rob could see it coming.

"Surely, you can find *something*, Jeanna." he said, almost pleading. Even though he could see it coming, he knew there wasn't that much he could do to resist her.

"You know I can't, Rob. What is there for me to do… hoe cotton? I am not goin' down that road. Remember I got a high school diploma and I'm not goin' to the fields again in my life." She allowed herself to get worked up before she paused and turned her back to him. Just as she was about to walk away, Rob stopped her.

"Have you asked your brother, for money?" He inquired desperately.

"No way. He'd tell Aunt Pearl and then she'd be all over me. She's still mad at me for not going to college this fall."

Rob sighed, looked down at his worn shoes and asked the one question he knew he shouldn't ask. "How much you need, Jeanna?"

"Rob, I need a lot," she paused, gauging his response, "pay it back by Christmas," she finished.

"How much, Jeanna. Just tell me," Rob asked impatiently.

"I need a hundred and fifty dollars," she responded while staring hard at the crack in the sidewalk. Even without looking, she could tell his mouth was wide open and that he was about to let her have it.

"My gosh, Jeanna! What you gonna do with all that money?"

"First, I've got to have a ticket. That's one. Two, I've got to have some new shoes. Three, I've got to have two new dresses. You see, I've got a waitress job." She said, as if that would make sense of it all. Rob, just watched her count letting her get all the way to ten before telling her to stop.

"Look, Jeanna. I've got three hundred-sixteen dollars saved up for college and I need twice that much. Do you know what I've done without to get that money and how hard I've worked? No colored boy around here got that kind of money saved up." Now Rob was worked up. He paused and backed up trying to walk away from her. "Okay, Jeanna, if I let you have the hundred and fifty dollars, do you swear I'm gonna get it back before Christmas?"

What else could Jeanna say? "Of course, Rob. You know I'll get it back, every last dime." She was smiling inside.

Rob shuffled his feet looking down at his dusty shoes and finally gave in. "Okay then, I'll go on home and get it for you." Then Rob paused looking somewhat pitiful. "Look, do you think we can go out tonight?" he asked, thinking if ever she'd say 'yes,' now was the time.

Jeanna didn't hesitate, "Can't tonight, Rob. I've got to pack. I'm leaving tomorrow."

Rob shook his head and began the long walk home leaving Jeanna standing in front of the store.

Jeanna nervously paced the sidewalk for at least an hour until she saw Rob slowly returning up the road as he promised with a sack in hand. Running towards him, Jeanna welcomed him with a big kiss on the cheek and immediately stuck her hand out. "Is that it?"

"Yeah, this is it." Rob slowly opened the sack and counted the money out into Jeanna's hand. "Now, Jeanna…"

Before he could finish, Jeanna stuffed the money in her purse, gave him another swift kiss on the cheek, and reminded him that she needed to hurry home and start packing. So off she went with Rob standing in his tracks with an empty bag in his hand, watching as she turned the corner out of sight.

Well, the packing didn't take long because she had so little, but she knew too that would be different as soon as she got to New Orleans.

Standing in front of her small suitcase with her mind racing, she suddenly heard a knock at the door and was almost startled when two of her classmates came barging in her bedroom. They wanted her to join them for a night out on the town at the Club 45.

By now she had already mapped out in her mind her plans for this next day. She would get up by five o'clock, walk to the bus station, buy a ticket, and be New Orleans bound by eight o'clock. However, with an intermittent plan such as a long night out with the girls, would definitely pose a problem. But fellowshipping with friends before leaving town didn't sound too bad either. Justifying her decision, she figured she had worked hard to graduate and she deserved a good last night out, but only on the terms that they wouldn't stay late. Reluctantly, she agreed and grabbed her purse, fat with money Rob had just lent her.

As one would imagine, as the evening came they found themselves having a good time and time did slip by without notice. The girls were pretty much taken care of all night for any drinks by all the boys at the club and they never had to pull out money for anything, unless Jeanna offered to pay with her roll of cash. However, when time came to go, Jeanna could not find her purse. Someone had apparently stolen it along with all her money she had borrowed. She was terrified. All at once she felt as if she had been thrust into an abyss. All of her hopes were gone. How was she going to get to New Orleans to her new job now? How was she going to tell Rob? He had to have his money for college before Christmas. How could she have been so stupid? She knew better and was smarter than that, but asking her big brother Able or Aunt Pearl was out of the question. She would do anything but that.

Jeanna walked outside and sat on the curb while her friend went to find the club owner. As soon as she sat, she broke down and started sobbing desperately. As she wiped away her tears, she noticed a tall guy with his hat cocked to one side. For being half drunk he was trying his best to be as suave as he could. He had a cigarette in one hand and a beer in the other. She looked at him disgusted but when he asked her what was the matter she decided for some reason to explain what had happened. To her surprise the guy listened patiently before telling her he thought he could help her with her problem. As she rambled on about how she just had to get the money back, she didn't notice the guy looking over at a parked green Cadillac and then signaling with a nod.

Four

Yazoo City

ABLE, JUSTIN and Pete headed up the farm's dirt road enjoying the first mile in a brand new truck. It had now been several months with no word from Jeanna and Able was beginning to worry. She was always in the back of his mind.

No sooner than the three pulled onto the highway Able started explaining everything he knew about the town of Yazoo City. He told Justin that Yazoo City was a big town. Over four thousand people lived there, not counting the colored folks. This was the Delta everybody had always talked about. In the summer time, he told Justin, that dust flies up, creating whirlwinds a hundred feet tall. Able said it looks like big clouds of smoke, almost like tornadoes when the huge tractors plow up the fields. Sometimes it even looks like the high school marching band at a football game, only using tractors instead of people. Justin told Abe he bet he could learn to drive one of them big tractors if they had one on the farm.

"Well, if Mr. Cane ever gets one that big, Jussin, I bet you can too, and I gonna teach you how."

He reminded Justin that they were from hill country though. "We's kinda like hillbillies to Delta people, Jussin. The people in the Delta got money running out their ears. Some of them farmers got over five thousand acres in land and got houses as big as the County courthouse."

Justin couldn't believe people were that rich. He listened closely as Able told him some of the farmers had houses on both sides of the Mississippi River. Able told him that on River Road, most of the antebellum homes were three and four stories tall and unscathed by the Civil War because the Yankees claimed they were too beautiful to burn. He gestured that the oak trees lining the driveways were as big as the redwood trees in California.

As they drove down the road, Justin was having a hard time seeing out the windows at everything Able was pointing out. Pete kept telling Justin to stop squirming so much, but Justin didn't want to miss anything. Pete told Justin he couldn't enjoy his cigarettes with him leaning over in his lap.   Pete didn't need to smoke them old ugly "roll your owns" anyway, Justin thought.

"Able, reckon we can drive over and look at some of them big houses on the River Road you been talking about before we go back?" Justin asked.

"I suppose so, but we gotta get Pete to the depot first. Can't miss that train. Won't be another one coming till tomorrow."

Pete said, "Y'all b-b-better call Cane before y'all s-s-strike out somewhere. He may want you to come straight back to the house."

"Oh, we gonna do that all right," said Able. "Sure wouldn't do nothing like that without calling Mr. Cane first. Sho' wouldn't."

As they entered Yazoo City, the first thing Justin noticed were the streetlights. In their little town of Friendly, there were only three, all in a row. In Justin's mind this place was huge compared to Friendly. Yazoo City had paved roads running both ways with some streets made of brick. With a French influence, light posts adorned mainstreet. Most storefronts had colorful signs with one or two wrought iron benches located in front for old timers to sit on. According to Pete, business had to be good because people were shopping everywhere. The curious thing to Justin was that people seemed more dressed up than they did in Friendly. To him it looked, as if, everyone was going to church.

"Able, this is just like you said. Gee, this is great!" Justin said.

"I told you so, didn't I tell you so?" Able said, nudging Justin in the side with his elbow repeatedly. Pete was grinning too, watching Justin looking from side to side out each window.

"You sure did! Look at all the cars and people! Look at the houses. Look how many stores they got, Able," Justin said pointing in front of Pete's cigarette.

"Shoot, ain't no telling how many stores this town got. Probably got fifty," Able said.

"It's got at least that m-m-many." Pete took a drag off his ugly cigarette and blew a smoke ring. Justin looked over at Pete's mouth forgetting about everything momentarily, for he was impressed on how Pete could make smoke do that.

This was even better than Justin imagined. He had never been in a city like this before. Pete told Justin and Able to stop looking and talking so much and look for that train station. The streets were so busy that cars and trucks were cutting in and out of traffic with no regard, and that was getting Able a little nervous and frustrated. Able had to swerve several times to keep from having a wreck, including one time when a little lady ran a stop sign. That one was so close he had to throw the brakes on to keep from hitting her broadside. He stomped his brakes so hard that Pete dropped his matches all over the floorboard and the force threw Justin towards the dashboard. Luckily, Pete grabbed Justin by the belt. Justin wasn't hurt none, but Able sure was mad at that woman.

"Two more blocks and a stop light and we'll be there, Pete. I can see it coming up ahead now," Able said. "Do y'all see all these crazy fools over here? I tell you what. You couldn't pay me enough money to live in a big city like this. No, sir, sho' couldn't. I'll take Friendly any day."

The dust-covered red brick building with a slate roof was as typical as any depot in the delta. Bricks laid in a herringbone pattern made up the uneven sidewalks that cut a path to the building. Several people had already gathered to wait for the train. Able downshifted the new Ford pickup and coasted into the graveled depot parking lot, resting the truck's front tires against one of twenty or so crossties lining the perimeter. When the truck came to a rest, he cut the engine, looked to his left and pointed up the track.

"That train be coming down that track in about fifteen minutes, Jussin. You ever seen a penny smushed?"

"Sho ain't, Abe."

Able reached in his pocket and thumbed through his change. Amongst the dirt in his pocket was a knife, two quarters, a rabbit's foot, and a dime. Then he found a penny. Before he thought twice, he said, "Take this penny and run out there and put it on top of that track." As soon as the words rolled over his lips he knew he had embarrassed himself in front of Pete.

"No kidding?" Justin said, trying to climb over Pete, who was now staring at his hands.

"Don't you go near that track, Boy," Pete spoke forcefully and pushed Justin back. "Ain't nobody going to play on no train track." Justin looked at Able, and Able looked at Justin.

Pete got out, walked around back and got his suitcase. He returned to the window and looked inside at Able and Justin sitting there saying nothing, then walked over to the track. He reached in his pocket and placed a penny on the track, then slowly walked back to the truck.

"Able, after y'all get b-b-back from looking at them houses, come back and get t-t-that penny for Justin. You see where I put it, don't you?"

"Oh, yeah, I see right where you put it, Pete," Able answered.

"Jussin, keep your tail in the truck. Don't you go near that track," Pete said.

That was the first time Pete ever talked to Justin or Able like he had good sense. Come to think of it, this was the first time Justin recalled not smelling whiskey on his breath.

"Don't forget to c-c- call Cane now, Able." Then Pete walked off.

Justin kinda waved bye but he was more glad to see Pete get out. Pete wasn't any fun. Able reached down and cranked the truck. "Man, don't that sound good? Listen to that motor purr," Able said. Able turned his head to one side as if listening to each cylinder hit. With the approval of the sound, he put it in reverse and backed up.

When they got back on the road, Justin looked through the back glass and saw Pete somewhat bent over his suitcase with one foot perched on top of it. He had a serious look on his face as he stood there rolling another cigarette. There was no way to tell what was on the old timer's mind, but Justin knew he was looking at a mighty broken-hearted man.

* * * * *

Five

The Business

THE GREAT SOUTHERN Railroad ran the 800-mile trip from Chicago to New Orleans every other day. The train kept pretty much on schedule. It departed Chicago around 6:30 a.m., arriving in New Orleans approximately twenty-two hours later. The only three major stopovers were in St. Louis, Memphis and Yazoo City.

The train was usually packed leaving Chicago but lost at least twenty-five percent of the fares after leaving Memphis on its way to New Orleans. Going up line, it worked in reverse.

For a number of years, the fares had been increasing in the summer months and with school out, many families were taking summer vacations.

Their favorite choice was always New Orleans. The city was known for the blues, and everyone wanted to hear that good music. The blues were especially popular with colored people. Money was always short for them though. Listening to the blues was a way for them to enjoy themselves and forget the real world. In reality, the blues was nothing more than a poor man's jazz band, a collision of African and European cultures. Many of the Negro families dropped their kids off with aunts and uncles and grandparents in small Delta towns and then made the trip on down by themselves. Often, the men left their wives behind and went alone, saying they were going to experience the blues and enjoy a few days of gambling with the boys.

Like most things, the blues scene had a downside. Prostitution and bootlegging were high-dollar moneymakers around the top hangouts. Memphis and New Orleans were where the biggest blues and jazz performers like Johnny Lee Hooker and the flamboyant Guitar Slim were gathering. Rich Northern whites and coloreds, along with poor Southern coloreds, exchanged money for women like exchanging money for poker chips. Prostitution was big business, really big business. The people came, and the money flowed. The demand for prostitutes and bootleg whiskey was becoming greater, and the supply was becoming shorter. To fill the void, bar owners made deals with hoodlums in small Mississippi towns to supply young colored girls and bootlegged whiskey on demand. Many bar owners even searched across state lines to fill their needs. A smalltime local thug could make $1500 a week. To fill the demand, many girls were being kidnapped and forced into prostitution. The refusal to go along often meant death.

Even though they first resisted and had to be tied and stowed away for weeks or months, many girls later chose to stay in the business because of the money associated with it. Other girls committed suicide because of the guilt. Most of the girls were thrust into the business as young teenagers. Some were only fifteen years old. It was not uncommon for a young girl to be missing for months, only to be found dead later. Some were discovered drowned in a local creek; others on a lonely gravel road with their throats cut. Since all the law officials were white, it really didn't matter to them. No attempt was made to investigate. No one was ever arrested. Another dead colored was just that, another dead colored.

With the Memphis demand pulling from one direction and the New Orleans demand pulling from the other, new-sprung businessmen were getting rich. Regardless of the nature or size of the order, the request would be filled quickly and completely.

Tucked away from the mainstream and out of the spotlight of any major city was a big name supplier of prostitutes. He was called Big Doug. His operation was in Belzoni, Mississippi. Since Belzoni was located halfway between Memphis and New Orleans, it was the perfect location for sending girls and booze up and down the rail. Big Doug controlled as many as fifty girls. His hideout for stowaways was a Victorian home in Natchez. For the runaways, Big Doug used a rundown shack on a back road in Humphrey County.

To him, a girl's life meant no more than a rat's. He could kill one as easily as the other. Big Doug had already spent five years in the Mississippi Parchman Penitentiary for second-degree murder. That time a girl came up missing after many witnessed Big Doug and her arguing outside a nightclub. She was only eighteen. Big Doug knew a pretty young teen like her would bring double the money if he could bring her into the prostitution ring. Big Doug's lawyer said she ran away because of her abusive stepfather. The truth was that Doug had thrown her off the Yazoo River Bridge with a 300-pound car axle tied to her feet. She was never found. Girls paid big if they didn't do what Big Doug said.

Big Doug had his business the way he wanted it. He controlled everything. His size, weight, and reputation ensured that nobody crossed him.

How was Jeanna to know whom she had encountered? She had just turned eighteen. After the cool-cat guy with the tilted hat came across from the parking lot, he invited Big Doug to come over and introduce himself. Jeanna didn't have a clue as to who Big Doug was and didn't really give a flip. All she was worried about was the $150 dollars. She figured she would treat him just like all the other boys, string'em along. With few words, Big Doug said he would lend her what she needed and reached into his pocket and pulled out a roll of money. He peeled $150 dollars off the roll, leaving plenty more. He told her to pay Rob his money and return to the club the next night. She explained that she needed to be on the train to New Orleans the next day. After Big Doug asked her where she would get the money for a ticket, he let her stand in silence. Then he told her that he would lend her the extra money, but she would have to miss that train and catch the one the following day. The answer was not what she wanted, but any plan for New Orleans sounded better than no plan at all.

Jeanna dropped off Rob's money at his house while he was at work the next day with a note explaining that she appreciated the loan but she had changed her mind. On her way back home she had a funny feeling about the night coming and her next meeting with Big Doug. She realized she knew nothing about him. If only she had her mother to talk to. As Jeanna tried to push away the nagging feeling she was having, she recalled years before when she found out that her boyfriend was messing around her. Her heart broke so bad she couldn't go to school. That night she was sobbing in bed, not knowing her mother could hear her. Later her mother came in her dark room and sit on the edge of the bed. They talked for hours and she felt so much better the next morning. That was one thing she remembered so vividly about her mom. She just had a way of bringing a peace to her. There were other times, too.

Once, she had stolen some candy from Moffet's store and felt so bad about it later. It had gotten to point where she couldn't sleep. Finally, she confided in her mom. Even though she was punished and had to go back to face Mr. Moffet, her mother stood right there with her. "If you want me to be wrong," her mother said, "then go do something wrong. I'll never turn my back on you. Never!"

Her thoughts went back to Big Doug and she couldn't help but feel like she had done something wrong. For a minute she thought maybe she should have gone on and told Rob the truth rather than hiding it. Well, anyway, she figured, she'd be on that train headed to New Orleans soon. What was done was done.

Jeanna caught a ride to the Club and was almost surprised to find Big Doug waiting on her. Feeling out the dark, smoke-filled room, she let her eyes rest on a young girl wearing a cute skirt and blouse. She walked over and asked to sit down at her table and the girl nodded 'okay' as the girl sipped her beer. As the conversation began, the girl asked Jeanna who she was meeting and Jeanna said the big guy in the corner. Jeanna asked who she was and the girl replied that she wasn't from around there, just passing through. Jeanna didn't want to pry, even though she was curious. Maybe she had kin that she knew? Before Jeanna could ask, the girl whispered over her bottle top, "don't get messed up with Big Doug. Leave now and don't come back." But just as the girl had begun speaking, Big Doug had dropped a coin into the jukebox, the music drowning out the entire message. Jeanna nodded at the girl, though she had no clue the warning she'd just been given.

"What kind of beer you want?" came a voice from behind her. Jeanna jumped when she heard the voice, still trying to take in what the girl said.

"Huh, Coke," Jeanna making eye contact with Big Doug across the room. "All I want is a Coke."

The waiter turned and walked back to the bar as Jeanna's face grew pale.

"What did you say?" Jeanna asked the girl immediately as the man walked away.

"Can't, here he comes." Big Doug started moving towards the table with Cool-Cat beside him. Cool-Cat reached for the other girl, and she stood up and walked away with him, glancing back over her shoulder at Jeanna.

"Who was that?" Jeanna, throwing the question to Big Doug.

"Nobody important, just a friend of a friend you might say." There was a pause as the records changed. In the music's lull, conversations rose from the tables, bottles clanked, and for a moment Jeanna felt as if she'd been nervous for nothing.

"Oh, I see. Well, here I am, just like I said I would be," Jeanna said, smiling.

"Yes, I sees you are," replied Big Doug in a deep gravel voice.

"Well...what did you want?" Jeanna said pointedly. "You said you would lend me more money for a ticket to New Orleans, right?"

"Humm-huh. Sho did. Didn't I?" Big Doug smiling and puffing on his cigar. " I think that can be arranged." Big Doug nodding and looking down at her cleavage, which she quickly lifted her hand up to cover. He was really starting to give her the creeps.

"When you say you wanted to go to New Orleans?" Big Doug asked.

43

"I'm leaving tomorrow. Don't you remember our conversation?" she said. "Positively, tomorrow."

For a minute Big Doug didn't consider the sound of such a forceful answer from a young female. It was a definite sign of no respect.

"How you gonna pay me back?" he said, smirking.

"Well, it may take a while but I'll get you every dime. I'm an honest person. Do you know my brother Able Johnson?" Jeanna tried to throw his name in hoping he knew how big he was.

"Naw, sho don't." Jeanna didn't like that answer at all.

"What if I give you a job? A job where you can make some *real* money." Big Doug said.

"Like what?" she said, thinking, "I'm not sure. I got a job when I get to New Orleans. I'm going to be a waitress. I don't think I have time for another job," Jeanna said, acting naive the best she could and only wanting out of there without committing to anything.

"Look, Miss Johnson, I's give you the money and I'll see that you gets a way to New Orleans. How's that?" Doug responded a little agitated.

"Tomorrow," Jeanna stated firmly, interrupting him.

"Yeah, tomorrow. I's have Slim carry you down. He's going anyway. That might save you some money. You gots a place to stay?"

"I think so," she said, almost hesitant, but realizing the money she would save with Cool-Cat Slim carrying her down would certainly afford her a place to stay until she found a place.

"Okay then, Slim will pick you up tomorrow." By now, Cool-Cat Slim had reentered the room without the girl he left with and Big Doug motioned for him to come over to the table.

"Miss Johnson, tell Slim where to pick you up."

"When do I get the money?" she asked.

"Now's, if you want it. How much?" Big Doug said, reaching back in his pocket as Slim looked on.

"Two hundred will do." It was no use in getting to far in debt, she thought, but the extra fifty would help.

"Big Doug peeled two-hundred off the top and dropped it on the table and walked away, but not before giving Jeanna a long stare.

* * * * *

Six

River Road

AS PETE WAS reaching for the handrail to board the train, he noticed two young women ahead of him getting on the train too. Probably in their teens, both looked worried and somewhat frightened. Strangely, they were dressed expensively for colored women from those parts. Too expensively, he though. They were speaking softly and looking back over their shoulders as if hiding something. Just then Pete heard a horn blow and turned around just in time to see a green Cadillac pull off. The girls got real quiet then and didn't make another peep until that car was out of sight.

As Pete stepped inside the train, he got a glimpse of Able turning onto the street. Able had his arm resting on the windowsill and was talking up a storm. He figured they were headed to River Road, regardless of what Mr. Cane said. As the two began making their way back through town, Able kept on about how fancy Mr. Cane's new truck was. He said he hadn't ever seen a blue the color of that one. "Ford outdone themselves this year," he said, satisfied.

Of course, Able wanted everybody in Yazoo City to see him driving the new truck. He honked at every colored person he saw though Justin doubted he knew them all, and didn't think twice about coming to a complete stop to let white people walk across the street so they could admire him driving the new truck as well. When they crossed, he'd say, "How you do, pretty day, ain't it?" All-in-all, it took twenty minutes for them to go down Main Street.

When they reached the outskirts of town, Justin turned to Able and said, "Think I can drive, Abe?"

"Sure you can...one day, Jussin. You gonna have to get a little older first."

"Come on, Abe, you know I can drive. If I can drive that big hay truck, you know I can drive this little truck. Won't be nothing to it. You can rest up and leave the driving to me. Come on?"

"I don't know, Jussin, you done heard what Mr. Cane said to me about this truck."

"I know Abe, but how am I gonna learn if you don't teach me?" Justin said.

Able shook his head, "You sho' got me wrapped around yo finger, boy."

When he looked over, he saw just about the wildest grin he's ever seen plastered across Justin's face. It was a golden face, kissed by the sun. How could anyone turn that down? It just wouldn't be right were he not to give the boy a chance out here on the open straight roads. Anyway, just to let him get behind the wheel for a moment wouldn't hurt anything and it would give the boy something to brag about when they got back home, too. He thought back to the first time his dad had let him take the reigns of ole Buzzard, their mule. It wasn't a car or truck back then, but it was all the same. He was driving.

As they drove down the road, it was obvious that the rich loamy soil was producing another bumper crop. Even from the truck, Able could see the cotton balls were swollen as big as baseballs. It really was a sight to see and Able was sure glad he was the one who got to introduce Justin to it for the first time. Able found himself slowing down, pulling over, pointing and trying to explain everything he knew about the Delta so Justin would have a lot to tell his friends when they got back home. At one point, they stopped, walked into the field and scooped some dirt in their hands. As the dirt sifted into Justin's hands, Able told Justin he was holding the richest dirt on earth. He reminded Justin how lucky they were to have it right there in their own backyard. Not to many people ever get to experience something as beautiful, he said. As they stood there looking over the thousands of acres and up towards the blinding heaven, Able knew that all of this just didn't happen by itself. Oh, how he hoped God was comforting Pete right now, but then he changed his thoughts.

"You like chocolate milk, Jussin? I always like to try to drink me a cold chocolate milk when I'm going somewhere. Just does something for me. Makes me feel good inside. What kind of milk do you like?" Able said.

"I like white milk for breakfast, but sometimes Mamma will buy some chocolate."

"Well, I always buys Luvel chocolate milk. They make it the best. I've tried them other kinds, but they ain't nothing compared to Luvel milk. I could sho use one now. How about you, Jussin?"

"Suits me. I'll take one, if you want one," Justin said.

They drove a few more miles and saw a sign that read, "Country Store and Gas Station Ahead Four Miles."

"We'll stop up here at this store coming up to, get us some gas, and I'll go in and get us two of them milks, okay?"

"Sure! That sounds great," Justin said.

They drove a few more miles when they saw the country store coming up. As they approached, they could see that the store sold and repaired flats too. Outside the store two colored men were working. One had a stomach big as a barrel. It was so big his t-shirt only covered part of his belly. From what Justin could tell, he was changing a tire with another man who was as small and skinny as the other was big and fat.

Justin stayed in the truck as Able went inside to buy the chocolate milks, watching the two men change the tires. Justin could hear that the shrimpy-looking man sure had a foul mouth on him. Nearly every word was a cuss word. Justin noticed that he also had one of them old rolled up, ugly cigarettes in his mouth just like Pete. Again, Justin couldn't figure out why colored people didn't buy store-bought cigarettes in a pack like everybody else. They should know they look better hanging out their mouth's.

Justin couldn't hear everything they were saying, but he knew enough that they weren't talking about going to church. Rolling the window down a little more, Justin could hear that the shrimpy man was talking about somebody's sister and how she hit him over the head with a beer bottle. She said he was drunk and wouldn't leave her alone. His excuse was that he wasn't drunk and that he was only trying to help her fix a button that had come loose on her dress. He didn't bother to call her by her real name, but he referred to her as "bitch" most of the time. Justin knew what that meant because he had heard that word around the hay field many times. Seemed to him that was one of the colored folks favorite words. The shrimpy man was mad for sure. The bigger man just laughed and carried on and did what he could to egg the shirmpy man on. And wouldn't you know, the more the fat man laughed, the madder the shrimpy man got.

Then, out of nowhere, something blew up near the tire-changing machine. The exhausting sound of compressed air was like a plane going over. There was smoke everywhere and somebody was hollering. A bolt hit the front tire on the truck. Justin flinched and ducked down in the front seat hoping it wasn't a gun going off. Through the corner of his eye, he saw the shrimpy man fly up in the air at least six feet and fall backwards behind some tires. For a second Justin thought the fat man had pulled a gun and shot the shrimpy man. For the life of him, he couldn't figure out why he'd have done that.

As Justin peeped up to look over the window, he saw the owner of the store running out the front door shouting, "What the hell happened?" Able was right behind him with a chocolate milk in each hand. "Oh, my God!" the owner said. He paled considerably. So did Able, as much as Justin had ever seen a black man pale.

Able looked at Justin to make sure he was not hurt. As Justin, peering over the window, began opening the door of the truck, Able pointed and said, "Get back, not now, Jussin, stay in the truck." From the force of his voice Justin knew he meant it.

Seeing a cardboard box beside the store, Able picked it up and folded it three times and handed to Justin.

"Slide on over and put this under your seat, Jussin. It'll pick you a little bit. It's time for you to drive."

Justin was looking confused. "What happened, Able?"

"It was a bad scene. Real bad. You see, Jussin, whatever you do, be thinking of what might happen if things go wrong. That way you'll always be prepared if it does. In this case, that tire changer just got his head cut off."

"What?" Justin's mouth just dropped open.

"Yeah, sho did. Cut off clean as whistle. His head was five feet from the rest of him. Landed in a five-gallon bucket of oil. You see, he wasn't paying attention, just running his mouth just like you ain't paying attention right now." Able pointed for Justin to look at the road.

"Watch the road now. Ain't no road over here on my side," Able said. "Keep your eyes on where you are going. You can't be looking over here at me and driving the truck too."

"Okay, Abe, I'll watch the road, now tell me what happened." Justin said.

Justin immediately sat straight up in his seat, put both of his hands on the steering wheel and looked straight ahead. His legs were not quite long enough to reach the gas pedal but he was able to manage with his tiptoes.

"You see, Jussin, whatever that sorry cuss was doing, he sho' didn't have his mind on his job. It must have been somewhere else. He knew not to have that truck rim pointed at him. Everybody that breaks down a truck tire knows them rims are in two pieces. When you air' em up, you gotta be careful. Them tires got more than 120 pounds of pressure to them. If that rim ain't just right, that sucker'll come loose and blow apart.

"Is that what happened?" Justin asked.

"That's what happened. That rim was just like a butcher knife. Cut that man's head clean off." Able got a faraway look in his eye. Justin thought he saw something almost like a tear in his eye mixed in there. Then Able changed the subject, "Pull over up here, Jussin. This milk ain't sitting too good right now."

Justin started applying the brakes and slowing down. He reached down from the steering wheel with one hand and put his blinker on just like Able had taught him.

"Slow down now. Yeah, that's right. Okay, now stop and let me out here on the side of the road just a minute."

Justin pulled to the side of the road and stopped. Able opened the passenger door and stood beside the truck a brief moment before he turned his back to Justin, leaned over and started throwing up. Justin had to cover his ears or he was going to get sick too. Able stood there for several minutes taking in the fresh air before opening the door and slid back in. Justin was sure glad he didn't see what Able saw at the grocery store.

Able climbed back into the truck. "Now I feels better, Jussin. That was too much to look at back there and drink chocolate milk at the same time. Okay, let's get back on the road."

Justin looked both ways, and pulled the truck back onto the road. He shifted the gears nearly perfect that time. Only scratched one. Second gear was always the toughest because it was at the top. He glanced sideways at Able to see if he had noticed, but Abe just had his knuckles in his mouth like he was fighting back the urge to throw up again.

Able's stomach was still queasy so he adjusted his vent to direct the wind to his face. The fresh air coming in the truck was immediate relief. He turned to Justin and said. "Man, you done turned into a truck driving man."

"How am I doing, Abe?"

"Aw, you doin' just right, sho is," Able said. "You know, that was the only time Luvel milk didn't sit real good with me."

As Justin headed the truck down the road, he kept thinking about Able telling him about that man's head flying over into that bucket of oil. He wondered if it had killed him right off or if the man felt it when his head landed in the bucket. In a way, Justin guessed he might have drowned. He knew enough not to ask now, but he was sure going to ask him later what he thought about it. For the time, he figured he better keep his mind on driving. He sure didn't need his own head rolling down the road.

* * * * *

Seven

The Reverend

WITH IN HOUR, Able had put the incident out of his mind and was back to his old self. He started telling Justin a story about how he used to pick cotton over in Rosedale, Mississippi, back in the 40's. He said he was a hell-bound poor colored man back then. Said he could pick more cotton than any two field hands around them parts. One time they had a picking contest, and he picked over six hundred pounds of cotton. The next day he said his boss gave him a five-dollar bonus. To keep the money safe, he said he stuck the money under the wagon seat. But when he got ready to go home, it was missing. Able said at the time he had a good idea where it went and was sure mad about it. In the long run though, losing that five dollars was the best thing that had ever happened to him.

Justin gave Able a look to which Able responded, "it's a long story." Justin gave Abe another look, a look that said, 'go on.' So Abe continued.

The first order of business on his mind after the five dollars came up missing was to whip the person responsible for stealing his money. He knew who it was. The ole boy's name was Fred Reed. He had been picking cotton too and must have stole Able's money when he wasn't looking. Now, Fred was about to get it good.

Losing that money messed all Able's plans up. He had been planning on buying his little sister, Jeanna, a new dress for her birthday with the money. Able approached Fred and told him to come up with that money or he was going to beat it out of him. The boss man saw what was about to happen and fired both them on the spot. The boss man said he wasn't going to put up with no bad talk or fighting on his property. After the boss man told them that, it made Able so mad he wanted to kill Fred, and would have, if it hadn't been for Reverend Dikes.

Able had made his mind up that he was going to kill Fred that evening. He was sure laying for him. "I ain't ever been so mad in my whole born life," Able said. "That Fred had done messed me out of my money and my job, too."

Justin couldn't help but look over as Able told the story. As he turned his right eye towards Able, all he saw was that lean finger pointing him back at the road. This was better than going to the picture show, Justin thought. From Able's voice, Justin could tell he was getting mad all over again. Able told him he planned it all out, by first finding and cutting a Bodok tree limb and making a club out of it. He explained to Justin that Bodak was the hardest wood God ever made and he was going to let Fred be a witness to it. Able wasn't for sure, but he thought that Bodak wood was what Noah made the ark out of, too.

Anyway, he knew that Fred hung out each night at the Blue Goose lounge with all his sorry buddies, and that's where Able headed to beat his head in.

"I thought you said this was the best thing that had ever happened to you, Abe?" Justin said, impatiently at the detour the story had taken.

"It was; I ain't through yet, Jussin."

"Oh!"

"Well, let me finish the story now," Able said, more than a little perturbed that he'd been interrupted.

"Okay, sorry." Justin could tell by this new high pitch in Able's voice that he was getting worked up.

So anyway, Able started the story again and told Justin how on the way down to the Blue Goose, Able met the Reverend Dikes and his daughter going to the church revival. The Reverend asked him if he was doing anything, and Able told him that he was just walking. He told the preacher he was trying to think a few business things out. But the Reverend, noticing the throbbing vein on Able's temple and the Bodak club he held behind his back didn't believe him for a second. With that unbelievable answer, the Reverend told him to jump in the wagon and go with them. There was a little revival going on down at Mt. Good Hope Church. Just as Able was about to say thank you, but no, he caught a glimpse of something in the Reverend's back seat.

She was the prettiest looking thing he'd ever laid his eyes on. Her smile melted Able's heart right there on the spot. He said he looked at that Bodak club and knew he had to choose between introducing Fred to a Bodok stick or introducing himself to the prettiest girl in the world. He dropped the stick, climbed into that wagon and away they went right to the church house.

"You kidding me, Abe, ain't you?" Justin said, unable to imagine passing the opportunity to beat up Fred.

"Naw, I ain't either," Able said. You know, Jussin, the Lord's always looking out for you, didn't I tell you? When you think you're at the bottom and you're at the end of your rope, help comes in mysterious ways. If you're smart, you know that mysterious way is always the Lord's Working." Able looked straight ahead and started smiling, then finished his story.

"As I was just about to get up in that wagon I looked down on the ground, and 'lo and behold' there was a five-dollar bill laying there. Just like it came from nowhere. I knew then I was on the right track and somebody was watching out for me. I asked the Reverend if he dropped any money, and he said no and told me to put it in my pocket and count it as a blessing from God.

"Jussin, not only did the Lord give me that five dollars back, but I gotta bonus too. I winded up getting saved by Jesus that night and it wasn't but a couple of more months and I gots to married that pretty girl too. I call that a double bonus in my book. Been married now thirteen years to Lizzy. Best thing that ever happened to me. Sho' is."

Able laughed for a long time after telling that story and when he was done laughing, he just smiled. Justin sure was glad he was feeling better. After that, Able continued with his stories, but Justin could tell what had happened at the station had shook Able to his core. Sure he was laughing and telling stories, but Justin would bet that man's severed head was rolling around right in the front of Able's mind.

*   *   *   *   *

Eight

The Test

VERY FEW CARS were on the road, and Mr. Cane's new Ford pickup and Justin were doing fine. It certainly was an improvement over Ole Red. The engine sounded as quiet as a sewing machine and Justin kept the needle straight up on forty. He was now getting the hang of driving the truck out on the open road and found that it sure was easier than driving the hay truck. Able tried to explain about the different signs to watch for while traveling down the road. He explained to Justin how he'd need to watch for yield signs, stop signs, railroad crossings, where to pass and where not to pass signs, and above all, speed limit signs.

"Jussin, you ain't passed a car yet. Are you ready to try it?" Able smiled.

Justin's gripped the steering wheel tighter without saying anything and looked wide-eyed at Able. "Jussin, don't look at me, look at the road. You's gonna have to learn sooner or later. You might as well get ready and learn now. I done taught all the Cane boys to drive. You be the last one. I be done my job when I get through with you. I expect I'm a pretty good teacher when it comes to machinery. Ain't nobody failed my class yet," Able chuckled. "Now there's one right there."

Ahead of them was an old car just poking down the highway, slow as could be, a perfect car, according to Able, to learn how to pass on. The old orange '46 Plymouth looked like a June bug and reminded Justin of his grandma's, except he remembered hers was maroon. As they approached the car, Justin slowed the truck down to about twenty miles per hour. The road was so curvy that Justin couldn't see a way to get around it. In fact, he was pretty sure the old man driving the Plymouth was sick or something because he was weaving all over the road. When out of nowhere, a beer can flew out of the driver's window, bouncing and skidding across the road, Able gave a throaty "hmph."

"There's your answer," Able said. "He's driving *and* drinking."

As Justin processed this information, the car unexpectedly darted into the other lane, giving him a good scare. As his hands became sweaty, he could feel the panic began sinking into his gut. He couldn't shake the memories of the day he got the hay truck stuck.

"That guy is *bad* drunk, Abe. I think you should take over and drive now?" Justin said, nodding his head vigorously, his wide eyes glued to the chrome fender of the orange June bug.

"Oh, naw Jussin, you'll be okay. Just watch the road and be keeping your distance. Them people that drink and drive usually wind up killing themselves. We'll get around him. Just wait a minute." Able seemed way too relaxed to Justin, he was tapping out some music on the dash, and staring at the farms they passed.

Justin didn't mind too much the though of the drunk killing himself, he just couldn't figure out how they wouldn't be going right along with him. The car was now swerving from one side of the road to the other. All of a sudden, it went completely off the road running in the ditch, and then swerved back towards the road again. Dirt and gravel were flying everywhere as the car jumped back up on the pavement. One rock hit the new Ford's windshield. Able gasped for breath as he examined the windshield with his fingers. If it had broken the glass, Able would never have been able to talk his way out of that one.

"Old drunk cleaned that ditch out pretty good, Jussin. I ain't ever seen nothing like that," Able said, "He's *definitely* gonna kill somebody," with slight bit of a smile in his eye. Justin kinda got the feeling Able was messing with him and if he weren't so scared, he thought he might even get pretty mad at him.

"Abe, we ain't ever going to get around that car with me driving. You better take it back," Justin proclaimed.

"Oh, yeah we will. You just trust me. You the man for the job. Just settle down." Able stopped his tapping and laid his hand flat against the dash as if to calm the truck and Justin.

"But, Abe, I can't pass. I don't know how," Justin tried to explain.

"It ain't no problem. You just gotta keep your mind on what you doing." Justin couldn't help but think back to the man at the gas station. The fella who hadn't paid attention. The one with no head. You always got to remember that there is two sides to a road. The right side and the wrong side." Able continued.

Where was he going with this? "I know, Abe, but he's driving on *both* sides."

"Yeah, I know that too, but I got a plan. Now, what we going to do is use the right side to the maximum. When we get past this next curve, you pull way over here on my side. On the shoulder that is. And then gun it." The playfulness was gone from Able's eyes. He was suddenly very serious.

"But that's the *wrong* side Abe," Justin frantically explained.

"Jussin, sometimes you can bend the rules a little if you have to. You listen to me carefully now. You got just enough time between them speed limit signs to pass, so don't get over here and stall around 'cause we don't want to take out one of them signs. That won't look real good stamped on the front of Mr. Cane's new truck. So when I say go, you go and go hard. Okay?" Able looked real hard in Justin's eyes right then. Justin felt real grown up just then.

"Okay," Justin said, firmly, nervously grasping the steering wheel. Justin

Trying to get his nerve up, Justin watched the car swerve again into the other lane. The man had been doing this regularly since they got behind him. Out of control, the drunk would stay long enough to see another car coming and then jerk back over just in time. Justin couldn't believe Able's plan was to pass on the wrong side, but it did have merit. He knew they would never get around him like it was.

"Oh, my gosh, what am I gonna do, Abe? He's moving back in our lane again."

"Patience now, Jussin, patience. Just listen to me. Get ready. It'll be all right. Now, when I say go, you gotta go. You hear?" Again, Able looked at Justin hard and Justin knew it was up to him to do this right. He shimmed up in his seat, held his arms out straight and said, "I hear you."

Justin squinted his eyes in concentration and pulled closer behind the car just like Able said. Being on the man's bumper would allow him to get around in a hurry when the drunk man moved back in the wrong lane, he figured. Able's plan was starting to make a lot of sense. Justin started to relax a little; he knew what to do.

Then Able said, "Okay now, we just about ready. Now, go boy, go!" Go for it, Jussin!"

Justin's heart jumped but he stomped on the gas and turned the wheel to the right throwing up dust and gravel behind the truck. The dust looked like a stampede of cows coming down the road. Able was holding on for dear life. He had one arm out the window gripping the top of the truck, and one arm stretched across the back of the seat. He had a grip locked so tight on the truck seat that Justin could feel the seatcovers sink in behind his neck.

"Come on now, Jussin, you just about around him."

Then the unexpected thing happened. For the first time, the drunk man came over on the shoulder of the road too. He cut right in front of the new Ford truck. Able looked over and saw that they were doing sixty-five miles per hour. The speeding vehicles were on the shoulder of the road. The blue Ford was on the old man's tail, eating all the dirt the he could throw at them.

"Pull back on the road and go around, Jussin." Then Able yelled, "Plan B! Plan B!"

"Huh...What's plan B, Abe?" Justin hollered.

"Backwards from A!"

The noise of screeching tires and racing motors was just like a chase scene in a movie.

"I'm trying, I'm trying." Justin hollered again, squirming.

Justin could barely see over the steering wheel as it was and the cardboard was now working its way out from under his bottom. Dust was just a-boiling and wouldn't you know it, no quicker had he pulled back up on the road than the old man followed suit.

"Watch out, Jussin, the fool's doing the same thing. Go back to the shoulder."

"Okay, Okay" Justin hollered back. Justin was trying to focus on the shoulder again when he saw a huge transport truck coming.

"Oh, Lord!" Able said. "Jesus, we's coming to see you."

Able quickly looked at Justin to see if he was a scared as he was, then turned back and watched the drunk and the approaching truck. His eyes were as big as saucers. The big truck driver saw the drunk and the new Ford swerving together, so he immediately locked his air brakes, which made his truck start jackknifing. Justin pulled the steering wheel further to the right again, and the ole drunk came right with him. Headed for the ditch, both vehicles went off the shoulder slinging mud, grass, sticks, frogs, beer cans, into the air. Justin's dad's new truck was getting clobbered with everything that was being flung out from behind the old man's car.

"I can't see, Abe." Justin said.

"Windshield wipers, Jussin! The windshield wipers! Turn them on quick!"

"Where they at?" Justin hollered.

Justin frantically searched for the knob that turned them on. He mistakenly pulled the lights first and then the defroster. Finally, he found the windshield wiper knob and pulled it. The wipers started, only instead of cleaning the windshield, they smeared the mud from one side to the other.

By now, Able had his head out the window, trying to direct Justin and holler at the drunk. As he did, a big piece of mud dead centered Able in the forehead. He looked like he had been shot with cow crap. As funny as it was, Justin didn't even feel like laughing. Somehow he had to try one more time to get the truck back on the road.

"Jussin, pull back up or you gonna kill both of us," Able was raising up off his seat as he hollered at him.

"I know, I know, I'm trying." Justin said.

Justin pulled hard on the steering wheel, and the truck shot out of the ditch in one bolt and landed right back in the right lane. As Able looked to his right he could see the blue Ford inching past the drunk, who was now plowing the bottom of the ditch out. Able turned around as they passed and saw the old man and Plymouth just plowing deeper and deeper into that ditch.

Just as Justin managed to straighten up and get control of the situation, a highway patrolman sped by them. The patrolmen whipped his head around, spotting first Justin, then the old man in the ditch. Reluctantly, the patrolman pulled off the road and began reversing to where the old man was already staggering away.

"Abe, I ain't gonna pass nobody no more. I don't care if they are stopped in the middle of the road. I'm still not. Look at Dad's truck. It looks like we been cleaning out a chicken house or the barn with it. He's gonna kill us if he finds out I been driving and done this to his truck. Abe, we gotta clean it up before we go home." Able just smiled at Justin.

"Oh, we will, Jussin. Settle down. Everything will be all right, now. You done a good job," Able said. "You done a *real* good job."

Able pulled his handkerchief out of his back pocket and wiped his face. "We'll find a place right up the road here, and we can pull over and clean it up." Able closed his eyes and thanked the Lord for what he'd done.

Justin must have driven for twenty more miles before he came to a little town called Rolling Fork. There was a funny looking round filling station there. It was round shaped. They pulled in and Able asked the attendant if they could use the water hose to wash the mud off and get some gas. The man at the station said it would be alright, but asked what had happened. Able told him some story about some cows in the road, and how they had to take to a ditch to keep from hitting them.

"Ooh wee! Gas sho' is going up," said Able. "Clean out of sight. Look a' here, Jussin, at this pump." Able pointed to the numbers showing the price and shook his head side to side.

Then he turned slowly around comparing the tank to the sign. Able noticed that the gas pump said twenty-two cents a gallon and the sign said sixteen cents a gallon.

"If I wasn't the good Christian man I is, I'd go in that store and tell that man I was paying the price on the sign at the road, not the one on the pump."

"Well, he did let us use his water hose, Abe," Justin said. "We were really in a tight, wouldn't you say?"

"You right about that Jussin," Able said, "Remember what the Lord says in the good book, 'If you need something real bad, He's gonna give it to you, especially if you's in a tight.' That be Able 4:5."

Justin's mom made him join the Bible drill team earlier in the year, but they hadn't learned much yet. They had really only began. Justin figured they hadn't got to the book of "Able" yet. He'd have to look for it Sunday. It must be in there somewhere, he thought.

"Sure does, Abe." Justin answered back. He was trying to show Able he was learning the Bible, too.

As Able filled the truck up, Justin spoke up, "I guess I'm a certified driver now, huh, Abe?"

"You sho' is. I ain't ever seen no driving like today. In fact, I hope I don't ever have too again, either." Able rolled his eyes and then fell out laughing. He thought that was funny, but Justin didn't think it was very funny at all.

"Abe, I was scared to death. Were you? Oh, I guess you ain't scare of nothing are you?"

"Oh, yeah, I is too." Able said.

"Naw you ain't. What then?" Justin said.

"Don't like no bats. Never did like them ugly little devils. They give me the hibbie jibbies."

"Me, too. I don't like'em either." Justin said.

Able finished filling the truck with gas and went inside to pay. In a few seconds he appeared back at the front door with the owner. Justin noticed Able pointing to the sign at the road and discussing something with the man. Justin figured Able must have told him what he wanted to, after all. Then, Justin saw the man giving some money back to Able.

"Better let me take the wheel again, Jussin. We might meet that highway man again. Don't need to go to jail today. The last thing we need is to be stuck in the same jail cell with that drunk man and have to call your daddy to tell him he need to come get us."

Justin slid back over to the passenger side, as Able discarded the cardboard into a nearby garbage can. Able pulled out of the filling station and pointed the new Ford truck southward. The truck looked better now. It even looked new again. Able had to tell Justin one more time how that was the best color blue Ford ever made. No quicker than he got the words out of his mouth, he snapped his fingers and said, "Mr. Cane."

"Doggone it! I forgot to call Mr. Cane. I'll pull over again up the road and do just that." Able said.

Able said it wouldn't be long before they would be coming upon some of them big mansions and reminded Justin he best not to be falling asleep. The windows were down, and the hot day was beginning to cool down a bit. As the breeze blew through the cab of the truck, Justin started drifting off into a little dream about last Christmas of all things. He had just come down stairs and realized he had gotten a new shotgun. He was just about to pull it out of the box when Able spoke. "I believe I see some clouds up ahead, Jussin. Some real dark clouds too." Able said pointing out to his right. He laughed to himself as Justin jumped, straightened down his hair and replied,

"Reckon it's gonna to rain?"

"Oh, it's probably going to shower a little. Them crops out there, they need some rain anyway. They sho' look dry. You know Jussin, I wish ole Pete was here 'cause he'd tell us if it was gonna rain for sure." Able stretched his arms out across the steering wheel to relax as he pressed on the gas.

"Look at that dust out there, Jussin," Able said, pointing to a dust whirlwind. "It's just about to choke that cotton to death. Lord knows when to send rain though. Good Book says rain is not ever far away. Good or bad. You just gotta wait on it. Be patient, the Lord says, and he'll be patient with you. Moses 6:1."

As Able continued his lecture, Justin focused on the deepness of his voice. Soon he couldn't hear the wind outside or the sound of the wheels on the road. Just Able's voice. Slowly, his eyes fluttered shut. All Justin could think about was how nice a good glass of cold lemonade and nap would be. The wind was blowing perfectly across his face and he knew the ole "rack monster" was about to get him. That was a term his dad came up with when he got sleepy at night. His dad always said the "rack" was calling him. Somehow that turned into the "rack monster" and that's what it's been called ever since. Right now, his dad's rack monster was about to get him and he knew it.

Able looked over and saw that Justin's eyes had shut, though his small mouth hung open. For thirty minutes he tried to miss all the potholes in the road so not to awaken him. With Justin fast asleep he had time to do a little daydreaming too. He remembered back to his dad being tall like him but skinny and carried a deep baritone voice. He figured he got all his funny side from his mother, because his dad was a serious man. He and his dad always went fishing together back then. That was one thing he missed most about his dad and one thing he knew he needed to do more of with Bebop. Able laughed to himself and then out loud thinking how they didn't have a truck like Mr. Cane's but they sure had a good mule named Buzzard. When he did, Justin's eyes popped opened.

"Whatcha laughing at Abe?"

"Oh, I's just laughing to myself, I guess."

"What'd you do so funny?"

"Oh, I's just remembering back when I was little boy like you and my daddy had an old mule that would always run buzzards out of the pasture. That crazy thing hated birds and anything with wings. A chicken didn't have a chance in a pasture with him. We named him Buzzard."

Justin laughed. "You named the mule Buzzard?"

"Sho did. Fit him perfect, too. He was a good ole riding mule and gentle as a lamb but Jeanna would never ride him. She always wanted something we didn't have or couldn't afford. She said she wouldn't ever ride *no* mule, give her a *horse* to ride. 'Who wants to ride something called, Buzzard.' she'd always say." Able laughed again out loud. "Yeah, one day dad got tired of all that sass and made her ride that mule anyway. He said he was going to spank her butt good if she didn't ride him. He intended to teach her lesson to show her she wasn't any better than anybody else, so he put her on that mule and made her ride all the way to church, Sunday dress and all. She cried all the way and especially all the way home when she knew all her friends saw her. It was a funny sight but it taught her a good lesson. Sho' did and I learned one too. I's got the worst whipping I ever got for making fun of her, but I didn't care, it was too funny. From that day on we never heard another peep out of her about not wanting to do something that might slight her appearance some. It humbled her *real* good and me too."

* * * * *

Nine

Lipstick, Hats, and Shoes

COOL-CAT SLIM didn't have plans to carry Jeanna to New Orleans like Big Doug had promised her. Instead he was going to carry her by way of Natchez where he was going to introduce her to some of his business associates, as he called them before. It was about 8:00 PM when they arrived. Jeanna had dressed in her best Sunday dress for the ride but didn't have a clue as to what she was going on. Slim parked on the side street in his '57 Oldsmobile and walked around and opened the door for Jeanna. As Jeanna got out she could tell she was in a town that was more high-class than she had ever been in before. All she could see were big mansions and wrought iron staircases everywhere as they drove in. Slim came around and opened her door mighty gentleman like and they walked across the street together and into the foyer of the St. George's Hotel. Slim tipped his hat to a few people he recognize through the halls and they continued to the Blue Room in the back. It was obvious to her that he had been there before. Entering the Blue Room, the first thing Jeanna noticed was the smoke that filled the air. It was as thick as dust in a cotton field on a windy day, she thought to herself. As her eyes adjusted, she noticed that the room was filled with people. Most were smiling and carrying on conversations. They held drinks in one hand and cigarettes in the other. As she listened to their conversations, she figured that many were northerners and some were even foreigners. She was in awe. What really took her breath away, though, were the sumptuous fabrics of the elegant dresses the ladies wore. They were gorgeous. Jeanna was still taking it all in when a man of medium height came over to Slim and her.

"How are you?" the stranger said with a big courteous smile. He must have been proud of that gold front tooth, she thought.

"I'm fine, but I think I'm in the wrong place," she said and looked Slim directly in the eyes. Slim is mortified and he had to hold his hand to keep from slapping the girl. "Slim why don't we leave now?" Jeanna gave him a big fake smile.

Slim could tell by the awkward look in her eyes that Jeanna was the type who might cause a scene. It was time to set the girl straight. He kindly excused themselves and with his hand gripped around the upper part of Jeanna's arm, he casually guided her off to a place where he could talk in private. Once they were out of earshot he railed at her.

"Look bitch, you don't embarrass me like that!" he said. He took her so much by surprise that she audibly gasped for breath before regaining her composure.

"What the crap are you talking about. I don't know any of these people and why are we here anyway?" she said forcefully in a soft voice.

"Look around, Jeanna. What do you think's going on? You know you want this kind of life. Look at the jewelry, the pearls, the dresses these ladies have on. This is just the first glimpse of your new life." Jeanna's mind was reeling. Suddenly, everything made sense.

"Slim, if you don't get me out of here now, I gonna kick you in the balls and holler fire."

Slim looked up and smiled at a few guest and turned up one side of his mouth trying to keep from saying anything too loud. Once the people passed, he leaned in close to her ear and whispered harshly, "Okay, bitch. Let's go!" He jerked her by the arm and out the door they went.

Neither said a word until they got in the car. Jeanna was about to open her mouth when Slim back-handed her across the face. If there was any doubt left, Jeanna knew she was in real trouble. No man had ever hit her before. She had only heard of other colored men beating their wives. She even knew of some women who just thought it was part of an average marriage.

"Don't you hit me, you son-of-a-! " Jeanna, shouted and swung her purse, hitting Slim in the face with the handle.

Slim reached for his nose and found blood on his hand. "You damn bitch!" he said and immediately slugged her in the face and breast as hard as he could. Jeanna, started crying and trying to find a way out, but there was no way. She had not realized when he opened the door before that the inside door knob was missing. He pounded her repeatedly until she stopped making any sound at all.

Slim was so mad he carried her to the river and considered throwing her off the bridge. He was half way there when he changed his mind. He was too afraid of what Big Doug might do to him. He knew Big Doug had plans for Jeanna. He might not throw her off the bridge, but he sure as hell was going to make sure Big Doug knew what he had on his hands.

Knocked unconscious by Slim's heavy fist, Jeanna drifted in and out as he drove across town. Seemingly hitting every pothole in the road, Jeanna was dreaming she was back home riding on the back of a wagon headed for a cotton gin. In her dream, she and her friend, Girly, were jumping and playing. As Jeanna tripped, hitting her head on the side railing, she awoke to find herself not in a wagon, but on a soft bed covered with colorful linen sheets. The pain in her head was plenty real, though. She squinted, feeling for blood and lumps as she looked from one corner of the room to the other trying to figure out where she was. The room appeared to be spinning around slowly as she fought to maintain her focus.

She could hear a steady mumbling through the walls, but she couldn't quiet make out any words. As she raised her hand to her cheek pain shot up the right side of her face. She realized she was having trouble seeing because her eye was swollen. Someone had hit her! *Now* she was remembering. It was coming back. She pulled herself up and righted herself on the edge of the bed. Pausing for a few moments, she slid down and planted both feet firmly on the floor. Leaning against the bed, she looked down and noticed she was wearing pink satin pajamas. She rubbed the cloth in her hands, marveling at how soft it was before a red flush spread across her face as she realized someone must have undressed her.

As she reached over to the nightstand to balance herself, she knocked a full glass of water onto the floor. The water and glass went everywhere like a pond levee breaking. She yelled and fell back against the bed. Within seconds she heard the hurry of footsteps. The door flung open revealing the faces of four girls. She pulled herself back up.

"Honey, you alright?" a voice asked as Jeanna nervously looked from one face to the next, trying to figure out who had spoken.

Still dazed, Jeanna replied, "I guess so. Where am I?" All four girls charged and caught her before she fell to the floor.

" Honey, right now you just try to get back into this bed and rest. You not in the shape you think you is." the older girl said, holding Jeanna's arm firmly. "Now watch that glass, honey," she added, looking around at another girl to start picking up. "All you need is to cut'cha damn foot off. Then you gonna be in a hell of a shape."

"Who are y'all?" Jeanna asked the girls, as they tucked and adjusted the cover and pillow under head.

"My name is Ann and this is Becky, Rita, and Sally. We live here." Ann reached around to a bowl of cool water that Sally was holding and began patting softly around Jeanna's swollen eye with a damp rag. "We all work here too," still patting and looking above Jeanna's eye level and hoping she could put two and two together.

Jeanna didn't speak. She was still trying to put the puzzle together. Out of the four girls, she thought she remembered seeing two at the hotel, but the other two were strangers. Looking around the room again she could see that the apartment was filled with some of the finest furnishings she had ever seen. Covering a mahogany dresser were perfume bottles of all shapes, sizes and colors. Jeanna smiled, thinking she had fallen asleep and woken up in another world that was certainly better than the one she had come from. Once that smile spread across Jeanna's face, the girl's realized that she wasn't even close to putting two and two together. She either hit her head really hard or was more naïve than any of them had thought. Ann decided to break the news to her bluntly. She looked her square in the eyes and said, "Honey, we's hookers," "Hookers?" she cried out. She jerked up in the bed, pulling the covers up to her chin.

"Yeah, Hookers!" Ann's gaze dropped slowly as Jeanna's disgust hung in the air. She then raised her head and continued, "But that ain't all bad." Ann could see that Jeanna was horrified by the news, and was wondering if she had become a hooker too in the time that she had been unconscious. Ann explained to Jeanna how Slim had brought her to the house. When Jeanna looked down at the pajamas, Ann continued to say that the girls were the ones who had unclothed her and put her in bed. Ann had forgotten what it meant to have such modesty. Her heart ached for the new girl as she explained to her that they were *all* at Big Doug's mercy.

"I ain't at nobody's mercy." Jeanna said, smarting off. But the girls quickly explained to her the consequences and to be careful about speaking her mind out too loud if she wanted to live very long.

Then Becky said, trying to lift Jeanna's spirits, "Sweety, come let me show you these dresses I just bought." Jeanna shot a glare at all four girls.

The girls held Jeanna's arms, lifted her out of bed and walked her over to the closet. As Becky opened the door, the wardrobe unfolding before Jeanna was unlike anything she had ever seen before. Lining both sides of a ten-foot closet were so many dresses and evening gowns she couldn't even begin to count them all.

"My, gosh, look!" Jeanna said, dumbfounded with her mouth agape.

She walked closer, reached just inside and touched the sleeve of one of the dresses. She could tell it was new as new could be, and soft. She closed her eyes for a brief moment and allowed herself to imagine wearing that dress. She imagined herself as a young girl, twirling as her mother looked on, beaming.

"Jeanna. You have to open your eyes to see it," Becky said, smartly.

"No, I don't either. I can smell it, touch it, and know all there is about it." Jeanna spoke, keeping her eyes closed, and smiling at the scene that was developing in her mind.

"Okay, if you say so. But I think your brain is *still* a little swollen, if you ask me."

Jeanna opened her eyes and turned to her, "How long am I stuck here?"

"Don't know the answer to that one, Sweety, but the way you look… your curves and all, I'd say you gonna be here a while." Jeanna didn't like the answer.

"Tell me. What all do y'all have to do?" Jeanna asked.

"About anything your man says to do…but the money and food is good," Rita spoke up.

"I don't care about the money and food. What else do you do?" asking for a more detailed answer.

"Well, Sweety, it's like this. You put out and get paid for it."

"Not me. Nooo, not me!" she answered shaking her head and stepping back. "I might do a lot of things but I'm not going to sale my pretty between my legs for nobody."

"I hope you're right, Sweety, but if you don't, you'd be the first."

"Then I'll be the first," Jeanna smirked with the reply and walked back to her bed.

Jeanna's was still worried what might happen when she saw Slim again. She had no way to know when he would return. In the meanwhile as she rested more and regained her strength, she could hear her new friends leaving most nights and returning in the early morning hours. It was amusing to her to listen to them talk about their dates when they got back in. Once in while, on a free night, they would huddle up in one's room and compare stories until dawn. All the time Jeanna knew her day was coming when she might be the one telling the next story. Somewhere in all the false glamour she was seeing and hearing she resigned to the fact that her new friends were only making the best of a bad situation.

After a call one morning the girls got word to take Jeanna to the big city to buy new clothes.

"Where are we going?" Jeanna asked Ann.

"Don't worry about where we are going. Trust me. This will be more fun than you've ever had in your life. Just ruby up them lips a little and let's go."

It didn't take Jeanna but a quick look in the mirror and one swipe from a tube of lipstick and she was ready. She was more than ready to get out from behind the four walls she had been imprisoned in for so long.

The sky was the limit as the five girls stepped from the taxi and marched into the exclusive Bell Fonte' Clothing Store, located square in the middle of the French Quarter of New Orleans. The manager, a dark skinned New Yorker, recognized them immediately and delegated his top salesperson to wait on them hand and foot. With Jeanna's natural beauty, it didn't take long for her to get an audience. Everyone in the store stopped what they were doing and watched as she modeled thirty or more dresses, evening gowns, hats and shoes. When the day was over, a total of $4700 worth of merchandize had been charged to Big Doug's account

*   *   *   *   *

Stephen Cheek

Ten

Final Curtain

SLIM WALKED UP the brick sidewalk towards the sweeping wrought-iron rails. Beveled glass sidelights on either side of the nine-foot stained glass door adorned the entrance of the two-story Victorian home. He walked in unannounced, tossed his hat at a recliner and missed. He was looking for someone in particular and that someone was Jeanna. Not knowing where her room was, he quietly made his way up the winding oak staircase, peeking in each room. He was eager to see what the girls had purchased.

Jeanna was standing in front of a full-length mirror in a sleek red party dress. It molded over every curve of her body as if it were her own

84

skin. The pair of white high heels definitely enhanced her long legs and made her tower over the other girls. Turning in the mirror, she ran her hand over her buttocks, smoothing the last wrinkle down as the door opened.

"Ann, what do…Oh my God! It's you!" Jeanna hollered, backing away from the mirror and clutching her hands up to her breast.

"Hell, I ain't Ann or God but let me tell you one thing, Cinderella. You are one *damn* good looking broad!" Slim said, bowing and tipping his imaginary hat, as if she were the queen.

"What do you want?"

"Baby, I don't want nothing. I just came to look at the investment and I'll tell you what, I'm well pleased with what I see."

"Well, looking is all you get and you done looking. Now get!"

"Just a minute now. Don't' get all riled up. We got to have a little orientation and agreement first."

"Agreement shit! You damn near killed me you son-of-a- bitch!" Jeanna backed closer to the wall, taking off one shoe and holding it firmly in her hand, revealing the long narrow pointed heal.

"Shit, girl! That was just a little love tap I gave you."

"Just let me go home. I'll repay all I owe you. I swear I will."

"I know you will but you gonna do it on our terms and not yours. Now just settle your little lively ass down a little bit."

Jeanna stood in silence with a wry face as he walked behind her touching her neckline with his finger and running it down her back. She was doing all she could not to turn and swing, but she knew he would break her neck if she tried to move. She could feel his breath on her neck as he continued to fondle the lace at the small of her back, searching for the zipper. As he tugged the zipper downward, she prepared to swing. Just then, the door sprang open. To her surprise, he didn't even attempt to move his hand from her back.

"Well, if it ain't the damn devil himself." Ann said, smiling. With one hand on her hip and a glass of bourbon in the other hand. "Where have you been, you bad boy?" She strolled closer to him and whispered in his ear. "You know I'm the jealous type." Then she pinched him on the butt. "Now, where have you been keeping yourself?"

"Been around, Annie," Slim said, finally letting go of the zipper. As he turned to give his full attention to Ann, Jeanna took the opportunity to move closer to the door. "Business, as always, you might say."

"Well, why don't you just say we go take care of that little business and leave little Miss Red Dress here to play with her new presents?" Ann looked over Slim's shoulder and saw Jeanna mouthing, 'Thank you.'

Slim, welcoming the invitation, adding, "That's not a bad idea at all. Let's be about business then. It's been a long day." Slimed laughed as he reached for the glass of bourbon, which Ann handed him. Then they walked down the hall to Ann's room. When Jeanna heard the door close, she made a dash downstairs to the kitchen. She didn't want to be in the room when he returned. There was a small nook in the back of the pantry that Mannie, the housekeeper showed her, so she squeezed into it to keep out of sight. Luckily, though, Ann did such a good job that he only stayed an hour and was on his way.

Ann did most of the bookings at the house. It was the best job of a bad job. By doing so, she had the advantage of picking the best dates, but she also showed partiality to Jeanna. Jeanna held to her promise. She was hired out repeatedly and became a favorite pick, but she continually had a calculated contingency plan. Time after time, her date would be bringing her back in early for one reason or the other. It was usually a case of upset stomach or migraine headache, but sometimes it was an uncontrollable breakdown due to a death in her family.

Mannie reminded Jeanna a little of Aunt Pearl. Jeanna found it comforting to talk to her in the afternoons before going home. It was Mannie who always fed Jeanna a new excuse to use on a date. She warned her though, that one day she might get in a situation she couldn't get out of.

One afternoon when they were talking, Mannie reached under the sink and pulled out a table napkin wrapped around an awkward object. She unrolled the napkin and laid it on the table. Inside was a snub-nosed .38 Colt revolver. She handed the gun to Jeanna and told her to keep it with her. Mannie sensed that Jeanna might need it one day.

Many of Jeanna's clients were old men who just wanted a young, good-looking woman at their side at some public function. Those dates were fun. However, some men were more sophisticated and knew what they wanted before they picked her up. But with the skill she had mastered through high school, she was always able to out maneuver them.

She didn't know how long she could continue with her escapades, but she knew her time was going to finally run out. It wasn't until Ann turned on her that it happened. Ann had fallen for a very rich client who had always requested her. When he surprisingly requested Jeanna for a very prestigious dinner party, Ann was livid. She tried her best to persuade him away and even doubled the fee for Jeanna, but all her efforts were in vain. Her last option was to suggest that no one had ever made it with Jeanna and that Jeanna was the biggest con in the business. The man didn't believe it until time came to go to bed. That's when he found out the truth. He became furious with the thought of paying top dollar and not being able to receive her service. Jeanna told him she was terribly sick but he knew the truth and he intended to get what he paid for. He forced her down, ripping her clothes, and then threw her across the room crashing her against the furniture. He became a mad man. To stop the man's aggressions Jeanna pulled Mannie's .38 Colt on him. She shot twice, hitting him once in the leg and once in the shoulder. Luckily, he survived, though it would have been better if he hadn't. Slim rescued her and brought her back to Natchez. After the episode, Jeanna paid dearly. None of the girls would have anything to do with her after that. Eventually, the incident cost Big Doug all of his New Orleans connections. New Orleans was where the money was and without New Orleans, the girls were soon to become nothing more than third rate hookers.

Within three months, calls all but stopped in New Orleans and in the Natchez area as well. The news was traveling. The only business that was not affected was around Memphis and if word continued to travel the way it had, it wouldn't be long before it reached there, too.

Big Doug ordered Slim to bring Jeanna up to Belzoni. He was going to teach her a lesson that only he could give.

*   *   *   *   *

Eleven

The Race

ABLE LOOKED OVER and saw that Justin was still asleep. He reached over to brush a strand of that shiny blonde hair away from the boy's eyes. 'How sweet can an angel get?' he thought to himself, before his mind wandered to darker thoughts. Jeanna had been gone now for four months. Something in how she left made Able uneasy and that something sent cold chills down his spine.

Aunt Pearl who still lived in Belzoni, had grown anxious lately about Jeanna, too. Recently, the name "Big Doug" had been tied to the local gossip, and much to her horror and surprise, someone told Pearl that Jeanna's had been mentioned, too. Pearl didn't want to hear that junk and got pretty mad at the lady that told her. "Whatever those gossipers are talking about, they got it wrong," she said. She told them her Jeanna was working in New Orleans and would never do anything like they said she was doing.

Whenever Aunt Pearl got to feeling weak and started letting those rumors buzz around in her head, Able would reminded her that Jeanna was a smart girl. He guessed that she was most likely working in a good restaurant waiting on tables and having the time of her life. In time she'd get around to calling them when she had time. "That girl definitely got a mind of her own," he reminded her. "She's probably gonna make just enough money to say she's got a job and then come home."

Aunt Pearl knew Jeanna would never do that "whoring around stuff" that some of the other girls were doing. She convinced herself that Jeanna was just trying to enjoy life and make some money so she could go on to college.

* * * * *

By now Justin was dreaming of his mom's lemonade and fried pies that waited on him after school each day. They were the best in the world. Justin would come home and head straight for the refrigerator to get a big glass of his mom's lemonade, then head for the front porch swing grabbing pies along the way. Now he dreamed he lay stretched out crosswise in the swing with the breeze floating across his face.

Able looked over as the second rumble of thunder startled Justin out of his nap. Justin jumped so hard that he hit his head on the top of the door.

Justin's face reddening as he came out of the dream and realized they were sitting in the middle of a brewing storm..

"Sonny boy, that's what they call lightning," Able said, securing both hands on the wheel. "I'm afraid we's fixin' to get in some bad weather, Jussin. That black cloud is bigger than I thought."

"Abe, it sure is scary looking." Justin said.

"Yeah, it sure is." said Abe leaning closer to the windshield and lifting his eyes up to get a closer look at the clouds.

No sooner had Able got the words out of his mouth, then the hail started. It sounded like a thousand drummers beating on a tin roof. The noise was deafening and then it stopped. They had moved from under the cloud.

"Think I'll speed up a little, and maybe we can get by them dark clouds before the hail gets us again. Sho' don't want this truck hurt." Able said. All Able could think about was how he was going to have to explain how he got four hundred dents in Mr. Cane's new truck.

Able pushed the accelerator down. The further they went down the narrow highway, the more the dark clouds surrounded them. Mist of rain started blowing in on the seats and as they frantically closed the windows, out of nowhere, a huge funnel cloud dropped from the sky. It appeared to be was sucking up everything in its path and coming right at them. This was a spooky sight for Able and Justin because neither had seen anything like this before.

"Keep rolling up your window, Jussin, the rain is blowing in on us." Able said, furiously cranking his arm.

"Look!" Justin pointed out the window. " A tornado!"

"Sho' is, and it's headed straight for us." Able pushed down harder on the gas.

"How fast we going, Abe?" Justin asked.

"It don't matter right now, Jussin. Just hang on."

Justin leaned over and saw eighty-five miles an hour on the speedometer, and it was still climbing.

"I ain't ever gone this fast before, Abe."

"Yeah, I know, and I don't think I is either. Don't peep a word to your daddy about this. This is just between me and you. You hear?"

"I ain't," Justin told him.

Justin looked out his right window, and he couldn't believe what he was seeing. A freight train was coming up right beside them. Able had not noticed but they were running parallel to a train track. It looked, as if, the train engineer was trying to do the same thing they were: outrun the tornado.

"I hope that train ain't planning on crossing the road up here somewhere." Able said.

"I swear I think it is, Abe. We don't have a prayer," Justin said. "If we don't make it first to the train crossing, we'll have to stop, and the tornado gonna get us. If we keep going, the train is going to kill us."

"Oh, hush up, Jussin, the Lord's going to take care of us. He's got a plan. I tell you he does," Able said, scolding Justin. What Justin was more worried about was not if the Lord had a plan, but if Able had one.

"We gotta plan, Able?" Justin asked. "What's *our* plan?"

"Look, Jussin. God, He made the man that made the train, and He made that tornado, too. He sees us right now, and I tell you He sees we in a tight, and He's gonna take care of us first. Lord always has and always will. The Good Book says, 'Don't get in too big a hurry thinking; have patience or you might be sorry...humm...or maybe it's 'don't test the Lord or He'll forget you.' Something like that," he said, talking to himself.

Able shook his head, trying to clear it. He was getting confused.

"I can't remember good right now, Jussin. I'm thinking too hard about that tornado out there. Must be's Jericho: 22:1." Justin looked at Able, thinking for the first time that Able might have made that one up.

The sound of the train horn was terrifying. They could both see the stone face of the engineer. He had a crazed look in his eyes with no plans on stopping. Stopping would surely mean the train would take the full brunt of the tornado. In the engineer's mind, he had the right-of-way and he was not going to let Mr. Cane's new truck show him up. No way! The engineer pulled his hat down and started gritting his teeth for a serious game of chicken.

By now, Justin had put his feet on the dashboard, trying his best to apply all the brakes that he could from his side. It was now a race between Able and the train.

Justin had his hands under his chin, praying, "Oh Lord, Oh Lord, help us now pleaseeeee!" Justin looked up and hollered, "We better stop Abe, we can't make it!"

Able hollered back, "Jussin, you ain't seen nothing yet. Keep praying." Then he pushed the shifter up to second gear and floored it. The thunder of the four-barrel carburetors kicking in pushed Justin back into his seat. He couldn't tell what was louder, the train horn or the truck motor. Justin closed his eyes as he heard the train horn right in his ear. He knew they were dead. Justin was screaming, knowing he was on his way to heaven or hell and didn't want to know which.

"Good gugly gue! Train man! You ain't fast enough for Ole Abe! Not in this new Ford truck." Able shouted and then let out a big old "YEEEEE...HI...as the front wheel hit the railroad track. The truck bounced so hard up in the air that the back wheels cleared the entire track and bounced two or three times on landing after it cleared.

"I swear, Abe, I could have touched that engine," Justin yelled. Able shook his head and grinned.

"Jussin, you didn't think this old truck would run, did you? This thing's gots power to spare. Under that hood is a Ford V-8, boy. Ain't no powder puff V-6. Henry Ford knows how to make a motor. Sho' does."

Justin couldn't say a word. He was totally paralyzed from fright. He sank further down in his seat, closed his eyes, and said his own prayer, "Thank you, Lord, for giving us another chance."

As Justin slowly opened his eyes, he could hear the sound of the train cars clanking on the track behind them and the horn still blowing, he muttered to himself, "Next time, boys, next time, victory will be mine."

Just as quickly as the storm had blown up, the funnel cloud vanished and clam replaced the storm. The caboose was fading out of sight as the clouds opened up to sunshine.

Strangely, the train reminded Justin again of Pete at the depot. He wondered about him on his trip to Detroit.

* * * * *

Twelve

The Straw Hat

THE TRAIN HAD left the station on schedule and was north
bound towards Memphis. Pete saw the two girls go to the
back of the coach and sit down. "Why not," he thought. He was curious
anyway, so he followed them and found a seat across from the two and sat
down. He was sitting next to the window and left room for anybody else
needing a seat to sit down beside him; however, he hung his coat over the
extra seat just in case he needed an excuse to keep some undesirable from
sitting down.

For forty-five minutes, the girls talked softly, almost secretly, but
the younger one appeared to be shaking and getting upset. Pete could see

a flood of tears coming down her cheeks and wanted so much to console her but knew he would probably do more harm than he would good. Besides, such an action would be completely out of character for him. She appeared to be no more than sixteen years old. The other was somewhat older, maybe nineteen. The older seemed to be the stronger of the two and in more control of her emotions. However, she was not getting anywhere with her younger companion.

As Pete tried to listen over the steady rumbling of the tracks, he managed to hear that they were going to Memphis. They mentioned two men were supposed to pick them up. The older explained that no matter what they did, they didn't have a choice. Getting off the train before Memphis was no option.

Gazing at their appearances, Pete figured they were working girls, but they must have been new to the business. They were just too young. He was trying his best to hear the meat of the conversation but was missing every other word. It could be money problems, or it could be about anything, he figured. So why was the girl crying? Why should he care? He was of the mind that people have to make their own choices in life. You live with them, and you learn from them. He had his own problems to worry about anyway, and he had sure made his share of mistakes in life, too. Besides, they were young and had time to learn from their mistakes. They'll recover, he thought.

Without warning, the younger girl fled to the restroom. She was becoming quite hysterical. Trying not to attract too much attention, the older girl reached for her but let her go anyway. Pete sat there a few minutes and then leaned over the empty seat to speak to the older girl.

"What's wrong with your friend? Y-Y-You girls, okay?" he asked.

The girl didn't answer but turned and looked out the window. She, too, started crying. Pete, hesitated, double thinking as to what to do. Giving it a second thought, he got up from his seat and sat next to he girl and asked again.

"What's wrong with your friend, young lady? Are you girls o-o-okay?" he spoke softly.

"It's something I can't talk about right now," she explained as she wiped the tears from her eyes.

"Anything that upsets you is w-w-worth talking about, ma'am. Believe me, it's best to let it out. Maybe I can help, and if I can't, m-m-maybe someone else can," he said, somewhat hopeful.

Dressed in his starched white shirt and paisley tie, Pete looked trustworthy that the girl slowly turned and looked at him with big tears rolling down her cheeks. Pete was at a loss for words.

"Sir, we are in trouble, I think." she said.

"Trouble, what kind of trouble?" Pete said.

"Big trouble," she said. "Dolly and I are supposed to meet two men in Memphis and stay with them for two days." She put her hands to her face, wiping back tears. She was embarrassed.

What's this, Pete thought. *Surely they knew the business they're in.*

"They're trying to make hookers out us," she said. "We don't even know these men, mister. We're being forced to do this by some bad people. They said if we don't do what they want, then they gonna kill our mommies and daddies," as she wiped her eyes again.

"Who these people, these b-b- bad people you t-t-talking about?" Pete asked, though he suspected he knew the answer.

"Where are you from, mister?" she asked in a frustrated tone. "Everybody in the Delta knows about Big Doug and his filthy operation. They shipping whiskey and women to New Orleans and Memphis just like coal. He's done killed three friends of mine and killed another girl five years ago for not doing what he said. He's got money to pay off anybody he wants and nobody is going to fool with him. The law turns their heads every time a corpse mysteriously shows up."

Pete couldn't believe what he was hearing. The picture unfolding was a lot more complicated than what he expected to hear. How could these girls get into this kind of trouble? Here were two girls in deep trouble, more trouble than anyone could imagine. Both were scared. Both were frightened out of their wits. Both are headed to a strange city to meet some scoundrels they didn't know anything about. If their performance report came back unsatisfactory, then there was a good chance their parents would pay the price and them too. He knew they had serious problems and for a moment, it shamed him to think how consumed he'd been by his own just moments ago. This was craziness. And these girls were just babies, like Able's little sister Jeanna. Pete felt his stomach bottom out as a horrible thought swept over him. Could these girls know Jeanna?

His mouth watered for a shot of whiskey. Two days. Two days without a drink. This was a new record for him. Right now he could definitely use a drink. On the other hand, he knew he had to offer some advice to the girl. Where were the words of wisdom she so desperately needed to hear from him? His mind was as clear as it had been in so many years and he still couldn't find the words. As he began to speak, a loud shriek echoed behind him.

"Come quick, anybody, come quick!" a lady hollered. "There's a girl hurt! There's blood everywhere!" The middle-aged woman that yelled was gasping for breath before losing her balance and falling into the conductor's arms.

Apparently, after waiting ten minutes or so to enter the ladies' room, she pushed on the door, revealing the young girl's torso lying in a pool of blood on the floor. The young girl had cut her wrists, evidently with a metal nail file.

Almost immediately a woman came from one of the seats and squeezed herself through the narrow door. The angle of the girl's body was keeping her from opening the door completely.

The older girl who had been talking to Pete pushed past him into the aisle and towards the back where her friend had gone just minutes before.

"Is she dead?" someone asked.

Pete worked his way back to the where several people had gathered. The conductor told some people to help with the lady that was passed out in his arms and then told everyone to go back to their seats.

The woman, apparently an off duty nurse, checked the girl's pulse, but it was too late. She was dead. The nurse looked up and saw Pete in the doorway and shook her head. The older girl pushed herself between Pete and the door and kneeled beside the dead girl. She pulled the limp hand from the pool of blood, held it to her neck and began whispering to the girl through her ears.

People started filing back to their seats shaking their heads in disbelief. Too much misery in this world, Pete thought. The urge for a drink came over him again. He could practically taste the whiskey on his tongue. But he had made it this long without a drink so why not make it a little more. He could always change his mind, he figured as made his way back to his seat.

Leaning back closing his eyes, Pete let the wind coming through the coach window wash over him. He tried to block out the sounds coming from the rear where the conductor tried to calm others down. He knew the feeling of being told someone had just been killed. He knew the pain, the heartrending pull on a person's inner soul that immediately attacks when the news of death comes. He felt so sorry for the older girl in her situation now and for the young girl's parents when they would receive the news of their daughter's tragic death. Did she have brothers or sisters? Again he thought about the possibility of these girls knowing

Jeanna. Thinking back, he remembered when Able was carrying him home, Able would mention how he was wondering why Jeanna had not called home from New Orleans. 'Surely, not?' he said out loud. Jeanna would never do anything like that, she was too much like her mother. Pete remembered how pretty her mother Candy was. She was absolutely gorgeous, much prettier than Dorothy or Pearl, not that Dorothy or Pearl were bad looking because they weren't. They were all pretty girls, but it was just that Candy was tall and everything was in proportion. Jeanna was growing up just like her. When she was younger, Jeanna stayed on Candy's foot-steps wherever she went, especially if she went shopping. Candy would always try to dress Jeanna in the best dresses they could afford, which was little. She was spoiling her rotten but Jeanna was the only baby girl in the family, so why not. If Candy wasn't buying her something then Dorothy or Pearl was. It was a girl thing, which a man can't figure out. However, to everyone's surprise, Jeanna turned out to be one of the smartest girls in school and best liked. She graduated with honors and made everyone in the family proud. It was too bad that her parents couldn't have been there for her. Pearl and Hugh did a good job raising the two after the accident. Pete shook his head and wondered why he couldn't have been there more for all of them? He hadn't even been there for his own son. "Matthew," he muttered to himself in grief.

For the first time in years, with his eyes still closed, he said a short prayer. Moments later he opened them again and tried to clear his mind. He thought about Able and Justin. Surely they were on their way back.

Somehow he smiled, thanking God they were in their world and not the world he was in at the present.

Pete was sitting pretty much by himself. All the windows were down on the passenger cars. The steady breeze was still steamy, but cool at times. The sky was pretty much all blue, no clouds in the sky.

Within thirty minutes the train made an emergency stop at Clarksdale where the local funeral home hearse was all ready waiting to accept the young girl's body. The older girl got off too. She was taking a chance on escaping the wrath of Big Doug. "Good girl," he whispered as she cautiously stepped into the street.

The local sheriff's deputy came on board the train, made a fast investigation of the scene, and left. Considering it was a colored girl, it was just a formality. The orderly didn't take long to clean the restroom and the train was back on its way.

Pete thought again about easing back to the lounge and taking a nip. Maybe it would help him rest and relieve some tension. Instead, he dozed off again.

The train passed right on through Memphis without waking Pete when it stopped. The sound of the tracks were hypnotizing and comforting as the train reached full speed towards St. Louis again.

Pete started waking when a man with a straw hat walked beside where he was sitting, leaned over, and said. "This seat taken?"

Pete was off guard, realizing he had pulled his coat off the seat. He couldn't remember if he had gone through Memphis or not. He was sleeping harder than he thought.

"Naw, it's not," replied Pete.

"May I?"

"F-F-Fine with me." Pete looked over at him and offered a "How you do?" The man returned the greeting with a smile that immediately made goose bumps run up Pete's spine.

"Where you headed?" said the man with the straw hat.

"Goin' to see my boy. We got to Memphis yet?" Pete asked, changing the subject, but noticing the neatness of the man's suit before he turned to the window and waited for a reply.

"Well, that's nice. I'm going to see mine, too. Hey, my name is Barnes, John Barnes from Memphis, and yes, we left Memphis about thirty minutes ago."

Pete stared out the window at the farmland rolling past for a long while before turning back absent-mindedly towards the man, "Pete Dodd is mine." Pete began running his finger tips along the top of the forward seat and before adding, "Excuse me, but I guess I was sleeping h-h-harder than I thought." Pete was wondering if the man could tell something was wrong by his fidgeting.

"Well, my pleasure, Mr. Dodd. My boy just graduated from Chicago University." Pete could tell that Barnes was beaming without looking at him. Then Barnes added, "How about yours?"

"Afraid not, sir. M-M-Mine's dead. I'm going to his funeral."

"Oh, gosh, I'm sorry," said the man. "I didn't know. What happened? Do you mind me asking?"

"I really don't care to talk about it." Pete folded his arms and turned again to look out the window.

"Oh, I understand, and again, I'm sorry for asking you."

The man could tell Pete was upset. The man sat there without saying a word, trying to build Pete's confidence in him. Pete didn't say much as he stared at the floor and occasionally looked out the window. Speaking softly the man seemed concerned about what Pete was saying and tried to get Pete to open up. He listened carefully as Pete started rambling and finally began telling his story.

Pete started by telling him how he had really loved and missed his boy. He hadn't seen him but twice in the last five years since things in Mississippi had gotten so bad. The Klan was burning crosses and churches and generally doing everything they could do to scare the colored folk. Two colored boys had come up missing around Vicksburg and everybody knew the Klan had killed them. But nobody had done anything. They were found in the Mississippi River, tied to an old car motor. The court acquitted the accused.

Pete said he knew all white people weren't bad, but he just couldn't understand that much hate. Rubbing his head with a handkerchief, he said, "Mr. Cane. Cane is what I call him; once run them K-K-Klan off his property years ago and swore he would kill any of'em if they ever set foot on his property again. He meant it too. It's a long story why I calls him Cane, but m-m-maybe I'll get around to that later. Anyway, he's the man I works for back in Friendly. He's a g-g-good man, a God-fearing man, and probably the fairest man there is. When he says something, you can take it to the bank. Yes, you can." Pete continued as if trying to get it all off his chest. Starting at the beginning maybe he could justify having sent Matthew away.

*   *   *   *   *

Thirteen

Pete's Story

S O PETE BEGAN his story. *Well, you see it went his way. One night the Klan showed up at the Cane farm and tried to get Mr. Cane to go to one of them meetings they'd been having, Cane wanted no part of it. No, sir, he didn't. The Klan said they had four thousand members in four counties, and they needed Mr. Cane to be a p-p-part of the brotherhood, but Cane told them over and again that he didn't want no part of hating.*

That kinda insulted their leader Bo Green. So as they were about to leave, they said they would be back. Bo told Cane to think about it, but Cane didn't need to think about it. He knew too well where that kind of junk would get somebody. Cane remembered too well when he was standing behind bars at the city jail in Macon, Georgia. He was seventeen at the time and was going to be a senior the next year. Somehow his mother managed to arrange so that he could go to his cousins and spend one week with them. He had always wanted to, but he had always had too many farming chores to do. Mr. Dewy, Cane's dad, wouldn't let him take off even one day. Never in his life could he have imagined what was going to happen.

It was the night before he was supposed to come home and his cousin and a group of friends had gotten some beer and were having a good time. One thing led to another and someone suggested burning a cross in front of Mt. Pilgram Church, a colored people's church. That stirred up Cane because he had no hard feelings against colored people. Maybe he was raised different or thought different from the people in Georgia but he knew deep down it was a wrong thing to do. Nevertheless, with him being seventeen and them being his cousins, he went along with the plan. The boys stole some lumber from a work site not too far from the church and made their way to Mt. Pilgram. They had figured out that two boys would dig the hole; two would be lookouts; and two would nail and set the wood on fire. Everything was going pretty much as planned until the boy carrying the gas can decided to put a little more gas on the cross after it was already lit. Well, the flames backed up on the gas can so fast that the boy stumbled and caught on fire. Cane was close enough to kick the can away and beat the flames off the boy's pants. The can, however, flew toward the church. Knowing what was about to happen, the boys panicked and high-tailed it out of there. Them boys knew they were gonna be in a heap of trouble. By now Cane knew the church was engulfed in flames and he sat there and wanted to be back in Friendly more than anything. All he could remember was that his dad had told his mother that when boys get together, then there is always going to be trouble. Boy was his dad ever right. Pete shook his head just thinking about it.

Cane's only salvation was that maybe nobody saw them. Well, when they got back to the cousin's house they didn't stand around long, because the party was over and everybody wanted to forget the whole ordeal.

The next morning though, Cane's cousin got a call from the police department and wanted him to come down to the station. Their minds started racing and they immediately started conjuring a story up, but it was useless, because when they got to the station there stood all the other boys. Cane could only hear his dad's voice over and over.

As it turned out all the boys got jailed, but it didn't take long before all 'em got bailed out. Most of 'ems folks came that same day, except Cane's. Cane stayed there for another three days before his dad showed up. That wait was ever more tough on that boy. I tell you it was!

Well, on the third day, Cane heard his dad in the front office talking to the jailer and a little while later his dad came walking down that hall for him. His dad didn't say one word except 'get your things.' Cane knew then that the silence was going to be worst than a beating. Walking out of the jail they walked across the parking lot to his dad's old dusty black Plymouth. Once Cane got in the front seat, he stared straight ahead. But then he decided to watch his dad walk behind the car back to the driver's side. When he turned to look over the front seat he jumped and hollered to the top of his lungs at the sight of someone in the backseat staring at him. He turned white as a ghost. Once he regained his composure his dad opened the door and he didn't say anything nor did anyone else the entire ten-hour trip home.

Well, it was about dusk when that black car came rolling down the gravel drive towards Cane's house. Cane's dad turned the engine off and told Cane to go inside and that he would be back in a minute to deal with the problem. By the time Mr. Dewy let me out at my house I was crying. I told Mr. Dewy that Cane was a good boy and not to hurt him, that somehow they musta talked him into doing what they did, but Mr. Dewy didn't say one word. He told me he'd see me later and told me to stay out of trouble.

I-I-I don't know what he did to Cane but I bet one thing; he never went to see his c-c-cousins in Georgia again. Pete laughed once and shook his head. Then he rubbed his lips with the palm of one hand as he gathered his thoughts.

Now, where was I? Trying to remember the story about the Klan.

Oh yeah, so anyway Cane told Bo to hit the road, but that didn't stop 'em from coming back several more times. Cane keep telling them, no. Finally, one summer night, four pickups showed up with a colored boy in the back of one. The young boy had been beat up a little and was scared nearly to death, saying not a word. The Klansmen were carrying torches and they called Cane to come out and told him to come to the 'swing.' That meant watching the man s-s-swing from a rope. They said they had caught the boy peeking into Mrs. Dickens' house, watching her daughter, Tammy Faye, take a bath. They said they were fixin' to hang them a darky for sure..

Cane knew better. He knew they picked the boy up on the road, probably walking home. Bo was lying. After Bo made his spill, Cane questioned him.

He asked Bo, 'Where did you find that boy?'

Bo said he f-f-found him hiding in the woods behind Ethel Dickens' house. She called them and told them to get over there quick. Said her girl was scared to death. Said the boy tried to climb through the window. When they got there, they saw this d-d-darky running into the woods, and found him hiding behind the tractor shed. Caught him red-handed, Bo said, and now they were going to fix him.

"Then Cane told Bo that that was a good story but asked Bo how he was going to explain Tammy Faye being over at his house getting homework up with his boy, William.

As Cane was saying that, Mrs. Kate, Tammy Faye, and William walked out on the porch. No way she could he be in two p-p-places at one time. Pete lowered his head and looked over at Barnes. Barnes nodded in agreement. Pete continued.

Well, Bo's cheeks turned red with rage when he saw that he had been caught in a lie. Even his buddies knew then that Bo had misled them.

He told Cane, they were gonna fix him anyway, just to show the other d-d-d-darkies around there who was running that place.

Well, before Bo could say another word, he heard a gun cock. Ole Able walked around from behind the truck and pointed a double barrel shotgun right at Bo's head. Pete straightened up in his seat a bit as his voice got a little higher pitch with excitement. *Now Mr. Barnes, you gots to understand that Able, he's the biggest black man you ever gonna see in your whole life time and he works for Mr. Cane.* Barnes grinned enjoying the story. He could tell it was about to get good. Pete continued. *Then the barn doors opened, and B-B-Bud, Cane's oldest boy, walked out with a shotgun.*

Cane smirked when he told Bo that it sounded like he got the wrong man.

Bo didn't say nothing. He was getting madder by the second, but he knew not to m-m-move a muscle. Then Able cocked that other barrel. That's when Cane told Mrs. Kate, Tammy Faye, and William to go back in the house. I tell you, it was sho' getting tense around there then. Nobody knew what was going to happen. Pete began wiping his lips again.

Mrs Kate told Tammy Faye and William to go b-b-back in house quick, just like Cane said. Then Cane hollered over at Bud and told him to show Bo that new D-D-D-8 dozer he just done got. Everybody knew Cane had the biggest dozer in ten counties for clearing land.

Bud told him he would be glad to. Pete laughed a little.

Cane told Bo his dozer weighed forty thousand pounds and could knock a forty-inch oak tree down with one grunt.

Pete leaned over and whispered into Barnes ear, *and if it f-f-farted real good, it could take a sixty-incher down. You will have to excuse my language, but that's just the words he said.* Caught off guard, Barnes stiffened a bit, but Pete continued on.

Then Cane asked Bo if he wanted to see how it worked, but Bo didn't say a word, mainly because Able still had that shotgun pointed at his head. Then Bud climbed on that dozer, pulled that throttle out, and hit the starter engine. I tell you that night air split like a watermelon when he pushed that starting button and throttled up. I can hear it now. When he opened her up, fire and sparks boiled out that eight-inch exhaust stack like a volcano blowing. I was watching Bud close. It took both hands for him to pull that left brake lever back, but when he did, that big dozer started swinging around and it shook the whole world I believe.

Mr. Barnes was captivated by the story as Pete told it. Even a little boy sitting behind him had his head over the seat listening. Pete leaned forward in his seat some to rest his back and continued.

Next thing that happened was that Mr. Cane motioned for Bud to move the dozer towards Bo. So Bud did as he was told, and we watched that dozer leave a set of three-foot tracks as it crawled towards him. The ground was shaking like an earthquake. It was, I tell you it was! Pete started shaking his hand back and forth imitating the ground movement as he spoke. *Bud kept his eye on his dad until he got within two feet of Bo. We could see Bo was sweating bullets 'cause he didn't know what was fixin' to happen, and neither did we. About that time, Bud dropped that blade right at Bo's feet, missing the end of his shoes by about a foot.* Pete held his hands apart indicating the distance. Barnes, astonished, could only stare at Pete's hands. *Bo was so frightened that he was gasping for breath. Cane sure had a way to g-g-get everybody's attention. He was a man of control and when he spoke, it was like G-G-God speaking.* Barnes looked to the side and stopped making eye contact with Pete when he said that. Pete turned and looked at the little boy whose eyes were now as big as saucers.

Cane asked Bo what he wanted? He was going to let it be his choice. The problem was that Bo didn't understand w-w-what Cane meant.

Then Cane told Bo it looked like Bo was fixin' to hang an innocent man and wanted to know what that was worth, a foot or a t-t-truck.

Bo started pleading with Mr. Cane, telling him to please not hurt his truck and all that junk of how it took three months to get it and so on. Cane didn't care about that stuff. Cane said that he'd just take a foot then if Bo wanted the truck so much. When he said that Bud raised the four-ton blade about eighteen inches high, and Able nudged Bo to where his foot was right up under that blade.

Cane told Bo the way he s-s-saw it, was that Bo could always have his truck rigged to where he could operate it with one of them hand clutches. Anyway, it didn't matter to Cane which one he chose, because he was fixin' to bury one of 'em that night. Yes, sir! A foot or a truck was fixin' to become Cane property. Pete couldn't help but grin as he said that and looked around and then added. *Now Cane may have added a few words here and there a little stronger to get his message across good to Bo, but I'm leaving them words out.*

You see, everybody standing around now knew that Mr. Cane meant business, 'cause he seldom cussed, but when h-h-he did, he knew just where to put them bad words to get the most out of them. One thing about it, Cane was not a fooling man. Pete was pointing his finger now. *Any man best be getting out of his way if Mr. Cane was in one of them moods.*

Pete stopped where he was and said, "Y'all sure wants me to go on with this story, its pretty long?"

Barnes chimed in quickly, "Oh, don't stop, Pete, go ahead." Looking around Pete could see the nodding of others responding the same way.

"Okay then. Tell me hush when you wants me to." Pete shucked his shoulders and continued.

At that point, nobody knew what Cane was going to do next. He was in total control. Was he bluffing? Nobody knew. I t-t-tell you right now, it had done got quieter than a mouse walking across a bale of cotton.

Now Cane demanded for Bo to talk him. You could see the veins popping out on his neck. Then Cane started counting, '5,4,3,2,' and Bo hollered, 'The foot, I w-w-want my foot, Mr. Cane! Please Mr. Cane, I want my foot.'

That's when Cane walked up within two inches of Bo's face and whispered in his ear. I'm not going to say what he said, but I tell you it got Bo's attention good. Then Cane stepped back.

'Dirt it, Bud,' Cane said, as Bo stood there as rigid as a tree.

Cane looked over at Bud, and nodded. Bud pulled back on that leaver again and started backing that big Caterpillar up. Again we could feel that awesome power and the weight of that machine. He swung around and positioned the blade right over the cab of the t-t-truck. He waited for a moment. That wait seemed like an hour. Then Bud looked at his dad, and Cane nodded. Bud dropped that huge steel blade on the cab of the truck and it folded like a sardine can. Pete popped his hands together and immediately laughter sprung throughout the coach.

No, sir, Bud didn't stop there, y'all, no he didn't. He drove over on tops of that truck next. Laughter again rang out. He must have drove over it five times until it was no more than twelve inches high.

By now Bo was crying, but he was still under the barrel of Able's shotgun. Seeing what just happened, he fell to his knees and then face down into the ground. Then when Bud called himself finished, he turned down the throttle for more instructions and Cane said, 'Good job, Bud. Dig a hole in the pasture and bury it.'

Bud said 'Yes, sir,' and dropped the blade on that D8, pushed the remains of the Bo's truck to the pasture and did what his dad said. It didn't take but twenty minutes and he was finished.

After all of that excitement, Cane walked back over to Bo and told him to stand up and told him he was fixin' to give him two pieces of good advice. He told him to listen up good." Bo was so much in shock now after watching Bud bury his truck that he just nodded a yes.

Cane told him to get off his property and never to step foot on it again, or better yet, drive by it. N-N-Number two was if he ever heard of them fooling around with this kind of junk again, well, let's put it this way, Bo would be the one coming up missing. Cane assured Bo, no one in Friendly would miss him either.

Cane asked Bo if he understood, but B-B-Bo didn't say nothing. Then Cane asked him again and grabbed him up by the collar.

When he did, Bo just squealed, 'Yes, sir, I hear you, Mr. Cane.'

The little boy behind Pete started laughing. He thought that was funny.

Cane told him, 'Good' and told him to get off his property.

I t-t-tell you, those guys got out of there like nobody's business. After that, I carried the young boy home that Bo had done messed with and told the boy he didn't have nothing to worry about. I think his family moved after that though. Wasn't but a few months later they say Bo got in trouble down in Gulfport, Mississippi. Rumor was his car ran out of control going over the Pascagoula River Bridge, jumped the rail, and was never seen again. Alligators probably had a good meal off of him. Pete shook his head, making a screwed up face thinking about that alligator.

Mr. Barnes asked, "Mr. Dodd, you okay?"

Pete laughed under his breath, thinking back about the incident. "Yeah, I'm all right, I guess. I was just t-t-thinking about how good it is to know a man like Cane. Cane, he sho' takes up for people. He just don't tolerate no junk. Do you know what I mean?" Pete stared at Barnes waiting on an answer.

Barnes gave him a nod.

"It's unusual in this day and time. W-W-White man stands to lose a lot siding with a black man. But to Cane, it don't matter. Right is right and wrong is wrong."

Pete looked around and saw that four or five people had been listening to him. The little boy had come around the seat and was leaning over Mr. Barnes's lap, and the boy's mother was now leaning over the back of the seat. The people across the aisle were beginning to lean so they could hear better too. Pete tilted forward in his seat to get more relaxed and continued with his story.

After that incident with Bo and the Klan, I thoughts it was best to send my boy to live with my sister up north. I was just too scared that Bo and them others would take revenge on him and do something bad. That took a lot out of me. With these words an old woman sitting across the aisle reached and patted her grandson on the leg and pulled him closer for a hug. The few people still carrying on private conversations seemed to notice the quietness sweeping through the car and looked to see what the source was. Pete pursed his lips and shook his head slowly from side to side displaying his deep emotions. He remained silent for a few moments and then continued after clearing his throat. He could see that Barnes was waiting.

Now my wife, Dorothy, she was one of the sweetest and best things that ever happened to me. We went to church every Sunday. We never missed, and we were always the first ones there. Now, that girl, she could cook, too. And if anyone forgot to bless the food, well, they better not forget! Not only was she a good cook for me and my boy, but she was a good cook for the whole Cane family. By now Pete was unaware of his captive audience. He spoke as freely as if he had just left Dorothy at the train station. His eyes followed the tilting of his head as he moved from aspect to another. He never looked directly at anyone, but seemed to ramble on as if he were casually whittling on a stick.

She helped Mrs. Kate, that's Cane's wife, every day, cooking, cleaning, canning, and washing around the Cane house. With all them boys it took a lot of help. You name it; they did it. Her and Mrs. Kate made a good team. Each day when eating time came, she made sure the meal was on the table good and hot. During the meal, she would always take her post in the corner of the kitchen to make sure everyone had just what they needed. And she was right there in every conversation, too. Sometimes, too much. She sure didn't mind giving her opinion. She sure didn't.

She could fill your ears up with what she thought was right and wrong. She could get away with telling Cane stuff that he would have scorned anyone else if they said it. Many times Cane just shook his head and said, 'Okay, Dorothy, you win. Just let me finish eating in peace.' She was usually still talking when everyone excused themselves from the table. She loved her work, and the Cane family was her family just like her own.

She worked until two months before she died. It was real hard on everybody, especially on the kids. She had been right there with all of them growing up, loving and whipping them just like Mrs. Kate did.

Now, my nephew's wife, Lizzy, is doing all the maid work. You know I told you while ago about Able. He was the one with the shotgun at Bo's ear. Well, her and her husband Able's doing just like me and Dorothy did there at the farm. She's helping in the house and Able he watches the farm.

Pete had a lot on his chest. It seemed okay at first to tell this stranger everything when he couldn't tell anyone else. Maybe it was because he knew he would never see him again. But by now, everyone around him on the train was his audience. Strangely it didn't bother him anymore. It felt good.

A girl who was about thirteen years of age asked Pete, "Where did you meet Mr. Cane?"

Pete rubbed the top of his head again, glanced out the window and saw farms, tractors, white cotton, and a lot of memories go by. When he turned back around, everyone was just waiting on his next word so he continued.

Well, you see, I went to work for Cane when I came out of the army. It was in the army that I saved Cane's life that second time. The first time was when Cane was about ten years old.

The little girl said impatiently, "What happened?"

"Hold on, honey and I'll tell you," Pete said, patting at the little girl's hand.

You see, Cane and his little sister were down at the mill pond. That's a pond where all the white folks would go swim and cool off. Cane and his sister were not supposed to be there, 'cause nobody was there to watch 'em. Anyway, colored folk couldn't go down there, you know. That pond was just for white boys and girls.

That day Cane was walking out on a minnow trap.

"What's that?" the little girl asked.

Pete tried to explain.

A minnow trap was something like a pier, but had a net attached to it. Minnows could be raised, but fish couldn't get in and eat 'em up. She seemed satisfied with the answer, so he continued. *Well, as he walked out on it, a rotten board gave way, and he fell in. His sister, Rita, tried her best to save him, but he went under water too fast. So she ran as hard as she could to the top of the hill. When she got there, she saw me riding my old bicycle down the road. She ran up and pulled me off that bicycle before she could finish telling me what was wrong. At first, I thought she was crazy and trying to kill me, so I fought her off trying to get away. I done decided to leave my bike and make a run for it, but then I realized she was frightened to death and needed help. When I got her calmed down, she told me what had happened. I asked her, 'Where is he?'*

She couldn't talk, just pointed, and we both started running down the hill as fast as we could. About half way down I stopped and hesitated for a second because I knew I wasn't supposed to be down there, but figuring this was important enough excuse, I took off running anyway to the pond's edge. I outran Rita and got there first. I stopped and looked. The water was calm and spooky looking. I told Rita I hadn't ever gone underwater before. I just been swimming on top of water and was still trying to learn to go under.

Pete stopped and laughed. *I told her my brothers always teased me about swimming like a tadpole. Anyway, she pointed and told me I was going to die a tadpole if I didn't get out there on that pier.*

So I walked out to the end of the pier, placing one foot in front of the other. I couldn't see no bubbles nowhere. The water sho' looked dark and scary to me, but I knew I had to jump in. I paused for a few seconds. 'Well, I guess it's time you learned to swim like a fish now,' Rita said, and pushed me in. I didn't have time to think. As soon as I hit the water, I was trying to find and hold on to the edge of the pier.

As I held on to the wood planks, I tried to feel down below with my feet. The water was too deep. My mind was racing. I knew I was fixin' to have to go underwater. I tried once, but as far as I got was my eyes underwater, and then I shot back up.

I told Rita I couldn't go under. Rita hollered at me and told me I could; to just try again. She was running back and forth on the minnow trap, out of control. I knew her brother was probably gone by now, but I had to try anyway. I took a deep breath and went under. Rita could see my feet splashing as I turned my head down. Then I was out of sight. 'Would I find him?' was running through my mind as I saw nothing but total darkness. Then with a big splash, I was back on top, gasping for air.

"Can't find him. You sure it was here that he went under?" I asked Rita.

'NO! Go out further,' she said.

I could feel my own eyeballs growing in my head now. Okay here goes, I told her.

I turned back down again. Ten seconds passed, twenty seconds passed, thirty seconds passed; then all of a sudden I came up with Cane's head under my arm. "Help me quick," I was gasping for air. I told Rita hurry up and help me because I couldn't hold him no longer.

Rita tried to reach out to get her brother's arm but she couldn't.

By now, Miss Guthrie, a neighbor, had heard all the commotion and had run down to the pond. She jumped right in. She grabbed Cane and pulled him on out. What a sight. I swam out right behind her, dog paddling the whole way, just like a tadpole.

We both watched as Mrs. Guthrie turned Cane on his stomach and pumped that water out of him. He was blue as a catfish. She must have worked on that boy three or four minutes before he came to. Then he coughed and started crying. By now me and Rita were both crying. We were scared to death and happy at the same time. Even Mrs. Guthrie started crying when Cane started breathing.

Mrs. Guthrie looked up at me and said, 'Boy, whoever you are, you have done the bravest thing in the whole world. You should be proud of yourself.'

By then, several other neighbors gathered around and helped carry Cane back up the hill. Several of 'em patted me on the back. They wrapped him in blankets to keep him warm and I remember one old man said, 'Wrap him good tonight. Probably gonna get the pneumonia.'

Well, Cane never got the pneumonia and was up like a chicken the next morning. His mamma said he didn't say two words as he walked through the kitchen and went outside, straddled his new bicycle, and took off.

Rita asked her mom where he was going and her mom told her she thought she knew. He rode his bike straight to my house.

When he got there, my daddy was cutting firewood. My mom came out on the porch and just stared like she had seen a miracle because she had done heard what had happened. I remember it just like it was yesterday. I had come out from behind the house with a bucket in my hand because I had been feeding the chickens. Several were still following me, pecking at the bucket.

Cane walked up to me and stared at me face to face without saying a word. We stood ten or fifteen seconds, just looking at each other. I noticed we were about the same size. He seemed smaller when I pulled him out of the water. Maybe because I was so scared.

Then Cane told me, 'Pete, I'm John, John Cane. You saved my life. I ain't ever gonna forget it. I owe you all I got and all I'll ever have, but for right now, I want you to have the only thing I own. Bought it with my own money last year. Paid thirty-five dollars for it. It's yours.' He let go of the Western Flyer bicycle he rode up on, and I caught it before it fell over.

'You don't have to do this, you know,' I told him.

Cane just said he knew that and then pushed the bike towards me. 'It's yours now.' he said.

Cane stuck his hand out to shake my hand. I hesitated first, then stuck my hand out to his hand. I turned to look at my dad, and he started grinning with approval and looked at Mom. They were so proud of me for what I did. I can still see.... Pete held his hand over his mouth to cough, stopping midway in his sentence and trying to hold the thought. Then he continued. *I can still see Cane turning and walking back up that road.*

And there's one point I forgot to tell. That was, when Cane started walking away, he stopped and turned around and told me, 'Hey, Pete, remember, that's just a down payment.' Then he walked on home.

"Wow!" Said the girl who had asked Pete the question. "But I thought you said that was the first time. You said you saved him two times."

"I did, but surely y'all don't want me running my mouth anymore, do you?"

One woman spoke up and said she had never heard a story like that in her whole life. She was in tears. "Sure we do, tell us how it happened."

Pete reached for a glass of water on a nearby tray and took a deep swallow. He flushed the cool water around in his mouth for a few seconds to help quince the dryness he had built up talking.

He looked around and saw everyone waiting. "Okay, her goes."

That was the first time and now you know w-w-why Cane was so embarrassed and ashamed that d-d-day we all came back from Georgia when he took part in that cross burning. He knowed he had done my people wrong that day, especially after I done saved his life.

And yes, there was a second time, too. You see, Cane joined up in the army in 1941, and so did I. The United States had done declared war on Germany and Japan, and we were both fighting over in Europe. Of course, we were in different branches of the service, so neither one of us knew that the other was over there.

The way it turned out, as I understand it, Cane kept getting promoted because all his upper officers kept getting shot up. He said it seemed like one day he was a private, and then the next day he was a private first class. Then in about a month, papers would catch up with him, and he'd find out that he was promoted to a sergeant.

Well, in December 1944 Cane was in France and so was I. It was the coldest winter I think I ever remember. I tell you it was cold. Bad cold! Both of us had done been overseas three years then. Neither one of us had talked to our wife's or family since we left. Just a letter here and there would catch up with us once in a while. That's about the way it was with all of us.

I tell you it was tough on our familys' back then. Cane only had one boy, Bud, then, but I think Mrs. Kate was expecting William when he left. All I had was my Dorothy.

Anyway, Cane was like the rest of us soldiers' over there. None of us thought we were coming home. Pete's face was taut as could be. *Well, the way I understand it, Cane's whole company got surrounded somehow and no support looked like they were coming at all. It was just his company against a whole battalion of the Germans. The cold was so bad at night that all the wounded were just freezing to death. Those medic couldn't do nothing.* Pete just shook his head more.

Caught in a crossfire and pinned down good, it wasn't but one thing left to do Cane said. Somebody had to make his way up to the top of one of them ridges and take out a position. It was suicide and he knew it.

Well, if you know Cane it was understandable when all he told his men was 'cover me.' He jumped out of that foxhole and started running up that hill as fast as he could. Them guns sounded like fireworks going

128

off on New Year's Eve he said. He was jumping, falling, shootin', and everything else he could do to stay alive. Somehow he managed to get about half way up before he got hit in his left arm and then his leg.

Pete looked at Barnes directly in the eyes. *Lead shootin' through you is just like eating hot coals. It burns you all the way down. It feels like your insides are on fire.*

Well, all he could do was cover his head. Artillery had been called in on his men's position and from where he was it looked as if his unit took a direct hit from a mortar round. If he had stayed, he'd be dead with the rest of 'em. The whole place just went up in pieces he said. Now, he said he feared for his life for the first time. He figured it was all over. His only two choices were bleed to death or freeze to death. Neither was an option he desired, but that was just the way it was.

'What a place and a way to spend your last days,' Barnes whispered to himself.

Pete tilted his head agreeing with him and continued. *"He knew he needed to stay conscious so he started trying to focus and remember all the good things that had happened to him in his life. I guess you'd say his life was passing before his eyes. Anything he could remember he was trying to bring to mind. He tried to think about Mrs. Kate and Bud, the farm, growing up, and all the things he had taken for granted. He remembered the grocery stores, the clothing stores and every store on the town square. Then he tried to remember who worked in the stores. He remembered his pastor coming to see him the day he left and how they prayed for his safety. He remembered the last meal he had at home with his family. He tried to remember all of his teachers from first grade through high school and his teammates on the baseball team. Just anything to keep his mind awake was what he was doing.*

Then he said he thought about me. Yeah, me, Pete, and the day I saved his life a long time ago when we was only twelve years old. He said he prayed and thanked God for givin' him a second chance in life, even though it was windin' up like this.

He said after that prayer, he looked at his blood soaked coat and his shot-up arm and legs and realized he couldn't even get his .45-caliber pistol out of the holster to take his own life. He knew then he was down to one option and that one option was freezing to death. So he just lay there as the firing continued. He figured it wouldn't be long now 'fore some German would walk up and put a slug in his head. Then the gunfire picked heavier than ever.

'Please, God let me go this time. I can't take any more!' he cried. But God didn't listen to Cane that day, y'all. He said he heard soldiers coming. He tried lying still so that maybe they'd pass over him.

As he lay there, seconds seemed like hours, and minutes seemed like days. He was preparing for the final call. He said he closed his eyes and listened. He was fading, but he kept resisting the comfort of giving up. In the background, he could barely make out the sound of the clank, clank, clanking of tracks, the sound of tanks getting closer. Then, the clanking stopped. Then he heard another stop and then another. There was silence he said. All that could be heard was the turning of the turrets atop the tanks.

Pete used his finger and made the gesture of turning. *One by one they were marking their targets.*

Then he heard an al- out cry, 'Take the hill. Take'em out!' As he tried to make sense out of it, he opened his eyes in revelation. That was an American shouting!' The guns opened up again, but this time he could tell more lead was being shot up the hills than being shot down the hills. The fire power was awesome. The thunder from that tank division was blowin' trees, mud, rocks, and armored vehicles to bits. Craters, the size of houses, were taking the place where them German artillery had been. Whoever that was, they were coming in numbers and with big guns for sure. Then, it stopped. He was confused. There was silence again, and then footsteps coming as the firing started again. The German guns opened up. About that time, a heavy body just crashed in on top of him taking cover. It didn't even hurt he said. He was so numb from the cold nothing mattered anymore.

Can you believe it was me that fell on top of him. Of all the people in the whole wide world to jump in a hole with, I never expected that we'd meet up like that. My wife, Dorothy, had told me she had seen Mrs. Kate, and she mentioned that Cane was somewhere in Europe, but she didn't know where. She asked Dorothy to write me and tell me if I ran across him, to be sho' to tell him she loved him.

At the time, I thought he was just another dead soldier until he moved. That's when I hollered, 'I have a live one!' I turned him over and told him to talk to me if he was alive because I wasn't hanging around long. I knew more of them German soldiers were on their way and would be breathin' down our necks pretty fast. When I turned Cane's head, I couldn't believe my eyes and neither could he.

I said, 'Mr. Cane! What in the heck you doing here, man?' Then I saw how shot up he was. It was a bad sight but I knew we had to get out of there fast. It wouldn't be long before that whole hill was going to be blown up. We needed to get the heck out of there now. So I heaved Cane on my shoulder, and down the hill we went.

As soon as I jumped up, them Germans opened fire again. Pete gritted his teeth and shook his head displaying the velocity of the gunfire that surrounded him. When two waiters' trays clanked as they passed in the aisle, Pete jumped and hollered. When he did, John Barnes jumped and hollered, too, for he was caught up in the story. Pete paused as the lights began to flicker and dim throughout the car. As the audience looked around at each other scanning the room, an eerie look crossed their faces. Pete waited a few moments and then the lights brightened. He looked at John and then scanned the room and continued. *I didn't know if we would make it or not because the gunfire seemed to be everywhere I stepped. That's when I told him, 'Kate said she loves you.' He didn't know what I was talking about, but I said it anyway. I sho' wanted to tell her if I made it and he didn't, that he got the word.*

'What you say, Pete?' Cane groaned, *trying to make sense out what I was saying. I mean I was in a full sprint with him on my shoulder.*

'I said yo' wife said she loves you.'

'What did you say, Pete?' Cane muttered again.

Before I could answer, I fell in a hole, and we both tumbled. The next thing I knew we were both laying there looking at each other. So while I was catchin' my breath, I told him again real slow.

'Sir, *yo' wife saw my wife, and my wife told me to tell you that yo' wife loves you. Got it?'*

He didn't say nothing. He had passed out. Can you believe that? He still didn't get the message. I figured I told him anyway, regardless if he heard me or not. Kinda like we do our kids today. We tell'em but half the time it goes in one ear and out the other. There was a chuckle a few rows up and a few couples bumping the arms of their kids in agreement with the statement. Pete smiled, as John nodded in agreement. *So I picked him up again and waited until the firing slowed down. I pulled myself out of that hole and ran as hard as I could. It was just like those suckers knew I was going to jump out of that hole, though.*

Bullets started hitting right behind me. In fact, the sole of my shoe got shot clean off. Now, that is as close as it can get. I must have carried him three hundred yards back down that hill before ,I got him to the medics.

I went over to the stretcher to see how he was doing right before they hauled him out of there, and I could tell he was coming and going in and out of consciousness. He opened his eyes and tried to say something, but I cut him off and told him, 'Man, you better stop usin' up all them lives. You gonna run out one day.'

Cane tried to speak back to me trying to reach for my hand, but all he could say was, 'Not as long as you're around, Pete. Thanks.' Then he passed out again.

Well, that was it. Pete straightened up in his seat thinking that was probably enough of his jabbering but the captive audience had not had enough yet. They wanted to hear more, so reluctantly he went on with the story.

I thought about him almost every day until the war ended. I knew he made it, but I didn't know what kind of shape he was in. I only got one more letter from my Dorothy, and she said she hadn't seen Mrs. Kate to find out, but heard he was sent to a hospital somewhere.

We didn't see each other again until one day in Washington. It was almost spooky the way it happened. We were both present for a ceremony for soldiers recognized for valor. Of course, neither one of us knew the other was there. You see, he was a Marine, and I was Army. When my name was announced, Mrs. Kate said he started looking hard to see me across the field in my regiment. As the awards made their way around, and they called his name out, I started looking to see him. That's when we both saw each other for the first time since that day. Harry S. Truman, himself, pinned that Silver Star on me and the Medal of Honor on Mr. Cane that day.

After we were dismissed, Cane, Mrs. Kate, little Bud and their newborn, William, made their way over to where I was standing. I could tell Mr. Cane still had a pretty good limp when he walked, and his arm was still in a sling. But he looked good considering what he'd done been through. We looked at each other just like we did that day when Cane brought me his bike. We just looked at each other with no words. As I reached out to shake his hand, Cane embraced me. The emotion was too great. As I looked at those painful lines in Cane's face, I could see in his eyes that he had aged ten years and so had I. We stood there and hugged each other just glad to be home again.

I tell you we were glad to be home and alive. Cane, asked then what I was going to do now that the war was over.

I said, 'I guess I gonna go back home and try to find a job.'

Cane told me it wasn't no use in looking no further for work as long as he had a farm and was alive. He said it would be awhile before he could do a good day's work, and he could sure use the help. That's when Mrs. Kate spoke up and said she could use help too, and welcomed Dorothy to help out too.

I told Mr. Cane, if keeping him alive meant keeping a job, then we'll take him up on that offer because I sho'had a good track record.

Then he said, Cane, my friends call me Cane.

We shook hands again and smiled glad to be alive. Then we went on our separate ways. Pete held both hands up and said, "No more. That's it."

By now several people listening to Pete's story were crying. The thirteen-year-old girl said, walking back to her seat and wiping away tears, "That was so wonderful, that was a beautiful story." Pete turned his head towards the window and everyone went back to their seats.

Barnes, the man with the straw hat, was touched by the story and said, "Well, Mr. Dodd, where is Cane now?"

"Well, I'm still with him," said Pete.

"You don't say," said Barnes.

"I'm guess you might say I ain't the man I supposed to be, though. He's held his end of the bargain but I ain't done mine."

Mr. Barnes, pulled opened his coat and handed Pete a small Bible tract. Pete looked down and read it. It said, *Yea, though I walk through the valley of the shadow of death, I will fear no evil, for thou art with me, thy rod and thy staff they comfort me.*

Mr. Barnes said, "Pete, everything is going to be all right. I assure you God knows what you are going through right now, and you're not supposed to be able to figure it out. You and your son Matthew were close, and I know that. God knows that, too. Matthew loved you. Matthew knew why you sent him away, and he loved you for it. He didn't resent you for that. Why the Lord works the way he does, no one will ever know, but you must remember, God stands for what's good in this world. So whatever he does, we must trust him. God can use whatever happens to us for the good of all people. You believe that, Pete?"

Pete didn't say anything. He just sat there with a distant look in his eyes. Then Barnes got up, gently put his hand on Pete's shoulder, and walked to the back of the train.

Pete read the verses several more times. Each time he read the words, he felt a little better. Even though he had lost all that had mattered to him, first losing Dorothy and then his only son, he felt a peace coming over him. It was almost like a supernatural feeling. Although it was a strange feeling, it was a good feeling. Pete immediately stood up and started looking for the man. He made his way completely through the train, stopping several times asking people if they had seen a man with a straw hat on. Each person said, "No." Finally he asked the conductor if he had seen the man.

The conductor said told Pete, "I don't recall a man fitting that description. Humm, what was his name?"

"He says his name was Barnes. John Barnes. I believe he says he was headin' to Chicago."

"Humm! Let's see here," the conductor said, running his fingers down the passenger list. "No, I'm sorry. There is no man on this train named John Barnes headed for Chicago. Could it be another name."

Pete told the conductor that he was sorry. Maybe he had misunderstood the man. So he went back to his seat and sat down, staring out the window as they approached the next town. The train didn't stop. It just passed on through. As it sped by the station, Pete got a glimpse of a man with a straw hat, standing in front of the depot. The man made eye contact with him, smiled, and tipped his hat. Then he remembered, he never told the man Matthew's name. How did he know?

Pete was now headed towards Detroit. The train stopped in Chicago for about an hour and then headed east. A cold chill came over Pete. He was thinking again about Matthew and what had happened. He was feeling a little sick and decided to walk about. As he was going through the diner, he spotted the nurse sitting by herself, drinking coffee. He saw her look at him for a quick moment before turning back to the book she was reading. Pete asked the waiter for a cup of coffee, which was unusual. He would usually be asking for a drink. He found a table, sat down and began sipping his coffee when noticed the lady look at him again. This time it was no coincidence. She was watching him. Placing his empty cup down, he started walking back to his seat, when by mistake she dropped her bookmarker on the floor. As he bent over to pick it up for her, he noticed the white nurse shoes and her uniform under her raincoat.

"I'm sorry if I knocked that out of your book, ma'm," Pete said.

"Oh, no, you didn't. It was my mistake." There was something familiar about the woman.

"Ma'am," said Pete. "Do I-I-I know you from somewhere? I know I saw you earlier, but it didn't d-d-dawn on me then due to the situation, but now..."

"I don't know if you do or not." She looked at him closer. Now she was thinking that she may have crossed his path before.

"I swear I've seen your face before," Pete said. "You look so familiar, but I just can't p-p-place you. Where do you live?"

She said, "Detroit. And you?"

"Oh, I-I-I'm from the South. I'm from M-M-Mississippi."

She looked harder at his face. "I could tell that by your accent." she said not surprised, but still trying to connect. "You do look familiar, too. Were you ever in the military?"

"Sho' was."

"Overseas?" she asked.

"Yep. July '41 to A-A-August '45." he said, still studdering.

"Ever stationed in England or France?" she asked.

"Yes, I was." Pete was hoping she had figured it out.

"Humm, I was there too. I was with the Red Cross. I tell you, all the nurses were so proud of you guys. It was so horrible though. I saw so many young men die, and I saw so many others make it, only to wish they hadn't. It sure hurts when you can't do anything but watch. "

"Yes, y-you are right. There were a many dads, sons and brothers lost." Pete looked down and gazed into his coffee as if speaking to it. "There were very few bright days then. We just did what we could. I guess it's like everything, not everybody's suppose to make it back from war. Some gotta die." Pete looked back at her, watching as she closed her eyes. She just shook her head slightly. Pete could see something was wrong.

"Oh, I'm sorry. Did you loose somebody?" Pete apologized, touching her hand.

"Not in the war. I lost my younger brother in an accident when he was small. He slipped through the ice where we were playing, and no one was there to save him. I tried, but I was too small." She shook her head again.

"I-I-I'm very sorry," Pete said.

"It's not your fault. When you said, 'some have to die,' then cold chills ran up my back." Pete was listening. "I guess I know the pain of what many of the families have gone through after the war." Then with a sudden smile she said, "But you know what? Life goes on, doesn't it?"

"Yep, it sure does?" Pete said, smiling back. "She shook her head, still in disbelief of the tragedy. Then she used her napkin and wiped her eyes and placing it on the table beside the bookmark.

Pete could tell it was still hard on her, regardless of what she said.

Trying to change the subject, he asked, "I didn't catch your name?"

"Naomi Washington," she said, grateful for the change in subject.

"That's, a l-l-lovely name. I-I-I'm Pete Dodd from Friendly, Mississippi." He nodded, as he smiled and extended his hand.

"Well, good to meet you, Mr. Dodd. I'm glad you were one of the lucky ones," she smiled, too, and shook his hand. "I've never been to Mississippi, but one day I would like to go."

"Well, if you do go, stop by Friendly. It's a good little place to visit."

Naomi looked down at Pete's hand and saw the silver wedding band on his finger. She really didn't want to ask and kind of hesitated before saying, "Mr. Dodd, where is Mrs. Dodd?"

He looked down, smiling. "Long story, ma'm."

"Look, you don't have to call me 'ma'm.' My name is Naomi, okay?" she said, laughing.

"Okay, whatever you s-s-say," replied Pete. He took a deep breath before answering her. "Well, I lost her about three years ago."

"What happened?" Naomi asked, frowning.

"I knew something was wrong because she was hurting so bad. We were having our second c-c-child. It just wasn't like the first. This one k-k-kinda slipped up on us. It had been almost eight years. Do you know what I mean?"

"Oh, yes, I do," Naomi said. "Go on."

"Well, it was getting time, and her water broke about 11:30 that night. I-I-I grabbed her bags we had already p-p-packed and took off to the hospital. On the way, somebody's cows were out in the road. I tried my best to m-m-miss them and nearly did, but I broad-sided one anyway. It just caved the front fender into the wheel of the truck. Of course, it blew the tire out too. The damage was so bad that the truck wouldn't move.

"Matthew, my boy was with us. He was crying so b-b-bad that he couldn't catch his breath. I was in a panic. I knew Dorothy was suffering, but she didn't complain. She wasn't that type. She was always cool-headed. We weren't far from Mr. John Cane's house. He's the man I work for. I told M-M-Matthew to run to his house and get him up and come q-q-quick. I stayed with Dorothy until him and Mrs. Kate got there, but it was too late. Dorothy was nearly gone. I placed her in the b-b-back of Mr. Cane's truck and told Matthew to get up front with Mr. and Mrs. Cane. I can still see that boy's eyes peering out the back glass, watching his mamma die. Mr. Cane drove that truck so fast that I was sure thinking he was going to kill everybody. That man loved Dorothy as much as I did."

"When we got to the hospital, Mr. Cane ran inside and t-t-told them to get a doctor fast. It was just too late. Everything seemed to go wrong. The doctors said she would have had a hard time anyway, regardless of the delay. She was hemorrhaging and they couldn't s-s-stop the bleeding. They must have worked on her for three hours or more. My baby girl died too. We buried Dorothy and baby T, T was for Teresa, two days later on the farm. We b-b-buried them together.

"Mr. Cane said that was where she belonged and offered a spot in the family cemetery for her and the baby. M-M-Matthew had a hard time with the death of his mom. He always thought that if he could have run harder and faster, it could have made a difference. I'm afraid he has carried that with him all his life. It wouldn't have made no d-d-difference at all."

Pete looked down at his wedding band and stared, "She was a good woman. A good woman, and I loved her, too."

Naomi looked down at her hands and then out the window at the tall grass blowing. Pete cleared his throat before standing up.

"Pete, are you all right?" she said.

"I guess I have to be until I finish this life. I just don't know how much more I can take." He then paused.

"Look, I'm gonna get a drink. Do you w-w-want one?" he asked.

"No, I don't drink. You go ahead though and get what you want."

Pete stood up and walked back to the bar and ordered a whiskey. He needed one, bad. As he got the drink, he handed the round-faced bartender one-dollar and turned to look back at the booth where they were sitting. To his surprise, she was gone. He stepped by a few people standing in the isle and made his way over to the table. Looking down at the table he noticed the bookmark. He turned it over hoping to find something on it but didn't see anything. He tilted his head back as if to take a swallow of his drink but stopped before the cup even neared his lips. "Do I really need this drink?" He slowly put the drink down on the table beside his coffee cup and picked up the napkin she had used to wipe her tears. Examining it closely, he was confused about the whole scenario. He folded it and put it in his coat pocket and waited for another thirty minutes but she never returned. Moving back to his seat and adjusting his seat back, he closed his eyes to the sound of the tracks echoing through the car.

* * * * *

Fourteen

A Dime's Worth

JUSTIN DIDN'T KNOW whether he was alive or dead after the tornado passed. "See there, Jussin, the Lord can make a new day just that fast." Able snapped his fingers. "When the world seems like it's gonna cave in, don't give up. Trust in the Lord. Alexander:1:1. That's my motto. I always live by it." Then Able started grinning and tapping his fingers on the steering wheel.

Justin grinned, knowing he was learning about a man who lived day-to-day by faith and was having the time of his life. Now he knew why his dad liked Able and Lizzy so much. He had never seen this side of

Able. Able had opened up to him and showed him that worrying about everyday things can do nothing for you. You have to have faith that the Lord is going to take care of you.

"'If the Lord is in control, who can be against you?' Humm. That almost sounded like scripture," Justin told himself. Then he thought, "Had he been around Able too long or had he learned that in Bible drill?"

"You know, Jussin, we ain't told your dad we gonna be late and what we're up to. Reckon we better stop up here and give him a call," Able said.

Able slowed down coming into the small community of Isola. There wasn't much to the place except for four or five old brick buildings and a yellow grocery store. The store had a name across the front painted in big green letters, "Pettit's General Store and Grocery." Some of the railings across the front porch were missing, and the steps going off each end were not in the best of shape. The double front doors apparently stayed open most of the time. That aided the ceiling fans in creating enough turbulence to rid the store of flies and fleas. A couple of beagle hounds slept at the front door, and anyone coming or going had to be careful not to trip over them.

Able spotted a pay phone hanging on the corner of the store, so he pulled the truck into a parking space and stopped. He and Justin could see some commotion inside, but they really didn't think much. It sounded like people were laughing and carrying on. Able told Justin that he'd be back; he was going to call Justin's dad. So he got out of the truck, leaving the motor running, and walked up to the pay phone digging for a dime. With no luck, he felt around in the coin return on the phone to see if anybody had left a dime. Lucky for him, there was one there. He turned to Justin and pointed up as confirming the Lord was watching out for them. With that bit of blessing came a big old grin across Able's face and a snap of his fingers.

No quicker than Able got the dime in and the phone to his ear, there was a Bang! Bang! Bang! Justin looked over his shoulder and saw a crazed man running toward him with a gun in his hand. As the man approached the truck, he stuck his hand through the truck window, put the gun to Justin's head, and told him to move over. He quickly jerked the door open and got in, throwing the paper sack full of money on the seat. He looked at Justin and said, "Drive."

"Mister, I'm only twelve years old; ...I can't drive."

"You do what I tell you, boy, or I'm going to blow your brains all over this seat."

Just then Mr. Pettit, the owner, came out the door yelling, "We've been robbed! We've been robbed!"

"Move! Now, boy! Move! I said! Quick, get under that wheel!"

Justin instantaneously slid under the wheel as the man slammed the door. Justin intentionally started fumbling with the gears because he saw what was about to happen.

"Hey! Hey, you. I'm talking to you!" The man heard a voice speaking outside the passenger side.

The man turned and looked through the passenger window to see where the voice was coming. When he turned, all he could see was a huge black fist the size of a basketball coming right at his nose. It was split second timing. Justin felt the concussion all the way over on his side of the truck. Able hit the man so hard that the gun and several teeth flew right past Justin's nose, heading out the opposite window.

The semiconscious man starting fighting his way over Justin to get away, but Able's big hand came back through the window and grabbed him by the collar. The man squalled like a chicken. He was kicking hard as he could as Able dragged him out through the passenger window. When Able got him out the window, he held him by his belt and throat about two feet off the ground. The man was just dangling there as Able pulled him closer to his face and spoke almost whispering.

"Don't you know better than to go trying to hurt a little kid and be telling him you gonna blow his brains out? What you think his mamma would do if you blowed her boy's brains out all over that truck seat? Huh?"

The man didn't say anything. Able squeezed a little tighter around his neck. "I'll tell you what I think. That would mess his mamma's mind up. Mess his daddy's mind up too." Able paused as he examined his grip on the man neck. "Yeah, Mister, you lucky today, 'cause that didn't happen."

Obviously, the longer Able talked to the man, the madder he got and the harder he squeezed the man's throat. The blood vessels in the man's neck and forehead were pulsing furiously. Justin had never seen Able this mad before. He was trembling. Able looked around to see who was watching. Justin just knew he would snap the man's neck at any moment.

"Yeah, you sho' lucky," Able said again, raising his voice. "See you lucky cause I's might let you live. But you's could be unlucky today too, because you gonna wish you were dead when I get through with you. Let me introduce myself. I be's Able. Right now I can be Able to let you live or I can be Able to let you die. Now what's it gonna be?" Able wanted to kill him right there. If it had been years before he wouldn't have hesitated. Like the time he was in high school and some boy made a comment about Jeanna. He knew what the boy said wasn't true, so he went to the boy's homeroom and called him out of class. The teacher thought Able had been sent by the principal to come get the boy, so she sent him off with Able. As soon as that boy walked out of the class, Able threw him up against the lockers. The boy's body slammed against the metal so loudly that the teacher ran out to see what was going on. It took that teacher and three more teachers to pull Able off the boy. Needless to say, Able got suspended for the incident. Later, he considered himself lucky. He knew they should have thrown him out of school altogether and would had if his parents not just been killed. He was man of the house now and he wasn't going to let anybody mess with what little family he had left. He felt that kind of rage now, too. Justin was as close as family and that man had tried to take him away. Able squeezed harder and the man struggled for air.

People in the store and others who had stopped in their cars were gathering to watch Able. Able slowly turned around towards the gas pumps, meeting the gazes of the curious onlookers.

He continued, "If I wasn't a God-fearing man, I'd soak you in that gas and set you on fire. But I is a God-fearing man, and I'm gonna let you live. Mister, you gonna get on your knees and tell that man and woman in that store you just robbed that you sorry for what you done." Able eased the man to the ground, still gripping him on the shoulder and pushing him down. The man looked at the couple with fear of what might be coming next.

"I...I...I... I'm sorry for what I did ma'am...mister. I don't know what made me do it."

"That's pretty good. Now tell this kid over here you sorry for telling him you was going to blow his brains out." Able said. Saying that, Able's eyes turned blood red with anger just thinking about it.

"I...I...I'm sorry, boy," the robber said.

"That's all you gonna tell the boy?" Abe said tightening his grip again.

"No," said the man. "I wasn't gonna hurt you, boy. I was just trying to scare you. I promise. I swear," the man was weeping out of control.

Able turned to the crowd as if he were a politician.

"I think everybody here accepts your apology, mister." Able said as they reluctantly nodded, okay. "Now, it looks like you done taken care of all the apologies except for mine. The way I see it, nobody's been hurt, nobody's lost nothing, except me."

The man looked up with a blank look on his bloody face because he couldn't remember doing anything to Able. All he remembered was that Able hit him through the window. Then Able spoke.

"You see, I was over there making a phone call and because of all this commotion you started, I lost my dime and my blessing in that phone machine. So you see, I lost something I needed. That was going to be a very important phone call," Able said. "So, I'm gonna get my dime's worth out of you."

With that, Able picked the man up two feet higher over his head, twirled him around, and then threw him head first into the gas pump. The man's head hit the side of the pump so hard that he put a dent in it as big as a watermelon. The man bounced off and just slithered down to the ground as everybody cheered. He was out cold.

Old Mrs. Pettit ran through the people to Able and just grabbed his hand, crying humbly and told him "Thank you, son. God bless you. You are a Godsend to us. Oh, thank you so much."

That made Able feel good when she said that. He took a big breath in and smiled, then told the lady it wasn't nothing to it. Then he walked to the truck, reached in for the sack of money and handed it to her. He told her and her husband he was glad to be of help. Justin felt ten feet tall. As

Able and Justin walked back to the truck, Justin couldn't keep a straight face. He was grinning so much he couldn't hold it back. He knew he was on the winning team. Abe was his hero!

* * * * *

Fifteen

The Picnic

L ET'S GO, JUSSIN. We gonna be late if we don't hit the
road. You all right now?" Able asked.

"Yeah, I'm okay,"

As they drove off, they met the same highway patrolman they had
met about an hour earlier during the tornado. He was coming to assist in
the arrest of the knocked-out robber. As they passed, the patrolman did a
double take. Able and Justin both looked straight ahead. Justin could see
right away that this was going to be a trip he would never forget.

"Jussin, we'll make that call again later down the road when we stop and get us somethin' to eat," Able said. "Right now, my stomach says it's gettin' pretty close to lunch time."

"Mine too, Abe. I could sure use a good hamburger."

"Shoot, I think I could eat a cow right now I'm so hungry. 'Just knock it in the head and bring it on,' I say." Then Able chuckled his usual way. He knew he was funny sometimes.

As the Ford truck cruised down the road, the sun was bearing down full blast with the temperature approaching one hundred degrees. Justin looked down at his new Timex and saw that it was almost 12:00 p.m. His mom and dad had given the watch to him for his birthday two weeks earlier. He had turned twelve on July 5th. In one more year I'll be a teenager, he thought. Being a teenager would make him just like his older brothers.

Before long, they saw Pap's Dixie Kream hamburger stand. "Let's stop here, Jussin."

"Fine with me," Justin responded.

Able asked Justin what he wanted. "I'm buying," he said. Of course, Justin knew his dad had given Abe money before they left.

"I want one hamburger with nothing on it. I eat 'em plain. Get me some French fries and an RC, too."

Able looked at Justin funny.

"Be sure to tell them nothing on it, now," Justin said again. "Get me some ice cream too, Abe."

Cane and Able

"We ain't got enough money for ice cream. Come on and help me get the food. I can't remember all that order. We fixin' to fill these bellies up!"

The hamburger stand was just a little white building with an air conditioner hanging out one side. Two giant oak trees beside it provided a little shade. Inside the building, an old scrawny woman was reading a magazine. Justin was amazed by how her cigarette hung from her mouth barely missing her chin.

Able and Justin walked to the front of the stand and stood there two or three minutes, wondering if the woman would ever open the window. They knew she saw them, but she continued to sit on the stool as though unaware of any customers. She finally stood up and slid the window open with one hand. The cigarette was still dangling from her mouth.

"Can I help you boys?" she asked.

"Yes, ma'am, you sho' can," said Able. "This here boy wants one burger with nothing on it, just the meat and bread."

"You mean he don't want no pickles, no onion, no tomatoes, no mayonnaise, no ketchup, or no mustard?" asked the old woman, cutting her eyes down at Justin.

"That's right, ma'am. The boy just wants meat and bread. That's all," Able said.

155

"No wonder the poor boy is so skinny!" she retorted. "Hamburger is sixty-five cents, and fries, fifteen cents. You want fries too, honey?" she said looking straight at Justin.

"Yes, ma'am, and an RC, too," Justin said.

"Is that all?" she asked, taking a big drag off her cigarette.

"Oh no, ma'am," Able spoke up with a big grin on his face. "I wants a Spam sandwich." He paused. "Sho' do!"

"Sir, we don't have *Spam*," the old woman said in a very deep condescending voice that sounded like she had a lizard wedged in her throat. The way she put the emphasis on the word, Able knew she wouldn't be eating none. Her loss, he figured.

About that time, Justin saw ashes from her cigarette fall onto her writing pad.

"Humm. Well, you got any lonny?" Able asked.

"You mean *bologna*, sir?"

"Oh yes'am, that's right, lonny," Able said smiling.

The woman grunted under her breath and told Able she could make him a bologna sandwich and that it would cost twenty-five cents. That was music to Able's ears.

"That's what I want. Make it four of them, if you will, ma'am?"

"Four?" she said, questioning what she heard him say.

"That's right, ma'am, four of 'em," Able said again. " And give me a bag of chips to go with that, too.

"All right then. What you want to drink?"

"Oh, just give me some water," Able said.

"That's all for you fellows?" she said.

"That'll do, ma'am," Justin told her.

"All right then. It'll be a few minutes. You can pay when you get your order."

The old lady slid the window closed and walked to the back. They could see her giving the order to her cook. They decided to walk back to a picnic table that was under one of the big trees. No sooner had they sat down than a long white Cadillac drove up. It must have been brand new because it was shining just like the new Ford truck.

"Man, look at that car, Abe," Justin said, punching Able in the side.

"Yeah. Now that's a fine automobile there, Jussin," Able said.

A man wearing a black hat, suit, and tie got out of the car and walked slowly to the window of the stand. He looked over at Able and Justin and nodded before looking back briefly at the car. Justin could tell that the passenger was a woman. She had rolled the window down about halfway, probably hoping to catch a breeze. He knew she was something special. From what he could see, she had shiny blond hair and was wearing a pink dress. When she draped her hand out the window, Justin noticed diamonds on her fingers that were as big as rocks. Her bracelet looked like something a queen would wear.

"Check that out!" Justin whispered to Able. "Wow! Who you think that is?"

"Don't know, but she sho' looks prettier than a yard full of speckled puppies. I mean she is some kinda beautiful," Able whispered back.

"I bet she's important, don't you think, Abe?"

"Sho' 'nough important, I mean," said Able.

"She sure is," Justin said.

Justin couldn't help himself staring at the lady. He was totally mesmerized, and Able knew it.

"Abe, there's something my mamma told me to never do, but I just can't help it."

"What's that, Jussin?"

"Mamma told me never to stare."

"Jussin, as you go through life, you gonna make many mistakes, but I promise you this one will be okay," Able said, staring at the lady as hard as Justin was.

Then Able nudged Justin in the side. "Look'a there. She's pointing at you, Jussin, to go over there." Able's mouth hung open as Justin kicked small rocks over the grass, his head down, hands in pocket.

Able looked up at the car, then back again with his mouth still open.

"Go on now, see what she wants, Jussin. She's callin' for you," Able whispered.

Justin believed what Able said, but he was frozen in place.

Getting frustrated, Able said, "Go on, boy. Go on over there and come back and tell me who she is."

Able was all but picking Justin up by the arm and nudging him in the direction of the car. Justin took a few steps, stopped, and looked back at Able. Able motioned with his hand for Justin to go on.

As Justin made his way to the car, he was steadily working to tuck in his shirttail. He looked back at Able two or three more times for reassurance. He didn't even realize that the back of his shirttail was still hanging out. Able motioned for him to tuck in the back and to keep going. He then put one arm across his chest and held the other up to his mouth as if to push it closed. As Justin approached the car, the lady spoke.

"Hey, young man, what's your name?"

"Justin, ma'am, but Abe over there calls me 'Jussin.' I think it's easier to say."

She looked towards the oak tree, and Able made a welcoming gesture to her.

"Well, that's a nice name. You got a last name, Justin?"

"Yes, ma'am, sure do. Cane. Spell it just like sugar cane."

"Where are you from, Justin?" she asked.

"Well, I'm from Friendly, ma'am."

"Friendly?"

"Yes, ma'am."

"Is Friendly very far from here?" she asked.

"Oh no, ma'am. It's about two hours that way," he said as he pointed back over his head. He was still trying to get his shirttail in the back of his pants without her seeing him.

"Oh, I see. Well, what is a young man like you doing out here so far from home?" she asked.

"It's a long story, ma'am, but me and Abe there," pointing again to Able again under the tree, "had to take a man to the train station in Yazoo City. His boy got killed the other day. He's going to the funeral."

"Well, that's terrible," she said. "It sure is nice of you and Abe to take him to the train station. I was hoping you were from here so I could ask you what you recommend to eat."

"I don't know, ma'am. Wish I could help you, but we, uh, well, I'm gonna get an RC, hamburger, and fries, and Abe, he's getting a bologna sandwich with water."

The lady looked very amused. "Well, I think I'll have the same thing you are. Go tell that man wearing the hat to give me the same thing you are having and to pay for everybody's food."

"Oh, you hadn't gotta do that, ma'am. I'll tell him anyway."

"I want to, Justin. Go on now and tell Herb, my driver, to do just what I said."

"You know, I bet they got good ice cream too, ma'am," Justin said, trying to keep from grinning.

"Well, I won't have any ice cream, but you get what you want." She leaned closer to the window to see if Herb was ordering.

"You want me to tell Herb that too?"

"Yeah, tell Herb that too."

Herb seemed to be a man with few words to say. He was kinda like Pete. Herb rattled the window with the back of his fist for the woman to take his order. He could see her coming from the kitchen when Justin walked up to the window. Herb looked down at him curiously.

"Can I help you?" he said.

Justin pointed towards the car. "Herb, she said to buy her a hamburger with fries just like I got and pay for whatever Abe and I get too."

"She did, huh?" Herb looked back at the car, questioning what he had just heard. The lady smiled with approval.

"There is one more thing, Herb. She said to pay for my ice cream, too. She don't want none." Justin looked back at Abe just a-smiling, and Able raised his eyebrow. "Herb, make that two ice creams," Justin added.

Herb bumped again on the window, and the old lady came back.

"Yes, ma'am, I will be paying for the young lad's food and his friend's, also."

"You want it all on one ticket?" she asked.

"That's right. One ticket." Herb looked down at Justin, and Justin just grinned and looked back at Able.

The woman in the stand was peering very hard at the car and the woman in it. She was so distracted, she could barely write the order. She finally managed to put her cigarette out after missing the ashtray two or three times. Ashes had already covered the top of the salt and pepper shakers. As she nervously flipped through the pages of a magazine with

161

one hand, she held the phone to her ear with the other hand as she spoke to the operator. Then she stopped and went to the back again. This time she brought the colored cook to the front and made her look through the window.

Both women looked down at the magazine and then up at the lady in the car, time and time again. With a quick move, the old woman placed the magazine next to the window and examined it closely. She was still talking to the operator. Justin and Able could tell she was excited about something, but what? As she reached to get another cigarette, she realized that she already had one in her mouth. She looked at Justin and motioned for him to come to the back door. When he got there, she was standing with a Hollywood magazine in her hand.

"Boy, did that woman say who she was?"

"No, ma'am, but I swear she said she'd pay for me and Abe's food."

"Shut up, stupid! That ain't what I'm talking about. You mean you don't know who she is?"

"Uh, no, ma'am. She sure is a fine lady though."

The old woman was getting agitated with Justin's answers. "Boy, that woman is Jane Mansfield."

"Uh, Jane Manderbuild, who's that?" Justin said.

"No, stupid, Jane Mansfield. She's a movie star. Could you tell if she had a poodle in the car with her?" she asked, taking another drag off the cigarette as burning cinders fell on the counter.

"You mean a dog?"

"Yes, a dog! Look at this picture." The woman stuck the magazine rig

"I think so," Justin said.

"Can you believe Jane Mansfield is in my parking lot right out there, boy? Oh, God, I can't believe it. I can't believe I'm fixin' to make a hamburger for Jane Mansfield."

For an old woman who couldn't move fast at all five minutes ago, she sure is moving mighty good now, Justin thought.

No quicker had Justin returned to the front of the hamburger stand, three carloads of women drove up. The women jumped out all four doors as if the cars were on fire. They all headed for Miss Mansfield's car. Every one of the women had a magazine and pen in her hand. One after another, they asked Miss Mansfield for autographs, but she declined.

Miss Mansfield finally rolled up her window and motioned for Justin. When Justin reached the car, she opened the door and told him to get in. When he did, he immediately noticed her long legs crossed. His mouth just fell open. He had never seen such a perfect specimen of a woman in his whole life. Her lips were red as a watermelon, and her hair was as shiny as an angel on a Christmas tree. Justin couldn't move. The whole car smelled just like roses. He was star struck!

"Justin, if you will, go back and tell your friend to follow us when we leave," she said.

Herb was still standing at the window loading up with food and drinks. Justin was sitting there in a trance. He finally came to his senses and did as she had asked. Able got back into the truck, trying not to draw any attention, and Justin returned to Miss Mansfield's car. Herb paid the old woman for the food and headed back to the car. Obviously disappointed, the women climbed back into their cars. Justin couldn't believe how fancy the inside of the car was. He just wished Able could be riding in there too, knowing how much he liked cars and all. Justin had never been in an automobile that rode as smooth as this one. He reached up and touched the glass window between the driver and the back seat. Could this really be happening, he thought as they drove away.

Justin asked Miss Mansfield why she was in the area, and she said that she was on her way to the Mississippi Gulf Coast. After entertaining in Memphis all week, she said that she was tired and just wanted to be around normal people for awhile. She said show business was good, but she missed everyday living. To Justin, everyday living was in his dad's hay field. She sure didn't want that kind of everyday living. This show business life looked pretty good to him.

"Pull in at that roadside park, Herb. We'll eat there," she said.

Herb pulled the big Cadillac off the road near some big oak trees. Able followed them. Justin noticed that the new Ford truck sounded like a freight train compared to the smooth-running Cadillac.

Herb removed a red blanket from the trunk of the car and spread it on the ground. Miss Mansfield got out of the car and stood there looking across a lush green pasture. She smiled as she reached down to pull off her shoes. She then strolled over to a live oak with her arms extended.

She circled the tree, just as a little girl would. She then sat down on the blanket Herb had placed on the ground. Herb began to distribute the food in the sacks.

"Whose bologna sandwich is this?" asked Herb.

"Oh, the lonny sandwiches would be mine, Mr. Herb," Able replied as everybody else rolled their eyes over towards him. "Yes, sir, the Lord said bologna is the best part of a swine and should be eaten at least one time a week, specially on Friday."

"Why Friday, Abe?" Herb asked.

"Cause that was the day they all run in the water and got baptized. That was Good Friday. The Lord said, though, that it would be okay if we eat fish on Friday if we don't have no pork. Yes, sir, says it right there in the book of Caribbean 12:2."

"Sounds good to me," Herb said. Then he handed Able the bologna sandwich. They all watched as Able closed his eyes and started saying a prayer to himself. They immediately followed Able's lead and closed their eyes too. They didn't dare eat a bite until he finished his prayer of thanks.

The four of them picnicked under the trees for about an hour. Miss Mansfield told Justin and Able all about Hollywood. She told them that she knew Clark Gable, John Wayne, Audey Murphy and many more handsome men. Able asked her if she knew Lena Horn.

"Yes, I do, she is one of my best friends."

"No, ma'am, you gotta be joshing me. That Miss Lena Horn is one pretty woman. I tell you now, for sure," Able said.

Justin thought to himself that Miss Horn must be one fine-looking lady if Able was comparing her to Miss Mansfield.

Miss Mansfield was the prettiest woman Justin had ever seen. He just couldn't take his eyes off her. Of course, he was dreaming, but he fell in love as soon as he sat down beside her in her car. He didn't know if she would ever remember him, but he sure wasn't going to forget her.

"Another fifteen minutes and we're going to have to leave, Herb," she said. "I've got to entertain at Gus Stevens' club tonight in Biloxi and can't be late. You know, Herb, I just might come back through Friendly and see my new friends." Able turned his eyes up and looked at her. She was telling Justin just what he wanted to hear and she knew it. Able knew she was an entertainer and entertainers' are paid to work the crowd to make them want them more. But Justin couldn't believe what he was hearing.

"Let's go, these people have got a long way to go," Able said to Justin.

"Okay, Abe," Justin replied as he daydreamed about Miss Mansfield visiting them on her return trip.

Able knew Justin was star-struck and tried to reel him back into the real world. After they cleaned up from lunch, Miss Mansfield walked back to the car with her shoes in her hand.

"Justin, this was the best meal I've eaten in a long time."

She then leaned over and took a picture from her photo album and autographed it. She handed to him and took his other hand and shook it gently. Justin could have melted. "Justin, I won't ever forget this picnic," she said, graciously.

His knees almost buckled.

"It was most perfect." she said, smiling.

Then she rolled up her window and smiled at Justin while she motioned for Herb to leave. In spite of what she had said, Justin had the feeling that he would never see Miss Mansfield again.

"Well, we better get on the road, Jussin. We gotta lot to see before we head back." Justin stood there watching as the car went out of sight.

Able put the truck in gear and pulled back onto the road. Justin told Abe this has been the best day of his life and one he wouldn't ever forget. Able told him it was a day of opportunity for sure. Traveling with Able was giving Justin a feeling of independence, a freedom he had never had before. He was growing up by the hour.

" Abe, did you hear her say she was coming to Friendly?" Justin said excited.

"Don't get your hopes up, Jussin. Remember, a frog wouldn't bump his butt if he had wings."

"What's a frog got to do with her coming back?" Jussin said, confused and swelling up a little.

"Jussin. It ain't gonna happen. It just ain't gonna happen." Able shook his head still smiling.

Sixteen

ABLE 4:5

JUSTIN LEANED OVER and turned on the radio. He didn't think Able wanted him to drive again, so he didn't ask. They continued down the winding road and noticed a lot of construction going on by the river. There were dump trucks hauling dirt, earthmovers moving earth, and bulldozers pushing down trees. Justin figured that construction was something he'd like to do one summer when he got older.

Able told Justin that all of the construction that he saw was the levee system the United States Corp of Engineers had started building. He told him how all the surrounding land flooded in the spring every year and how the new levees were supposed to hold back the mighty Mississippi

River. He said he remembered one time when he lived in Greenville, Mississippi, as a kid, that the flood picked up a sharecropper's house, and it floated all the way to New Orleans. He said the sharecropper, his guitar, and his dog floated down the river on the roof of the house for seventeen days straight, just like Noah in the Great Flood.

When the water finally went down, the man was in New Orleans and said he would never go back. He said he'd never been out of Mississippi before, but always dreamed of going to New Orleans where the blues was always playing. He guessed the Lord found a way to get him there before he died. He said he wasn't going to upset the Lord and go back to Mississippi after all that trouble. Able said the man is probably dead now, but that was a true story because he knew the old man's boy. The boy's name was Leonard, but everyone called him Leo. In fact, the boy was spending the night over at his house the day the rains came, and the boy couldn't get back home because the roads where so bad. Able said it rained for five days and nights. Got thirty-one inches of rain in all. It must have been a 1800-year record, he thought. Nobody could get anywhere. Cows, horses, pigs were all drowning. The crazy chickens were the only animal that could make it. Chickens lined the roofs of every house and barn in a hundred square miles. He said it was darn near funny looking. Every house looked like as if it had twenty-five weather vanes on it. Chickens were walking up and down the roofs like they owned the houses. That's why the chicken is so plentiful today, Able figured. The best he could come up with, was that Noah put two chickens in the boat, and the rest just caught a ride on top. He laughed and said Noah's ark must have looked just like a chicken coop. Chickens must have been all over that boathouse. He added maybe that's why peoples use 'em as weather vanes, to remind them of the flood.

Then he went back to telling how it finally quit raining enough to get Leo home. Able said his dad rode Leo back by mule to his home place but they never could find the house nowhere. It was gone. They rode up and down the river for two days, looking and asking everybody if they had seen old man Skinner and his house, but nobody had seen him.

Leo's mamma died when he was born, and he didn't have any kin, so Able's dad didn't have any choice but to call an orphanage to see if they could take him. He just couldn't raise another kid. He was having too hard a time as it was for his family, and it was going to be double hard now that the crop had washed away. The orphanage was located in New Orleans. They waited another two weeks just in case somebody found out some news, but after two weeks, the floodwaters had gone down, and still nobody had heard a word. Able's Uncle Frank had a car and volunteered to take the boy to New Orleans. Uncle Frank asked Able if he wanted to go too because it might make the trip a little easier for Leo. Able agreed to go.

The next morning Able gave Leo his best Sunday shirt because he figured Leo needed it more than him. He knew he could always work and get another one.

Cane and Able

They left Greenville early that morning and headed down Hwy 61. When they got to Vicksburg, they stopped and filled up with gas. They told the people at the station what they were up to, but everyone said they hadn't seen nothing either. The owner said he felt sorry for Leo but added that twenty-six people from their area had also died during the flood. Hearing those words didn't make Leo feel any better. Leo, in his worn jeans and Able's oversized white shirt, just sat there silently with his arms crossed. He was looking out at the leaning willow trees, a reminder of the flood along the road's edge.

Able said Leo didn't say two words after that. He felt so sorry for him, not just because he was his friend, but because Able knew how much he loved his own dad, and now Leo didn't have one. Leo would tear up ever so often, but he would never let it out. As he wiped his runny nose with fingers, Able noticed how Leo's hands were shaking the same way his did when he got his hand slammed in the car door one time. Able kept telling him to let it out, but he never would.

When they got just about to New Orleans, it happened. The car overheated, and they were forced to pull over. Everybody was tired, and it looked like the car was tired too. The old car had been burning oil from the time they left Greenville. Sometimes it looked almost like a fog machine going down the road. They had two flat tires on the trip that day, ran out of gas once, and everyone was just exhausted from talking, walking to the nearest filling station, and changing tires.

Uncle Frank had two old whiskey jugs in the trunk that he used to put water in when something like this happened. This must have been a pretty common thing because he went straight for the trunk and the jugs without saying a word. Frank saw Leo's condition in the back seat and told Able to go down to the bayou and fill the jugs up with water and take Leo with him to help.

Able reminded Leo to be watching for gators while he filled the jugs up because he was going to have to wade out some. Able pulled his shoes off and fought back the reeds and bamboo so he could get to a clear spot to dip water. When he broke through, they were flabbergasted with what they found. There, sitting fifty feet in front of them, was that purple house of Mr. Skinner's, with chickens lining the roof.

Leo jumped for joy and forgot about the gators and started hollering in the direction of the purple house, but nobody came. They quickly filled the water jugs and hurried back to the car where they told Uncle Frank what they had found.

Uncle Frank couldn't believe what they were saying and went back with them to see for himself, and when he saw the house floating like a boat, he looked at Able and shook his head. He said he'd lived a long time and seen a lot of weird things, but he believed this one was gonna take the cake. It was exactly what the boys had described.

They hurried back to the car as fast as they could and Uncle Frank put the water in the radiator. Leo was so excited, but still a little scared, too, because nobody answered when he called. Surely, if the house made it that far, maybe his papa had did as well. After several more trips, they finished filling the radiator with water. Uncle Frank still couldn't believe what he had seen and went back down to the water's edge one more time to make sure he hadn't imagined it.

"Sure enough," Uncle Frank said to himself as he looked out over the water. "That's it all right. Can't believe it. Sho' can't. I'll be a monkey's uncle. Now Lord help us find that boy's papa."

Uncle Frank hurried back to the car and said, "Let's go up the road a little to the nearest house and see if anybody knows anything." He slammed the hood with both hands, jumped in, checked the heat gauge, and headed down the road looking for any sign of life. About a half-a-mile down the road, he saw a little wood cabin with a crooked chimney, so he pulled over. It was a neat looking place tucked under all the live oaks. The trees were full of Spanish moss, giving the secluded area a ghostly feeling. No one appeared to be home, so Uncle Frank went around to the back of the house. When he turned the corner the first thing he saw was Leo's papa sitting on the back porch. Leo ran past Uncle Frank and made a dash for his papa, almost knocking him out of the rocker. The old house had just drifted to shore a few hours before and the white people were good enough to feed him and let him wash off before they carried him to town to call back home.

"Can you believe that? I tell you, Jussin, the Lord works in mysterious ways. Of all the places for that old car to run hot, it decided to run hot right in front of that floating, chicken-covered, purple house. We could have drove right by that crib. Now, I tell you this. If the Lord didn't want old man Skinner in New Orleans, then my name ain't Able Johnson, III."

Able looked Jussin straight in the eyes. "Jussin that should be a lesson for us all to follow. Have faith in the Lord and never worry about where you is going and how you is going to get there. He will always provide." Then, Able said, his brows furrowed as if searching for something, "That be Moses 25:25."

Able carefully watched the line of cars that drove in the other direction. Occasionally, he'd lazily lift a finger up off the steering wheel in a gesture of a wave. He was so proud he was behind the wheel of a good-looking truck. Every once in a while he would see the skeletal remains of old wooden tenant shacks buried amongst briars and weeds. Most of them were leaning to the point of falling in. He made a point to show one to Justin and explain that they used to be the homes of one-time slaves. Just looking at the state of those structures filled Justin with horror as he thought about the winter months. Every time they passed one, Justin's head just followed it until it was out of sight. Looking at them, himself, Able was glad that he never had to live in those conditions. He *knew* he was blessed.

"You know, Jussin, we gotta stop here pretty soon and call home. Mr. Cane can get pretty wound up if things get out of whack. There's a filling station up ahead. We'll pull over there, and I'll call."

Justin was trying to open his eyes from the nap he'd been taking.

"You awake, Jussin?" Able said.

"Yeah, pretty much so," Justin said, rubbing his eyes.

"You had a good little nap back there, didn't you? We done been forty or fifty miles."

"Where are we, Abe?"

"Well, I thought we might just ride up here to Belzoni. There's a man over there that I want to talk to about some business. I haven't seen him in a while, and since we just out riding, we might as well ride over there and see him."

"What kind of business?" Justin said, with a curious look on his face.

"Oh, just a little business." Able turned to Justin nodding as if he knew just what he was up to.

As they approached Belzoni they saw a tall metal-covered bridge ahead spanning the Yazoo River. Justin was quick to lift his feet and hold his breath for good luck as soon as the front tires of the truck touched it. Then he held it until the truck made it across.

"Made it!" Justin said, red in the face and gasping for fresh air.

"I thought I saw you breathe," Able said, teasing him.

"No, you didn't either. I made it all the way across. I swear I did."

"Naw, I was kidding. You made it all the way, Jussin. Sho' did. I was watching you."

"I think that was the longest bridge I've ever been across, Abe."

"Probably, so. But that *Mississippi River Bridge* is one *big* bridge you need to see. That sucker will make ten of this one. No way a person can hold their breath over that one. A man would pass out first."

"It must be a big one then."

"It is! It sho' is! Maybe one day we can ride over there and see it." Justin was hoping it might be this trip.

A few more miles up the road and they saw the city limit sign of Belzoni.

"First time I ever been here, too, Abe," Justin said.

"Jussin, I be's showing you the whole country, ain't I, boy? If Mr. Cane let me use this truck for a week, I bet I could show you the whole United States of America. Why don't we just wait and call Mr. Cane when we get to Big Doug's house, okay?"

"Who's Big Doug?"

"Just an acquaintance. I don't remember exactly where he lives, but I gots a good idea. A man the other day tried to tell me. It was down this road somewhere, I think."

They cut off the main paved road and got onto a little dirt road. By now Justin's T-shirt was pretty soaked with sweat and sticking to his back. So was Abe's. The temperature was really rising fast.

"Man, this Ivory soap ain't doing much for my sweating," Able said. "It says on the box that it supposed to keep you cool, clean, and refreshing for twenty-four hours."

"Yeah, I don't think so either, Abe. It ain't doing a whole lot of good right now. You sure you used some?" The cross wind was about to kill Justin.

Able said, "Sure I did, but this heat done sweat it all out. It don't matter anyway right now, Jussin, that's not what's important. You just listen to me right now. Okay? Now, when we get up here, you just sit here in the truck, and I'll be back. It won't take me long to get what I need."

"Whatcha gotta get, Abe?"

"Jussin, my little sister might be there, and if she is, I gonna bring her home."

"Well, why didn't you say so, Abe?" Justin asked, excited about meeting Jeanna.

"I just didn't want to say nothing because I don't know for sure if she's there. We'll see."

They drove about four miles on the dirt road before arriving at a little wooden shack. Justin couldn't believe anybody would live there. It looked horrible. From what Able had told him about Jeanna, Justin doubted she'd be inside that place! The way it appeared to Justin, if a strong wind came by, it would fall down. From the road, it appeared that the tin on the house was bent up in several places from previous storms. It had to have leaked. Somebody had made an effort to tar some of the pieces back down, but it apparently was not a permanent fix. The tar bucket sat abandoned on the roof.

The broken wooden steps with missing handrails were in keeping with the rest of the house, and so was the yard. There wasn't a single blade of grass in it, only sinkholes where dogs wallowed. Beer bottles were broken and strewn everywhere. The stench coming from a burning fifty-five- gallon drum in the front yard was unbearable. It could have been garbage, but it smelt worst than that. The pungent smell of it burning, mixed with the summer heat and swamp, was enough to make Justin gag.

As they drove up closer, Able slowed the truck down and watched carefully. Justin could see a big fat colored man whipping one of his dogs with a piece of leather. The old dog apparently had the mange and looked as if he had not eaten in weeks. The man had a pearl-handled pistol on one hip and a bone-handled knife on the other. He looked mean, too, weighing over four hundred pounds. His feet were as wide as they were long, and his shoes had been "customized" so the tips of his toes would come out the ends. Justin shoved his elbow at Able and laughed about the man's old shirt was undone and his huge belly was exploding over his belt. The man certainly didn't miss a meal! That had to be Big Doug, Justin thought.

"Is that Big Doug, Abe?" Justin asked.

"That's him, alright," Able said, closing his mouth shut tight. Justin didn't like the look of Big Doug, and by the flexing Able was doing with his jaw muscle, Justin figured Able didn't like the look of him none either.

Big Doug stared a minute, then kicked the dog again. It was then that Able moved the truck, though Big Doug couldn't make out who was in the cab. Just then, another man came out of the house doing up his belt and putting his shirt tail in. The man stopped and argued with the fat man about something but then gave him some money. Justin looked at Able, confused about what was going on. Able pulled the truck up a little and stopped closer to the house. Justin could see Able's veins in his neck beginning to swell.

"What's wrong, Abe?" Justin asked.

"Just what I thought, Jussin. Some things just ain't right in this world. Some peoples are just too plum sorry and always trying to mess it up. They's too sorry to live the right way. All they know is how to use somebody and live the ways of Satan."

They sat there another minute and watched the one man drive away. The fat man, Big Doug, was watching them closely as Able inched his way to the front of the drive and stopped.

Big Doug stood there long enough for a woman to come out the front door. Justin could tell she had been beaten. They could tell she was begging.

"Please let me go home! Please!" the girl said, as the big man ignored her request.

"Look, bitch. You've cost me a fortune, so you might as well get used to this place."

"You, sorry bastard. I hate you!" she hollered, trying to kick at him. He laughed as she planted her foot in his shin, then he swung at her. She ducked just in time to miss his heavy fist, but tripped backwards and fell. He then kicked her down the broken steps. When she fell to the ground, she hit her ribcage on a crosstie. He cussed her some more and told her to get back inside.

"I'm leaving. Kill me, I don't care!"

As she tried to stand up, she hollered up at him saying, "Is that somebody out there that you want me to screw for you?"

"If I say so, yeah!"

"I'll rot in hell first. I just threw up on your last man and if I have to, I will shit on the next." she hollered back him. Big Doug wanted to kill her now. All she had been since he met her was trouble. Why he had not already eliminated her already was beyond his own reasoning.

Through the side of his eye he was still watching the new Ford truck in the entrance of the drive. He motioned for them to continue to come on up the drive. Justin was putting things together now and could tell this man was in for a big surprise.

"Is that girl, Jeanna?" Justin asked Able.

"Sho' is."

Then Big Doug pointed to the door and commanded her to go back in the house. She slowly stood up, holding her side and pulled herself up onto the porch. She lay back down and continued to sob. She didn't have the strength to stand any longer.

The fat man started walking towards the new Ford truck wondering who it was. As he approached Able's side, Able opened the door and got out. Height wise, they were the same, but Big Doug was twice as heavy as Able. The fat man was surprised all right.

"What can I do for you?" Big Doug said, in a deep voice.

"I coming for my sister." Able said.

"So, you the big bad brother, I been hearing about?" Big Doug stepped back and looked Able over from head to toe. "I think you need to get back in this shiny truck and go about your way, mister."

"I's not looking for trouble. Jis' want my sister, is all." Able nodded and looked at the ground in a humble way and then back up at Big Doug's face still nodding and pursing his lips.

About that time, Jeanna pulled herself up on the steps and cried out for Able.

She said, "Is that you, Able?"

Her eyes were so swollen that she could hardly see. Able started to walk over and help her.

"Yes, it's me, sister, and I'm here to take you home."

As soon as Able said that, Big Doug hit Able right in the ribs. Able fell backwards and hit his head on the side mirror of the truck. Blood started coming down Able's head almost immediately. The powerful blow almost knocked him out. It startled Justin so much that he jumped back against his door, but there was nowhere to go.

Justin jumped out of the truck and ran around to the porch to help Jeanna. Doug was in his back swing to hit Able again, when Able came up with a punch that could have knocked a bull down. Doug fishtailed so far backwards that he stumbled and landed against a pile of firewood. Able, thinking he had Doug down for awhile started walking back towards Jeanna. Just then Doug picked up a piece of firewood and scrambling to his feet, started at Able's backside. He used it like an axe and swung downward, striking Able across the shoulder. The force nearly tore Able's shirt off, gashing his upper arm, and forcing him to slump over. Able didn't know what hit him, when another lick to his stomach brought him face to face with the ground. Doug walked over to Able lying on the ground and straddled him as though a horse. He squatted putting all his weight on him, all four hundred pounds. Able couldn't move. Then Doug began pounding Able's head with his fist.

Justin was struggling, trying to hold Jeanna back from the fight, but she got away and jumped on Doug's back, screaming, cussing, and biting. Big Doug threw her off like a fly. She flew across the drive, landing in the woodpile, knocking herself out cold.

Big Doug sure didn't fight fair, Justin thought. He knew boys weren't supposed to hit girls.

Able was hollering for Justin, "Do something, Jussin! Do something!"

"What can I do, Abe?"

"Anything, Jussin, anything! He's killing me!"

Big Doug was cussing and smiling as he continued pounding Able in the face.

By now, Justin was so scared that he was about to pee in his pants. All he could do was hold his hands between his legs and run back and forth. From Able's vantage point, he looked like a chicken running around in a circle..

"Justin, stop that running around and do something, boy!"

"I gotta go, Abe! I can't," Justin said, about to explode.

"You better do something boy!" Able hollered.

Then Justin thought, *Better on Big Doug than on the ground*, so he backed up about three feet away from Big Doug's head, unzipped his pants, and yelled, "Hey, Fatso! Get this!"

Justin sprayed Big Doug right in the face with a force of pee that could fill three coke bottles. Big Doug instantly closed eyes and tried to deflect the pee with his hands. That gave Able a chance to clobber him one good time. He sent Big Doug tumbling back a good ten yards, but Big Doug had more left in him. He wiped his face with his forearm and yelled like a Confederate soldier going into battle. He charged Able, hitting him square in the chest. Able's feet flew out from under him, landing by the back tire of the truck. The weight of Doug crashing down on him knocked his breath out of him. Able's strength was sapped. Big Doug wiggled around enough to pull Able's arms behind him so he couldn't get loose. Then he started pounding Able again with his mighty fist. With the remaining stamina Able had, he hollered again to Justin.

"Come on, Jussin! Help me! Quick!"

Justin put his hands on his head and tried to think. Then he ran up beside Big Doug and let out a high pitched, blood-curdling scream directly in his right ear, surely bursting Big Doug's eardrum. Big Doug grabbed his ears and then swatted backwards, knocking Justin in the air. That gave Able another chance for a powerful lick against Doug's fat head. This time, it didn't do much good. Big Doug swayed backward avoiding the full power of the punch. Justin was air born to the woodpile and landed on his back beside Jeanna. He looked over and saw that her eyes were still closed. He tried to wake her by shaking her, but it did no good.

Then he hollered, "Jeanna, wake up! I need some help!" He was stumped; he couldn't think of anything to do. Then he remembered what Able said one time, "The Lord says, 'If you need something real bad, he's gonna give it to you, especially if you are in a tight. Book of Able 4:5.'"

He looked up and said, "Lord, if you listening and Abe's anywheres close to being right, we sho' needs some help down here fast. Lord, we are in the worst trouble we've ever been in. Help us, please!"

Able was barely conscious after repeated licks from Big Doug. He mumbled, "What you doing, Jussin, looking up in the air? Man, do something."

"I am. I am. I'm thinking Abe," he hollered back to him.

Big Doug was tiring and slowing down but Justin could still hear every lick. Justin, nervously standing on tiptoes, started repeating, "Come on, Able 4:5, I need you now. Show me a sign, Lord! Oh, Lord, help us before this big giant kills Abe and all us." Then it hit him, "Giant" that was the key word. Justin looked down, and there on the ground was a rock. It must have weighed twenty-five pounds. He looked at the truck and then the rock. That was his answer. The Lord was giving him a plan.

He ran over to the rock and tried to roll it, but he couldn't budge it. He looked again at Big Doug and watched him deliver another blow to Able. Big Doug was swearing every other word. It would be only moments before Able met the Lord in person. Justin knew he had to work fast. He ran to the back of the truck and let the tailgate down and tried again to lift the rock onto the tailgate. Time was ticking. It was too heavy. He had to hurry, or it would be over soon.

"Come on, Able 4:5, I gotta get this rock in this truck."

Justin looked around and saw a big plank on the ground by Jeanna's crumbled body. She was still out cold. He dragged the board over to the tailgate and placed one end up in the back. Then with a big grunt, he pushed with all his might. The rock started rolling, and he heaved it up on the board. Then, with a loud Able 4:5, he pushed again until he managed to get it up in the bed of the truck.

With a bewildered look, he thought, "Gosh! It worked."

Repeatedly, he sang out, "Come on, Able 4:5, Able 4:5, Able 4:5, YES! YES! YES!"

Justin jumped up in the back of the truck and down on his knees. He started rolling the rock to the front of the bed as fast as he could. Sweat was pouring down his forehead and down his red cheeks as he rolled the rock over and over again to its position. He looked over the edge of the pickup and he could see Big Doug still cussing and hitting Able below him. It was a perfect target.

"Okay, Able 4:5. Let's go. Let's go. Let's go. Give me strength."

With a big grunt, he managed the big rock up onto the fender weld and then onto the edge of the bed. He had to balance it there until the time was perfect.

"YES!" he hollered, knowing the Lord had given him strength to balance the rock.

Able was lying face up and getting pounded with fists every few seconds. Doug was trying his best to finish Able off, but his punches had lost their sting. He was wearing down. Though his eyes were swollen, Able could see for himself what Justin was doing. He knew he could be the target, if Doug moved. What did it matter anyway? He was going to die one way or the other if something didn't happen soon.

"Come on. Line up," Justin said, talking to the rock. He was waiting for a perfect shot.

Big Doug, tired and bored of beating the man with his hands, reached around into his back pocket and pulled a gun. Drawing it out, he forced the gun in Able's face.

Able closed his eyes, waited. "Here I comes, Lord, to see you," he mumbled. He knew this was it, and Justin saw it too.

Justin closed his eyes and pushed the rock. When it hit, he heard a thump. It was a cracking sound almost like the sound of a tree branch cracking in a storm.

Big Doug didn't know what hit him. The rock hit him right in the top of the head, collapsing him onto Able.

Big Doug's fat face fell against Able's face. The combined smell of urine and cigars was putrefying. Able began spitting and grunting trying to get out from under Big Doug heavy body.

"Get this hippopotamus off me," Able said, pushing. Big Doug rolled over face up on the ground.

"Is he dead?" Justin asked, as he peeped over the truck bed.

Able, still on his knees turned around and looked up at Justin. "What do you mean, 'Is he dead?' You hit him, not me."

"Afraid not, Abe. I didn't hit him at all. The Lord did. Goliath 25:25."

"Well, son, that scripture carries a lot of weight. I's got to use it sometime." Able chuckled as he picked himself up. He stood up and lifted Justin out of the truck and put him on the ground by Big Doug. "Shoot, Jussin, where you get that strength to pick that rock up?" He reached down to feel his muscles. Able rolled his eyes up and looked up to heaven and said, "Thank you, Lord, for your great little servant. Thank you, Thank you."

Able kneeled beside Jeanna and spoke to her. When he did, she started coming to. Justin found a cloth and wiped her face off. She had a pretty good bump on her head from the fall and was still feeling the affects of it. Able helped her to her feet and told her everything was going to be all right. She was safe now. He walked her to the truck and she slid over in the middle of the seat. Before getting in, Justin took a good look at Big Doug to make sure he wasn't dead. He was breathing.

"Abe, let's get out of here. This place is creepy," Justin said.

"That's what I say too, Jussin."

"That what I say too, Justin," Jeanna said in a soft voice and held on to Able's arm.

As Able backed out of the driveway backed onto the dirt road, he noticed in his rearview mirror that the old dog that Big Doug had been beating was now leaving his own mark on Big Doug.

After leaving, Justin told Able he didn't really care for anymore of his business deals.

Able looked at his sister and said, "Well, that ain't exactly the kind of business I was planning on. But you know, it was sho' nuff a successful today, wasn't it? Little sister?" Able smiled and put his arm around her. "I guess I's just a good business man, huh, sister?" Jeanna closed her eyes and didn't say anything. She was just thankful to be alive.

Justin slowly glanced over at Jeanna. Realizing she was nearly unconscious, he began surveying her battered and bruised body. Immediately, he noticed the deep cut over her eye and swollen top lip she had gotten when Big Doug kicked her down the steps. He leaned a little forward, noticing that there was blood oozing from below one of her knees. Her big toenail was nearly torn off. Horrified and embarrassed to have seen what he had seen, he straightened back up in his seat. He managed not to look over at her again for a few miles, but then he made a slight cough and looked over at her dress. He could see that her light blue dress was torn, especially around the fringe and her blouse neckline was ripped exposing the upper part of her breast and shoulder. He couldn't tell if she had a bra on or not, but he didn't think she did. He looked out the window casually before looking over at her arm. For the first time, he noticed the color of her skin. He wondered, how could Abe be black as tar and she be darn near tan? To him, she was a bunch-more lighter than Abe, except for one real dark spot behind her shoulder. That was the color she was supposed to be. Studying her arm more, he wondered if Abe knew that. Something wasn't right, he guessed. Maybe she was adopted or maybe the babies got swapped up somehow at the hospital. One thing for sure though, she was kinda pretty for a near-bout colored girl. Of course, he couldn't ever tell anybody that, not even her. Whites didn't supposed to say things like that about colored people. Maybe she wasn't colored at all. He recoiled. The thought scared him at first, then he was relieved when he remembered her hair. If she weren't in the truck he'd have had to pop the question to Abe. He'd just have too.

Then, Justin looked out the window thinking of what he was going to tell his mom and dad. He knew they were going to be in trouble.

"You know, Jussin, we never did use that phone. We gonna stop up here when we get back to Belzoni and call Mr. Cane. What time does that new watch of yours say?" Able said.

"It's about 3:30." Justin said.

"Well, we've been gone now about, let's see, humm, shoot, Jussin, you add it up; I got both hands on the wheel."

Justin started counting the hours on his hand: thumb, index, middle, ring, thumb, index, middle, ring. "I think nine hours, Abe," Justin said.

"Okay, then what we's gonna do first is drop my baby sister off over in Tchula. It's not but about thirty miles up the road, and she can stay there with Aunt Pearl. She'll be safe there until she can get away from here." Able patted Jeanna on the shoulder.

Able knew Big Doug would come looking for her as soon as he could. Able also knew he'd find her too, if they didn't send her way. They would have to act fast.

As the trio traveled over the flat delta highway, the sun had moved over to the west allowing a cool southern breeze to come through Justin's window. Jeanna noticed Justin's blond hair whipping in the wind. She smiled at him and told him his hair was pretty. Justin wasn't sure he liked his hair being called pretty, but he knew she'd meant it as a compliment. She asked him where he got such a golden tan, and he told her in the hay field. Then Justin asked her if she ever had a mule named Buzzard.

Jeanna turned around and hit Able on the arm. "Well you did learn a lesson, didn't you?" Able laughed.

"Well, you the one that got the whipping, not me. I rode ole Buzzard, didn't I?" she smiled as if she's gotten him back.

" I guess you right, and you sho' was a pretty sight in that white dress with lacey white socks and black shoes," Able said, shaking his head. "Daddy said ole Buzzard never looked so good in his whole life." Jeanna hit him again just like two kids would do.

Justin was loosing his breath laughing so hard and thinking how much fun it would be to have a kid sister to hit sometimes instead of all them brothers. If he did maybe his mother wouldn't be so protective of him, she could spend time with his sister, teaching her how to cook and stuff. As it was, the only time he did anything much fun was when he went fishing with Able and Bebop or shooting tadpoles with his slingshot. His dad only knew one thing and that was work. When he grew up, he planned on being a ballplayer and pitching for the New York Yankees and he was going to play ball with his boy everyday. If they couldn't play ball, they were going to the picture show and eat all the popcorn they could hold. One thing for sure he was not going to do. He was not going to be a farmer and live on some old farm.

Able began to tell Jeanna about how Justin had done most of the driving that day. He had picked up driving better than any of his brothers had at that age. That made Justin feel good.

Justin had his arm hung out the window, and was trying to forget what had just happened. He was pretending that his hand was an airplane flying in the wind. It would dive down and then go back up. He was thinking about how neat it would be to be a pilot. One day he might be one, he thought. It would be great if he and Able were pilots, and all they did was crop dust the big Delta fields.

As they got closer to Tchula, Able's good nature dissolved and he became very concerned. He told Jeanna not to go outside the house. He said Big Doug might be watching. She agreed, knowing he was right. Able reassured her that everything was okay and that she didn't have to worry. He would go back to Friendly and come back in a few days with enough money to get her a bus ticket so she could go to Atlanta where they had kin. She smiled and told him that she didn't know what she would have done if he and Justin had not shown up. She started to tell Able what she would have done had they not come, but he just put his arm around her, pulled her close and planted a soft kiss on her forehead. "Don't even speak them words, Jeanna."

As they approached the edge of the Delta, where the flat land took a sudden steep incline, they could see the town of Tchula ahead. It was mounted majestically on the Delta's edge, high on a hill. The old silver water tower was the highest point in town and could be seen miles away. Across the front of it was written *Tommy loves Linda* painted in John Deere green, a sign of school kids desperately trying to have fun in the small town.

"Jussin you see that big hill up ahead?" Able asked.

"Sure do, Abe."

"The Lord let a big block of ice come down right beside it about a million years ago. They called that block of ice a glacier. It pushed so hard that it pushed all the trees and bushes down and bladed all the hills down with them. When that thing finally got gone, it was flat as a flitter around here."

"What's a flitter, Abe?"

"Humm! A flitter is something real flat. Anyway, when it got down to New Orleans, it went right on out in that Gulf of Mexico."

"Where's it at now, Abe?" Justin said.

"Well, I think it made it all the way to the South Pole and is still there today. But the good thing about it is that when it came through, it brought all that good Yankee soil with it from up north."

"Them hills must be rich up there in the north, Abe."

"Oh, yeah, they are. Now I can't say if they's richer than the Promised Land back there in Adam 26:26, where it flowed with milk and honey, but it's right there amongst it, I think." Able rolled his eyes out his window to keep from looking at Justin and trying to keep a straight face at the same time.

"How you know so much, Abe?" Justin asked, cocking his chin up towards Able.

"Shoot man! I've been around." Able looked over at Jeanna one more time and smiled. He sure was proud she was sitting beside him. As he turned off a side road and traveled a couple hundred yards on a dirt road, he announced with a grin.

"Well, here we is, kids," He turned in a driveway to a small house.

This house was a complete contrast to what they had just left. It was clean and tidy in every way. It looked like a picture out of a magazine. An old colored woman was bent over hoeing around a bed of gardenias in the front yard. She was wearing a big straw hat, working gloves and a white apron. The house was light green and had a freshly painted white picket fence across the front yard. There were roses and flowers everywhere. Obviously, she loved her flowers. A closer look revealed she was dipping snuff 'cause her mouth was pouched out some. That was a close runner up to Pete's cigarettes in Justin's book.

As they drove in, she stopped hoeing and turned around to see who they were. Able pulled up, stopped, and got out talking as he pulled up his trousers and pulled his shoulders back.

"Hey, Aunt Pearl, it's me, Able."

She leaned on her hoe trying to focus on who was in the truck. When she heard Able's voice, she immediately recognized him. A big smile came across her face and she dropped the hoe beside her. She was smiling so much that the snuff started running down one side of her mouth. With her apron in her hand, she briskly made her way towards Able, wiping her mouth and lips.

"Is that you, Able?"

"Yes'm, sure is. And look a-here, I've got a surprise for you," Able held the door opened so Jeanna could get out. "It's Jeanna, Pearl."

"Oh, my goodness, girl. Lordy, look a-here. Where have you been? Come here and let me hug you." Pearl kept walking as fast as she could towards her. Jeanna immediately ran to her and hugged her as hard as she could.

"Aunt Pearl, I'm so scared."

Able had to wipe his eyes. He was glad she was safe now. Aunt Pearl could tell by the look in her that she probably hadn't been doing no waitressing. She was bruised and had been in trouble. She looked Jeanna in the eyes. Then she looked up and down Jeanna's thin body. As Aunt Pearl registered the torn clothes the glow of happiness in her eyes turned to look of pure rage.

"Jeanna who did this to you?" Pearl demanded.

"Aunt Pearl, I'm so sorry. It was Big Doug. I didn't mean to. I'm a good girl and a fighter. But I ain't got no fight left in me now. I'm sorry." Jeanna started crying and sobbing on Pearl's shoulder. "If Able hadn't come got me, then I'd be dead. I was going to _."

"Shush, baby," Aunt Pearl said.

" How could somebody do that to me?"

Aunt Pearl held her close and smoothed over her hair. Over the top of Jeanna's head, she barked at Able, "Where's that sorry no-good-for-nothing Doug?"

"Uh" Able spoke up, "He's not with us and won't be coming either."

"Well, I'm glad. If I ever see him, I'll kill him myself," Pearl said.

" You won't have to, Aunt Pearl. I'm gonna kill'em first," Jeanna blurted out.

"It's gonna be all right now. You go inside now and clean up and rest. You hear? That man ain't coming around here," Pearl said, nudging her.

Jeanna began walking to the house. When she got to the door, she paused and turned around looking at Able and Justin.

"Thank ya'll." She turned and stumbled inside.

Then Aunt Pearl wiped her eyes and turned to Able and said with a bright smile, "Who you got here with you, Able? He sure is a fine looking boy."

"Aunt Pearl, you know Mr. Cane's boy." Able pulled on his trouser again and smiled.

"No, that can't be the baby. Oh, he's grown so much. Is that you, Justin?" Aunt Pearl held both of his arms and bent her knees some to look in Justin's eyes. He could see the tobacco juice tucked under her bottom lip beginning to ooze out the side of her mouth. Then her straight mouth turned into a big grin revealing a mouth full of stained teeth and tobacco.

"Yes ma'am, sure is." Justin said, smiling and hoping she wasn't going to hug him.

"Well, boy, you's tall as I am. You all ready growed up. Oh, Justin, I love your mamma and daddy." Rejoicing, she looked over her shoulders for a basket of plums to give to Able. "Here, ya'll have some fresh plums. I just picked them."

Justin put one in his mouth and said, "Man, these are good!" He told Pearl they were the juiciest plums he'd ever had.

"Get all you want now. There's plenty for both of you."

Able reached in and got a bigger handful than Justin's.

"Yes, sir, Mr. Justin, your Dad and Mom has been mighty good to us. I just can't tell you how good a people they are, especially after the fire and all." She was referring to the time when her husband Hugh was hurt in the cotton gin fire.

"What'cha talking about Aunt Pearl?" Justin asked.

"You mean no one done told you this story? Well, before I do, let's head for that porch swing and get out of this here hot sun. I'm burning up!"

On the porch, Able beat Justin to the rocker, so Justin and Aunt Pearl settled down in the swing together. Justin could still smell the tobacco juice over her breath as she continued to talk to him. He wanted to hold his nose but he knew that wouldn't be good manners. So, he let Aunt Pearl push a little with one foot and he wrapped his arms around his knees and pulled them up to his chest, as if to show her he were getting comfortable for a good story. When, in all honesty, he was trying to wedge his nose between his knees. Able reared back and got easy in the rocker and fanned himself with a newspaper that was lying beside him as Aunt Pearl started.

* * * * *

Seventeen

The Gin

*H*ONEY, YOU SEE, *up the road there, there was a cotton gin over in Rosedale, where everyone carried their cotton for ginning. Hugh, my husband, was the only man that could work the cotton press. It was a very dangerous job. Ain't just anybody could run that thing. If a man weren't careful, he could fall off in it and come out in a bale of cotton.*

One day, something happened to spark an electrical fire. Gins are always catching on fire because of all the lint hanging in the roof. This time the whole place was up in smoke. Some say smoke could be seen fifty miles away up to Greenville. Well, the fire got up into them rafters and danced from one rafter to the next in no time flat. In minutes, it was everywhere. No one really got injured except my Hugh. Hugh was trying to shut the electrical system down when a beam up in the roof fell and hit him. It knocked him down, but it didn't knock him out. He barely escaped falling in the press where all the knives work back and forth. If that had happened, he would have been a goner for sure, but the beam landed across his leg and pinned him down. Aunt Pearl paused and patted her forehead with a handkerchief that she pulled from her apron. Then she shook her head side to side as if she was right there looking at the grisly scene.

When everyone was outside and clear, the gin operator, Mr. Clarence, realized that Hugh was not out. Mr. Clarence was much a big white man. He had the biggest hands of anybody I'd seen. Much man he was. He had been running gins all his life. He knew right where old Hugh was supposed to be, so he ran to the water trough where all the mules were watering and dipped two cotton sacks in it, one for him and one for Hugh. He made sure they were soaked good, then covered his head with the sopping bags. Then he ran right in that fire. No man could go in such a fire like that and come out. Smoke was choking him, and fire was falling from the burning webs of lint everywhere. It looked just like a million spiders had made nests in the ceiling and they were all on fire.

Justin looked over at Able, and he just cringed. Able was making an ugly face. Justin guessed he was thinking about them spiders.

Somehow, Mr. Clarence managed his way to where my Hugh was on the floor. He looked up and saw another beam hanging, and just about ready to fall.

He told Hugh, "We gotta get you out of here."

Hugh told Mr. Clarence, "Save yourself and let me be. This tree on me ain't gonna let me up."

Mr. Clarence didn't hear a word he said. He wasn't going to leave my Hugh, even though the beam had him pinned. Mr. Clarence tried his best to pick the beam up, but there was no way he could get him loose. Then he saw an axe on the wall. He hated to suggest such a thing but he had no choice.

He said, "Hugh, how much can you take? I don't have time to cut this beam, but I can get you free with one lick"

Hugh, he knew the situation. In a matter of minutes, it would be too late. This was the only option.

"I can take it, Mr. Clarence, go ahead." Mr. Clarence, holding the axe in his hands, looked carefully at Hugh's leg and then the beam. He had no choice. In seconds they were both about to die.

"Put this over your head, Hugh," Mr. Clarence told him.

By this time, Justin was squeezing his knees closer and clenching his jaw. By now, he had forgotten all about the smell of tobacco juice as she spoke.

Mr. Clarence helped place the soaked sack over Hugh's body and head. Then with one mighty blow, it was over. Hugh's voice could be heard for miles. Everyone thought they were both dead men. The women, children, and the men outside all yelled with fright.

Hypnotized, Justin stretched his leg out and rubbed it to make sure it was still there. Able glanced over at him and slowly raised his hands as if he were holding an axe and grinned. Justin cut his eyes back at him with a serious look and waved him away.

Mr. Clarence tied his belt around Hugh's nub. He then made sure Hugh had a sack over him and then picked him up and climbed over burning debris and burning cotton to fight their way out. Finally, Mr. Clarence got out. As soon as he cleared the steps of the building, the whole building fell. Mr. Clarence fell to the ground with Hugh in his arms. He was completely exhausted.

It was a terrible sight, I tell you, Pearl said. *Hugh was lying there on the ground, and Mr. Clarence started praying over him, waiting for the ambulance. It took so long to come that Mr. Clarence threw Hugh in the back of his own pickup truck and hauled him to the hospital. When he got to the hospital, he carried him in his arms, kicking them doors wide open, telling them nurses and doctors to get their asses, I mean rear ends over there now and help this man. They did too, cause they knew he meant business.*

Blood was everywhere. Mr. Clarence looked like he'd been shot. He had black smut all over him and his white shirt, what little not burned off, was covered with blood.

Well, it was four days before they knew if Hugh would make it. He had lost a lot of blood. Mr. Clarence, he checked on my man every day. Some people would have said it would have been better for my Hugh to die in that fire because you see, Justin, colored folk is always used to hard work, and when you ain't got but one leg, it means life is fixin' to change and get harder for you.

I always reminded Mr. Clarence I'd rather have Hugh with one leg than no Hugh at all though. I always thanked him every time I'd see him. Mr. Clarence, he would usually just chuckled a little and not say too much. That Mr. Clarence was a good man for saving my Hugh, yes, sir, he was. I just think Mr. Clarence felt guilty for having to cut Hugh's leg off like that.

That was where one good white man helped us, but here is where Mr. Cane comes in, Justin. Your papa knew about the fire and also knew Mr. Clarence too. I guess the story about the fire covered them ten counties pretty fast. It wasn't long after then the hospital administrator was wanting to know how we was going to pay that bill. We didn't have no money, and Mr. Clarence had done all he could do. Hugh was still in the bed. He couldn't even feed himself. If we didn't come up with a way to pay, then the hospital was going to have to move Hugh out. I knew if they did, then it would kill him.

"Justin, we didn't have nowheres to turn. Them people at that hospital were mighty ugly to us. I told my twin sister Dorothy what was happening, and she knew we were in trouble. She came and stayed with

me five days 'cause I was just plum exhausted. I was trying to work all day, teaching at school, and then come in and stay with Hugh at night. It was just so hard on me. Ole Hugh, he just couldn't eat no more from worrying. I think he had given up.

Then one night about 6:30, the doctor told us he was sorry, but we were going to have to get out to make way for another paying patient. It was nothing he *could do, he said. I knew then that I was fixin' to lose my Hugh. If I had to carry him out of there, he would be dead in no time.*

That's when the miracle came. Justin, that's when your papa spoke up.

Pearl smiled, spit across the porch into the yard and patted him on the leg. Justin looked down at his leg where she touched him and then into the yard, impressed at the distance she could spit. Then he looked back her as she continued. *I looked around and saw this tall, dark, handsome man standing at the door. He had dark hair and blue eyes and a farmer's tan. I guess he just let himself in. I didn't know him from nobody else, but I had heard of him through my sister Dorothy. Mr. Cane asked the doctor what the problem was. The doctor started explaining.*

That's when Mr. Cane cut the doctor short. 'Doctor, don't you worry about that man's bill. I'll take care of it. He's gonna stay right there in that bed until he's well. You got a problem with that, Doctor?'

'Not if you can pay the bill. The problem is, how do I know you can?' the doctor said, smiling with a smirk of doubt.

'Well, that's about what I thought I'd hear, young man. That's why I brought my local banker with me. May I introduce you to Mr. Bowles, President and Chairman of the Board of the Plantation Bank. Do you know each other?'

The doctored looked shocked. *'Hello, Mr. Bowles…how are you?'* said the doctor.

'I'm fine doctor, and you?'

'Huh, fine sir. Huh, I don't know if you remember me; I'm Doctor Lindsey, Mr. Bowles. I was just in your bank last week.'

'Not really, but, well, Dr. Lindsey,' Mr. Bowles said in a very deep slow Southern drawl. *'Looks like we got a very sick man here, don't we?'*

'Yes, sir, we do, but…'

Mr. Bowles cut him off. *'How old are you, son?'*

'I'm finishing up my residency, sir. I'm twenty-nine.'

'Well, I'm not going to tell you my age because it none of your damn business. However, I do want you to remember this night the rest of your professional career. I'm not only the Chairman of the Board of the Plantation Banks, but I also occupy a nice seat on this hospital board as well. I believe it's in your best interest and this hospital's best interest to let this patient have whatever health care is necessary. Mr. Cane has explained to me that this man is a decorated war hero. I don't think we here at Delta Hospital are going to subject ourselves to any ridicule over kicking a war veteran out on the streets, no matter what color his skin is? Is that your opinion, too, doctor?'

'*Oh, yes, sir! We can't do that,*' *said the young doctor.*

'*Further more, for your information*' *Doctor, Mr. Cane here has a substantial amount of, let's say currency in my bank, and he can damn well pay this bill, if he says he can. So let's not hear another word about this patient's bill because I don't want to lose a good account over such a trivial matter as this. You understand?*'

'*Oh, yes sir. I sure do.*'

'*One more thing, Dr. Lindsey, when you see Mr. Brezeale, your hospital administrator, tell him he needs to come to the main bank tomorrow. He and I will need to talk,*' *Mr. Bowles said.*

The doctor all but ran out of the room, knowing he would probably lose his job the next day.

*Mr. Bowles walked over to Hugh and said, '*Son, I stretched that a little, but don't you worry about that. You just get well, you hear.*'*

*Mr. Bowles turned to Mr. Cane and said, '*Anything else I can do for you, Lieutenant?*'*

'*No, sir, Colonel.*'

'*As you were, then,*' *said Mr. Bowles as he walked out.*

'*I tell you what, Mr. Cane sure knows how to do business. I guess it all goes back to Pete saving your dad,*' *Pearl said.* '*Mr. Cane would always do what was necessary to help Pete's family. No matter what the call. I just figured Dorothy must have told Mrs. Kate, and then Mrs. Kate told Mr. Cane and then on down the line. I guess it don't really matter. The bill got paid, and I got Hugh home.*'

Do you know that Mr. Cane even paid that rehabilitation bill? Pete carried Hugh every other day for a solid six months to Memphis so Hugh could learn to walk on that new artificial leg. Can't nobody tell me Mr. Cane ain't a fine Christian man. And that ain't all, Justin, I want you to grow up and be just like him. He's the glue that holds all these families together. And you will be, as long as you keep the Lord first and read your Bible.' Justin, to the Lord we all one big family and we really are you know...maybe a different color but we really are one big family." Pearl looked up at Able and smiled. Able tucked his head some, knowing she was right.

Able spoke up, "That's right Aunt Pearl, I'm teaching the boy all I can about the good book." Justin looked up at Able and smiled. He hadn't heard a word Able had said. He was wondering what kind of man his dad really was. His mind was going in circles. He knew his dad was good, but to do all of what Aunt Pearl said was unimaginable. Why hadn't somebody done told him about all of this? He couldn't wait to get home and tell his brothers.

* * * * *

Eighteen

The Wait

MR. CANE AND Kate were anxiously waiting at the kitchen table trying to figure what was taking Able and Justin so long to get home, but Mr. Cane knew Able too well.

"Naw, nothing is wrong, Kate. It's just that Able's wanting to drive that new truck around the whole state of Mississippi," Mr. Cane told her.

"Well, that's what I'm afraid of. They need to be getting back in here. Able knows not to be keeping Justin out too long. Why haven't they called?" Kate asked.

Cane and Able

"Now, Kate, Able's not gonna let a flea hurt Justin. They'll be home shortly. Sometimes it takes a little longer to do things. Who knows? They may have missed the train all together. They may be in Vicksburg for all I know. The way Able talks, he probably drove right on by Yazoo City." Mr. Cane turned up a brow and glanced over at Kate with a grin.

"Kate, what you think is going through Pete's mind right now? It seems that he never gets the breaks he deserves. He's always caught the bad hand of stick. I don't understand why bad luck always follows him."

Mr. Cane walked over to Kate where she was sitting at the table and began rubbing her neck. He watched as she turned her head to one side and then the other to make it feel better. The massage was helping relieve the tension that had built up.

Then Mr. Cane continued. "You know, I shouldn't be here today, Kate. I should have died when I was twelve, but for some reason Pete was pedaling his bike down the road that day. He had no idea when he left his house that his timing would be so perfect. Again in France, Pete's timing was perfect. Not close to perfect, but on-the-dime perfect. Honey, I can't figure out why Pete was always there. I guess one day I will. Think about it. Without him, we wouldn't have any of our kids, our home, this farm, or anything. We wouldn't even have us, would we?"

"We have a lot to be thankful for honey," Kate said, "and Pete's one of them. We have so much more than most. But we shouldn't dwell on the why, just be grateful and live each day to its fullest," she paused and moved her head around more to better feel Mr. Cane's finger tips. "You know, we need to start doing more together. I mean the whole family. We haven't been on a real vacation in I don't know when." Then she rolled her head side to side with satisfaction. "If you want to call going to Uncle Claude's funeral on the coast a vacation then I guess that was the last time I remember. Gosh! He died twelve years ago. John Wilson Cane, do you know we have not been on a vacation since Justin was born?"

"I know, I feel bad about it too," Mr. Cane added. "The boys haven't seen any big water except Grenada Lake, as far as I can remember." Then he paused the massage for a brief moment, "You're right, Kate, we need to plan something next year," he said, thoughtfully.

Even though he knew Kate was right about dwelling on the past, he still couldn't help but think of how unfair life could be. Here Pete had saved his life and look at the hand Pete got. Down deep he felt that he didn't do enough to repay Pete to make his horrible life a little easier to live.

Kate spoke up softly. "I just hope Pete can pull it together. I'm scared he won't be with us much longer unless some miracle happens."

"Well, don't give up, Kate. A miracle may just happen. The Lord has worked in our lives, and he will work in Pete's too," Mr. Cane said, as he patted Kate on the shoulder.

Mr. Cane walked out of the kitchen and stood on the large front porch that overlooked the farm. *I just don't understand, Lord*, he said to himself, *but thank you anyway*. The field hands were finishing up the hay for the day and were about to head in. Bud was pulling the baler and William was raking. He thought, *I am a mighty blessed man.*

Mr. Cane stepped back in the kitchen and told Kate that he was going in town.

"It looks like Bud's got everything under control with the hay. I'm going to ride into town to the mercantile for a little while. I'll be back shortly."

"Okay, honey, but you better hurry. You don't have much time. I'll see you at supper," Kate said.

Mr. Cane turned the key and cranked Ole Red as he had for so many years. He realized he had made a good decision not to trade it in. When he arrived at the mercantile he got out of Ole Red and paused for a moment. He wondered about his new truck and where in the world it might be. *Who knows?* he said, aloud, an answer to nearly every though flowing through his mind. Then he pulled the brim of his hat down and walked in the front door.

Opening the door to the mercantile you could tell that five o' clock was near even without looking at his watch. Everybody looked tired and ready to call it a day. One of the clerks was closing his register, and the colored helpers were putting up their dollies. Close by looking at some ticket sales was Mac, the owner-manager, propping his feet up on the very same desk his grandfather had sat at seventy-five years earlier when he had started this business. Behind the desk was a large picture of

Main Street taken in 1903 showing cotton wagons and buggies parked in front of the store with colored hands sitting a top the cotton. That day in the picture appeared to have been a busy day. The old mercantile building, with its brick entrance and arched glass transom above the doors, was a museum in it's own rite. Still there were a variety of antique tools hanging on the walls. Everyone who came into Friendly saw the mercantile as the first sign of the business district and many stopped for directions each day. Of course, one street light and a glance in the rear view mirror also showed them how small a business district Friendly had, too.

"Hey boys, what's new in the feed business?" Mr. Cane said.

"About the same, Mr. Cane," said a tall lanky boy wearing a pair of overalls behind the counter.

"Well, I hope this weather holds out until I get my hay up."

"If you do, Mr. Cane, you'll be mighty lucky." The boy said, looking up briefly before dropping his head to continue counting money from the register. "This weather has really been acting strange lately. They say a storm popped up this morning around Rolling Fork, and someone spotted a funnel cloud over there."

"You don't say," said Mr. Cane. "Nobody hurt?" For some reason, Cane let his mind wander to Justin and Able.

"Naw, nobody hurt. A highway patrolman came in earlier this afternoon and said he was trying to haul in a drunk that cleaned out a ditch though. He said the storm came along and picked that man's car up and threw it about a hundred yards or so down the road. He said he barely had time to get the man in his car before it all happened. Funny what a drunk man will say for an excuse. He said the drunk thought he was being chased by pickup with no driver.

Crap, I've heard it all!" Mac said, bringing his left leg down and balancing his right foot against the edge of the desk.

Mr. Cane said, "Yeah, no kidding? What kinda truck was chasing this old drunk."

"He didn't say. He was too scared by the tornado. Besides, you know as well as I do that he was making every bit of it up. The crazy fool was drunk is all," said Mac, as he tipped himself back in his chair.

"Yeah, you're right," said Mr. Cane. "That whisky can really play tricks on a man's brain." Then, getting to business. "Tell you what, Mac, you better go on and put me down for twenty tons of feed for this winter. I don't want to take a chance on the price getting any higher."

"Will do, John. Anything else?" Mac asked as he tipped forward, planted both feet on the ground and swiped the pencil out of the corner of his mouth. He looked up at Mr. Cane while he scribbled the order down in his book.

"I guess, nothing right now. I'll probably see y'all tomorrow to get some fence supplies." Business taken care of, Mac reclined again and continued gnawing on the pencil.

"Oh, Mr. Cane, I hear that Pete's son got killed. What happened?" one of the clerks spoke up.

"Yeah, I'm afraid so. We don't really know what happened. Somebody called Able yesterday and told him Pete's boy got hit by a train. We don't know any more details than that. Pete left this morning headed up to Detroit to find out what happened. He'll be gone a few days I expect."

"Well, that's mighty bad for Pete," Mac said. "He's had a hard time, hasn't he? First, it was Dorothy and now his son." Silence filled the room.

"Yes, he has. In fact, he's had a real hard time," said Mr. Cane as he turned and walked out to the truck. Opening the door to the truck, he thought to himself again about the truck chasing that drunk man, then he shook his head in disbelief, *Naw, surely not!* He cranked Ole Red, pulled onto the road and headed home.

*   *   *   *   *

Nineteen

Plum Hungry

AUNT PEARL SAID, "Able, let me fix that shirt for you right quick while y'all here." His shirt was in miserable shape. One sleeve was torn nearly off and the smell on it was awful. Able pulled it off revealing his huge muscular frame.

"Boy, if Lizzy don't stop feeding you so good, you is going to swell up and pop. I'll be back in a minute. Y'all help yourself to more of them plums."

Able and Justin, grabbed some more, and Able told Justin he wanted to show him the prettiest vegetable garden he'll ever see. Justin liked the idea and followed Able around to the back of the house where

Able opened a white gate. When they turned the corner, the view opened so beautiful that Justin could not believe it. It was beautiful. The two stood overlooking five hundred acres of rich bottomland as a Blue Jay chased a Mocking bird right before them. Justin could see for miles it seemed. There was a crab apple tree filled with small red apples cascading over the fence to their right and a old clothes line with a one broken strand wrapped around the pole beyond that. In the far back, beyond the pasture, were woods Able said had more squirrels in it that any woods in Mississippi. Aunt Pearl's garden was just inside the fence, overlooking the pasture. Able pointed to a soaring Hawk high in the sky looking for field mice.

Justin was amazed that a Hawk could see that well from that distance, but Able said he could, so it must be true, he figured. Her garden was not a big one, but boy was it ever neat. Each plant was grouped within a box of crossties. At the center of each box was a crapemyrtle, which had clusters of blossoms hanging like grapes all over it. Some boxes were rectangle and some square. She had tomatoes in one box and maybe peas in another. She even had an assortment of roses ranging in colors from yellow to salmon and orange Zinnias and gold Marigolds in other ones. There was no way to see the whole garden from one angle because the view was always cut off by something growing tall like staked butter beans. Able was right. There was not another garden like Aunt Pearl's, nowhere. .

Aunt Pearl was back out in twenty minutes, with a shirt that looked like new. "It's going be a little wet now, Able, 'cause I got some of that dirt and smell washed out. Here, take this cloth and wash your underarms and face off. You look like you've been rolling around with the pigs. Smells like it too. Goodness, boy!" Aunt Pearl screwed up her face real good and fanned her face with her hand.

Justin and Able looked at each other and Able spoke up. "Aunt Pearl, we's really got to be going or we ain't ever gonna get back."

"I understand now. Don't you worry about Jeanna. She'll be all right here with me. I'll take good care of her." Her face was serious now.

"I know you will, Aunt Pearl, but I'll be back soon. You'll be hearing from me in a day or two."

"Okay, honey. I love you now and y'all be careful, now. You hear?"

Aunt Pearl picked up her hoe, as Able and Justin started walking for the truck.

As they backed out of the drive, Pearl hollered to Able. "Justin, you come back. You welcomed any time. Wait a minute, Able," she said and Able stopped the truck.

"Here, y'all carry the rest of these plums with you." She handed the basket through the window. "Y'all can eat'em on the way home."

"Thank you. Aunt Pearl!" Justin exclaimed.

As Able and Justin pulled back onto the road, Able asked Justin to figure what time it was.

"It's about 5:30 according to my watch, Abe. You reckon Dad's going to be upset with us for being late?"

"Shoot, naw, Jussin. He'll be just fine. We'll just tell him we took a tour around them cotton fields and forgot what time it was."

"You think he'll believe that, Abe?"

"Sho' nuff!"

"You know, he knows I got a new watch," Justin said, squinting up at Able.

Able looked puzzled. "Well, we will just tell him you took it off and put it back on upside down. He'll believe that, won't he?"

"I don't know, Abe." Justin responded, amused. Then out of nowhere Justin said, "Say, Abe. Did you know you and Jeanna are different colors?"

"Do what, boy?" Able craned his neck to look over. The muscles in Able's neck were straining and his eyes were just about popping out of his head. Justin swallowed hard before continuing.

"You sure are. She's light chocolate and you kinda darker than chocolate," Justin raised his eyebrows looking at him mighty proud to have figured that out.

Able didn't know how he was going to answer this one. He was thinking real hard and fast.

"Oh, I know what you talking about now. See Jussin, sometimes the first born baby gets all the color when it's born. Just like a cow or dog. You seen some spotted animals, ain't cha?"

"Yeah," Justin said.

"Well, the oldest always gonna be darker than the other ones. Just ain't enough of them pigamons in the blood to go around. Sho ain't. I've seen some babies be's snow white before. They call them babies albinos."

"Gee, that sounds like a Mexican name," Justin said.

"Probably is. I think all them medicine words are Mexican."

After Able told Justin that, Justin started looking at his own arms up and down and trying to remember if he was lighter than William or if Bud or had any spots on him. He did remember that his dad had a dark spot behind his shoulder about the size of a quarter, but his dad said that was birthmark. Able was hoping Justin wasn't going to ask anymore questions like that. The boy was doing a lot of thinking for sure. Too much thinking and it was gonna get uncomfortable for Able.

In a few minutes, Able started pushing down on the accelerator.

"How long is it going to be before we get home, Abe?" Justin asked.

"About an hour or less," Abe said. He eased on down again on the gas pedal. "We going get on this here Highway 49, and it will be a straight shot to the house."

"Well, I can't wait," Justin said. "Because my stomach is feeling kinda funny."

"Whatcha mean, you stomach is feeling funny?" Able looked over at him. Justin had begun turning white as a ghost.

"Oh me, boy, you ain't fixin' to get sick on me, are you?"

"I think so, Abe"

"Huh, is it the 'call of the wild feeling'?" Able asked, somewhat hopeful that the boy would say, 'no.'

"Whatcha mean, 'call of the wild feeling'?"

"Going to the bathroom sick. Do you have to go to the bathroom?" Able responded, impatiently. Whether it was going to come out the top or out the bottom, Able knew it couldn't happen in Mr. Cane's new truck.

"Not yet. My stomach is just hurting right now."

"Well, I better shower down a bit more then," said Able. "We ain't got no toilet paper, you know?" Able pushed down on the accelerator more. The turbulence through the window was picking up inside the cab again as it did when the tornado was coming.

"How fast we going, Abe?" Justin asked.

"Oh, about sixty miles per hour and a little." Able looked down at the speedometer. The needle was crossing the eighty mark. "You just hold on and be still, Jussin. Don't be letting nothing loose. Ole Abe gonna have you back home before you know it."

No quicker than Able had said those words, something hit him right in his own stomach. A sharp pain in his lower gut. Able's face turned as white as Justin's.

"Uh, Oh!" Able was thinking. "Darn plums," he said.

"What did you say, Abe?" Justin couldn't hear what he said for the wind.

"Them plums done made both of us sick," he hollered back.

"You too, Abe?"

"Sho' nuff!, I mean."

No quicker than Able got the words out of his mouth they met a highway patrolman car. Able looked in his rearview mirror and gritted his teeth. He braced himself as he saw the patrolman turning around.

"This is bad, Jussin."

"What you mean?" Justin asked nervously, his mind filled with images of the plums that had made his stomach hurt so bad.

"Just believe me. This is bad."

Able looked at Justin and said, "That law man we just met, well he's turning around after us."

"Do what?" Justin turned around and looked out the back window. "He sure is, Abe. What'd we do wrong?"

Able didn't answer, instead he pulled his hat off and started hitting the back seat and back window. He was swinging his hands and arms every which way and started pulling his shirttail out. Justin couldn't figure out what was wrong with him.

"You gone crazy, Abe. What you doing?" Justin said.

"Tell you later. We gonna pull over now. It's probably nothing."

Able pulled over on the side of the road and stopped. He immediately jumped out of the truck swinging, dancing and swatting at his arms and legs. He was like a crazed man. Then he stopped and began rubbing his back trying to look in pain and then started walking again towards the patrolman.

"Say, there, boss. How...how you doing?" Able said, as the officer got out of his car cautiously and approached him. The officer was wondering why this huge man was so excited. He'd never seen this kind of activity before, so he kept one hand on his gun.

"Why you driving so fast, boy? Do you know you were speeding?"

"Oh naw, huh, sir! Well, I don't rightly know if I was or if I wasn't." Able was acting in pain and trying to reach behind his back with one hand.

"Now what do you mean by that?" the patrolman asked.

"Well, he's gone now, but there was one bad yellow jacket wasp in the cab of that truck, and he was tearing me some kinda up, sir. That sucker done got down in my shirt and was giving me fits. I guess I might have speeded up a little on the gas, but I sho' wasn't trying to break no speed limit. No, sir, sho' wasn't. It was just me and that wasp." Able paused, shaking his head and then looked up at he patrolman, "You know what, officer? I think the wasp won." Able chuckled, trying to convince the patrolman.

"You got any license?" the patrolman said with a straight face.

"Oh, yes, sir. I sho' do." Abe pulled his license out of his billfold and handed it to the officer.

The officer looked closely at the license. It matched Able all right: NAME: ABLE JOHNSON, WEIGHT: 240, HAIR: BLK, RACE: C, HEIGHT: 6'5".

"Well, who you got up there with you, Mr. Johnson?" the patrolman asked, turning his attention to the boy in the passenger seat.

"Oh, that's Mr. Cane's boy, from over there in Friendly." The officer walked up to the truck window and noticed that Justin was pale as a sheet.

"How, you do there, sonny?" the officer said.

"Huh, okay, I guess," Justin replied, holding his stomach. The officer walked back to Able.

"Yeah, Johnson, I've heard the name Cane before. This the boy's daddy's truck?"

"Hum, yes, sir, it is. Brand new. It sho' is pretty, ain't it? I believe that's the best color I ever seen on a Ford pickup, don't you?" Able said.

"Yeah, it is. Can't beat these Fords," the patrolman said as he walked to the rear of the truck. "Be sure to tell Mr. Cane he needs to hurry and get a tag on this new truck. He's only got a few days. Able looked down and could see it was missing. "You know, I met a truck just like it this morning over around Rolling Fork," said the patrolman. "Y'all been over there?"

"Excuse me officer, that wasp feels like he is still stinging me." Able reached again to his back avoiding a direct answer to the question.

Then he changed the subject completely. "You like plums, sir? My aunt back up the road here," Able pointed from the direction they had just come, "she just gave us a mess of them. In fact, we got a few left. How would you like to carry a mess home with you?"

"They look pretty good there," said the patrolman looking over into the bed of the truck. "I guess I'll take a few." The officer handed Able his license back. "Say, is that boy ok?"

"Yes, sir, he's fine. Just a little carsick is all." The patrolman reached in the plum bucket for a hand full and popped one into his mouth. Able seeing that might be all he was going to get spoke up quickly, "No, sir, now, you go on and have'em all. We done ate all we can," said Able. "They sho' some fine eating." Able reached over in the bed of the truck and handed the patrolman the entire bucket of plums. With the kind offer and satisfied, the officer walked to his car, opened the back door and put them on the seat. Before the officer shut the door he grabbed another big handful and put them on his front seat. "I appreciate the plums, and y'all hold that speed down now, you hear?"

"Oh, yes, sir, that wasp he's gone now." Able breathed with relief, but with care. His stomach was in knots. He walked back to the truck carefully and saw Justin leaning against his door.

"Jussin, how's your belly?" Able asked, as he got back in the truck.

"Not too good, Abe."

As the officer turned around in the middle of the road, Able watched though his mirror, the officer bit down on another juicy plum.

"Well, we ain't gonna have to worry about no more policeman. Let's go!" Able gunned it and pulled back onto the road "Judgements 12:6, 'Always give fruits of the earth with a loving spirit, and the Lord will be kind to you when he judges you.'"

"What did you say, Abe?"

"Nothing, Jussin, you just be still until I gets you home."

It was about 6 o'clock when Able and Justin pulled in the driveway. Mr. Cane had just gotten back from the mercantile and was standing beside Ole Red.

"That's pretty good timing, Mr. Cane," Able said, as he got out of the truck.

"Where in the He__, heck you two been?" Mr. Cane said to Able.

"Oh it's a long story, Mr. Cane, but right now little Jussin needs some medicine. He's been sick all day. We done stopped under every tree between here and Yazoo City."

Able went around and helped Justin out of the truck. Able put his finger up to his mouth and shhhh for Justin not to say anything and just remain quiet.

"Jussin, I'll tell them later about today. Let's not get everybody nervous now. We knows they worries too much."

Kate heard the trucks drive up and walked to the front porch. When she heard Able say Justin was sick, she ran over to the truck and helped Justin into the house. She was asking Justin how long his stomach had been hurting when Able saw him go in the door. Able crossed his fingers.

"Y'all get Pete to the train, Able?" asked Mr. Cane, somewhat brusquely.

"Oh, yes, sir, no problem. No problem at all."

"Able, I thought I told you to put that tag on that truck this morning."

"Oh, I did, Mr. Cane, but you see them screws didn't look too good and so I took it back off. Sho' didn't want to lose it."

"No, you don't," said Mr. Cane. "That tag cost $45."

Able rolled his eyes and looked at the ground, wondering where in the world that tag was.

Then Mr. Cane said, "I know you're tired Able if you've been taking care of a sick boy all day. It's been a long day for me too, so go on home to Lizzy and get you a good cooked meal. I'll see you tomorrow. By the way, she carried a good plum pie home this afternoon. Get you a piece before you go to bed. It'll make you sleep good. It sure is good."

"Oh, yes, sir! Mr. Cane. That, sounds just like what I need. If it be all right with you, I'd like to carry your new truck to the house and wash'er back up for you. We got in a little shower coming home."

Mr. Cane raised his eyebrow a little and gritted his teeth. "I guess it'll be all right. Go ahead, but you go straight home now. Don't be driving that truck around town."

Mr. Cane was glad to see his truck again, but he hated to see it leave again so fast.

"Oh, no, sir. I's just gonna shine'er up a little. Huh, Mr. Cane. Tell little Justin I'll check on him tomorrow."

"Okay, I'll tell him, but, Able, one more thing," Mr. Cane paused and looked down at the ground not knowing what he was about to say. "Think you can get Lizzy to come in early tomorrow and watch Justin? Mrs. Kate's going to carry me to Jackson to the eye doctor, and we don't want Justin here alone."

"Oh, yes, sir, I'll get her to ride in with me."

"What a relief," Able thought, sweating bullets. He knew Mr. Cane didn't like no fibbing, and that was just what he was doing. Then Able drove off in the new Ford. Mr. Cane could hear the radio playing as Able turned out to the road. He shook his head, smiled and walked into the house.

The next morning Able arrived at the house a few minutes late. Lizzy was driving her old car behind him. He usually got to the farm around 6:00 a.m., but today he wanted everyone to know he had carried Mr. Cane's new truck home over night. He certainly didn't want to beat anyone there. As Able drove through the front gate, he made a grand entrance for the other hands. All of them were proud to see Able driving Mr. Cane's new truck. They were just talking back and forth to each other and pointing.

"That Able's done moved up to the top," one man said. "Look at him."

In a sense, it made most of the colored feel proud that one of their own could be trusted and achieve something like that. "Able done carried the boss's new truck home," another colored said, taking his hat off and slapping his knee with it. "We gonna make it yet, sho' is," he said.

After making the grand entrance, Able pulled in Mr. Cane's drive, got in Ole Red and drove to the barn.

All the help was standing around the hay barn when Mr. Cane walked up.

He told Able, "We got a lot of hay to get up today." Then he looked over at the boys, "Bud, you and William, we're gonna work late if we have to, so don't plan on having no dates tonight." He looked hard at them to make sure his point got across. Bud shook his head in defeat.

"That rain just missed us yesterday, and we sure don't want another one coming along and messing us up. Able, we need to get it all up today, understand?" Mr. Cane said.

"We can do it, Mr. Cane."

Then, pulling Able aside, Mr. Cane added, "Able you need to put that tag back on today, too. Mrs. Kate and I are taking the car." With those few words, Mr. Cane walked back towards the house, leaving Able wondering how he was going to find the tag to the truck.

"Okay, everybody." Bud hollered, stretching his arm out to pull one of his gloves on, "Let's hurry and get this hay up 'cause I got a hot date tonight that won't wait!"

William, knowing it was going to be a hot morning, started pulling his shirt off over his head revealing his rib cage. He knew he might as well go ahead and get rid of it now, because the heat would be up in an hour. With one leg of his pants riding above his right boot top, he grabbed the fender on the tractor and yanked himself up. . "Me too!" he shouted back to Bud.

Minutes later Able saw Mrs. Kate and Mr. Cane pulled out of the drive and head towards Jackson.

Like clockwork, Bud checked his oil and got on the John Deere tractor, pulling the baler. William got on a smaller Ford tractor, pulling the rake. Able told Bebop, his ten-year-old boy, that he would have to fill in for Justin in the haul truck. He liked that idea. He knew he could drive if Justin could.

"We's got a lot of hay to bale today, boys. It's sho' gonna be a long one, so let's get at it!" Able shouted.

Able hopped on the hay truck to show Bebop what to do. He knew Bebop was going to have the same problems all the rest had learning. "Slow down, son. Alright turn her left. Turn her right. You got it. And, straighten her up now," Able said, helping Bebop get the hang of it.

* * * * *

Twenty

Lunch Time

IT WAS 10:45 when Lizzy came out to the field and stood by the fence. When Able saw her, he told Bebop to hold the wheel steady. He jumped off the truck and went to her, wondering what she wanted.

"What's up, honey?" Able asked. Lizzy had a strange look on her face.

"Able, a highway patrolman called a few minutes ago and said he needed to talk to Mr. Cane." She was working her hands and her brows just as high up as could be.

"No kidding. What did he say, Lizzy?" Able was doing some powerful thinking and trying to keep a straight face at the same time.

"Nothing really. Just said he needed to talk to Mr. Cane." She looked up at him with a glint in her eye, asking him without asking him.

"Humm," said Able. "Did he leave a name?"

"Sho' did. I got it right here." She reached in her apron and pulled out a piece of paper with a number scribbled on it.

Able thought for a second. "Well, Baby, just let me have that number, and I'll take care of it. I bet it's something Mr. Cane needs to know about his new truck." Able pretended he might know what it was. He paused and then acted like he had an idea. "Yeah! Now that I think about it, sho' is.

"Well, I got plenty to do. I don't need to be talking to a highway patrol," Lizzy said. "Wouldn't surprise me if Bud hadn't done got another speeding ticket."

"Well, now that you mention it, it sho' might be, Baby. Yeah, you right. I might better run some interference for Bud before he gets in trouble. I'll just call that patrolman at lunch time."

Lizzy handed the folded paper to Able and started walked back to the house.

Lizzy turned around, arched her brow and said, "Lunch time won't be long now, so y'all don't be late. You hear?"

"Don't worry. We won't." Able replied, rubbing his stomach and smiling.

Dinnertime came pretty quick, and everyone was glad of it. They had made five loads to the barn and they were tired. Five was a record. They had never made more than four loads before. So far, the heat was not a factor. There was a slight breeze out of the west that helped, but a breeze usually meant rain was not far off. Regardless, of the consequence of rain, it helped.

Since Mr. Cane and Mrs. Kate were gone, Able and Bebop ate inside with Bud and William around the big breakfast table. Lizzy had fixed a meal of cornbread, sweet potatoes, blackeyed peas and pork chops.

"Lizzy, how is Jussin doing?" Able asked, about to finish up.

"He's doing all right if he can just stay out of the bathroom." Able knew the problem. He'd spent most of the morning in the woods himself.

"Whatcha think y'all got, Able?" said William.

"Probably something we ate yesterday. Them hamburgers may have been bad we gots at that snowball place."

"What was the name of the place?" William asked Able with a mouth full of food.

"Shoot, Mr. William, you know I can't read too good, and besides I was too hungry to look. Just one of them places you kids hang out at all the time."

As Able took his last gulp of tea, he looked up and saw Justin staggering into the kitchen. He still had his red striped pajamas on

"Well, look a here, Jussin. How you feeling?" asked Able.

"I think that 'call of the wild' done got me, Abe."

Able looked down at the table, and Lizzy looked at Able, wondering where Justin had heard that term. Bud and William looked at each other too and started smiling.

Lizzy stood up from the table and said, "I swear you men are all full of foul mouth sayings." She tightened her lips, putting her napkin down and said. "I think you all come in the world like just a like. Correction! Alllllll, but Mr. Cane. He's decent and upright. Now y'all all get out of my kitchen! Go on, get!"

After she ran everybody out of the kitchen, she turned to Justin, looking in his puny eyes and said," Baby, you feel like eating anything yet?"

Lizzy was going to make sure he was taken care of. She loved Justin as much as her own son, Bebop. Justin told her he wasn't up to eating anything yet, but maybe later.

* * * * *

Twenty-one

Perfect Timing

ABLE WATCHED FROM the porch as Bud and William got back on their tractors, and one of the other hands opened the door for Bebop to jump back in the truck. He stood around on the porch a minute, then turned and walked back in. He walked over to the phone, but hesitated about picking it up. He pulled the number from his shirt pocket, staring at it hard, trying to make his mind up as to what to do. Not sure he was making the right decision, he picked the phone up several times to his ear and then quickly placed it back down before the operator had time to answer. It could mean trouble if he did call, but it could also mean trouble if he didn't.

About the third time Able repeated this ritual, he had the receiver to his ear only a moment before the operator came on and said, "Number please?" His heart jumped. He'd made the call.

"Oh huh, ma'am, I needs to call 582."

"Okay, just a minute, and I'll connect you," she said.

Able could hear the phone ring on the other end as he stood there wondering what he was going to say.

"Hello," came a voice on the other end.

"Huh, is this here the Highway Patrol station?" Able said.

"No, it's not, but this is Patrolman Campbell. This is my home. Can I help you?"

Able started walking the floor.

"Huh! Mr. Campbell, this here's Able Johnson. I's work over here for Mr. Cane. Huh. Mr. Cane is out to the doctor today, and Lizzy, my wife, says you's called about something, and since I's in charge while Mr. Cane is gone, I figured I better come right on in here and call you." Able was rolling his eyes, knowing he was going to be killed if Mr. Cane found out about yesterday.

"Able, didn't I stop you yesterday about that tag on Mr. Cane's truck?"

"Huh, yes, sir, you sho' did. That was me all right. Me and little Jussin."

"Well, we found a tag today, and it matched up to Mr. Cane's truck."

235

"Oh! No kidding," said Able. "Huh, where did you find it, sir?"

"Well, that's just it. We found that tag mounted on the back of a stolen vehicle this morning. Didn't you tell me yesterday Mr. Cane didn't have his tag yet."

"Yes, sir, sho' did, but you see." Able was havin to think fast. "Officer, he got that tag and give it to me when we got back. I betcha them car thieves got it off that truck last night, sitting in my driveway. I shined Mr. Cane's truck up good last night, and I think I put that tag on there. Now, it might have fallen off that truck between here and there."

The officer realized he was getting nowhere with the conversation.

"Well, Able," said the officer, "I'll drop it by the house for you this afternoon. I'll be out that way."

"Oh, I'll be glad to come get it now," said Able.

"No, I'll drop it off. I'll be out that way anyway patrolling."

Able was grasping for words. "Okay then," said Able. "One more thing. Huh, Patrolman Campbell, I sho' appreciate the fine job you officers are doing."

Campbell just looked at his receiver, not believing what he had just heard.

"Well, thank you, Mr. Johnson," Mr. Campbell said.

With his forehead covered in sweat from anxiety, Able hung up the phone and gave out a sigh of relief. Looking upwards, he exclaimed with clasped hands, *"Ask and you shall receive,* says the Lord!" Able started walking towards the door with a slight bounce in his step and a big smile plastered across his face.

"What are you so happy about Able?" Lizzy inquired, as she came into the den. "I thought you done gone back to work?" She said, putting her hand on her hip.

Able turned around and said, "Everything, Baby, everything. It's a good day to be alive. Yes, it sho' is!" as he headed to the field.

As Lizzy watched him skip off the porch back into the field, she mumbled, *"That man's ain't right."*

As Able stepped on the running board of the hay truck to check on Bebop, he exclaimed, "Yes, sir! Things sho' shaping up, Bebop." Bebop just looked at his dad and smiled.

For the next couple of hours, the hay crews made good time. When Able looked up and saw a cloud of smoke coming from the gravel road his first thought was Mr. Cane. But as the dust cleared, he could see a big red light atop the car and the "Mississippi Highway Patrol" logo scrawled across the hood and side.

"Oh, yeah! Mr. Campbell, you saved my day!" Able told himself, grinning and jumping down from the truck. He turned and told Bebop to carry the load on to the barn when they got it loaded.

"You sure I can do it by myself, Pop?" Bebop asked.

"You gotta do it sometime, boy. It might as well be today," Able said, making long strides toward the house.

Patrolman Campbell stopped his car along the hayfield, and watched Able walk towards him with a speed. Campbell got out of his car slowly, adjusted his sunglasses and stood there with the truck tag in his hand. He knew it was Able coming because of his huge size. When Able got to the road, he crossed over a barbed wire fence and a little ditch and extended his hand to Patrolman Campbell for a big handshake.

"Pretty hot out here today, ain't it, Mr. Johnson?" said Patrolman Campbell, shaking Able's hand.

"Sir, just calls me Able. That's what everybody around here calls me." Able looked down at the ground and then spoke up again, "Whew! What you talking about?" he added. "It's hotter than I can ever remember, Mr. Campbell. We done drank up the whole well today. Betcha Mr. Cane ain't gonna have no water tonight to take a bath." Able laughed.

"Yeah, I can't ever remember it being this hot either. In fact, it's been so hot that I've done seen the highway buck up in three or four places in the last few days. The highway crews have been pretty busy cutting those bad places out so the cars can get by. I've worked one wreck caused by it, today."

"Sho' nuff?" said Able.

"Yeah! I sure have. We sure needed that rain they got over in Rolling Fork the other day, but without the high wind."

Able said, "Yes, sir, I heard they had some pretty bad storms over that way."

Campbell spoke up, "Sure did, I seen that twister pick a man's car clean up out of the ditch. If I hadn't just arrested him for being drunk, he would have died. No question about it. You know the Lord sho' works in mysterious ways, don't he, Mr. Johnson? If I hadn't come along just when I did and arrested him, he could be standing before the Lord right now, still trying to come up with a good reason to tell the Lord why he was there."

Able just laughed. "Yes, sir, it sounds like you sho' nuff saved that man's life. Maybe he can get straightened out now after that close call."

"Maybe so, but don't count on it. Some people just don't ever learn."

"You right about that now, Mr. Campbell. You sho' right there." Able said looking down at Campbells's hand. "Huh, is that there the tag you gonna give me?" Able said.

"Yeah, it is." Campbell, handing the tag to Able. "Put that thing on good now, Able. You don't want to lose that thing again," said Patrolman Campbell opening the door to his car.

"Oh, no, sir, sho' don't want to do that. I'm gonna put it on real good this time. Ain't nobody gonna be able to get it off. Not even a good thief."

Patrolman Campbell got in his patrol car and rolled his window down, "Good luck on getting that hay up, Able. Maybe that rain won't catch you."

"Appreciate that, Mr. Campbell. We gonna get it," Able laughed, "or Mr. Cane gonna get us."

Campbell smiled, put his car in gear, and headed back to the highway creating a cloud of dust along the way.

Able immediately went to the tool shed and found four 1/2-inch bolts, four lock washers and eight nuts. He dug around in the toolbox until he retrieved a screwdriver and wrench, then walked back to the house where the new Ford truck was parked. He put all four bolts through the tag and used the four lock washers with two nuts on each bolt.

"Now, you sucker," he said. "Come off now!" He tightened down as hard as he could.

He stood up and looked at the tag and said, "Mr. Tag, before you come off now, Mr. Cane gonna have to take you to the machine shop and get a blow torch to get you off. I done put a Able hold on you ain't nobody gonna get loose."

Looking around Able could see that Bebop had made a successful trip to the barn and was heading back to the field in the old hay truck. With the mid-day heat coming down, the barn had turned into an oven, drawing out what remaining water each man had in his body. When Bebop got beside the water hydrant under the tree, he rolled to a stop. Nearly everyone was in slow motion walking to the tree. Each man slowly bent his knee beside the hydrant and began drinking and splashing water onto his head to cool off. After doing so, they stood around a few minutes to get their blood circulating again and then boarded the truck back to the field.

Bebop drove by his dad as they made their way back through the old gate.

"Papa," Bebop said, "Two more loads and we'll have it all in."

"Hang in there, Bebop. Bring it on home. Mr. Cane ain't gonna believe we done all this today." Able shouted. "No, sir, he sho' ain't!"

Able didn't go back into the field. He turned and walked back to the house. Lizzy greeted him on the front porch with a glass of cool iced tea.

"Mr. Johnson, you a good man." she said, handing him the glass.

"That's right!" He smiled mischievously. Lizzy snapped her dishtowel at Able, catching him on the leg. To which he replied, "Yes, Mrs. Lizzy, you the perfect woman, too."

"Now, Able, I ain't no *perfect* woman. Look at these hips and butt on this girl."

"Honey, I didn't say you were perfect for everybody. I just said you were the perfect woman for me." He leaned down and kissed her. He was still standing three steps down. "We sho' mighty blessed, Lizzy. Look at Bebop out there only ten years old. In his mind, he's twenty-five, driving a transport truck headed to Shreveport. He's sho' proud of hisself."

Lizzy spoke up, "Yes, I'm proud of him too 'cause he's just like his daddy." Lizzy held Able's hand up to her lips and kissed it.

In the distance Lizzy and Able could hear a few hands hollering, " Bebop, slow down, you killing us back here, boy!"

Able looked at Lizzy and said, " Love you, girl."

"I love you too, Mr. Johnson." Then Lizzy said, "You better get out there and slow Bebop down, or you gonna have to finish picking up all that hay by your ownself."

"You probably right," he said. Able handed her the empty glass and started walking briskly back to the field. When he crossed the fence back into the pasture, he looked down. There below the wire was a copperhead snake coiled up ready to strike. He eased back and saw to his right a stick lying on the ground. He reached down and picked it up without taking his eyes off the snake, raising it up slowly so as not to scare it. When he raised the stick to deliver a deathblow, he suddenly had an uneasy feeling. Shaking the momentary thought from his mind, he struck across the snake's head, killing it with one blow. Then he picked the snake up with one end of the stick and carefully draped it over the top strand of the barbed wire fence. He dropped the stick, stepped over the fence and started walking in the direction of Bebop and the crew. When he got halfway across the field, he saw William driving towards him on the tractor with one foot perched on the dash. He had his straw cowboy hat tilted back and Able could see that his front side was already turning red from the sun. In a few minutes William rolled up to him and turned his tractor off. He removed his leather gloves, wiped the sweat from his forehead and smiled. "I'm through raking, Able. I believe I've got all the rows up and finished. I'm gonna get one more drink of water, and then I'll come back and help load."

"That'll be good, Mr. William. You done a splendid job of raking. Don't think I've ever seen anybody rake and get them rows looking so pretty. I tell you, that really helps Mr. Bud out too while he's baling. When them rows are straight, it sho' cuts all that twisting and turning to get that baler lined up." William's face began to swale with pride.

"Well, Able, I see it like this." William leaned back in his tractor seat and pushed his hat back further on his head, "When you need the best, you gotta get the best man for the job."

"You absolutely right there, Mr. William, and I promise I'm gonna pass that right on to Mr. Cane, so he will know where to come to when he needs anything done." Able smiled knowingly.

"Na'ah! Don't do that, Able. We'll just keep that between us, okay?" He lowered his hat fast, cranked the tractor, and drove off.

Able just chuckled and said, "You Cane boys, y'all sho' something else. What I's gonna do with you?"

Bebop had made his last turn in the field, and there were only two long rows of hay remaining when he hollered out at Able. "This is gonna be the last load, Papa."

"Good, Bebop! I see Mr. Bud finishing up too; he gonna make that date tonight after all. That boy done baled some hay in the last three days." Able said and turned and hollered to the other hands, "Y'all about ready to get through?"

243

"Yes, sir, we sure are!" they all hollered back.

"Then let's see how fast we can load this last truck." With that, Able joined in on the pick-up line. He was picking up two bales to everyone else's one.

Somebody yelled out from behind, "We been needing you all day, Able. Where you been?"

Able could throw those bales all the way to the top with no problem. William jumped up on the truck to help stack because the hay was coming too fast for one man to stack. As they turned at the end of the row, Bud parked his tractor and joined in on the pick-up line. The sun was just starting to settle deep in the horizon and a cool breeze was lifting up across the field.

"I've been looking for this row all day long," said Bud, referring to the last row of bales on the ground. You could hear everyone saying, "Me too, me too. Thank the Lord."

As they picked up the last two bales, Able looked and saw the cloud of smoke appearing again over the road. "Wellllll, look a-yonder," he said. "That looks like Mr. Cane and Mrs. Kate coming. I guess they done got down there to Jackson and got back."

"Man, he knows how to time it," said William.

"He sho' does," said Able. "He sho' does," looking to the heavens.

Having loaded up the last few bales, Bebop turned the old truck towards the pasture gate. Able was hanging on the running board giving him instructions as he did Justin. Bebop was trying his best not to miss any gears. "Slow down here, Bebop, in front of the house and let me off. I need to talk to Mr. Cane," said Able.

Bebop didn't like that idea at all because he had made it through all the gears and certainly didn't want Mr. Cane hearing him scratch any, if he had to start over.

"That's good, Bebop," said Able as he slowed down." I'll just jump off here. You keep going and keep it in the second all the way to the barn."

That was a relief to Bebop.

As they drove by Mr. Cane in front of the house, Able jumped off and for show, hollered, "Take her on to the barn, Bebop!"

Bebop sat as high as he could so Mr. Cane could see him driving.

"Able, ole Bebop's driving that truck real good. He's coming along. He's gonna make us some good help." Mr. Cane said, taking his handkerchief out of his pocket and wiping his brow. "He's certainly growing up, Able. I remember when he wasn't that tall." He held his hand down about his waist. "It seems like yesterday."

"Yes, sir, Mr. Cane. They grows up fast."

"Yeah, they do, Able, and get more expensive at the same time."

"You got that right, Mr. Cane!"

They both laughed.

"Say, Mr. Cane, you got a minute to talk?" Able looked over at Mrs. Kate.

She opened the screen door and walked inside, waving goodbye over her shoulder.

"What's on your mind, Able?"

"Well, Mr. Cane, you remember my sister Jeanna? Mr. Cane got a knot in his stomach. Pretty girls were always trouble. He was thankful for his boys.

"Oh, yeah. Sure I do. I haven't seen her in quite a while though."
"Well, you see, Mr. Cane, she's got a man following her and she needs to get away. I mean, an evil man. I'm afraid he's gonna hurt her. Matter of fact, he already has. Right now, she's staying at Aunt Pearl's house. What I really need is to borrow some money to get her away from here. Something terrible's gonna happen if I don't."

"I see," said Mr. Cane. "Well, let me ask you this, Able. Is she safe with your Aunt Pearl now?"

"I think so, Mr. Cane, but not long. That Big Doug Carter is involved."

"Who's Big Doug Carter?" Mr. Cane removing his hat slowly and running his hand through his hair, thinking as if he had heard the name before. Then it came to him clearly. "Able, I think he killed a girl over in the Delta four or five years ago, didn't he?"

"That's right, Mr. Cane. That's him." replied Able.

"I thought that sorry slug was dead or in prison."

"No, sir, he ain't. He got some fancy lawyer to get him out of all those robbery and killing charges. How my little sister got hooked up with him I don't rightly know."

"She may not have had a choice," said Mr. Cane. "Somebody like Big Doug can scare a young girl into about anything, and besides, it doesn't matter how she got hooked with him. The main thing is to get her unhooked from him. Where you are going to send her?"

"She says she'd feel safe with her cousin Missy over in Atlanta."

"Well," said Mr. Cane, wiping his head again, "That should put enough distance between them. I tell you what, Able? I'll lend you what money she needs, but I'd have her catching the bus over in Kosciusko rather than Belzoni. You go by there tomorrow and find out the details when the next bus is leaving to Atlanta. Then you go get Jeanna and come back here. If Big Doug finds out she's skipped town, he'll check the bus station in Belzoni, first. Without any clues, he might just think she's still around the area."

"Good thinking, Mr. Cane. I sho' appreciate it."

"No problem. Glad to help, Able." Mr. Cane wiped his head again and looked across the pasture feeling real good about the hay being up.

As Able walked off, Mr. Cane wondered if Able even had a clue. Did he sense that their closeness ran deeper than the bond between two men? "Able, y'all did a good job today. Looks good. Looks like you broke a record or two, didn't you?"

"You can credit Mr. Bud and Mr. William for that."

"Really?" said Mr. Cane.

"Yes, sir! Girls can get any man in high gear," Able said. Then he heard Bebop coming back from the barn.

Able yelled out to him, "Bebop, park over there under the shed now. We through for the day." Then under his breath, Able muttered, "Thank the Lord!"

About the same time Mr. Cane spoke up and Able turned around. "Oh, Able, when you go over to Kosciusko, carry Ole Red. Let's leave the new truck here for me."

"Oh, yes, sir!" Able grinned. "I was gonna do that anyway."

Mr. Cane smiled back him and walked into the house where Justin was standing in the kitchen with Kate and Lizzy.

"Well, big boy, how are you feeling?" Mr. Cane asked Justin.

"Much better, Dad." Justin said.

"I got a lot of chicken soup down him, today, Mr. Cane." Lizzy chimed in.

"That chicken soup of yours can sure fix about anything, Lizzy," Mr. Cane replied.

"Well, Mr. Cane, I think he'll be good as new tomorrow." Lizzy walked over and rubbed Justin on the head.

"Too bad they got all the hay up, Justin," Mr. Cane told Justin.

"Yeah, that's too bad! But I ain't gonna miss it at all," Justin said in a softer voice.

"I thought you'd say that for some reason," Mr. Cane laughed. "Don't worry, we'll find something for you to do." Then as routine would have it, Mr. Cane walked into the den and turned the TV on to watch the evening news.

Kate and Lizzy were in the kitchen talking and Lizzy mentioned she needed to put Justin to bed. "Lizzy, you go on now, it's no use in you hanging around any more today. You've put a long day in. I'll see you in the morning, and I do appreciate you coming in early this morning to watch after Justin for me." Lizzy didn't argue because she was tired.

"No problem, Mrs. Kate. You sure there ain't nothing else I can do? I'll be glad to help you put up them groceries."

"Oh, no! I've got them. You've had a long day. Go on home now, Lizzy."

"Let me get my purse then." Lizzy grabbed her purse and started out the door telling everyone good night as she parted.

By the time she got to her car, Bebop was already stretched across the front seat sound asleep. She had to wake him to make him move over so she could get in to drive.

"Move over, Bebop!" Lizzy grunted. When he moved, he left a trail of dirt on the seat from his dust covered pants. Lizzy saw it and said, "Boy, we gotta get you a big bath when we get home."

"Oh, Mom, I'm too tired," Bebop answered.

"I know you are, but you've had a big day, and that bath will help take all the soreness out. You will sleep a whole lot better."

"Oh, Mom!"

"You heard me now, no arguing!" Lizzy said.

As Lizzy and Bebop headed towards home, the clouds of dust lifted off the gravel road behind them. Not far behind her was Able in Ole Red. He figured he'd give Ole Red a good shin'in before he headed off to Kosciusko for Jeanna's ticket.

Once at home, it didn't take long to get Bebop fed, bathed, and off to bed. It had been an extremely long day for everyone and everyone was exhausted.

Lying in bed, Able told Lizzy he was going to Kosciusko the next morning to check on getting a bus ticket for Jeanna. He told her about his conversation with Mr. Cane and how Mr. Cane figured it would be safer to go get her and let her leave from there.

"You know Lizzy," he said. "I hadn't felt good about Jeanna all day. I sho' wish Aunt Pearl had a phone so I could call her." She asked why and he said, "just 'cause." He didn't know how to explain about seeing the snake in the field and how it shook him to the core.

Able didn't say anything for several minutes. He just laid still and thought about the situation to himself. Then with confidence, he burst out. "Well, tomorrow when I goes to Kosciusko, I'm gonna swing by and I'll talk that girl into coming home with me."

"You're a good man, Mr. Able Johnson, you just trying to take care of everybody." Lizzy said with admiration in her eyes.

"I tries," Able said. "but, baby, it's mighty hard sometimes. I guess the good Lord He knows how much we can takes. I's just gotta have faith that he's watchin' over us." He took a deep breath and reached for the bedside light.

As they lay there in the darkness, Able said, "Baby, sometimes I don't think the Lord knows me as good as I does."

"Hey, Mr. Johnson, don't go doubtin' the Lord," rolling over on her side and patting his stomach.

"I guess you're right, Lizzy," he said. Then he placed his big hand gently on hers. "Baby, you go on to sleep now. I gonna lay here and thinks a little bit."

Able, lay there for two more hours worrying about Jeanna before he finally fell asleep.

* * * * *

Stephen Cheek

Twenty-two

Tragedy On The Hill

THE SUN WAS just coming up, and the old Blue Jay was chasing the Mocking bird again, but in contrast to the making of a peaceful promise of a new day, Jeanna had had a restless night. Nightmares that Big Doug had found her had awakened her time and again. Trembling each time she awoke, Jeanna pulled the bed covers closer, hoping that the linens would protect her. At one point, she turned on her bed lamp to lessen her fear, but it hadn't helped. She imagined that he was watching her through the window, waiting for his chance to attack. She prayed that daylight would calm her fears.

252

At nine o'clock in the morning, Pearl came in Jeanna's room with breakfast. "Child, I want you to lie here and rest. Don't do anything until I tell you to. You gonna need your strength before this is all over." Pearl had a feeling things might get worst before they got better.

Jeanna raised up her head and said, "Thanks, Mamma." Aunt Pearl stopped in the doorway and looked back over shoulder at the child who had become a woman. Then Jeanna continued, "Y'all have been so good to me and Able. You raised us like your own after we lost mamma and I just want to you to know how much I appreciate and love you for it."

Tears started streaming down Pearl's face. She had wanted to hear those words for eighteen years.

"You and Able couldn't have been better babies to Uncle Hugh and me. I just wish Uncle Hugh could have lived to see you now. I never regretted that we couldn't have any children of our own, because you know what, girl? We didn't need any. We couldn't have had any young'uns we coulda loved more than you."

Pearl walked over to the bed and sat beside Jeanna and hugged her neck. There was a special feeling about her hug. Jeanna always felt safe and warm in Pearl's arms.

"Darlin'," continued Pearl, "you don't know how that warms my heart to hear you say them words. That makes me feel so good. There ain't no flower in my garden as pretty as you. Do you hear me? No flower at all!"

They continued to talk as mid-morning approached, and Jeanna could still hear the birds singing outside.

"It's gonna be a beautiful Lord's day today, Jeanna. Look out there at that bright sunshine and the beautiful soil in the garden. Most of all, I got you home again where you belong. I love you so much and don't you ever forget it, you hear?"

As Pearl got up from the bed, she wiped the tears from her hard, worn little face and whispered to herself, "Sweet Jesus, you are so good to me, but now I need to get out there in that garden, or the day will gone before I know it."

As Pearl walked back into the kitchen, she sensed a presence behind her . . . as though someone was standing there. No sooner had the fear crept up her spine and neck than she felt a piercing pain in her back and the heat of steel piercing her small, aging body. Pearl didn't even have the strength left to turn around; the blow was too powerful.

She collapsed to the floor and lay there motionless, blood oozing from her wounds. Her hand began twitching on the floor as the intruder walked by her, stepping in her warm blood. The footprints could prove the attacker's identity. Size fifteen shoes.

Jeanna could hear someone moving around outside the bedroom door. She called out softly, "Mamma, can you bring me some more orange juice?"

The door was flung open, and there appeared the monster that Jeanna most feared. She screamed, but there was no one to hear her screams.

"Where's my mamma, my Aunt Pearl?" she screamed. "Mamma, can you hear me?" Jeanna screamed again. "You didn't? Doug, tell me you didn't!"

"Had to," Doug said. "She got in the way and fell right there on that knife blade. I couldn't do nothin'."

"I hate you! I hate you! I hate you! I hate you!" Jeanna exclaimed with agony, as she pulled back against the headboard with her knees in her arms.

Big Doug just laughed. "Come on, baby, we goin' home. Daddy's come to get you. But before we go, Daddy needs something."

Jeanna was crying and calling for help to the top of her lungs, but her cries were futile. No one could hear her. Big Doug forced her down, gagged her and tied her hands.

When he finished Doug forced her through the kitchen towards the car. Jeanna noticed that the white petals of the gardenia bloom that Pearl was still clutching were beginning to turn red in the pool of blood beside her.

Wearing nothing but her nightgown, Jeanna squirmed and kicked as Big Doug dragged her towards the back of his car. After several attempts, Doug managed to open his trunk. Inside were beer bottles, car parts, oil cans, assorted garbage, and a rotting dog that Big Doug had killed. He planned to throw these things in the river. The stench was stifling. Sensing the danger of the open trunk, Jeanna struggled to free one hand and reached for Doug's face. Her long nails sunk into his angry flesh.

"You bitch," he protested as blood streamed from his cheek and eye. He grabbed her around the waist and threw her into the trunk.

Thrust into total darkness, Jeanna worked her hands free and removed the gag. Although she couldn't see anything, she could smell the pungent motor oil that was spelling from the rusty cans. Groping blindly to get her bearings, she searched for any object that might be used to free her from the trunk. Surely she could find something like a knife, a car tool, or a screwdriver. Instead, she nicked her finger on a broken whiskey bottle. Instinctively, she put her finger in her mouth to stop the bleeding. Then she felt hair brushing against her leg. Her first thought was that it was a human head. When she felt the paws, she was sure that this must have been one of the dogs from Doug's house. Considering the offensive odor, Jeanna feared that the dog had been in the car long enough to be infested with maggots.

"Oh, God, help me, please!" she cried. "Don't let me die like this."

Doug had killed a dog the day she left. He made a sport of killing stray dogs after he had nearly starved them to death. This was just another of the sick games Doug played.

To play the game, Doug would first wait for a dog to beg for food. In response, he would tie the dog to a tree with food just out of its reach.

Days later, he would release the dog from the ropes. As the dog ran towards the food, Doug would shoot the dog in the head from his front porch.

He had often threatened Jeanna with the same treatment if she ever left him. After killing a dog, he would place the emaciated remains in the trunk of his car and throw it into the river.

As she lay there, she thought, he's heading to the river to dump the dog. She imagined he would probably dump her as well. The though relaxed her. She imagined that the river could be a blessing compared to what she could face were he to keep her alive.

She felt every bump in the road and was somewhat nauseous from breathing the exhaust fumes. Suddenly, she felt something moving in the trunk with her.

"Oh, my God! Please, Lord, don't let this thing bite me!" pleaded Jeanna as her resolve was tested again.

She beat on the metal above her head and started screaming, "Doug, stop! Let me out!" In response to her cries, Doug drove faster. He saw the blood on his hand from the stinging face wound and cursed Jeanna again.

When he arrived at the house for stowaways, Doug stopped the car, walked to the back, and opened the trunk. Jeanna lay motionless across the dead dog. She was terrified. He laughed at her pitiful state. Maggots were crawling up her leg, and a three-foot water moccasin was resting on her breast.

"Bitch, that snake don't want you."

He reached in and grabbed the snake behind the head and threw it to the dogs. The ravaged dogs fought for the snake and devoured it in seconds.

"Bitch, you need to clean up," Doug said. "Even them dogs won't even have you the way you smell. Go in the house and clean up."

Then he said, "Stop!" He picked up the water hose lying beside the dog pen. The dogs started barking and growling so he turned the hose on them to shut up them up. He told Jeanna to be still and sprayed the maggots off of her.

Then he said, "Now, go in and clean your sorry ass up, bitch!"

Jeanna was still crying.

Big Doug was in need of money. He had missed several opportunities to put some big deals together because of Jeanna's earlier escape. This time he was going to make sure she wasn't going anywhere.

When she finished washing off, Big Doug forced her to the bed and strapped her legs and arms to the bedpost. He would teach her a lesson she would never forget.

In the room, roaches were feasting on crumbs and juices from potted meat cans and beer bottles. A lone bulb danged in the bathroom, the only light. The rain from the previous night had leaked through the ceiling, soaking the end of the mattress and causing water to puddle on the floor.

Jeanna was terrified. She vowed that if she could get loose, she would cut her wrists.

As she lay there, she heard a car drive up and doors slam. From the sound of footsteps on the porch and muffled voices, Jeanna knew that Big Doug was making a deal with someone outside. Big Doug demanded money "up front or no deal." Moments later, the door opened, and two young, white males stepped into the doorway and peered into the dark room. Seeing their silhouettes against the porch light, Jeanna guessed that the taller one was about twenty-five years old and that the other was several years younger.

Big Doug cranked his old Caddy and drove away, probably to get more cigars.

The two walked in cautiously, letting their eyes adjust to the darkness. Both had been drinking heavily and were still carrying their beers. One walked to the bed and looked down at Jeanna; the other stood back.

"What's your name, pretty girl? Are you ready for some good loving? I can love you like nobody can or ever will again as far as that matters," the older man boasted.

He laughed as he pulled her gown down to her stomach and reached for her breast. "Uhmm! This looks sweet. I can't wait to have me some of this."

The older one was doing all the talking. The other acted somewhat shy and confined himself to the darkness.

Jeanna didn't say anything at first but then spoke, "Don't touch me," she said, gritting her teeth.

The older boy slapped her and told her to shut up. "I've paid my money. You're mine for a little while." He slapped her again and told his companion that they had a wild one to tame. Jeanna recoiled and licked the blood from her lips.

"We ain't planning to hurt you. We just gonna have a little fun." The older one told the younger to come closer and look at her beautiful body.

"Boy," he said, "you ain't gonna find nothing in these parts like this. Feel the breast on this heifer."

The younger man moved from the corner of the room and looked at her but would not touch.

"Come on now, boy, how you gonna find out what it's like if you don't try it?" the older one said.

Shaking, the younger boy reached out. Then the older boy grabbed his hand and made him grasp her breast. The boy knew what they were doing was wrong but he was overcome by the driving desire to feel the flesh of this naked woman.

"Feels good, don't it, Johnny? You watch me and I'm gonna show you what it's all about." The older boy's eyes gleamed as he worked to unbuckle his belt.

Then Jeanna spoke, "Look, I'm sorry, why don't you untie these ropes some so I can do you some good? I just want to hurry this up, okay? I'll give you your money's worth."

Without much hesitation, the older boy complied and began untying the ropes from her wrists as fast as he could. Johnny went back to the corner. While the older boy was removing his shirt, Jeanna noticed a broken beer bottle on the nightstand. To keep him distracted, she began telling him the trash he wanted to hear.

"Let me feel what you got down there, big boy." She reached and pulled him closer and pushed her hand down into the top of his trousers and began fondling him.

"Oh, baby, yes! That feels good. Keep *on!*"

"Don't you get off too quick now, big boy. You gonna have to wait on me." She kissed him on the neck and pulled him closer.

With her hands free, she reached for the bottle and slipped it beneath the sheets.

"What are you going to do, stand there?" she asked in a cocky voice. He immediately started dropping his clothes to the floor. With only his underwear on, he climbed into bed. In the semi-darkness, he sought only one thing.

Responding to a primitive instinct, he sucked her lips and neck. Then he squeezed her firm breasts with his dirty hands. The smell of liquor, sweat, and stale cigarette breath was almost choking Jeanna. She knew, however, that she had to go along with him for the moment. Then he sat up some and finished ripping her gown open, and began biting her breasts.

She whispered to him, "Let me on top. I can do you better that way."

"Alright! That's what I want to hear," he said, with excitement in his eyes.

He rolled over, and the young beautiful Jeanna straddled him. Looking into his eyes, she gripped the broken bottle in her hand and lowered it behind her back.

"Come on now, baby, move down a little. You way up too high. Move down so I can do you some good," Jeanna said. Letting her take control, he slid down in the bed.

"Honey, I'm fixin' to put something on you that you ain't ever gonna to forget," she said.

The younger boy stood there silently watching because he had never seen or been this far before with a girl. He twitched and bit his lower lip with reserved excitement as his buddy was getting ready to show him something he had never seen before.

"That's what I want to hear. Put it on me." He licked his lips and closed his eyes.

With the skill of a butcher, Jeanna grabbed his testicles in one hand and used the broken bottle to give a powerful upper cut with her other hand. At first, the man didn't feel the pain. Then his eyes widened in horror. With his eyes fixed on hers, Jeanna raised her bloody fist above her head. With a deep, guttural groan, Jeanna shoved the handful of organs and skin into his face.

Screaming, he kicked Jeanna onto the floor and grabbed his groin area. He floundered on the bed, searching frantically for his pants or anything to stop the bleeding. He hollered for Johnny to help him; but Johnny had stumbled backward from the position he had taken to one in the corner of the room. The castrated boy fell on the floor, curled up in a fetal position, and cried for help.

Jeanna grabbed a few pieces of clothing to cover herself. Clutching her clothes to her chest, she opened the door and looked out to see if Big Doug was back. He wasn't. She jumped off the porch and ran into the woods behind the house. As she ran deeper into the woods, she could still hear the man's screams from the house.

* * * * *

Twenty-three

The Funeral

IT WAS 9:30 a.m. when the phone rang. The morning mail had run and Mr. Cane was thumbing searching for a feed bill. When it rang, he tried to put the mail down beside the phone on the small table but dropped half of it on the floor. His temper flared shortly, but he managed to recover and answer the phone in a courteous manner.

"Huh, hello."

"Cane, this is Pete," Pete said in a melancholy way.

"It's good to hear your voice, Pete. I'm glad to see you made it." Mr. Cane said Pete's name out loud so Kate could her.

Kate was holding a drying cloth and a plate in her hands, when she heard the name, and glanced from the kitchen.

"Yes, sir, it was sho' a long ride, I-I-I had some pretty good company on the way. That kinda passed the time along," Pete said.

"Well, where are you, Pete?"

"Right now, I'm at the funeral home. It's a lot of p-p-people here. It looks like Matthew had a lot of friends."

The thought of a child in a coffin made Cane's whole body numb.

"I bet he did, Pete," said Cane. "Well, have you had any time to find out any details on what happened?"

"Yeah, I did, Cane. M-M-My sister, she tells me Matthew had a little paper route up here and on the way home, he and his two cousins stopped beside a railroad track to put some pennies on it. You know how they do, Cane."

"I know. We've all done it." Mr. Cane shook his head thinking about how his own boys had done it, too.

'Well, his foot didn't get caught in that track l-l-like somebody told me. What happened was that the train was carrying a load of paper wood and when it passed b-b-by, a piece of that w-w-wood was hanging out too far, and it hit him. He didn't know what hit him, Cane. He was the only one hurt. It was just a freak thing and a miracle no one else was hurt. It was just an accident was all. 'Being in the wrong place at the wrong time,' you might say. Rather than bringing him back home, we decided it best to b-b-bury him up here. We figured he should be where all his cousins and little friends are. He would want that. His little cousins were just like brothers to him. Matthew was the oldest, so it's making it real hard on t-t-the little ones."

There was silence for a moment. Mr. Cane was at a loss for words. If only Pete really knew how sorry Cane really felt.

"Kate and I are real sorry, Pete, and if there is anything we can do, you pick up the phone and call us, you here?"

"Well, I believe the funeral is going to be at 1:30 this afternoon, and then I suppose I will be heading back, f-f-first chance."

"You got everything you need, Pete?" Mr. Cane asked, referring to money.

"Oh, yes, sir, I got everything I need."

"Okay then, call me if we can help. Kate and I are praying for you."

"Thank you, Cane. Tell M-M-Mrs. Kate that everything is okay."

Pete placed the phone on the receiver and looked up. The small room, illuminated by only a few lights, felt so heavy. He held his hand over that phone for a while before walking out to where the others were. Beside the casket, his sister and brother-in-law were standing together over his boy. He reached for his sister's hand. It was nearly noon now. Soon the funeral home would be closing and they'd have to leave Matthew. They all held on to each other and wept.

As they stood there, Pete spoke up, "You know it s-s-seems like the Lord is punishing me for something I've done."

"You can't say that, Pete," his sister said.

"W-W-Why not? It's true. The Lord, he done took everything I ever needed or wanted. I'm a beat man. I don't believe I can go on."

Pete could not hold back the pain any longer. Leaning closer to his sister, he broke down. Over and over in his mind he replayed memories of Matthew. His mind jumped from pitching baseballs to that first Christmas when Matthew was a baby and things had been so wonderful.

Meanwhile, Mr. Cane was in the middle of telling Kate what Pete had said when Able knocked on the door.

"Mr. Cane," Able said, "I guess I's ready to head on to Kosciusko to check on them tickets."

Mr. Cane looked at his watch. "You're right, Able. It's about ten o'clock now. You better head on. It's a pretty good drive over there, so you need to hurry on so you can be back before dark."

"Oh, I's gonna do that. Just let me finish up a few things, and I's gonna be out of here."

"Say now, Able," Mr. Cane said with his head tilted downward, but looking upward, "that's Ole Red now, not New Blue on this trip," reminding Able not to even consider taking the new truck.

"Oh, yes, sir. Me and Ole Red, we gets along just fine. Ole Red will get me there and back. No problem at all."

Able walked back to the barn and finished instructing Bud how to change the air filter on the John Deere tractor that the two had started earlier. He told Bud he was going to Kosciusko on some business and he'd be back that afternoon, so he couldn't hang around any longer. He told Bud to watch William change the other tractor's filter, too, to make sure it was done right.

It was important to check and change all the oil and air filters after so many hours of work with the equipment. That was the life of the machinery. Mr. Cane had taught that lesson to Able early and Able was passing the lesson down to the boys.

After seeing that Bud was on the right track with the maintenance, Able cranked Ole Red and let him sit there a minute and idle. While adjusting his radio, the same eerie feeling came over him again that he had the day before. This time though, it gave him chill bumps. He looked across the pasture and could see the dead copperhead still hanging on the fence. Oddly, the wild coyotes had not bothered it through the night. As he started at the carcass, he remembered that there was something he needed to do before he left. Walking to the side kitchen door, he poked his head in.

"Lizzy, say, Lizzy," Able said, slightly opening the screen door and knocking.

Lizzy walked to door and said, "What you want, big boy?" carrying on with him. "You out here making all this racket, and we women up in this here kitchen trying to get some work done." She was wiping one hand on her apron and trying to hold a pan in the other one.

"Baby, I'm fix'in to go now and check on them tickets for Jeanna. I'll be back late this afternoon. That is, if Ole Red don't put me down." Able looked over at it. No doubt about it, there was no comparing Ole Red to the new Ford.

"You can get that new Ford out of your mind," she said, exasperated. "But if you gonna be late, you find a phone and call me before I leaves work," she added, as she pointed her finger at him. "You find yourself a pay phone, now. You hear me, Mr. Johnson?"

"Loud and clear." Able looked down and grinned and looked back up at her. "I's hear you real good, Mrs. Johnson. That mean you gonna be waiting on me when I gets home to night?"

"Able Johnson, you better leave right now before I throw this pan at you. Mrs. Kate might hear you talking that trash."

Able turned and walked back to the truck. It cranked on the first try. He patted it on the dash, as always, and said, "Good, boy, you do that all day for me now and we gonna get along just fine."

Ole Red didn't stir up any dust on the dirt road because of the little rain that had fallen overnight. Able turned onto the highway and sped away heading towards his destination. As he adjusted his seat some, he thought about Pete and what he might be going through. He really felt sympathy for Pete, and said a quick prayer for him.

As the services began, the funeral director and assistants rolled the white casket to front-center of the room. It was ordained with red and white roses. There was standing room only. Sobs were coming from all over the chapel as the choir, dressed in blue robes, began singing "The Old Rugged Cross." When the song ended there was a stillness that broke every heart present. The minister began by saying, "God loves his little children. 'The kingdom of heaven belongs to these, the Lord said.'" Then he continued with the eulogy. The funeral lasted over two hours with many different people speaking about Matthew. Pete's sister stayed by his side as one after another stood. One of Matthew's schoolteachers stood up and said a few words to the congregation about how Matthew was an outstanding and talented student. She commented on how he never got into any sort of trouble and how he was the one who had set an example for all the kids to follow. Hearing those words only deepened the wound in Pete's heart, but made him very proud of his son as well.

Later, at the graveside service, a young girl walked over to Pete. She was wearing a blue dress, white shoes, and had a red ribbon tied in her hair.

"Are you Matthew's dad?"

"I-I-I am," Pete said, looking down at her.

"Matthew carved this." She handed him a small wooden cross. She said Matthew had made it for her but she wanted Pete to have it. On the back, Matthew had carved his initials, PMD, Jr. Her little face was glowing but still showed the hurt as she looked up at Pete.

"Matthew was my best friend, Mr. Dodd."

She told Pete that Matthew talked about him all the time and mentioned that his daddy was a war hero.

"I thought you might want to know that," she said.

She went on and told Pete how Matthew was always talking about living in the South and how his town had more fishing holes than he could count.

Pete adjusted the ribbon on the little girl's head.

"What's your n-n-name, honey?" Pete said.

"Tina."

"Tina, I'm so glad you were Matthew's friend. I didn't get to speak to him much after he moved away from Friendly. I'm glad he had a friend like you." Pete smiled. "You know? He was right about all those fishing ponds." He turned his head from the little girl and wiped his eyes.

The little girl reached up for Pete's hand. She held it for a moment and then walked away towards her dad, who was waiting. Most of the friends and students were dispersing when Pete's sister asked when he would be returning to Mississippi.

"I guess I need to leave tomorrow. We got a lot of work to do back home," Pete said. "Got some catching up to do." Pete was thinking how hard a time he had given little Justin and Bebop along the way. The boys were just kids and all they wanted was a few answers. That's all. In fact, he should have done more for his own nephew Able, after he lost his parents. Pete shook his head in shame. Condemnation was becoming his friend it seemed.

"Have you checked the train schedule to find when the next train leaves?" she asked.

"No, I haven't."

"Then, why don't I go with you to see?" his sister said. You really need some rest though. This has been a long, hard, twenty-four hours for you. I know it has for me."

As they walked back to the car, it was beginning to rain. His sister had her umbrella in hand, so Pete took the handle and ducked down under it, and they walked back to her car.

"Can you use some coffee, Pete? There's a nice little spot up the road."

"I-I-I guess so, sis," Pete said.

On the way he explained how everything always seemed to go the wrong way for him and how good things never last long anymore. She listened as he told her that life didn't mean much anymore after the loss of Matthew. He was willing and ready to go to the other side, if only the Lord wanted him. In his mind, waiting around wasn't doing anybody any good.

His sister could tell he was down on his himself, but she also saw a wonderful and humble man inside that blue suit.

"Pete. You did the right thing sending Matthew away. Don't you know that?"

"How can you say that? Look what *happened*."

"I can't argue with that, but you must understand something just as bad could have happened back in Mississippi."

"Well, I would have been there to protect him."

"No, you couldn't! Remember that's why you send him here. Things done got too bad down there! You know that."

"Sis, I just don't know. I'm all confused. Everything I do, I screw up."

"Matthew was a fine young man. He had you to thank for that. He had good common sense. Pete, he got that from you and with that, he touched many hearts. Don't take that away from him. He was supposed to be here. It was for the best. I know it."

Pete was glad to hear those words. It was comforting to him.

"Here's the coffee shop ahead," his sister said, pulling her car into a parking space. "What do you think? Can you eat a donut, a late breakfast, or anything?"

"M-M-Maybe some coffee," Pete said.

"Okay then, that's a start," she said.

By now, the rain was coming down harder and they knew they would have to make a run for it. Regardless, they were going to get wet trying to get inside the restaurant. They looked at each other and said together, "One, two, three, GO!"

Without an attempt to open the umbrella, both jumped out and made a dash for the entrance. When they reached the front door, they had water running down their faces and water in their shoes. They looked at each other and laughed.

"Sis, you remember that time I-I-I poured that water on you head." Pete said laughing.

There had been a play at school and Pete was supposed to throw a pail of water at his sister. Not a real pail of water, but a pail of cut up paper. However, Sis had told on Pete two days before for sneaking out of the house. As his father hit him over and again with his belt, Pete got an idea of how to get even. Well, payback was a pail of real water when it came time to drench her in the play.

"Yes, I do, and I still owe you for it too," she said, holding the door for Pete to enter.

"No, you wrong little sister, I got paid back, twice, remember. Daddy tore me up again that night!"

"Well, you deserved it anyway and I guess you're getting around to saying I look like I did on that stage that day, huh?"

"Yeah, I-I-I guess you might say that," Pete said smiling.

By now the two were soaked. They walked in, placing the umbrella in the corner as they looked for a booth.

Finding a booth, they sat down and ordered coffee. Pete was not ready for a meal but thought he'd have a piece of the tasty looking coconut pie that he spotted on top of the counter. The waiter returned with the coffee and pie and told them to motion for her, if they needed anything else. One cup of coffee lead to another and the next thing they knew, ten minutes turned into an hour, and then an hour turned into two hours. Pete told Sis pretty much his life story after Matthew came up to live with her. He had not dated another woman since Dorothy had died. He had generally remained to himself, he said, living in a broken down farmhouse for the last three years.

He and Dorothy had a home, but he gave it up once Matthew left. He figured he didn't need anything nice anymore. Pete confessed he started drinking heavily as soon as Matthew left, and the world just seemed to slip right on by him.

Pete told Sis he guessed there was nothing left now. She reached across the table and held his hand. She told him there was always hope too. She reminded him that there is always a bright day coming again in everyone's life after the darkest day had passed. For some reason, he believed her. She made him feel better and was making sense. His sister always was easy to talk to.

She squeezed his hand again. "Let's get out of here.

Pete paid the bill and the two splashed through the puddles in the lot on the way to the car. It had stopped raining. A white slip of sun was burning a hole through the clouds.

* * * * *

Twenty-four

Bad News

W ITH THE WINDOWS down and the bright sun coming through the windshield of the Ole Red, Able made his way on to Kosciusko. As usual, he had the radio cranked up as loud as it would go. Carl Perkins' new hit, "Blue Suede Shoes" was blasting through the car. Able was patting that dash, beating the seat, playing the guitar and driving all at the same time. Ole Red's eight-cylinder engine was purring like a kitten and running a straight-up fifty-five miles per. The V-8 in Ole Red was a good one, using a little oil, but not enough to matter, which proved itself to be too good of a truck for Mr. Cane to trade in. Although it had a dent in the door, it still looked great.

There was always a need for an extra truck around the farm anyway. Besides, Justin still had a lot more learning to do yet.

In the back of Able's mind, something still wasn't right. He couldn't figure out if he should go by Aunt Pearl's first or wait and go after he had gone to bus station. The time was the same so it probably would not matter. " I's think I'll go on to Kosciusko," he proclaimed. No quicker than he said those words, he noticed a patrol car coming up behind him. He looked down and checked his speed. As the car eased up behind him, he saw the red light come on.

"What have I done now?" he groaned. He sure had seen plenty of that patrolman.

Able pulled Ole Red over onto the shoulder of the road and killed his engine. Being colored, he knew to get out and walk back to the patrol car. He was surprised though to see Patrolman Campbell.

"Mr. Campbell, looks like we meet again." Able smiled.

"Able, Mr. Cane called in and told the dispatcher for us to try to stop you and tell you to head to your Aunt's house immediately. He said to be quick about it."

Able's face showed what he most feared.

"If you want me to, I can escort you there," Mr. Campbell offered.

Able knew the worst had happened, or Mr. Cane would not have called and tried to stop him. The question for him was, Could Big Doug have found Jeanna? Able's blood boiled as he thought about Big Doug again. "I should have killed him while I had the chance. If Justin had not been with me, I would have. Well, the Lord says it ain't right to kill. Get behind me devil," Able said aloud. Able tried not to think about it. Besides, he didn't know for sure what the problem was.

"Yes, sir, Mr. Campbell, you better do just that."

Able got back in Ole Red and Mr. Campbell sped away leading the way to Aunt Pearl's. With the patrol car's red light flashing and siren blaring, cars were pulling off the road coming and going. Observing the hood on Ole Red just a-vibrating, Able stayed right on the bumper of the patrol car, not letting Mr. Campbell out of his sight. Abe looked down at the speedometer and saw the needle pass eighty miles per hour as he passed from Attala into Carroll County.

"Come on, Red, don't let me down now. I need you," Able whispered, patting the dash.

The roads were curvy, but Campbell didn't let up. He continued his fast pace through the country roads. Able watched his gas hand continue to move lower as he knew the 4-barrel carburetor was sucking the gas out of the tank in every straight away. Now, he was wondering if the truck had enough gas to get to Aunt Pearl's. All that was remaining was a quarter of a tank.

Lord, you's been good to me. Jist let me make it.

Able was right on Patrolman Campbell's tail, riding his bumper as hard as he could. Campbell glanced in his rearview mirror and could not believe how well the old red truck was doing. Then, without warning, smoke started coming out from under Campbell's hood and pieces of black something shot out from under his car. The car was apparently overheating. Campbell pulled over to the side of the road and Able pulled behind him skidding his front tires some because the front right wheel grabbed when applying the brakes. Able jumped out of Ole Red and ran to Campbell's window.

"What's the problem, Mr. Campbell?" Able said, panting hard.

"Darn fan belt, I think. She's running hot. I heard something pop back up the road and figured that might be what it was. I was right. Let me radio back to the station and tell them where the car is and that I'm going on with you."

Able eyes grew as large as two cue balls. After Mr. Campbell called, he hurried towards Ole Red.

"Huh, you gonna ride with me, Mr. Campbell?"

"Heck naw, I'm driving. Get in on the other side, boy!"

Campbell sat down in the driver's seat, and Able got in the other side. Able knew one thing for sure, nobody was gonna give Ole Red a ticket today.

Popping the clutch and shifting gears from first to second, Campbell burned rubber when Ole Red hit the pavement. He nearly did it again from second to third. Able was impressed with how well Patrolman Campbell could speed-shift the gears. He'd apparently had done this before in his earlier years. At their rate of speed and how Patrolman Campbell was driving, Able figured it would only be another thirty minutes before they got to Pearl's.

Able's mind was racing like a clock. He was trying to think through every scenario that might have happened. He knew Mr. Campbell didn't have a clue of what was going on. One thing for sure was that they both knew it had to be serious, or the dispatcher wouldn't have called.

Trying to show Mr. Campbell the way, Able was giving directions as they came to different crossroads and intersections. Mr. Campbell, for sure, was not holding back as he broke every rule in the book when it came to stopping, passing, and speeding. It seemed it was just a little while ago, that Able was having the same reckless trip with Justin driving. If he made it through one more, it would certainly be by the Hand of the Lord.

Oh, how Able wanted to know what had happened, but without a radio now, it was impossible to know what was going on until they got to Pearl's.

On the way, he tried his best to explain to Mr. Campbell about what had already transpired concerning Big Doug and Jeanna. All he could do was hope this was not going to be a rerun of the past event.

"When you get up here where that sign is, turn. It's a short cut in the back way," Able said.

Campbell started downshifting and applying the brakes to Ole Red..

"Turn right here!" Able shouted.

The truck practically turned on two wheels as it fishtailed through the curve taking both sides of the road. Able was holding on for dear life, as Patrolman Campbell was losing no time gunning it again in another straight away. Besides the gas problem, Able was now beginning to worry about Ole Red's motor too. Patrolman Campbell had been running it hard for more than thirty minutes and there was no sign of him letting up.

"There it is, right up ahead. It's not much further!" Able, hollering above the engine noise.

Campbell hit the brakes and slowed down again. Gravel was flying out from under the truck as he applied the brakes. Ole Red's front brakes always pulled a little to the left, and Campbell had to fight the steering wheel to stay out of the ditch.

In front of them, they could see the scene unfolding. The Humphrey County sheriff and two deputy cars were in front of Pearl's house along with an ambulance. The ambulance surely meant real trouble. That kind of trouble had been on Able's mind the whole trip. Campbell pulled alongside one of the deputies' cars, and immediately a deputy came over to the truck about to ask him to keep moving. He was caught off guard when he saw the highway patrol uniform and Patrolman Campbell stepping out of the truck.

Campbell spoke up, "What we got here officer?"

"Looks like a homicide, sir."

Several detectives and deputies were walking around the house searching the grounds. Earlier, one of Pearl's friends, Lucy Arnell, had stopped by for a visit. When she knocked on the door and didn't get an answer, she went inside and discovered Pearl lying with a bone-handled hunting knife in her back. Lucy Arnell was in a state of shock when the sheriff and his deputies arrived. Her custom was to come by once or twice a week to check on Pearl and have a cup of tea with her. She lived about two miles down the road from Pearl and always walked. She said the exercise was good for her.

The officers searched the grounds thoroughly and found a set of fresh tire tracks in the drive. Fortunately, due to the rain, it was easy for the detective to take a plaster cast of the tracks. With the plaster molds made of the tracks, matching the tire prints might be found. The tracks were mud grips, usually indicating a truck, but fortunately, one tire had a noticeable notch in it. With luck, they hoped they might match that one easier.

The sheriff knew to call Mr. Cane about the murder because Pearl had mentioned on many occasions how good her boy turned out and that he ran the Cane farm in Friendly. Pearl was a retired schoolteacher and was always bragging about Able to everyone. She was smart enough to know that spreading that word just might come in handy some time. She was right.

Mr. Cane and Lizzy where heading out of the drive when Kate ran to the truck.

"John, be careful, now. I need you and so do your boys."

"It'll be okay, Kate. I'm just carrying Lizzy to Pearl's. If the highway patrol didn't catch Able, Lizzy might need to answer some questions for the authorities. Don't you worry about us? We'll be back."

"I wish it were that easy," she said, wishfully.

Mr. Cane and Lizzy backed out of the driveway and headed up the gravel road towards the highway. When Mr. Cane reached the highway, he let the hammer down on the new Ford truck. It was imperative that Mr. Cane or someone got there in time to talk some sense into Able before Able went out of control and headed alone after Big Doug. Just thinking about it made Mr. Cane press on the accelerator more. Lizzy's held her hand on top of her head trying to prevent her scarf from blowing out the window.

"You're not scared of my driving, are you, Lizzy?"

"Not at all, Mr. Cane. Speed up if you likes too."

That was all Mr. Cane needed to hear, so he pressed the accelerator to the floor. Lizzy sat up straight in her seat and began smiling because she had never gone that fast before. For precautions, before leaving, Mr. Cane had put his rifle behind the seat although Kate didn't know it. The situation was unclear as to know what he might be in for. He was wise enough to know that he never wanted to be in a situation where he didn't have the advantage. He learned that lesson in the military.

When Able heard the word "homicide" he opened the truck door and bolted for the front door of the house. As he approached the house, he was hollering.

"Pearl! Jeanna! Pearl! Jeanna!"

When he got to the door, he slowed down looking to the left and then to the right before entering the door. He slid his hands down the walls approaching the kitchen. Cautiously, he inched further until he saw blood on the floor. He stopped. There, he saw Pearl's foot twisted in a way that could only mean something terrible had happened. Able paused as he saw the officer pulling a sheet over her head.

"Oh, no, Aunt Pearl! Who, done this to you? Who done this to you?"

As he walked beside her, he lowered one knee to the floor, pulling the sheet back very slowly and carefully. Trying to prepare himself for what he was about to see, he closed his eyes and opened them slowly. Pearl had a calm look on her face, as if she were sleeping. Able began weeping and the officer reached over and, put his hand on Able's shoulder, giving him a gentle pat before walking away.

"Aunt Pearl," Able said holding her hand so gently, "You knows you was the only mamma I ever really had. You and Uncle Hugh, y'all took me and Jeanna and raised us like we were your own. You didn't have to do that, and I always thought about it a heap of times. I can't say thanks you enough. But I tell you, I been trying to be good just like you always taught me to," Able paused and tried to keep his composure as he wiped his eyes, then he continued, "I still reads my Bible every day and tries not to say any of them bad words. You's with Jesus now, and I know that. You don't worry about me. I'll be okay. I all grown up now, but I'll always remember what you taught me. You know I will. I love you, Aunt Pearl."

Able lowered his head down on Pearl's face and wept more. As big a man as he was, he looked mighty small just then, knelt beside her body. He stayed that way for some time with his head bent before he shot up right quick as if he'd suddenly remembered something. "Jeanna! Where's Jeanna?"

"Who's Jeanna?" a young officer replied as Able shook him by the shoulders.

Able let the officer go and ran through the house hollering for Jeanna. He ran out the back door and hollered out across the pasture. A lone old milk cow and a few chickens stirred around. He ran to the fence and scared the old milk cow into bolting down the hill. The bell around her neck rang with every step as she jogged along.

"Jeanna! Jeanna!," he continued shouting to the top of his voice.

Able hit his hand on the top of the fence post in total frustration and stared across the open field in the direction the cow was running and said, "Big Doug, you gonna be mine. If I's find you, I's gonna slay you with more than just a jawbone of an ass. I swear to it."

As he stood there, Able heard Mr. Cane calling from the front of the house. He turned and saw him coming around the corner of the house, walking towards him. Mr. Cane could see the emotion in Able's eyes as he got closer. He knew that Able could get in trouble over something like this if he were not careful.

"Able, you listen to me now. You listen to me good." Mr. Cane put his hands on Able's shoulders and looked up at him. Able eyes were filled with tears and anger.

"Able, you let the law take care of this. You hear?" He shook Able a little because Able did not respond. Able just stared down at the ground with his fist clenched.

"Able, look at me. I said let the law take care of this."

Lizzy put her arms around Able's waist and held him.

Mr. Cane continued, "Able, you got too much to lose to do something stupid. You got Lizzy and Bebop to take care of. You gotta think about them, Able."

Able spoke softly, "I know, Mr. Cane, but that Big Doug done got Jeanna." Able looked at Mr. Cane like a child. It was almost too much for Cane to bear.

"We don't know that for sure, Able. Yes, it's a good chance, but we don't know yet. She might have gotten away," he added hopefully.

"Yeah, and he might have done the same thing to her as he did to Pearl," Able added.

Lizzy spoke up, "Now, Able Johnson, you start using your head now. Don't you be thinking with your big foot. You gonna have to let the law take care of this. You gonna have to. I ain't gonna raise Bebop by myself whiles you be up in some prison. No, I'm not!"

With those words, Able broke from the trance and said, "I guess y'all right. I's be better on the farm than I would be trying to find Big Doug."

"Wheww! That's right," Mr. Cane said, relieved. "Able, you can help right now by going back in there and telling the officers about Jeanna. Tell them everything. Okay?" he emphasized, fearful that Able might leave out details he might have felt would harm Jeanna's reputation. This was no time for pride.

"I gotcha, Mr. Cane." Lizzy and Able started back for the house.

Mr. Cane just stared over the pasture towards the woods wondering if Jeanna was out there somewhere. He sure hoped she was and that she was looking up at the same beautiful sky he was looking at.

*   *   *   *   *

Twenty-five

The Hunt

BIG DOUG PULLED in the drive looking at his watch. He figured the two johns had about five minutes to finish up. He got out of the car and leaned against the door and lit a cigar. Before he could even exhale the first drag, he noticed the dogs were barking uncontrollably. "Shut up," he barked back, adding in a low growl that usually sent them whimpering off. For some reason, they ignored his warning. Something had bothered those dogs so much that Big Doug couldn't spook them into shutting up.

Big Doug took another draw off his cigar and gazed at the deep shadowy woods and then back at the house. Something wasn't right. He paused a moment, threw his cigar down and hurried up the steps, bursting through the front door. He gasped as he saw the naked boy sprawled across the floor holding his crotch as if trying to reattach what had been cut off. The dead boy's testicles were still clutched in his bloody hands. The walls, floor and bed were covered in blood. The younger boy had a blank stare on his face. He was shaking and squatting on the floor in the same dark corner he had occupied during the incident. Only the liquid below him indicated that he was still alive.

"That bitch is going to come here right now and clean up this mess!" Big Doug muttered. He marched through the rooms before realizing she was gone. He ran out the front door and looked at the dogs staring at him from the pen. "Shut up!" he yelled as he got into his car and sped off.

Big Doug had a plan but he was going to need more help. He knew he couldn't track Jeanna by himself, but he knew a coon hunter named Henry who could. Coon hunter Henry was nothing but white trash, but had one of the best bloodhounds in the parts. If anybody could find her, Henry's bloodhound could. Doug had used coon hunter Henry's services before finding escaped girls and so far, had a one hundred percent track record. As far as Big Doug was concerned, the chase was on. He smiled to himself thinking, in a few hours, he would have her back and boy would she pay!

Big Doug pulled his car into Henry's drive and honked the horn. Henry knew the sound of that Cadillac horn anywhere. It was distinct, more like a train horn than a car horn. He walked onto his porch, pulling his overalls up and leaned slightly over the railing. Henry had been sleeping off a night of heavy drinking and late night poker with the boys.

"Stop blowing that darn horn, Doug. You liable to wake up my chickens."

Henry didn't have his shoes on. He walked down his steps, through the mud to Doug's car window and asked him what he wanted. Big Doug explained the situation. Henry didn't seem too anxious to help, but Doug pulled out two one-hundred-dollar bills, flashing them in Henry's face and told Henry they were his, if he found the girl. Then, he pulled up his shirt and showed Henry the butt of a handgun. It didn't take Henry long to make his mind up. He told Big Doug he would be at the stowaway house in about thirty minutes. Big Doug handed him one of the bills as a down payment

"Thanks, I can use this," Henry said, taking the bill.

"Good! You'll get the rest when you find the girl," Big Doug said, spitting out his window.

"Well, don't get too attached to it, because I'll have her back by the end of the day." Henry laughed, then turned and spit, too.

Big Doug smiled and told him that was what he wanted to hear and backed out of the drive. Coon hunter Henry smiled looking at the hundred dollar bill in his hand and watched as smoke billowed from the tailpipes of the old Caddy as Big Doug made his way up the muddy road.

After Big Doug returned to the stowaway house, he went inside and found that the younger boy, Johnny, was gone. It was just as well. That way Big Doug wouldn't have to deal with him. The dead boy was still in the middle of the floor. Big Doug walked around the corpse, picked up the fire poker and examined what was clutched in the boy's hands. He shook his head and walked back out of the house to the front porch for a breath of fresh air. After a few moments Doug returned to the room and began looking about, when he noticed part of Jeanna's gown on the floor. He studied it a moment, then picked it up folding it gently before putting it in his back pocket. Seeing the half-filled oil lamp and a box of matches on the mantle, he removed the globe and lighted it, then rotated around the room, illuminating it as the roaches ran for cover. By now, with the heat of the day, flies were already finding their way to the dead boy's private area. Disgusted, Doug tossed the lamp onto the bed and watched the bed burst into flames. Within seconds the old curtains caught a fire and spread to the walls, which were like gas-soaked kindling and then spread up to the ceiling. The house was an inferno within five minutes casting flames through the roof. Big Doug stood by his car contemplating and lit another cigar while waiting for Henry to arrive.

In a few minutes, Big Doug saw Henry coming up the muddy, winding driveway in his old black '48 Chevy pickup with two dog boxes in the back. As he got closer, all Big Doug's penned dogs began barking as they usually did with any vehicle approaching.

Henry rolled to a stop and gave a kick opening the somewhat-sprung door and got out in knee-high rubber boots. From the other side of the truck, two of his helpers emerged. One was his own boy, and the other was just another hunting buddy. All three were still drinking beer and carrying on from the night before. After some small talk Henry walked to the rear of the truck and dropped the tailgate. Henry's boy, Herman, reached and unlatched one of the dog boxes, and out peered a large four-year-old bloodhound. Herman snapped a leash on him quickly and gave him a big yank. "Come on out of there, Blue." The old dog did what Henry said, and with one hop, he was on the ground.

As Herman led the dog to the front of the truck, the other hunter, Jamie, opened the remaining dog box. This dog reacted differently from the last one. It was growling and not wanting to come out. The snarling sound was not like the baritone bark of the bloodhound, but more haunting. With some abusive verbal language from Jamie and encouragement by beating on the top of the box, the dog finally stuck its head out. It was clear the Doberman was not a dog for hunting coon, but more, one for hunting people. Aggravated and excited, the Doberman displayed its long power fangs that could easily cut through human flesh as Jamie tried to leash it.

"Get back, you black son-of-a-bitch!" Jamie hollered, swatting at the dog's head with the end of the leash. With a protective glove on, he snapped the leash on the dog and jerked him out of the truck. Then he led him to join the others.

"Okay, Doug, we're ready," Henry said. "What do you have that ole Blue can track?"

Doug reached in his back pocket and handed him a piece of the Jeanna's gown. Henry, first held the cloth to Blue's nose and then to the Doberman's, making sure both dogs got a good whiff. Almost immediately, they started barking and began pulling the men in the direction of the woods. Henry gave a smile of pleasure knowing the dogs had a good scent and that he'd have the other hundred dollars in a few hours. Big Doug's penned dogs were having a fit wanting to join the two, so Big Doug walked to the dog pen and unlatched the gate. When he did, ten husky cur dogs stampeded out chasing the other dogs.

* * * * *

Twenty-six

Germans Are Coming

O N THE CANE farm, everyone but Justin and Bebop were gone, making it a perfect opportunity for them to have some real fun playing in the hay barn. Justin was playing with a stick, which he pretended was a machine gun. Bebop used another for a bazooka. Soon, they had a full-fledged war going on between the Americans and Germans, which carried over to the hay truck, placing Justin behind the steering wheel and Bebop hanging out the side window. In their minds, Germans were everywhere.

"Bebop, the truck is gone dead," Justin said, playing.

"Justin, get it cranked before the Germans get here. I see'm coming now!" Bebop hollered.

Justin reached for the keys and turned the ignition. The old truck cranked better than it ever had before. They both paused and looked at each other. *Why not?* they thought. In their minds it was nothing but open pasture ahead anyway. What could it hurt?

Bebop said, "Hurry, Justin, we ain't got no time. We gonna be blowed up!"

Justin looked at the Cane house and saw that the coast was clear. He didn't see his or Bebop's mom anywhere, so he put the truck in gear and pulled out of the hay barn. As they gathered speed, Justin shifted to second gear and then the third. The small circle around the barn eventually grew to a large circle around the field. They were having the time of their lives as they pretended to shoot every cow they passed.

Pep, Justin's dog, was having as much fun as they were barking and chasing cows. "Slow down, Justin." Bebop said. "I see one over there. Bamm! Bamm! Bamm! I got him. Keep going."

As the war carried further across the pasture, the boys became too preoccupied with shooting cows and weren't watching where they were going. As they topped the hill in third gear, they saw the farm pond directly in front of them. Immediately, reality sank in. Justin frantically tried to put the brakes on, but the brake pedal slammed to the floor with no results. The hay truck never needed much of any brakes because it was always driven slowly around the field and to the barn. It was to be used on the farm only and not on the highway.

"Uh, oh! We in trouble now, Bebop. I can't stop the truck! We got no brakes!" Justin yelled.

"Do something, Justin! Pull back on the shifter or something."

Bebop reached over and began helping Justin pull the gearshift back. With Justin forgetting to push the clutch in, the two pulled with all their might in vain, as the truck continued gaining speed barreling down the hill. Finally, with a sudden pop, it jumped out of third and into neutral. Now the truck was going too fast to go back into another gear. There was no way to slow down as the truck was picking up more speed.

"Help me push it back in gear, Bebop!"

"I can't. It won't go!"

"Push the clutch in!" screamed Bebop.

"I can't reach it!" Justin hollered back.

As they gained momentum down the hill targeting the pond, they looked at each other horrified. There was nothing else they could do. The truck was bouncing into the air and tossing off the remaining few bales of hay that were on the back, as the cows between the truck and pond scattered at the sight of what was coming. Kicking and bucking, the cows retreated up the hill as the truck plowed through the middle of group. The boys were screaming at the top of their lungs in desperation. They looked from each other to the pond then back to each other. There was only one thing to do. Simultaneously, they grabbed their door handles and jumped clear of the truck, rolling and tumbling down the hill. They watched as the hay truck continued out of control, bouncing and veering from one side to another. Then, with a huge splash, it crashed into the water. For a moment it seemed like it might float. As they watched, though, the hay truck slowly tipped forward. Angling up higher before beginning its slow descent out of sight, one word came to mind, Titanic. Pulling grass and dirt out of their hair and brushing off their clothes, the two started crawling towards each other. Bebop watched Justin rubbed his head while getting onto his knees.

"Oh, shit!" Justin said, looking at the bubbles.

"That's what I was about to say, too. Shit! We in deep shit, Justin! We done sunk the hay truck!"

* * * * *

Twenty-seven

Homeward Bound

PETE'S SISTER CARRIED him back to the train station, telling him all the way that she wanted to come back to Mississippi and visit sometime soon. He told her he thought that was a good idea and he knew her kids would love seeing all those ponds Matthew had told them about.

Just then he felt the weight and power of the train behind him, as it vibrated the ground coming into the station. "You know I don't want to leave, don't you, Sis?"

"I don't want you to either, Pete. I'm afraid I won't see you again."

"Well, there's a few things I-I-I got to do first, but don't you worry about that. As soon as I can, I'll call you, and w-w-we'll talk some more." He touched her hand and looked into her sparkling eyes before turning, and walked toward the passenger car of the train. A few feet from the steps he stopped and turned and looked at his sister one more time. As he jumped on the last step he could see the tears coming down her face.

She missed her brother so much and she missed her home, too. Just talking and seeing him made her really know how much she missed that place. She waved and wiped her eyes with her handkerchief as she stood and watched the train speed south.

Pete walked down the aisle until he got about halfway into the passenger car. He placed his suitcase under the empty seat and slid next to the window. It didn't take him long before he dozed off. He began dreaming he was back in Nantua, France, where he had saved Cane. This time, however, was different. When the fighting was over, he realized he had been the one shot, not Cane. He was bleeding, and a nurse came to his aid. It was Naomi. He was in a Red Cross tent, about to go into surgery, and the last thing he remembered was looking into Naomi's eyes and saying, "If I don't make it, tell my wife, Dorothy, I love her." Naomi assured him she would. While in surgery, he was able to see himself from above the operating table and could tell the doctors were fighting for his life. Things were not going well. More blood was needed. His blood pressure had decreased to 45 over 30. They were losing him.

"Hurry, Nurse, bring the plasma!" shouted the doctor.

"I can't find a vein, Doctor!" she shouted back, trying to administer the needle.

"Do something, Nurse!" the doctor shouted, then said, "Let me have it." He took the IV from her hand and tried nervously to find a vein in Pete's arm. He was desperate. Then he realized Pete's heart had stopped. He hollered for assistance and started CPR. He continued until another doctor finally pulled him away.

"It's too late. We lost him," the assistant said.

Suddenly Pete jumped in his seat. He was sweating and holding his arm.

The conductor was shaking him by the sleeve, saying, "Ticket, please. Sir, I need your ticket."

Pete reached inside his shirt pocket and pulled out a ticket. He slowly handed it to the conductor, still trying to shake the dream.

"Sir, would you like a glass of water or juice? You don't look well," the conductor asked.

"Yes, yes, I would. Thank you," Pete responded.

In a few minutes, the conductor returned with a glass of orange juice. He handed it to Pete and told him to drink it slowly and said the juice would make him feel better. The conductor started explaining that lots of people are scared of traveling on trains. He told Pete not to worry about anything. He said he had been conductor on the train for eighteen years and had never had a close call yet. Pete smiled and thanked him again, and the old conductor went on his way asking for more tickets.

Pete started thinking about what Sis had said and questioned if could really settle down and start a new life without Dorothy? So much had gone downhill for him in the last six years. Could he kick the drinking? Where would he stay if he got married again? He had no money. He had nothing. He buried his face in his hands. Condemnation was back for the ride home.

"Hello, looks like we meet again. Huh, that's Mr. Dodd, isn't it? Care if I take this seat?"

Pete looked up. The man with the straw hat had appeared from nowhere and this time he was smoking a pipe.

"Where did you come from?" Pete asked.

"Oh, it doesn't matter where I've come from. It's where I'm going that's important." The man with the straw hat sat down in the empty seat and continued to talk. "Did you know, Mr. Dodd, that we can't change the past or where we've been, but we can make a big difference in the future with what we've learned in the past? Do you believe that?"

Pete said, "Who are you?"

"Oh, Mr. Dodd, I come and go. You see, I ride this train quite often. Locomotive 505 it is. This train has been a good one. You know, I've seen a lot of happy and unhappy people ride these tracks in my lifetime." He paused and looked into Pete's eyes. "You're one of the unhappy ones, Mr. Dodd." Pete looked surprised. "You were easy to spot. One I've seen a lot." The man with the straw hat unfolded his newspaper, looked down and began thumbing through it. Then he continued. "You're unhappy and lonely, Mr. Dodd. You sure are. It's written all over your face." He waited for Pete to react.

"What do you know about loneliness?" Pete questioned the man. Pete was getting to the point that he didn't care for this man.

"Mr. Dodd, I know a lot about loneliness," the man with the straw hat said, speaking with authority. "I spot it everyday. I can tell when a man is so lonely, that he would rather kill himself than suck his pride up and do something about it." He paused, turned the page, and let his words sink in good before continuing. "A woman is the same, too. I can tell when a woman is so far down on her luck that she would rather turn to whiskey rather than ask God for help. And children get lonely too, Mr. Dodd." He paused again. "Loneliness will break your heart, if you don't do something about it." Then he summed it up. "Mr. Dodd, loneliness comes in all shapes and sizes. Most people don't understand that loneliness is one of the most powerful and dangerous things in the world. However, Mr. Dodd, there's still one other thing that can break your heart, and believe me, it's even stronger and more powerful than loneliness. Do you know what it is?"

"What do you mean?"

"Just what I said."

"Well, Mr. Uh… Barnes. I think that's your name. You can't sit here and tell me there's something more miserable and stronger than loneliness because I got it, and it's pretty darn strong."

"I didn't say miserable, Mr. Dodd. I said stronger. Love has just as much power as loneliness does, but the good thing is, it can heal loneliness. Love is the root of all good things. It's what makes people smile. It's what makes mothers cry when they see their newborn babies for the first time, and again when their babies leave home. It's what makes a grown man cry when he loses something more dear to him than anything in the world. It's what makes a young boy cry when he loses his little dog and a little girl cry when she gets confused and can't understand things. So, there you have it." Mr. Barnes folded the newspaper and tucked it beside him and took a draw off his pipe. "Loneliness and love are just about equal, but my friend, only one will kill you. Do I have to tell you which one that is?" Pete hung his head.

John Barnes was telling Pete to look to the future with bright expectations. He told Pete that his moment had finally come, and that God had seen his long suffering. It was time for Pete to reap some of the good deeds he had done in life and time to be forgiven for the bad ones. However, he reminded Pete that he needed to change, and if he asked, God would help him. The change had to come from the inside first, he said. In time, friends will see on the outside what God changed on the inside.

Pete lowered his head. "I-I-I don't know if I can. I think I'm too far gone."

"Oh, no, Pete. You still got a good life ahead of you, that is, if you want it. Give the Lord a chance. He's already found someone for you."

"Huh...what are you talking about?"

"You'll find out my friend. You'll find out."

The man with the straw hat stood up, and the conductor looked right at him and said, "Ticket please."

"Oh, yes, sir, I have it in my bag. However, I left it in the dining car. I'll get it for you."

Pete turned to see him walk back to the dining car. He wondered more than ever now *who* this man could be. He was too scared to think about it, and even more afraid to say the words he believed in his heart.

* * * * *

Twenty-eight

Savoring The Moment

LIZZY DID WHAT she could to comfort Able, but there wasn't much she could do. Words wouldn't help. They had gotten home late and figured it was best not to tell Bebop the bad news about Pearl until the next morning. Lizzy made Bebop a peanut butter and jelly sandwich for supper and sent him to bed. He didn't complain about wanting to stay up. All he could think about was the disastrous day he had been through with Justin and the hay truck.

Able bathed and went onto bed, while Lizzy finished some cleaning in the kitchen. He was still awake when she came to the bedroom, so it didn't bother him when she turned the light on so she could make her way to the bed. After she climbed into the bed, both found themselves staring into the darkness. Lizzy finally fell a sleep but Able tossed and turned so much that he knew he was wasting his time. At four o'clock he gave up, found his pants by the light of the moon coming in the window and headed for the kitchen to make a pot of coffee. Moments later, he heard Lizzy's footsteps coming from their room. She couldn't sleep anymore either, so the two sat at the table sipping coffee and discussing what Able needed to do that day. Lizzy knew the day would be a long one for him having to go back to Belzoni to make funeral arrangements. He told her he might stay overnight, if she didn't mind. He said he'd just like to sleep in his old bed another time and clear his head. Lizzy was not keen on the idea but didn't say anything. There was always a chance he would change his mind before the end of the day, and if he didn't, that was okay, too. She placed her coffee cup down on the table and walked behind him while he sat in his chair. She put her arms around his big shoulders and leaned over and gave him a big kiss on the back of his head and told him she loved him. He told her he loved her too and continued on about how he needed time to get his thoughts together. Staying at Pearl's would help, he said. He told her he knew the old home place would not be the same anymore without Pearl, but he couldn't imagine it without Jeanna, too. Worried sick about her, he sat at the table and waited for the sun to rise.

By 7:00 a.m., Able was ready to leave. He told Lizzy to tell Mr. Cane that he needed to borrow Ole Red for the day, but not to worry. She said she'd tell him the first thing when she got to work and reassured Able that Mr. Cane would understand. Able told Lizzy he planned on going by to see whether Mrs. Lucy Arnell might help him with the planning. Lizzy thought that was a good idea and helped him finish packing a small suitcase. Pouring the last cup of coffee from the pot, she listened as Able fired Ole Red up in the drive. She knew he would be patting the dash twice, as he traditionally did and telling Ole Red, "good boy." When the motor warmed up, she heard him drive off.

Able left the radio off, as he drove up the road. All that he could hear was the purring of the V-8 engine as he thought about Jeanna. He knew she would fight to her death or even kill herself before letting Big Doug force her back into the whoring business. Mentally, he tried to prepare himself.

Within thirty minutes Lizzy had driven to the Cane farm and found Mr. Cane walking to his truck. He stopped and watched her wheel in and park by the plum tree like she did every day. She was running a little late, but Mr. Cane didn't mind. He was more concerned with where Able was.

"Mr. Cane, I hopes it's all right, but Able needed to use Ole Red again to run back to Belzoni this morning to make funeral arrangements for Aunt Pearl. The poor boy didn't sleep a wink last night. All he did was roll around in that bed, tossing and tumbling like a bull. I told him it would be all right to take the truck, but he wanted me to ask you anyway."

Mr. Cane looked amused as he listened to Lizzy. He always said she had a unique ability to ask and answer a question in the same sentence, not to mention that she talked ninety miles-an-hour.

"Lizzy, you were right. It's okay. He didn't need to ask me. Able's been too valuable around here to have to ask in a situation like this."

"Well, that's what I told him, too, Mr. Cane. But, you know? I'm so worried about him. I'm afraid he might go off and do something stupid."

"Aw now, Lizzy, Able's going to be all right. He just needs some time to clear his head good."

"I sho' hope you right, Mr. Cane. You always is, you know?"

'Well, that's kind, Lizzy. I hope I am, too, this time." Mr. Cane opened his truck door and cranked the new Ford. "I'll see you in a little while. I have to run somewhere for a few minutes, but I'm coming back to get Justin."

"You look good in that new truck, Mr. Cane," Lizzy said as she stepped onto the porch. Mr. Cane smiled and backed up.

It wasn't long before Able got to Miss Arnell's house. No one was there, though, so he went on to Aunt Pearl's. As he drove in Pearl's drive, he saw Mrs. Lucy out front, sweeping the front porch. He honked and pulled in the drive. He could tell she had been crying as he walked to her. She had picked some fresh gardenias and had placed them in a vase on a stand by the front door.

"Able, I hope you don't mind me pickin' these flowers of Pearl's."

"Shoot, naw, Mrs. Lucy, you go on and pick all you want. Aunt Pearl wouldn't mind, you knows that."

"Oh, Able, who would do such a horrible thing to Pearl? She never hurt nobody in her whole life." She lowered her head to wipe the tears.

"I don't know, Mrs. Lucy, but I guess it would be somebody that don't love people." Able wanted to say more but was scared he might frighten her. She composed herself and told him she had cleaned up everything in the house. Able told her he appreciated everything she had done but that he needed something else, too.

"Huh, Mrs. Lucy, I's got one real big favor to ask you if you don't mind."

"What's that, Able?"

"I'd really like for you to go with me to the funeral home and help me make the arrangements for Aunt Pearl. See, I ain't got nobody with me, and I sure could use some help. You know what I mean? I's just don't really know what I's in for."

"Sure, darling, I'll be more than glad to help. I would be honored to do that."

After helping Mrs. Lucy into the truck, Able cranked Ole Red and backed out of the drive. It was only a fifteen minute drive to the Belzoni city limits. As they slowed down for traffic they passed a few storefronts and Able watched as several old colored men recognize him and Ole Red. Out of respect, they tipped their hats to him. Through his mirror, he continued staring as he drove down the street. The news traveled fast and especially, since it was bad news. Everyone knew. Mrs. Pearl had been loved and respected by all the people in Belzoni. She was one of few Negro college graduates in the whole county. She had taught history at the Humphrey County schools for thirty years and always told the kids that history was the most important subject the human race could learn and that every one of her students would know it before they left her class.

She always said, "If you don't know where you come from, you haven't a chance of knowing where you are going." Able smiled as he remembered her telling him that repeatedly. Aunt Pearl drilled that quote in to the head of every kid that came through her class. Her students would remember her for that one thing, if not for anything else.

Able pulled into the funeral home parking lot. It was gravel with a few shade trees spaced around the perimeter. It appeared as if, he and Mrs. Lucy were the only ones there, except for a pickup parked at the end of the building. Just having Mrs. Lucy with him made the experience easier for him. They parked under a tree and went inside. As they entered, a Mr. Dickens, the funeral director, met them at the door and introduced himself. He told Able he was sorry about the incident and hoped that the person who did it would be brought to justice soon. He then explained to Able about the different burial plans. He said, however, that Mrs. Pearl had already pre-paid her funeral services some time back and had taken care of all her financial obligations. Mrs. Lucy and Able were dumb-founded. Mrs. Lucy told Able she knew Pearl was the most organized woman she had ever met, but this was unbelievable. With the plans already made, everything else only took about an hour. Able was awed by how smart his Aunt Pearl was and how she had always planned ahead. She was the kind of person who never wanted to impose on anyone. Mr. Dickens went to the vault and came back with a letter addressed to "Lucy" and handed it to her.

"Mrs. Arnell, I believe this is for you," said Mr. Dickens. "Pearl told me to give it to you in case."

Lucy opened the letter and read. *"Lucy, if you are here with Able, please comfort him. I feel as if he will come to you first. He's a big man but has a soft tender heart, and this will be extremely hard on him. It will be harder on him than Jeanna because he was always my baby boy, and I made sure he knew it. He won't have a clue for what to do. You will have to do everything, however, I hope I've tented to the most part. Believe me, Able will be doing all he can just to hold it together. In my lower drawer in my bedroom, you'll find my pink floral dress. That's the dress I wore when Able graduated from high school. It's still my best dress. Put my cameo earrings on me, but take them off later and see that Jeanna gets them. Put my "Star Teacher" pin on my dress so my students will remember me. Don't put my glasses on me. They will make me look old. Do put fresh gardenias in my hand. I always loved the smell of the gardenia. I hope heaven will be filled with them. I love you for what you are doing for me, Lucy. You've always been my best friend. Love, Pearl.*

It was all Lucy could do to finish the letter. As heart-broken as she was, she found the strength to make the final arrangements with Mr. Dickens before she and Able went back to Pearl's house for her things.

Stephen Cheek

The funeral was scheduled to take place in three days, at the Mt. Hebron Church at 2:30 p.m.. Able was glad to have all the funeral business behind him. He thanked Mrs. Lucy and carried her back home, where she asked him in for a sandwich. He thanked her but said he needed to go back to Pearl's. She understood and waved bye to him as he pulled out of the drive and headed up the gravel road. For some reason, he decided not to stop but ride past Pearl's house and ride around for a while. Maybe, just maybe, he would run into someone who had seen Jeanna. When he entered the city limits again of Belzoni, he pulled over at Moffet's Family Grocery to pick up a few things for his supper. He went inside and looked around and decided on a couple of cans of potted meat and bread. He was pretty hungry, so he got a pound of bologna and some sliced cheese to go with the other. After he paid, he picked up his groceries and walked out of the store and across the parking lot towards Ole Red. He had gotten to the truck and was about to open the door, when a deputy sheriff drove up beside him. Able stood there as the deputy stepped from his car and approached him. Able didn't know what to expect so he didn't say anything. He knew, though, that a colored man being approached by a white police officer was never a good sign in the South. *What have I done wrong?* he thought to himself.

The deputy rested his hand on his gun as he spoke. "Able, I met you yesterday out at Miss Pearl's. I just been back out there looking for you."

"What's up, sir?" Able said.

"Well, we don't really know. We went out to Big Doug's place this morning and there ain't nothing left but ashes of the place. It's burnt down to the ground. No sign of Big Doug, nowhere. You ain't been out there have you?"

"Oh, no, sir, sho' ain't. Me and Mrs. Lucy Arnell been busy all day up at Aunt Pearl's and then the funeral home. Hadn't been time for nothing else."

"I see," said the officer.

"You say Big Doug's place done burned to the ground?" Able asked to make sure he heard right.

"Yep, that's right, and that ain't all, Able, but first I need you to steady yourself."

"Okays, I'm steady," Able said with a puzzle in his eye and clinching the groceries he had just purchased.

"Alright, here goes," the officer said looking Able in the eyes hesitant. "In them ashes, we found some human remains." Able looked surprised, thinking the worst. "Now before you go getting excited, we don't whose they are yet. Don't know if it's male or female. The sheriff done called the coroner to come in and make an investigation of the whole thing. Maybe two or three days before we know anything. Probably have to carry the remains to Jackson to the lab."

Able leaned back on the truck, shaking his head. That's all he needed to finish knocking the wind out of him. "Thank you, sir. Y'alls find out anything else, y'all let me know, will you? I sho' don't know how much more I's can take though," Able said.

The officer offered his condolences again and then drove off. Able stood there for a while before climbing back in Ole Red and put his head on the steering wheel and prayed.

Oh Lord, you's know how much I can take. Surely, I'm at my end by now. No man can take much more. Lord, please don't take little Jeanna from me. Save my baby sister. Please save my baby sister.

Then Able thought about Job in the Bible and the test and struggle he went through for the Lord. "Job, I don't know how you made it, man. The Lord sho' expects a lot out of us peoples down here." Then he clutched Ole Red slowly, put it in gear, and drove back to Pearl's to do some more soul searching.

Instead of going inside Pearl's house to eat, Able dropped the tailgate on the pickup and decided to eat outside. Sitting there, he noticed a crop duster coming in overhead returning from spraying cotton. He wondered what it was like to be able to fly in the sky like a bird. It would sho' would be nice sometimes, to get away from it all down here, he thought. Within thirty minutes the crop duster had filled its tanks and flew back over. It headed into the sunset. When it did, Able saw the pilot look down and wave at him.

It was getting dark when Able heard the crop duster come back over from its final trip. He listened closely as the pilot cut the engine and glided onto the runway somewhere close by. With no instruments to guide the pilots' home, most followed landmarks such as lights and highways to find their way back in.

It had been a long day and Able decided not to stay up late. He needed the rest because he was exhausted, mentally and physically. He went to his old bedroom where he had spent many a night as a young boy and looked around. Facing him on the bed stand was a picture of Jeanna and him when they were kids. He was riding Uncle Hugh's back, and Jeanna was in Uncle Hugh's arms. What a memory, he thought. Tacked on the wall across the room was a picture of Jesus and a second place ribbon that he had won in the 4H Club. He still remembered the old cow he fed and groomed for a year. He remembered that he learned a lot in the 4H club, not only about animals but about people, too. Now, he knew why Aunt Pearl wanted him to join and why she always said, "Animals just like people, Able. You never know what to expect out of 'em, but always expect something you didn't expect."

That quote never left his mind as he grew up; hardly a day ever went by that he wasn't reminded of it. Thinking back what seemed like hard times, he could see where he had really had a good life after all. Maybe better than he would have had with his real mom and dad.

Wandering from room to room he spent some time looking through old pictures and the family Bible where Pearl had documented things about his real mom and dad. She had never showed it to him, but it was exactly what she had always told him and Jeanna through the years. Aunt Pearl never wanted to take credit for being Able's and Jeanna's real mom.

She always said, "You got only one mamma. Nobody can ever replace her."

Pearl would always tell them stories about her own sisters when they were young. Most of them were funny stories. They were always getting into trouble, most of the time with one other. She said their mom would have to straighten them all out with a strapping most of the time.

It had been a long time since Able had spent the night in his old bed. It felt good as he pulled the sheets back and climbed in and turned the lamp off. Remembering the good times helped. As he lay there, he knew Pearl was in a good place now, but he hated that she had to go like she did. Even though she was old and may not have been around much longer, it was nobody's place to take her except the Lord. There was no question of what happened and who did it. Then he remembered what Aunt Pearl had always made him do. He reached for the lamp again and turned it back on. He pulled the sheets back and got down by his bed on his knees and began to pray.

"Dear Lord, I's just a man. Me and you's done talked a whole lot right here. You knows I's ain't real smart like other peoples, but I's know where my strength comes from. I's hadn't got no right to ask you for nothing 'cause you done give me more than I's can ever thank you for. Lizzy, Bebop, Mr. Cane, Mrs. Kate, Bud, William, little Jussin, and Pete, they may be all I's got now but they's all the world to me and, Lord, please be with them always and keep them all safe for me."

Then he added "Now, Lord, wherever Jeanna is, I's got to ask you to watch out for her. If she's with you right now, tell her I'm so glad for her and tell her I loves her. Tell her she's been the best little sister any brother could ever have. Tell her I'm sorry I couldn't help her in time. But Lord if she's still here with us, please protect her, build a tall hedge bush around her little self and not let anything happen to her. Let her know I's coming for her and that I ain't gonna give up till I find her and she's back in my arms safe and sound. Please do that for me, Lord. Thanks you, Lord. Amen. Oh yeah, Lord, tell Aunt Pearl I loves her, too."

Able got back up on the side of the bed, wiping his eyes. His big hands were quivering. He rubbed his eyes and then lay back, fixed his pillow and fell asleep just as he had when he was younger.

* * * * *

Twenty-nine

On The Run

JEANNA HAD BEEN in the woods for nearly fourteen hours. The sun was coming up, and she was tired of running. The woods had turned to a swamp and she was crossing one slough after another. She had no idea where she was and was afraid she might be turned around because there had been a cloud cover all night. In the distance, she could hear the sounds of cars, but they seemed to be a long way away. There was no choice, she had to follow the sound and hope she could get help.

Coon hunter Henry dogs still had a strong trail going and figured he'd have Jeanna within another four or five hours.

"Good," Big Doug grunted.

The bloodhound and the Doberman were pulling coon hunter Henry and his buddy steadily through the woods, with the cur dogs barking and following. Once in a while, one of the mangy cur dogs would jump a rabbit and distract the others. But after a short pursuit, they would always fall back behind the bloodhound and Doberman.

The Doberman was strong as an ox and wanted to run out front of the bloodhound, causing Henry's buddy to struggle to hold him back. The problem was that the Doberman could wind better than the bloodhound, but he just wasn't as reliable. He would lose the track every few hundred yards and would have to go back to where the bloodhound was in order to get started again.

Henry's bloodhound, Ole Blue, was a tracking machine. Unlike the Doberman, the bloodhound kept his nose to the ground and would bark about every ten seconds. The Doberman kept his nose high in the air, swinging his head from side to side trying to catch a scent. He barked only when ready to attack. In times past the combination of the two usually cut the tracking time in half.

Jeanna continued pushing herself, knowing there was no time for rest. She knew that Big Doug wouldn't just be following her, but that he would do anything to catch her and punish her. She had heard stories about him tracking runaways before and how the girls were never heard of again. She had no intention of letting that happening. She waded through bayous that were waist-deep and swam the deeper ones. The shallow waters and low-lying limbs were infested with water moccasins; one wrong move and she could be bitten.

Nothing would stop her. She was determined to make it, but the swamp was so confusing. The creeks snaked back and forth so much that she would become confused as to what side she needed to be on. She knew that if she stayed in the swamp much longer, she would be caught. It was important that she find an opening soon so she could make a run for it.

Another hour passed and then she saw what she was looking for. It was faint at first and then she saw the opening through the trees. Her heart was racing at the thought of an open field.

Only a hundred more feet through the dense briars, and she would be out of the swamp. As she broke through the briars, she could barely see a cotton picker or maybe a tractor working in the field. The problem was, it was going the opposite way and the field seemed miles long. It might take an hour to go to the end of the row, turnaround, and start back. Then it would take another hour for it to get to her. She was so thirsty, hungry, and exhausted that she wished she could lie down and die.

"Please, Lord, help me," she said.

As the machine made its way across the field, the sound of the pickerr faded, carrying what hope she had with it. Standing there in desperation, she strained to hear something faint and in the distance. First, she thought it was a housedog barking, but after making a full 360-degree turn, she realized there was no house around. Then it hit her. It was the sound of hunting dogs coming from the same way she came through the woods.

"Oh crap! It can't be Big Doug!" she screamed.

She immediately started running through the cotton field in the direction of the machinery. There was no time to wait. The end of the day was nearing soon and the sun had started its path down behind the trees. She knew she had to get to the farmer on the machine quickly. The cotton was about three feet high, and the stalks were cutting her legs, feet, and arms as she scrambled through the dense crop. Her dress snagged and ripped as she crossed over row after row barefooted. She was falling and crying in vain. As she reached to pull her hair out of her eyes, she felt a leech clinging to her neck. She hollered with pain and pulled it off and squeezed it until blood squirted between her fingers.

"Oh, my God, Lord, help me, please!" she screamed.

As she ran, she could see in the distance that the tractor had not turned around but continued on out to the gravel road and kept going. The driver was apparently going to get more fuel before returning. She screamed as hard as she could, but to no avail. She had to make a decision and make one fast. The choice was either stay in the field or go for the woods across the fields. The woods provided cover; the field would not. The woods would have to be her answer. She knew if she were spotted in the field, it would be only minutes before they would catch her. Plus, Big Doug may have somebody watching the road from where the tractor came out. She ran as hard as she could, hoping the night would provide her some extra protection. Although another night in the darkness was not what she really wanted anything would be better than being caught by Big Doug. She had no way of knowing where he was, where she was, or how far she had traveled in the last twenty-four hours. If her instincts were right she had gone maybe ten to twenty miles and was heading northeast.

She remembered that Aunt Pearl's house was overlooking the Delta bluff. If she could get that far, she could get help. She remembered how it was always fun as a kid to ride cardboard boxes down the bluff behind her house. Every day after school, her friends would come over and play until dark. Aunt Pearl would always get on her and Able about the grass stains in their good school clothes and the shoes they had forgotten to bring home. What she would do now for a pair of shoes, she thought! Her legs and feet were all scratched and bleeding. The path wasn't stopping her, but it had slowed her considerably.

As she reached the edge the dark woods, Jeanna stopped to say a quick prayer. She remembered the talk about a black panther that hunters had seen. They said it screamed just like a woman giving birth to a child. There were many things to be afraid of in the woods, but she had no choice. She had to go in.

* * * * *

Thirty

Madness

A S THE TRAIN pulled into St. Louis, Pete woke up as it came to a halt. He looked around and saw a few people getting off; most were staying on. He noticed the conductor making his way to the front of the car scribbling something on a pad. A young boy trailed behind him, mimicking his actions. Pete chuckled as he watched the youngster's mother head after him, catching him right before he disappeared into the next car. With a swift swing of the hand, she tanned his behind. The small boy pouted as his mother ushered him back to the seat and plopped him down firmly beside her. Pete turned to look out the window and saw his reflection. So far it had been a long and hard trip and one he never wanted to live through again. He was ready to go home. A few luggage carts loaded with boxes and suitcases still passed by the windows for the new arrivals. He strained his eyes to see past the carts to where he thought he could see three soldiers trying to make the train before it departed. The ticket manager, who had seen them too, jumped off his stool, pencil in hand, and ran to the back door. All the while they hollered out to the conductor to hold up. The soldiers would make the train after all. Amidst the chaos, Pete could've sworn he saw the man with the straw hat walking along the depot dock, twirling his umbrella. "Was he seeing things or was he needing a drink," he thought. The man turned, as if sensing Pete's gaze and tipped his hat with a smile. Then, as if someone had poured warm water on Pete's head, he felt a spiritual presence so strong that he broke into a cold sweat. Pete reached for his handkerchief in his coat pocket but found instead scripture written on a small piece of paper.

"Where did he come from? Come on, what could this mean?" Pete asked, aloud. The scripture was Ruth 1:2. He read it aloud and it said, "'and the name of his wife was Naomi.'"

Frantically, he reached into his other pocket, found his handkerchief, and wiped his forehead. He then turned in his seat and looked out the window at where he had seen the man with the straw hat standing, but he was gone. A forced smile came over Pete's face. *What happened,* he thought? He felt so clean inside. Where did the urge for a drink go? He had not felt that good in twenty years. He was like a new man. He knew something was different for sure. Where was the depression? Where was the anger at the world...at the Lord? That was it! Then his smile turned into a solemn, gentle look and one of remorse.

He knew now what was behind this change. He put his face in his hands and whispered, "Thank you, Lord. Thank you." The train continued to pick up speed heading southward towards Yazoo City.

* * * * *

IT WAS NEARING suppertime when Mr. Cane saw Justin creep up into his bedroom. Something was off with the boy. He followed him in and asked, "Justin, where you and Bebop been today?" Justin froze and then spoke.

"Oh, just playing, Dad." Justin put his hands in his pockets and tried his hardest to meet his father's gaze.

"Y'all stay out of trouble?" Mr. Cane asked.

"Huh, boys will be boys, you might say, Dad," Justin replied. He had no idea what the phrase meant, but his mother had often uttered it with amusement after Justin or the other boys had gotten into a bit of trouble. Under the circumstances, it sure felt like the right thing to say.

—

"Well, Justin, Pete called today and said he's gonna be in Yazoo City in the morning, so we better go over there and get him. Reckon you still know the way?" Mr. Cane said.

"Huh, I don't know, Dad. I slept a lot that day and I was sick too, remember?"

"Yeah, that's right, you didn't look too good when you came back in. Well, I think I can get us over there, if you can't. Ole Pete will be ready to get off that train for sure. He's had a long trip. That new truck needs another good breaking in run anyway."

"Yeah, I bet so too, Dad."

"Oh, by the way, Justin, that little hay patch Bud cut on the other side of the ditch will need raked and baled in the next few days. So, you didn't miss out on all the truck driving yet. I'm real proud of you, son. You're really growing up fast. Able said you sure have turned into a good hay truck driver."

"He did? Abe said that?" Justin was excited until he remembered where the truck was. He turned pale just thinking about it.

"That's right. That's what he said. Now you eat a good supper tonight, and we'll head out in the morning." Mr. Cane looked closer at Justin. "Justin, you all right? You're not getting sick again, are you?"

"Oh, naw, Dad, uh, just hungry."

* * * * *

WITH DARKNESS APPROACHING, Big Doug was furious that they had not caught up with Jeanna. With the delay, Herman was also having doubts about getting the other hundred dollars that he was promised. Jeanna had been doing a good job of crossing the river and backtracking to confuse the dogs. The driver on the cotton picker returned but didn't help Big Doug any. He just asked a lot of questions. He wanted to know what they were tracking, how they were tracking, and so on. They made an excuse that they were tracking a rabid fox that had bitten one of their dogs. The driver talked their ears off for twenty minutes, the twenty minutes they needed. With the loss of precious time, they were forced to camp for the night.

It wound up being a long, mosquito-infested night. Al and Herman had gathered wood for hours to keep the fire roaring, and for a while at least, there was enough smoke to run the mosquitoes away. Their defeat was obvious the next morning when they looked at each other's faces, swollen from bites. Everyone awoke restless and irritable, as it appeared that Big Doug's plan was heading south. Tension was building. Coon hunter Henry was cussing Herman; Herman was cussing Al; and Al was cussing the dogs.

By six o'clock, Big Doug had smoked another cigar to the stub and was stomping around the fire. He was ready to move. Henry was feeling the pressure. Big Doug knew that if they took much longer, someone would put two and two together and cause him real trouble. His original plan for being out of the state with Jeanna by now was gone.

"What's wrong with these stupid dogs?" Big Doug demanded.

Henry replied, "The trail keeps going cold, Doug, and they're having a hard time. Besides, the dogs done got hungry, and to tell you the truth, so are we."

Immediately Doug pulled his revolver from his belt and shot one of the cur dogs.

"Not now," Big Doug said. "Skin and cook that dog there and be fast about it," talking to Henry. Next time, somebody gets hungry and can't get the job done, then I'm gonna shoot'em." He kicked the fire again and walked off.

Henry, Al, and Herman all knew Big Doug meant it. The other dogs were licking the dead cur. Henry told Herman, and Al to hurry and pick up the dead dog before the others started in on it. Herman picked it up and kicked the other dogs away. He found a stump and laid the carcass over it.

Henry reached into his pocket and pulled out a switchblade. He pushed the button on the side and the eight-inch blade snapped open. He threw the knife at the stump, and it stuck in right beside Al's hand.

"Hell, hang him in that tree there, Al," pointing to a red oak. "Wash that meat down in the river when you get him skinned and throw them guts to the other dogs."

Al and Herman pulled the dog over to the tree. Herman still had a leash in his pocket and used it to throw over a limb. They tied the dog's rear legs up and pulled him upward. The cur weighed nearly forty pounds.

After tying the legs off, Al started cutting the skin down beside the inside of each leg.

"Skin him just like a deer, boy. Ain't no difference," Henry said as he lay up beside a stump rolling a cigarette. "Just gonna taste a little twangy is all." Then he laughed.

Herman was not laughing. He knew this was not the time to whimper because he knew he could wind up like the dog. Big Doug went to relieve himself and was back in a few minutes.

"What's the problem here?" Big Doug said.

"Ain't no problem, Mr. Doug," Herman said. "We'll have us a sho' nuff hot dog in a minute or two," Henry laughed as he got up to cut some sticks. Big Doug didn't say anything.

In a few minutes, Al came back with the meat and began cutting it up into little pieces so they could cook it over the fire like marshmallows. Big Doug was standing there thinking. He had something on his mind.

"Y'all keep on tracking, I'm cutting back," said Big Doug. "There's a cutoff road a few miles ahead. I'll go get my car and meet y'all. If you know what's good for you, you better have that girl with you when I get there." Big Doug started walking back in the direction he came from fading into the woods.

"Let's eat. I'm hungry," Al said.

"Better eat fast or it's going to be our last meal, if Big Doug's got anything to do with it," said Henry.

Thirty-one

Them Ducks

O KAY, JUSTIN, TIME to rise and shine. We gotta get on the road soon. It's about 8 o'clock." Mr. Cane said, entering Justin's room.

"Aw Dad, do I have to go? I think I'm sick."

"Sick or not sick, you gotta get up. Go wash your face and come on down for breakfast."

Justin struggled to the bathroom and looked in the mirror. His blond hair was sticking straight up. He rubbed his hands through his hair and grumbled some, then washed his face and slicked his hair down. As he went down the stairs, he was still trying to get his shirttail tucked in his pants.

Waiting for him on the table was a plate of pancakes and bacon that his mom had cooked. That was one of Justin's favorite breakfasts. He sat down in a hurry and poured a mountain of syrup over his pancakes and dug in. As he was eating, he heard Lizzy coming back in. Mrs. Kate looked out the kitchen window and saw Bebop coming up the steps behind her.

"Hey, Bebop, where you been?" Mr. Cane asked, holding the door open as the boy ducked in under his arm.

"Oh, Mom made me come with her since my cousin had something else to do. I've been sleeping in the car." Looking at Justin eating, he said, "Hey, Justin, what you doing today?"

"I gotta go with Dad to get Pete at the train station. You want to go with us?" Before Bebop could answer, Justin said, "Hey, Dad, can Bebop go with us? We can ride in the back coming home."

"All right with me as long as it's all right with Lizzy."

"Shoot, get them both out of here, and maybe I can get something done for once," Lizzy said with her hands on her hips.

Bebop was not excited about being around Mr. Cane no more than Justin was. He was afraid the hay truck would come up in a conversation, and was afraid he wouldn't know what to say. He would much rather take his chances around the farm than being in close quarters with Mr. Cane.

"You hear that, Bebop? You can go, too." Justin said.

"Yeah, I heard, thanks. You're a great friend," he said under his breath.

"Justin, hurry up and finish them pancakes and let's get going," Mr. Cane said, as he came back in to get his keys.

"Okay," Justin said as he washed everything down with a glass of milk.

As Justin and Bebop went to the truck, Bebop asked, "Justin, why you want me to go? You know I didn't wanna go with y'all. When your dad finds out about that hay truck, he's gonna whip me, too."

"I know. That's why I want you with me." Justin put his hand on Bebop's shoulder, and Bebop pushed it off.

Mr. Cane, Justin and Bebop loaded up in the truck and said bye to everyone. As they backed out of the driveway and headed up the gravel road, Lizzy made the remark to Mrs. Kate that they looked like a man driving with two knots sitting beside him.

"Well, Justin, you know the way, don't you?"

"I told you, Dad, I was sick." Justin was looking out the window.

"Oh, yeah, that's right. I almost, forgot. By the way, you sure are in a bad mood there. Hope you get better soon. Bebop, you gonna have to do all the talking, I guess."

"Huh, yes, sir."

"Well, I'll turn right here, boys, and hope we go the right way." Mr. Cane turned onto the highway and then reached over to turn on the radio and heard, "I wonder where the yellow went, when I brushed by teeth with Pepsodent" the Pepsodent toothpaste commercial going off. After a few miles up the road he turned the radio down and tried to make conversation again.

"I'm telling you boys something. When y'all start driving, you're not gonna find a better truck on the road than a Ford pickup. This truck rides so good it's just like riding on water. Smooth sailing. What do y'all think?"

Bebop looked over at Justin, and then they both said at the same time, "Sure does." Mr. Cane knew then that it was going to be a silent trip; he reached and turned the radio back up.

* * * * *

ABLE HAD SLEPT good and had not woken up a single time. He opened his eyes and for a moment forgot about where he was and about all the worries of the day. As his mind cleared, it didn't take long before he remembered.

After lacing up his boots, he walked into the kitchen to see what he could find. From the refrigerator he poured the remaining milk from the bottle into a glass and thought about how quickly things go back to normal as he tilted his head back to drain the glass. The milk hit his mouth not cool and blank, but velvety and sour. He spitted the contents of his mouth into the sink, washed his glass out and then filled it with tap water. So this is how the days gonna be, he thought.

He looked out the kitchen window at the old milk cow grazing and a few chickens stirring about. He opened the back door and stepped out onto the back porch. Leaning against the house, he gazed across the lower forty. It was a beautiful sight. The dew was rising. A few ducks headed for the river. He thought aloud again how nice it would be to be able to fly up in the sky. *Only the Lord knows and them ducks and that crop duster,* he thought. With the words barely out of his mouth, a huge smile spread across his face. Able had an idea! He quickly put his shirt on and hurried out the door.

He cranked Ole Red up and headed towards Mrs. Lucy's house looking all around to see if he saw a landing strip anywhere between her house and Pearl's.

It wasn't long before he was standing at Mrs. Lucy's house pounding on the door.

"Mrs. Lucy! Mrs. Lucy!"

"What on earth do you want, Able?" Mrs. Lucy asked, adjusting her robe and looking questioningly up at the sky as if to verify that the sun was low and the man was out of his mind.

"Who owns a plane around here, a crop duster, Mrs. Lucy?"

"Well, that's Mr. Williams' plane. Why you ask that, Able?"

"Which way to get there? I ain't got time right now. I tell you later." She pointed past her house about a quarter-of-a-mile. Able turned and ran to the truck. Then he stopped and turned around. "Oh, yeah, Mrs. Lucy. Thank you."

Mrs. Lucy watched as Able jumped into the truck and spun out the drive, shaking her head. *Boy ain't right*, she thought.

Able went a few hundred yards down the road to the first drive he came to and turned in. He drove another hundred feet and stopped along side a small tin building where he saw in a distant field a mechanic working under a plane. He stopped for a second wondering if he was doing the right thing, said a short prayer. As he stepped out of the truck he adjusted his pants, adjusted his hat and thought, here goes nothing.

The pilot, holding a wrench in one hand and a rag in the other, was somewhat surprised to see Able, jump out and start running towards him. The closer Able got to the pilot the more he slowed down. As he neared, he slowed down to a fast walk. The pilot walked out from under the wing of the plane to meet Able. He used the sleeve of his shirt to wipe the grease from his face. Able stopped in his tracks and stared in awe at the bright red and blue 1926 Curtiss Hawk I, bi-plane. The prop and wheels were yellow; the wings were striped with blue. Across the fuselage, the letters spelled "Red Devil." A cartoon of a devil and pitchfork were painted on both sides of the nose.

"Huh, how you do there, sir?" Able asked.

"Hmm, I'm all right and yourself." The mechanic squinted up at Able, using his hand to shield his eyes from the sun.

"Couldn't be no better and have less, I guess. Well, let me change that a little, if you don't mind. I could be better if had a little more," Able said, and smiled.

"Well...that makes more sense to me. I know what you talking about now." The man started wiping his hands off with the rag, finishing up what he was doing.

Able stuck his hand out, "Uh, my name's Able Johnson from over at Friendly, sir."

"Well, Able, I'm Gene Williams. It's good to meet you. What can I do for you?"

"Say, huh, what you get for a plane ride?" Able asked smiling.

"Don't give plane rides. What else can I do for you?"

"Say you don't, huh?" Able looked down at the ground, somewhat dejected.

There was a pause and silence, and then the man spoke up.

"Yeah, that's right. My insurance won't cover nobody in the plane but me. If I hire out for rides, that changes my coverage, they say. I crash the plane, the people won't be covered."

"Oh, I see." Able cheered up little because he thought it was because he was colored. "Well, I appreciate your time there, Mr. Williams."

Able started walking away and then turned and said, "That's a mighty fine looking plane you got there. Where did it get that name, Red Devil?"

"Well, it's been kinda good luck to me, believe it or not. That name was the name of my plane on the aircraft carrier Hornet back in the war. It got me through that hell, so afterwards when I started this business, I needed a name for my plane. There you have it. I haven't crashed yet. I've come close a few times but not enough to damage her or me. I guess it's kinda good luck. What you think about it?" Williams continued wiping his hand with the rag even though there was no grease left on them.

"Sounds like a good name to me. I wouldn't change it," said Able as he walked around it, looking closer.

"Why you want to ride in this plane, Mr. Johnson?"

"Well, it's a long story, Mr. Williams. Even against all indications, I feel likes my baby sister is still alive. I think there's a small chance she could be lost in the woods around here somewhere and I thought..."

William looked real hard at Able as if he were trying to piece something together.

"You any kin to Pearl up the road there?" he asked.

"Yes, sir, I is. She raised me and my sister Jeanna." Able pulled his shoulders back.

"I'll be darn. I've known Pearl and her friend Mrs. Lucy for eight years now. I sure am sorry about Pearl. You know, it's got everyone around here pretty shook up. You tell me you think your sister is still alive but out there in them woods somewhere?"

"That's right, and I just thought..."

"I know what you thought. Get in. We'll make a loop or two and see what we see."

Williams started to the back of his plane to make sure everything looked good underneath and told Able to start crawling over in the back seat.

"Watch your step now. Don't want you falling off my plane this low. You'd feel it a whole lot more." he laughed as Able looked bug-eyed him.

"I thought you said something about your insurance coverage," Able asked.

"Oh, they wouldn't know it anyway. You be done burned up by then," Gene said, continuing his preparation. Then he said, "When these things hit the ground, they go up in smoke pretty fast, especially with all these chemical. You liable to burn for a couple days before they get you out."

Now Able wasn't so sure the Lord heard him in that prayer he said back in the truck.

So again he prayed, *Now, Lord, I ain't got but a minute or two before I's gonna be a whole lot closer to you than I really wants to right now. So if you got any plans on me getting out of this plane 'cause you were out when I called on you little while ago, it's—*

With an ear-piercing screech like a tractor running straight pipes, the plane started before Able was able to finish.

"Put this cap and goggles on, Able. You gonna need them." Gene handed them over the seat to Able.

Able looked close at the leather aviator's cap. Then he tugged it on his head and over his ears. Gene started going over all the gauges and checklist.

"Okay, Okay, Okay, what the heck," Gene said, looking down at his gauges.

As they pulled out on the grass runway, Able closed his eyes and continued praying.

"What you say back there?" Gene hollered.

"Oh, nothing, just remembering a few things. Don't pay me no 'tention. *Shucks Lord, don't fail me now*," he continued praying.

Gene taxied the plane to the far end of the runway so he could lift off with the wind to his face. This was important because the runway was about seventy-five yards too short, and he needed all the lift he could get on takeoff. As he turned the plane into the wind, he pulled his goggles down, paused, and calmly lit a cigar that he retrieved from his leather jacket. He then revved the engine to full throttle for about thirty seconds before letting the engine idle down. Gene stood on the brakes with both feet to hold it still. Then he throttled up again. The noise of the Rolls Royce engine was deafening as Able closed his eyes. This time he let off the brakes and the plane immediately lunged forward, forcing Able's back against his seat. Gene was accustomed to this type takeoff because of the short runways on the carriers during the war, but for Able; it was his first ride in anything higher than a flat bed truck. The more the plane sped down the runway, the more Able's earflaps blew alongside head and the tighter his grip got on the side of the plane. Then, without warning, about halfway down the runway, the engine started missing. Gene quickly adjusted the fuel mixture and let out a string of curse words. As the engine leveled out, he pulled back on the stick and the plane miraculously became airborne, skimming a pine tree as it passed over it.

"I guess that added weight made us tip that tree back there." Gene remarked with interest.

Able's eyes were still closed.

Gene turned around and patted Able on the head and said,

"Hey, man, it's all right. We in heaven now." Gene fell out laughing. He took a big drag off his cigar as if saluting another perfect takeoff.

*　*　*　*　*

Thirty-two

Homecoming

M R. CANE SLOWED down to turn into the depot. He told the boys that the train carrying Pete would be coming down the track in about fifteen more minutes. Justin remembered Able saying those exact words a few days earlier.

Mr. Cane pulled the truck in a parking spot, and everyone got out and walked towards the depot building. Justin heard his dad jiggling his change in his pocket and it reminded him of the coin Pete had put on the track.

"Dad, can me and Bebop go look at the track?"

"Naw, not by yourself. I'll go with you."

As they approached the track, Justin was scanning the brick walkway beside it where Pete had put the penny. He was hoping no one had picked it up. Then he saw something that he thought might be it. A small piece of metal was turned up edgeways beside the track. He reached down for it and examined it closely. He then turned it over to look at the other side. It was twice as big as its original size and as smooth as the fender on his Dad's new pickup truck and so flat that the name was even blotted out. He had no idea a train was so heavy that it could do that to a coin.

As he looked at it, his dad walked over and said, "Whatcha got here, Justin?" Justin handed it to him.

"Looks like a smushed penny, Justin." Mr. Cane handed the penny back.

"Pete told me a train could do this to a penny. I think it's the same one he put on the track for me before he left."

"Probably is. You can put it on your dresser and save it to remember the trip."

"Let me see it, Justin," Bebop said.

Justin handed the coin to Bebop. "Man, this thing is smushed good. It's flat as a flitter." Justin rolled his eyes; he knew were Bebop heard that word.

"Will you put one on the track for me, Mr. Cane?"

"Oh, I guess, so, Bebop." Mr. Cane reached in his pocket and got a penny and put it in the same spot where the other one was. "Okay, boys, let's get back in the truck and wait for Pete." Mr. Cane put his hands on the boys' shoulders and steered them back to the truck.

As they sat waiting in the truck, the caution light beside the track went from green to red. The warning bell started ringing, which meant that the train was within two miles of the station. Then the crossing gate at the road came down to prevent any cars from coming through. It was exciting, even for Mr. Cane. All three's eyes were fixed looking north when they saw in a distance the big locomotive coming down the track. It was electrifying. It amazed Justin how something so heavy could run down two tiny metal strips? It was almost magic.

Justin and Bebop wanted to get out of the truck and get closer to the track, but Mr. Cane thought it would be better for them to sit on the hood of the truck, Justin flung the door open and he and Bebop ran to the front of the truck where Mr. Cane lifted each one onto the hood.

In less than a minute, they saw the big locomotive come into to full view with its light beacon on the front moving from side to side and the horn blowing long and short bursts. As it grew closer, they could feel the ground begin to tremble. The whole place seemed to be trying to move.

As the train sped by in front of the pickup, Justin was intently watching where his dad had placed the coin. The brakes were making a terrible noise as the train slowed down. It scared Bebop so much that he grabbed Mr. Cane's arm and turned away, hiding his face. Mr. Cane put his arm around Bebop and held him tight to assure him nothing was going to happen.

The clanking of railway cars and the awesome power was unbelievable. With all the shaking, Justin was afraid the coin might have fallen off the track before the train got to it. The long train continued to go by until it finally came to a slow crawl. "Look-a-there, Justin, I just saw Pete go by in that passenger car," Mr. Cane said as Bebop popped his head back around to see.

"I didn't see him, Dad. Which one?" Justin said.

"The third one, right there in front of the depot. Good, that will make it easy to get Pete's things. It won't be as far to walk."

"Did Pete see us, Mr. Cane?" Bebop asked.

"I don't know, Bebop. He might have."

After the train slowed to a complete stop, people immediately started moving towards it and the luggage handlers, with their distinctive hats and coats, started rolling the luggage carts towards the luggage compartments to unload the baggage. Stepping from the train, the conductor folded the steps down on the passenger car and passengers began filing out one after another.

"Maybe he missed the train, Mr. Cane," Bebop said.

"Oh no, he's on there. He'll be stepping off in just a minute. Just hold on," Mr. Cane said.

A few more people got off, and then Pete stepped in the doorway and looked out. With his six-foot slim frame, dressed in trousers and suspenders, he looked as dignified as a Chicago lawyer getting off the train. Justin and Bebop yelled to him.

344

"Over here, Pete, we're over here!" They both jumped off the hood and made a dash for him.

Pete started smiling as soon as he spotted the boys and Mr. Cane.

"Hey, boys, I'm sure glad to see y'all," Pete said as he lowered his luggage to the ground.

Bebop ran to Pete and hugged him. That was a surprise for Pete. He wasn't expecting such a warm welcome. Justin was surprised too at Bebop's actions. He figured Bebop didn't know him as well as he did. Trying to help, Justin tried to pick up Pete's suitcase but found out quickly that it was too heavy.

"Better let me get that, Justin. That thing is pretty heavy," Pete said.

By that time, Mr. Cane had walked over to help. Pete stuck his hand out.

"Good to have you back, Pete," Mr. Cane said, shaking his hand.

"Cane, I'm glad to get back. It's been a long trip."

"Oh, I know it has. Everything go all right coming home?" Mr. Cane asked.

"Yes, sir, in fact, it did. The whole trip went better than I expected, considering the circumstances and all."

Pete looked at his watch and momentarily wondered what Naomi was doing and remembered what the man with the straw hat had said. As he walked towards the truck, he carried his suitcase briskly as if he had more energy than usual. Mr. Cane was noticing it too.

345

"You looking better to me, Pete. I'm glad the trip was okay." They walked a little further and reached the truck. "Let's get her loaded and head home."

"That's what I-I-I want to hear." Pete said, looking back at the train and gently placing the suitcase in the back.

Justin and Bebop had already crawled into the back of the truck. Pete opened his door and checked that Justin and Bebop were settled down behind the back glass.

"Justin, did you and Able get that penny?" Pete asked, about to get in.

"Bebop, Dad! Wait a minute. We gotta get Bebop's penny," Justin hollered.

"That's right. We about forgot about it after Pete got here. Y'all stay here and I'll go get it."

So they sat in the truck a few more minutes until the train pulled away. Mr. Cane got out and walked back to the track and found Bebop's penny. It too, was smashed "flat as a flitter."

"You boys, sit down now. Don't be standing up," Pete said turning in his seat and looking out the window.

"That's right," Mr. Cane said, handing Bebop his penny.

"We won't. We'll be all right, Dad," said Justin.

As they backed out of the station, Pete again, looked back at the train moving south toward Jackson, Mississippi one last time.

Cane and Able

* * * * *

Thirty-three

Mailbox Road

JEANNA WAS TOO scared to stop and rest. As she ran, the deep swamp of thickets and canes finally started opening up to larger oaks and sweetgums. Then, out of nowhere, there in front of her appeared a small gravel road. She dared to get on it, not knowing whether Big Doug had someone scouting it. She didn't have a choice though; she had to take a chance, hoping, maybe someone else would see her first. *Right or left?* she asked herself. She quickly looked up at the sky and said a short prayer. *Lord, help me make the right decision, I don't know which way.* She thought a moment about what she had just said, *Okay, right it is.* Half-running and half-walking, she started up the road looking and listening for any sign of hope. After a couple of miles the road started looking somewhat familiar, but she wasn't for sure. She was hoping that it was the road behind Pearl's house where she used to sneak off to. If it was, she'd know soon because there was an old landmark where an old house had burned some forty years before. If she remembered correctly, there was an old bell mounted on a pole there. The bell pre-dated the Civil War. If there ever was an emergency, the tenants or servants would run to the bell and ring it, signaling for their neighbors to come help.

Jeanna walked on the edge of the road to prevent the gravel from hurting her feet. The moist silky sand was beginning to soothe her sore feet, but not long enough before she heard a car coming in the distance. She decided to jump back into the woods and lay on the ground. Whoever it was, was driving slow and apparently looking for something. After it passed and at a safe distance, she got back on the road and kept looking for some clue as to where she was. It had been a long time since she had seen the place and it was more than likely overgrown and hidden. How could she find it? Probably gone by now, she figured. Then she heard another vehicle coming and it didn't sound like a truck. It had a rattle that she knew all too well. She jumped back into the woods again to hide. As she stepped into the woods, a covey of quail flew. She screamed and jumped as if the devil himself had caught her.

"Crap!" she hollered and then dove just in time to keep from being seen by the person in the car coming around the curve. Peeping from behind a stump, she could see that it was Big Doug's Cadillac. The birds flew right in front of his windshield.

Big Doug sensed something spooked them. He slowed down and stopped right beside where Jeanna was hunkered down. He turned his engine off and listened. Jeanna was breathing so hard, she was afraid he would hear her, so she put her hand over her mouth. She didn't move a muscle as Big Doug looked carefully for something moving in the woods. He had a good hunch something was out there, but without dogs it would be hard to find.

Please, Lord, let him go on, she whispered to herself.

Then she heard a car door shut and the engine crank, but the car did not move. Big Doug took a long, hard look before throwing his cigar out beside the road. It was so close that Jeanna could smell its pungent odor. The car started moving slow and Jeanna heard the gravel popping under the tires as it went by. She listened as the car continued to the top of the hill; then stopped again. She didn't move. There was dead silence for a moment. Then she heard the motor crank again as the car continued over the hill.

Jeanna made a dash down the road and around the short curve until she was were she was out of sight. As she slowed down to catch her breath, she could feel her heart pounding in her chest. Time was getting short, and she knew it. She had to pick up her pace.

"There you are, you little road runner," a voice boomed from the edge of the woods. She turned around in horror to see Big Doug leaning against a tree.

"But how? You just drove off." Her mouth was open and she was panting hard.

"Mistake, little Jeanna. You don't think too much. Yes, the car is gone, but I wasn't driving. Don't worry, though. It'll be back in a minute to give you a lift."

"You sorry son-of-a-bitch. I'll rather rot in hell than let you take me again."

"Well, get ready for hell then, baby," Big Doug said, stepping out of the woods for her.

"Not in your lifetime." Jeanna began running back in the way she came. Then she stopped. There were only two ways: down the road the way she was going or through the woods. The woods had been good thus far and were probably her best chance again, but where was that bell? Quickly she scrambled. Instinctively, she started running down the road to put as much distance as she could between her and Big Doug.

Big Doug started walking in the same direction. He was taking his time. He knew Henry and the dogs would be out shortly and Shorty would be back in a minute with his car. Big Doug stopped to hear the dogs coming. He smiled as he stood there and lighted another cigar. He could hear them coming.

* * * * *

OVERHEAD ABLE quavered, "Mr. Williams, I's think the Lord don't want me up here this close to him."

"Mr. Johnson, settle down. The Lord's glad to see you up here visiting. If he sees you flying around like this, he'd be liable to make an angel out of you," Gene bit down on the cigar and told Able to hold on. He was gonna get a little closer to the ground to see better.

As Gene pushed the stick forward, the plane pitched a good forty-five degrees in a downward dive. Able hung on for dear life.

"Hey, Mr. Johnson, what we looking for?"

"Huh, how about a landing strip?" Able said.

"Naw, come on man, what we looking for? We're about over Silver City now."

"I rightly don't know exactly, but I guess first we need to be looking for Big Doug's Cadillac. When we find it, we'll find him. Most likely Jeanna won't be far either."

"Okay then, at least that's a start. What color is it?"

"You can't miss it. Lime green!"

"All right then, Red Devil, let's find us a lime green Cadillac."

Gene pushed the stick further down, and the plane's altitude dipped even more.

"Hold on now, Mr. Johnson, we gonna get down here amongst these trees."

Able was holding on for safety but was starting to enjoy the ride some. As they circled over Silver City, they passed over the smoking ruins of Big Doug's house. Everything looked abandoned and there was no sign of life or movement anywhere. From the air they were able to get a good view of the layout of the swamp behind Big Doug's house. The creek that ran through it, looked like a long curvy snake, with marshes and wetlands on both sides. Able figured it would be hard for a skilled hunter to survive going through it, much less Jeanna.

"Whatcha think, Mr. Johnson?" Gene turned to talk.

"Let's stay this-a-way over the swamp." Able pointed to his right. "If she's trying to get away, she's probably headed right in to it," Able said.

"Sounds like a winner to me!" Gene yelled as he turned back around in his seat. They passed over and circled the swamp area once again and cut back west towards Belzoni.

"You reckon she headed south?" asked Gene, talking over his shoulder.

"Don't know, Mr. Gene. She might have. I's just don't know."

"Well, we'll head towards Yazoo City after we finish here. It's further for her to go, but she might have gotten turned around. Who knows?" Gene said.

Gene leveled the plane off a couple hundred feet above the tree tops and continued looking. He figured if the Cadillac were down below, they would surely see it at that level. They continued on for another five

353

minutes, but with no luck, he pulled back on the lever, raising the plane twenty degrees to get more altitude and then dipped towards Yazoo City. It was

Punching Williams on the back, Able hollered over the roar of the motor, "Mr. Gene, this is sho' the way to travel. It don't take no time to get somewhere up here."

"You right about that, Able. The only problem is though, is that you can't get out when you want to." Gene said, with the cigar clinched tightly between his teeth.

"You right about that. I sho' ain't thought about it that way," Able replied.

"Let's try going back towards Silver City and Belzoni again and try Mailbox Road and see what we see there," Williams shouted back to Able.

"Sounds okay to me. You doing the driving," Able said.

As the plane passed back over Silver City, they turned east and headed towards Mailbox Road. Mailbox Road was a shortcut to Belzoni from Tchula that was used before Highway 12 was paved. It was gravel and dusty, but it cut four miles off the trip.

Sure enough, the first pass over it, they spotted the lime green Cadillac. It was parked in the middle of the road, and there were two men standing beside it talking. The two men never even looked up.

As Gene banked the plane to the left, he could see what the two men were waiting on. There was a pack of hounds headed their way, about to cross the road. They could see two other men were with the dogs.

Gene made a wide circle and came back around for another look. When he did, he spotted movement running along the edge of the woods. It was Jeanna.

"That's her!" Able cried out, scrambling in his seat for a better view. He was pounding on Gene's back.

"Okay, Okay, I see. Easy on the shoulder, man. I'll make another pass."

As they made another pass, Gene brought the plane down to treetop level and tipped the plane up sideways hoping Jeanna could see Able. At first, she didn't recognize who or what was going on. She crouched down to hide, for fear of another one of Doug's buddies. Gene made another circle and came back over again and that time she saw Able pull his aviator hat off and wave. She immediately started jumping up and down.

"Able! Help! Please Able!" she hollered. "Help me please, help me." She fell on her knees crying.

"We gotta get to her, Mr. Gene!" Able hollered, looking instinctively for a door.

"Well, if you jump out of this plane, you ain't gonna help nobody. Stay cool, Mr. Johnson. We'll circle back one more time.

Gene pulled the stick back, and the plane began to rise. They could tell that Jeanna was not far from Pearl's house. But they could also tell that Big Doug and his bunch would surely catch her before she got there. Rising to about 700 feet and circling, Able looked out to his left, and couldn't believe his eyes. Coming up Highway 49 was that brand new Ford truck.

Able started beating on Gene's back again.

"Will you stop that, Johnson? That's my bad shoulder and it's sore as hell."

"Can't stop, Mr. Gene. Look down there on that road. See that new Ford truck?"

"Yeah, I see it." Gene hollered back.

"That's my boss man, Mr. Cane, coming from Yazoo City."

"It is, huh? Well, let's just pay him a visit."

* * * * *

MR. CANE HAD told Pete what had happened to Pearl. It was disturbing to Pete and figured it was just one more thing to add to his list. But in the back of his mind, he kept remembering what the man in the white straw hat had told him; his future would change for the good.

"How old you reckon Pearl was?" Cane asked.

"Oh, I guess she was up there pretty good. M-M-Maybe seventy or seventy two or about."

"Now, Mrs. Lucy, she's not that old is she?" Cane asked.

"Naw, sir. Mrs. Lucy, s-s-she's not that old. I expect she is a few years younger than Pearl. I-I-I tell you what though, them two together can beat any p-p-pair of domino players in the Delta."

"No kidding," Cane laughed.

"That's right, I remember when Candy and Dorothy would try to beat them, but they never could. They were just too good a team."

"Yeah, that Candy…and Dorothy, we sure miss them." Cane said, sadly.

"Well, I-I-I believe it when they say the good die young." Pete remarked looking out the window.

"I agree, I agree with you on that," Cane responded. "Time flies, don't it Pete?"

"Sho' does." Pete said, as he squinted his eyes and looked up the road.

"Say, Cane, is that a bird coming at us?"

"Hell, I hope not. If it is, we in trouble. That sucker is bigger than this truck."

"Watch out!!!" Pete yelled ducking in his seat.

Cane turned the truck hard, running off the shoulder. Dust was flying out from under the truck as it ran another twenty yards getting back on the pavement.

"Man, did you see that?" hollered Pete.

"Did I? That son of a—" Cane stopped short. He glanced back at the boys before continuing in a near whisper. "He nearly wiped us out! Pete looked in the back. Both boys had been tossed to one side of the truck and were on their knees, crawling back to the front. Pete could see out the right side that the plane had made a circle and was coming again.

"Here it comes again! Get down kids," Pete shouted out the window.

This time the plane came across the windshield of the truck, missing it only fifty feet.

"Did you see that?" Cane paused and thought about it. "My gosh, Pete, did you see what I thought I saw?"

"I don't know. What did you see?" Pete asked. Cane didn't say anything.

The plane banked hard and was coming back again across the road in front of the truck. This time Cane ran off the shoulder again. He almost lost control of the truck, but he was able to get it back on the road. Justin and Bebop were rolling around in the back like two watermelons. That's when Justin started banging on the roof.

"Dad, Dad, that's Abe flying that airplane." Justin said, trying to holler in the side glass.

"Sit down, boy, before you get thrown out," yelled Mr. Cane to the boys and then looked at Pete and said. "What the hell? That's exactly what I thought I saw, too."

"I know. Me too," Pete glanced at Cane.

"What in the devil's going on?" Cane said.

"Don't know, Cane, but that ain't what a crop duster's supposed to be doing, for sure."

Gene Williams told Able, "Mr. Johnson, hold on to that stick in front of you and don't move it."

Able looked down and for a brief moment imagined he was a fighter pilot. "Yes, sir, Mr. Gene."

As soon as Gene let go of the controls, Able pulled back on the stick. The plane shot straight up. The higher he got, the harder he pulled back to hang on. The plane made a complete 360° loop in the air. Gene had to fight to get the control back.

"Johnson! If you're gonna fly tricks in this baby, let me know first. Look, just hold the damn controls steady, no forward or backward motions, just steady. Okay?" Able could barely get a word out. He had scared himself to death.

"Uh, yes, sir." Gene looked back over his shoulder again and gently let go of the controls. Able looked straight at the control stick, holding it with both hands trying not to move it. *Okay, Red Devil, it's me and you and the Lord this time.*

Gene reached down beside his leg and pulled out a chalkboard. He started scribbling on it. Then he told Able to let go, he'd take control again.

Able gently let go, wiping the sweat off his brow.

"Hold on, we're going back!" yelled Gene. Then he pulled back on the control stick. The plane rolled up and over, making a complete somersault again. Able closed his eyes and began praying as hard as he could.

As Gene approached the truck again, he could see Cane and Pete trying to crouch down in their seats, as the plane was meeting them head on. Just before he got to the truck, he pulled up and rolled and tossed the chalkboard out. It fell about fifty yards in front of the truck on the side of the road and tumbled down the shoulder of the road.

Again, Cane ran off the road. "Damn it, Able, you cause me to hurt this truck, I'm gonna kill your ...." He paused and changed his words. "We gonna have it out." Cane looked at Pete with a serious look his face.

"Naw, you won't have to, Cane. I'm gonna kill his black ass for both us."

"Thank you," Cane said. "That's what wanted to say."

"Cane, I think they dropped something out of the plane right there." Pete was pointing to the spot. Cane had not seen it fall. "Pull over, tight here," Pete said.

Cane hit his brakes, and slid to a halt as Pete jumped out and picked it up.

"What's is it?" Cane asked.

"Trouble. Looks like big trouble," Pete said, looking at the chalkboard. "'Says, Spotted Jeanna on Mailbox Road/ Running to Pearl's/ Big Doug behind her.'"

"Where's Mailbox Road, Pete?"

"Don't worry, I know just where it is. I used to pick Dorothy up there a long time ago."

"Show me the way then," Cane said. "Kids, y'all hang on tight."

Pete jumped back in the truck, and Cane burned rubber, throwing gravel everywhere. Justin and Bebop didn't know what was going on, but it didn't really matter to them. They were enjoying Mr. Cane showing them what his new truck would do.

The plane came back over the truck one last time and headed in the same direction of Mailbox Road. Gene tipped his wings to say, sorry. Justin and Bebop were on their knees, waving as hard as they could. Able was waving back and saluted. The boys saluted back. In a minute the plane was out of sight, though the boys continued to watch for it.

Cane pushed the accelerator down harder until the four-barrel kicked in on the Ford's V-8 engine. Bebop and Justin hunkered down next to the cab of the truck enjoying the trill of it all.

Patrolman Campbell was now patrolling Highway 49 en route to Yazoo City. He had noticed the crop duster making odd turns, but it was too far away to tell if anything was out of the ordinary. Crop dusters usually buzzed the skies of the Delta every day. An extra flip or roll didn't appear strange or send up any red flags for anybody in that area.

He was cruising about fifty-five miles per hour, his usual speed, and was enjoying the drive. He had just picked his car up from having the fan belt replaced and a wash-and-wax job at the downtown Gulf station in Belzoni. The police radio was silent, and it appeared that the morning was going to be a quiet one. In the distance though, he saw a vehicle approaching across the flat Delta highway. He could tell that it was speeding because dust was being whirled to the side of it more than usual.

He had an eye for that. He could usually spot a speeding vehicle within a mile away.

Well, so much for a quiet morning, he thought, as the speeding truck passed him, nearly blowing him off the road.

"What the hell!" Campbell shouted. He slammed his brakes, turned the wheel and did a complete U-turn in the middle of the road. When he did, he floored it. The patrol car fishtailed as it smoked the tires leaving two strips of burned rubber on the highway. He grabbed for his radio but hesitated. He figured he could handle it alone. In his mind he was saying to himself, "Damn idiot, I'll put your ass under the jail for this."

As Cane saw Patrolman Campbell approaching rapidly, he pulled over. The patrol car came up, nearly ramming them from behind. The car stopped inches from the tailgate.

Justin and Bebop stood up as soon as Patrolman Campbell stopped.

"Hi! Mr. Campbell. How you doing?" Justin shouted, as Patrolman Campbell got out, looking completely confused, but recognizing the kid.

"Uh, young fellow, we meet again" he said as he walked by removing his sunglasses, "and who do we have here?" Campbell walked up beside the truck very cocky, now expecting Able again.

Cane opened the door and got out.

Campbell was searching for words. "I thought this was..."

"Officer Campbell," Cane was squinting his eyes to read his badge. "I'm sorry for speeding and I don't know what you are thinking, but we're in an emergency situation here, and with all due respect, we need your help and at the same time need to get the heck out of here now!"

Patrolman Campbell was trying to make since out of what Cane was saying. "What do you mean, emergency?

Pete looked at Cane and told him, "Cane, you go to Pearl's, and I'll go to Mailbox Road with the patrolman . I'll explain everything on the way to him. Go! Go! Go now!"

"Boys, y'all jump up here with me," Mr. Cane said to Justin and Bebop.

Justin and Bebop hurried around and slid across the seat from the driver's side. Campbell and Pete ran to the patrol car. Then Mr. Cane jumped in behind the boys, put the truck in gear and gunned it. He threw gravel and dirt all over the front of Patrolman Campbell's newly washed car.

As Justin and Bebop looked through the rear glass, they could barely see the patrol car through the smoke screen created by the Ford truck.

Mr. Cane didn't waste any time reaching ninety-five miles per hour in the new truck. He told the boys to be still and keep quiet because he didn't have time to answer any questions. Sensing danger, Justin and Bebop did as he said and sat still. Patrolman Campbell was right behind them, with Pete filling him in on the details about the message they had just received from Able.

* * * * *

Thirty-four

The Save

CIRCLING THE RUNWAY, Gene Williams was trying to position the plane for a landing. "Hold on, back there, Able, we're fixing to have to do a little trick here," Gene hollered back.

"What you mean, a trick?" Able said.

"Just hold on."

Coming in at ninety miles per hour was no piece of cake on a 400-foot runway. The runway needed to be twice that long for a safe landing, but that was not what Gene Williams had. The landowner next to him wouldn't sell the acreage needed, so Gene didn't have a choice. Pre-load on take offs and hit hard on landings was the way he had to do it.

"Here we go, Mr. Johnson. You've been a good student so far. Let's see how you do for the final exam."

Able pulled his aviator hat down on his head and adjusted his goggles, as Gene banked the plane to the right and aimed the plane for the runway. He gently pushed the control in a downward motion until the plane was about sixty feet off the ground. The plane was all but skimming the sixty foot trees below. One slip of the control stick and the wheels could easily snag a treetop.

Gene slowly pulled the lever back, creating drag, which made the plane feel as if it were floating. By performing the unorthodox maneuver, he was within five knots of stalling the plane. But it was necessary to make the landing. As the plane cleared the last trees, he pushed forward again, and the plane dove sharply. The forceful blow of the front wheel hitting the ground jarred Able so much that he thought they were crashing. The plane bounced four or five times, violently, sometimes as high as twenty feet. Gene stood on both brake pedals as hard as he could, rising in his seat a good twelve inches. Able was preparing for the end when he saw the wall of trees coming at him. He knew with the speed they had, there was no way to stop. Then all of sudden, he was thrown to his side and pressed against the side panel of the passenger seat. The G-force was so great he couldn't stay straight. The plane turned around two complete times at the end of the runway, plowing up grass and dirt, before it came to a rest.

"Piece of cake. Done it a couple hundred times probably, but you know what? Never done it with a passenger before. What do you think about this Red Devil, Mr. Johnson?" Gene asked, turning around in his seat with his cigar stub clinched in his teeth.

Able didn't hear him ask anything; he was hanging over the side, spilling his guts out. Williams just chuckled as he crawled out onto the wing and jumped down. He never turned around to check on Able, knowing Able would feel better in a few minutes

*   *   *   *   *

JEANNA HAD RUN as far as she could down the gravel road before she headed back in the woods. Big Doug and Shorty would be coming soon. As she stepped in, she realized she was at the exact place she had been looking for all along. Surely, the Lord was at work, she thought. Fighting her way through the briars and under growth, she made her way to the old house site. Behind honeysuckle, she saw the bell nestled comfortably in the weeds. She could see that the bell still had a chain hooked to it. Apparently someone, maybe kids had played with it and rigged up a way to ring it. She didn't know, but didn't have much time to think about it. She scrambled to the post pulled away the vines that clung to it and grasped the chain in her hand.

She held her breath and said, *Lord, please don't let You be the only one hearing this bell ring.* Then she tried to correct herself. *No! No! I didn't mean that.*

She started again. *Lord, if no one hears this bell but You, then that's all right with me. You know best.*

With those few words, she pulled down with all her might. The bell rang out as loud as it had ever rung in years. It echoed through the hills and down the hollows. In all the time she knew of the bell, she had never heard it ring so beautifully. She pulled it again and again. She was smiling with excitement, as if she were ringing it for all the saints in heaven to hear. Then reality sank in. She had to run. Big Doug would hear the bell, too.

Patrolman Campbell and Pete had reached Mailbox Road, but they didn't know where to go, so they had pulled over to the side of the road and were standing outside the car listening for anything. The message from Able and the pilot just read "Mailbox Road/ Running to Pearl's/ Big Doug behind her." That was not enough. Then they heard the bell ringing.

"What was that ringing?" Officer Campbell asked Pete.

"I think I know!" yelled Pete. "That's the bell at the old Fletcher place. That's where she is."

Pete and Campbell jumped back in the car and spun out in direction of the Fletcher Place.

Jeanna couldn't stay any longer ringing the bell. She had to keep running. At least now she had her bearings. No sooner had she stopped ringing the bell and headed into the woods, then Big Doug and Shorty drove up. Some three hundred yards behind them in the middle of the road, straggled Henry and the dogs. They had just emerged from the woods and were on Jeanna's new trail. It wouldn't be long before they would have their prize.

As Able thanked Gene Williams, he heard the bell ringing. Gene wished Able luck. Able immediately knew where the sound was coming from and what it meant. He and Bebop had rang the bell once when they had been squirrel hunting. He had told Bebop about the old Fletcher house and told him why people had bells. Bebop wanted to ring it so Able found a broken porch chain in the truck and hooked it up. Bebop rang the bell so many times that before he stopped, three neighbors had come up to see what was wrong. One had come from two miles away. "Old timers" apparently never forgot about the importance of the bell. It sure made a believer out of Bebop.

Apparently, Jeanna hadn't forgotten either. He knew she didn't have much time but he hoped she'd have enough time to make it another quarter mile through the hollow to Pearl's bottom before Big Doug caught up to her. Dear Lord, help her, he thought? Able knew he had to make it to Aunt Pearl's and fast. He jumped in the pickup and began backing up when Gene hollered at him.

"Wait a minute, Johnson, I'm going with you." Gene ran around the other side.

"Better hold on, then, I'm flying this plane." Able said.

"Let her rip, then," Gene said, as he jumped in.

Able peeled out backward and called on Ole Red to give him all it had. Ole Red did just that too, as it sped off towards Aunt Pearl's house slinging gravel everywhere.

*   *   *   *   *

"GO GET'EM, BOY!" hollered coon hunter Henry. "Here, here now, look good, now." The Doberman was getting a strong scent. He was pulling and dragging both Al and Herman down and through the brush. Between the two of them, they could hardly restrain the animal. Every four or five steps, the old bloodhound would bark. Big Doug and Shorty were right behind Henry and the pack. They crossed the ditch, continued into the woods and eased down the first big hollow.

Jeanna, had made it through the woods and was coming up on a worn-down barbed wire fence. She could see Pearl's house from there, a straight shot up a long tall hill. It would take every ounce of energy she had left to make it to the top. She just hoped that she had enough time to make it before the dogs caught her. The old milk cow started walking towards her, its cowbell clanking around her neck.

As Jeanna started across the open field, Able and Gene wheeled into Pearl's drive.

"Hold on, Mr. Williams. I gotta go in and get an equalizer out of the house." Able said.

"Don't worry about me. I keep one right here in my back pocket. I never go nowhere without it." Gene reached in and pulled out the .38 caliber revolver from his jeans.

"Just hold on, I'll be right back, then." Able ran up the steps and returned with a .22 rifle. "Let's go!" As they started around the house, Mr. Cane drove up.

"Where's Jeanna?" Mr. Cane hollered.

"Don't know yet, Mr. Cane," Able hollered back. "We heading down the back forty and hope we finds her."

"Justin, you and Bebop take my truck," Mr. Cane was pointing in the direction of Mrs. Lucy's house. "Go down the road here to Mrs. Lucy's. Tell her to call the sheriff quick. She'll be the first house you'll come to on the right. Then y'all stay there." The boys stared back at Mr. Cane. "You hear me?" he repeated. "You go there and stay there."

"You want me to drive, Dad?" Justin asked honored to help.

"That's right. You can do it. I gotta good feeling this ain't the first time you drove this truck anyway." Mr. Cane said, as he looked down at him suspiciously.

Bebop looked at Justin, and Justin looked at Bebop. Bebop shrugged his shoulders.

"All right now, go, get, go, go! We don't have much time!" Mr. Cane shouted.

Justin and Bebop ran to the new Ford truck, and Justin got under the wheel. He put it in reverse and took off, peeling gravel. Bebop couldn't believe what he was seeing. Justin was handling the truck just like a race driver. They left the drive spinning gravel for all it was worth. Mr. Cane looked back over his shoulder at the boys leaving and then looked at Able. Able just shrugged his shoulders and said. "That boy sho' catches on fast, don't he?"

As Justin sped down the gravel road and into the first curve, the Ford truck got sideways. "Hold on, Bebop, here comes a big curve." Justin pulled down on the steering wheel trying to correct the sliding truck. It straightened up, but Bebop didn't loosen his grip on to the door. He was wondering how Justin could know all this from just the hay truck.

"Justin, you done learned how to drive good! How'd you learn this good and never drove this truck before?" Bebop asked.

"Bebop, I'm just good. That's all. Hang on." He stomped it, and the four-barrel kicked in as they hit the straightaway. "And I had a good teacher, too."

As they made the next curve up the road, they came upon a tractor pulling a two-row planter that was taking the entire road. Blowing the horn, Justin hit the brakes and got in right behind it. They slowed down to nearly nothing.

"What we gonna do, Justin?" Bebop said.

The tractor driver was smiling and looked with great pride. He was taking up the whole road and he didn't care. He wasn't about to pull over.

"Well, Bebop, I'm fixin' to give you a lesson in passing. Watch this."

Justin jerked the truck into the right-hand ditch and gunned it. The tractor driver didn't know what to do. He couldn't believe somebody would attempt to pass like that. Bebop was holding on for his life. The truck was leaning over in the ditch on its side. Mud was slinging out the back, and the powerful V-8 engine was screaming. Bebop could've touched the ground if he had of stuck his hand out.

The tractor driver immediately jerked his big rig to the left giving them room to get back on the road. As they passed, the tractor driver gave them some hand language that Bebop returned in an instant. Something else they had learned in the hay field.

"Way to go, Justin, we got him!"

Pete and Patrolman Campbell had entered the woods right behind Big Doug. They could hear the dogs. The hunters were yelling at each other. Big Doug was cursing every other word and sounded out of breath. He had reached the open area too and could see Jeanna scrambling up the hill.

"Let'em go," Big Doug said. Henry just looked at him in disbelief. "I said let'em go. Now!"

"Them dogs gonna tear that girl apart, Doug," Henry said.

"Who cares? She's done caused me more trouble than she's worth. Do as I said."

"But, Mr. Doug," implored Al.

Big Doug pulled his revolver out and stuck it to Al's head. "You gonna let them dogs go, or do I have to let this hammer go. Which is it?"

Al and Herman reached down and unleashed the Doberman. It immediately crawled under the fence and went for Jeanna. The dog had her in full sight. It was just a matter of time until he captured his prey.

Jeanna turned to see the dog coming. It appeared that the dog was leaping in ten-foot strides. She turned back around and looked up the hill. She would never make it. She was crying so hard that she couldn't catch her breath.

"Oh, Lord, please don't let me go like this!" she cried out loud.

No quicker had she said the words then she heard a voice. "Jeanna! Go for the barn!"

It was Able coming down the hill. Mr. Cane and Gene were behind him. Big Doug saw Able and then saw Mr. Cane and Gene. He knew his best bet was to turn back into the woods and head back to his car. The Doberman knew no difference and was now within a hundred yards of Jeanna. Jeanna turned to look again and stumbled, turning her ankle. She tried to crawl towards Able on one knee, but she could go no further. She was completely exhausted.

Able could see what was about to happen. He stopped long enough to get a shot but knew he couldn't stop the dog with just a .22

caliber gun even if he hit it. His only chance was to outrun the dog to Jeanna, so he threw the gun to Mr. Cane and started running down the hill as fast as he could.

"Come on, Able! Come on, Able, faster! Come on Able 4:5!" Able didn't realize what he was saying at the time, but he was quoting what Justin said when he put Big Doug out with the rock.

The Doberman was in full stride coming up the hill and was within ten feet of Jeanna when he made his final lunge towards her neck. His mouth was opened and ready to make the kill he had been trained for. Able leapt through the air, his hands and arms extended. As they both were in midair, Able's big hands reached for the dog's throat. With Able's momentum, he knocked the dog off balance, and the dog fell short of Jeanna. Able fell across Jeanna's bruised legs. He turned just as the Doberman lunged for him and caught him in the neck with one hand. With his other hand he pulled himself up and stood up. The dog flailed helplessly in Able's clutched fist. Jeanna was still trying to crawl away when Mr. Cane and Gene got to her to help. Able picked the ninety-pound dog up with one hand, as the dog was still twisting and trying to fight. He continued to hold the Doberman in his hand with his arm fully extended and began to squeeze. Gene could not believe the strength of Able as he heard the bones begin to crack in the dog's neck. Able clutched tighter until all the life had faded from the killer dog. Then, looking at Henry, he dropped the dead dog and started walking toward him. Henry and the others let their leashes go and turned for the woods. As the dogs ran forward, the men retreated.

Pete and Patrolman Campbell had started through the woods towards Pearl's when they heard someone coming. They stopped. They could see a figure moving but could not make it out. As they paused, they saw that it was Big Doug.

"Hold on, Mr. Campbell, this man is gonna be armed," Pete said.

Patrolman Campbell drew his revolver and moved slowly towards Big Doug.

"Hold it right there, mister."

Big Doug froze as Pete and Mr. Campbell walked over to him. Big Doug appeared extra calm, his pistol down by his side.

"You sure gotta a lot of guts coming this far after that girl," Patrolman Campbell said. "Now drop that pistol slowly or I'm gonna blow a hole in you as big as that Cadillac you drive."

"You sure talk big for a lawman," said Big Doug.

"Well, as long as I got this .357 on your ass, I can do that. It kinda goes with the territory you might say."

Then a voice came from behind Pete and Patrolman Campbell. "Lawman, your territory has just shrunk, and your ass now belongs to Big Doug because I got this here rifle pointed right at your head."

They turned around slowly and saw Shorty standing there pointing his rifle at them.

"You ain't so tough now, are you, big Lawman?" Shorty walked up to Campbell and hit him in the face with the butt of his rifle, knocking him to the ground. Pete flinched towards Shorty, but stopped when Shorty directed the gun at him.

Pete looked hard at Shorty, letting him know that he didn't like what had just happened. Big Doug reached over and picked the .357 up that had fallen when Patrolman Campbell was hit in the face. Then he placed his huge foot on the side of Campbell's head, pressing the side of his face in the mud. As the trooper's head sank, blood mixed with mud pressed out around his head. The more pressure Doug put on his head, the more blood ran out Campbell's broken nose. Then Big Doug cocked the .357 and put the gun to Campbell's head.

"Don't!" hollered Pete. "He hasn't done anything to you. He was only doing his job. He had a chance to kill you, but he didn't. Don't kill him."

"Yeah, you're right, bro. Maybe I'll let this whitey live out of the goodness of my heart."

Pete seemed to be relieved when suddenly the awesome sound of the .357 exploded. The splatters of matter went all over Pete. For a moment, Pete was scared to look at what was left of Campbell's head. Then he saw that Big Doug had moved the gun and shot a hole in the ground six inches from Campbell's head. It was mud on Pete's face from the explosion, not brains. No doubt, the explosion had blown Campbell's eardrums, but at least he was still alive.

Able had just crossed the fence when he heard the shot fired. He knew no one had a gun like that except Patrolman Campbell. Surely Campbell killed Big Doug, he thought. Able hurried faster towards the direction of the sound.

* * * * *

Thirty-five

Fletcher's Miracle

MR. CANE AND Gene helped Jeanna back to Pearl's house. Mr. Cane carried her inside and put her in Aunt Pearl's bed. Gene went to the kitchen and searched for some first aid supplies. He then hurried back to the bedroom with some antiseptic cream and clothes.

"These wounds need attention," said Gene.

"I know. If you will, huh— Mr. Cane searching for a name.

"Williams, Gene Williams," interjected Gene.

"Okay, Gene," said Mr. Cane. "If you will, stay here with Jeanna and do what you can. I've got to go find Able." Mr. Cane turned his ear to window when he heard gravel crackling outside.

"Must be Justin." He hurried to the door and saw Bebop and Justin getting out of the new Ford truck.

"Boy, I'm glad to see y'all! Have any trouble?" Mr. Cane asked as he walked over to them.

"None, Dad, everything was okay." Bebop looked at Justin and then the muddy truck. "We did just like you said. We told Mrs. Lucy to call the sheriff and tell him to get out here quick."

Looking at Justin squinting his eyes, Mr. Cane said, "By the way, I thought I told you boys to stay at Mrs. Lucy's."

"You did, Dad, but we thought you might need your truck."

Looking around, Mr. Cane saw that his truck was the only one there.

"Huh. You're right, Justin, Great! Okay now, y'all go inside and help Mr. Williams with Jeanna."

"Where you going, Dad?" Justin asked.

"I'm going to help Able. I'll be back in a little while."

"Can we go, Dad," Justin pleading.

"No way. You've already done enough. Good job! Both of you!"

Mr. Cane walked around the house towards the back pasture and down to the woods. By now, coon hunter Henry and the dogs had made a run for it. They wanted no part of what was going on.

Mr. Cane walked in a brisk pace down the hill towards the woods. His eyes were focused on the dead dog as he passed by it. He knew to be cautious and not to be in too much of a hurry, because that was how mistakes were made and mistakes can cost you your life. The closer he got to the wood line and fence, the more tense he became. It was not a good feeling. He had not felt that tense since the war. However, he reminded himself that he was the hunter, not the hunted.

By now Big Doug had Patrolman Campbell and Pete tied to each other with a dog leash. He couldn't make up his mind whether to shoot them or use them as hostages. He had beaten both of them. It was questionable whether or not Campbell would make it. He needed treatment immediately.

Shorty was griping that they needed to hurry because the law would be coming soon. Big Doug didn't like that kind of pressure. He was used to being in control. Now, he was also getting pressure from a short guy that he was growing to dislike by the minute.

"Come on, Doug, make your damn mind up. Whatcha gonna do? We don't have time for this. Kill'em and let's get out of here."

"Killing might be a mistake right now. I'd rather do it later," Big Doug said.

"Come on then, if you ain't gonna kill'em, just let me have the gun. I'll do it for you." Shorty was surprised when Big Doug threw the gun to him and called his bluff.

"Uh!" Shorty said changing his mind, "Look, if you want to leave them, we can."

"No way. You gonna do it," Big Doug said. "You said you would. Now do it." Shorty froze without saying anything. "Put your money where your mouth is," Big Doug grunted out.

Shorty looked over at Big Doug, then walked over to Campbell pointing the pistol at the back of Campbell's head. He cocked the gun. His hand was shaking.

"Pull the trigger, Shorty, you weasel. You pissant. You cop lover."

By now, Able had managed to sneak within a short distance of Big Doug and was watching Shorty getting his nerve up to fire, but he was helpless.

What do I do, Lord? I need help. This can't happen, Able prayed.

Then all of sudden and out of nowhere, a squirrel jumping for a limb in the tree above missed his mark and fell next to Shorty. It frightened Shorty so bad that he flinched and fired. Seeing what it was, he drew the gun up and fired at the fox squirrel scampering across the ground. He missed. Embarrassed, he started chasing the crazy squirrel through the woods, firing at it randomly and cursing. He was coming right towards Able.

Able was ready to make his move as Shorty came by. With one hand outreached from behind the a tree, Able grabbed Shorty by the throat and lifted him two feet off the ground, just like he had done with the Doberman. With one twist, he broke Shorty's windpipe. Able lowered Shorty to the ground gently. Shorty never uttered a sound.

"Hey, Shorty, where you at, boy?" hollered Big Doug. "Hey now, where you at?"

Big Doug started looking around, feeling uncomfortable when there was no reply from Shorty. He knew Able was near. He figured he best be making tracks fast. He walked back over to Pete and Campbell. Both were well aware of their probable fate. Big Doug pulled his other revolver and aimed at Campbell. Campbell closed his eyes tight.

"You sorry lawmen, you all need to die. You nothing but maggots."

As sudden as chimes of a cathedral sing and split a cold frigid air, equally, the ear-piercing sound of three loud rings echoed through the forest. "What in the— ? Who's ringing that damn bell again."

Big Doug turned around and listened closer, holding his hand over his injured ear where Justin had screamed in it. He knew that if he fired now, it would bring more attention.

"You two pissants are lucky," he said as he uncocked the revolver.

He left Pete and Campbell where they were and headed back through the woods towards his car. The further he went, the quicker he went. With his 400-pound frame he was winded and near exhaustion, but it wasn't much further to the car. The closer he got the more the bell sounded like it was amplified.

"Who is ringing that damn bell?" he thought. He stopped and listened. Then he heard footsteps behind him. He side-stepped behind a large walnut tree. As he heard the footsteps getting closer, he knew it had to be Able. He waited. It was hard for him to hold his breath so as not to be detected, but he remained still.   Then he saw a silhouette moving through the trees. If Able was behind him, who was ringing the bell, he wandered.

Again the loud deep sounding echo of the bell rang three times. This time it had an eerie cry that sent chills down his spine.

The sound of the bell was getting on his nerves. He knew if it continued it would arouse other's curiosity and they would come soon.

Again, the shrill sound of the bell rang three times bringing a sweat to his forehead and spooking a hoot owl from its roost.

"Who is ringing that damn bell?" he repeated to himself under his breath.

As Able walked right by the tree Doug was standing behind, Doug clubbed him in the head with the butt of his pistol. Able fell to the ground, but not before he grabbed Big Doug by the leg twisting it, bringing him down with him. It was like felling a big oak tree.

Big Doug's dropped his pistol as he tried to regain his balance. Quickly they both scrambled for it, but only knocked the gun further out of reach. Able then hit Big Doug as hard as he could, landing a fist against his skull. Able's powerful blow didn't seem to affect Big Doug much. Big Doug got to his feet as Able was doing the same. Doug immediately charged Able and pinned him against a tree. Then Doug reached around the tree and squeezed Able as hard as he could. Able heard a rib pop as he was being crushed into the tree.

"Boy, you don't know who you messing with. Listen to me. Your sister is my property, and I can do what I want with her. You hear me?" Big Doug told Abe as he continued to put pressure on him.

"I don't hear anything, but this." Able said.

Able managed to bend his knee as Big Doug adjusted for another power-squeeze. Able's knee caught Big Doug right in the groin. Big Doug let out a scream and doubled over in pain. Able connected with a mighty upper cut to the head, sending Big Doug reeling backwards. Big Doug fell right on top of his gun. Able didn't have time to react. Doug pulled the gun up and fired, hitting Abe in the left shoulder. Flesh and bone exploded as the force of the .357 magnum knocked Able against the tree. Big Doug fired again but missed. Able, still standing, managed to scramble to the backside of the tree while Big Doug fired three more rounds that ripped chunks of bark from the tree. Another round hit Able in his leg. Blood spewed out of his leg as the bullet left its gaping mark. Able was knocked to the base of the big tree. Big Doug walked up to him and pointed the gun at his head.

"Hey, you, Big Boy," a voice came from behind Big Doug.

Big Doug turned around. Before he could focus, a four-inch limb caught him right below the lip, smashing his jaw and sending teeth flying.

385

Mr. Cane had circled around, rung the bell for help and then moved back into the woods to find Able.

Big Doug hit the ground and then staggered back to his feet. Mr. Cane swung as hard as he could and connected again with a blow to Big Doug's shoulder blade. Big Doug hit the ground again. Mr. Cane knew he was no match for Big Doug, but he was making considerable progress with the stick. A few more blows and Big Doug would be out cold. He needed to knock him out.

Mr. Cane swung again, but this time, Big Doug stopped the swing with his forearm. The limb broke over his arm. With Big Doug's other hand, he grabbed Mr. Cane by the shirt and butted his forehead into his nose. Blood went everywhere. Mr. Cane fell to the ground with his face turning into a sheet of red muddy slime. Then Big Doug kicked him in the ribs. Mr. Cane immediately held his side and gasp for breath. As he lay there on the ground, twitching and gasping for breath, he spotted Able and tried his best to crawl towards him while Big Doug looked for the gun again.

"You alright, buddy?" Mr. Cane asked Able, reaching and putting his hand on Able's wounded leg. Able was barely able to talk but smiled, knowing Mr. Cane was there.

"I's be okay, Mr. Cane. It's just a little scratch."

Each man looked at the other and could tell they were both in bad shape.

"Your nose is broke, I think, Mr. Cane."

Mr. Cane kinda laughed. "I think my whole body is broke Able, not just my nose." Then they both laughed.

"Don't worry, Mr. Cane, the Lord gonna get us out of this mess. He always do.   Apostles 2:2."

"Well, Able, I hope you're right about that scripture. 'Cause we don't have room for error."

Big Doug finally found his gun and walked over to the tree where both men were lying. Able was lying against the base of the tree with his eyes closed. Mr. Cane was at Able's feet with his eyes opened, looking directly at Big Doug. Big Doug brought the .357 up and pointed it at Mr. Cane.

"So here's one for you, Mr. Cane and Mr. Johnson," said Big Doug aiming.

As Big Doug squeezed the trigger of the .357, Mr. Cane threw his body over Able's. The sound waves of the blast echoed through the forest as if in the Grand Canyon. Mr. Cane's body slumped on Able's leg. The shot had taken a good inch of meat off his side as it passed. Big Doug cocked the massive pistol again and aimed at Mr. Cane's head to finish him.

As he did, the haunting shrill sound of the bell rung three more times through the trees.

Big Doug paused as he heard the sound of the bell again. It must have been within forty yards now. He turned in the direction of the sound. Mr. Cane barely opened his eyes. The fire in his side was like a hot branding iron piercing through him. He heard the bell ring again, too. Then the wind mysteriously picked up.

The bell shouted again three times. This time, so loudly that it produced a rainfall of leaves.

Able put his hand on Mr. Cane's back and patted him. It was a pat like a father would give his son, letting him know he was secure. Able closed his eyes and started praying.

"Oh, Lord, takes care of Mr. Cane for me. We's all need him."

Big Doug was furious and started toward the bell. Every time it rang, his temper intensified. The piercing sound was getting louder and louder in his head. He was holding his ears, trying to block the sound as it rang. He was breaking limbs with his bare hands, raging and plowing through the woods. He still had his gun in his hand, aiming it in the direction of the sound. He staggered from tree to tree as if he were a blind man with the sound of the bell his homing device.

Then he saw it. The bell. He wiped his huge hand over his blurry eyes trying to clear blood for a better vision. Then the bell stopped ringing.

Standing there holding the chain with both hands was Justin. He didn't move as Big Doug stumbled from the woods, looking straight at him.

"So it's you, ringing that bell, huh, boy? Ole Rock boy! I believe I owe you a little something from the last time we met, don't I?" Big Doug rubbed the back of his head where Justin had landed a 25-pound rock.

"Come here, boy," Big Doug said. Justin didn't move.

"Can't you hear, boy?" He raised his voice. "I said, bring your nappy ass here."

Justin still didn't move. He gripped the chain and started slowly pulling it down. The bell barely rang at first. Then he pulled harder and rang it again. He was scared to death but kept pulling. Justin knew he was about to die, but he knew he needed help.

Big Doug brought his pistol up to aim at Justin. "Drop the damn chain, boy!" Big Doug shouted as he was trying to protect his injured eardrum with his other hand.

Big Doug moved forward, step by step, carefully placing one foot in front of the other. He walked to within thirty yards of Justin. He knew he had only one shot left, and he needed it to count. He stepped closer to get within range. Justin's small frame was shaking from head to toe; the chain still clinched in his grip. To pull the chain harder, he jumped way into the air to bring all his weight down on it.

Ring,

Ring, ring.

The bell started ringing. Justin had to jump off the ground to pull the chain each time. Each time he dangled from the chain, he closed his eyes and prayed. Beads of sweat had popped out on his forehead and were running down his flustered cheeks as he waited for the sound of the gun.

Ring, ring, ring.

Big Doug grabbed for his ears with both hands. "I said stop ringing that bell!"

Big Doug carefully lifted his pistol and drew a bead on Justin's little frame as it bobbed up and down. As he squeezed the trigger, suddenly, someone from his side hollered at him.

"Hey, fatso!" Alarmed, he swung around and fired his final bullet into the thicket, cutting a limb into right above Bebop's head. Bebop's eyes were as big as saucers. He froze, then jumped for cover like a rabbit. Big Doug began to lose his balance and stepped backward dropping his gun. When he did, his foot stepped through a rotten board and then another. The ground was giving way under him.

"What's happening?" Big Doug asked himself. His body started sinking into an abyss. Justin and Bebop didn't know what was happening to him.

Big Doug hollered for help as the ground continued to swallow him. He was trying to grab for anything, but he was too heavy to hold himself. His fingernails were digging into the wood planks that he had stepped on. The expression on his face was one of disbelief as the hole pulled him down the dark bottomless shaft. He screamed a blood-curdling scream as he lost his grip and went out of sight into the abyss. It seemed like a lifetime before they heard him hit bottom.

Bebop walked over to Justin. "Where did he go, Justin?" Justin slowly opened his eyes and saw that Big Doug was gone. He had vanished before his eyes.

Speaking very slowly, the words muttered from Justin's mouth. "I...don't know. I think to hell, Bebop. Yep, I think he went straight to hell." Justin said shaking and confused. "Bebop, we just saw a real live miracle. The devil got him."

"The devil got him?" Bebop said, bug eyed and scared to move an inch.

Standing in awe, the two were speechless. Then Justin remembered. He realized the old Fletcher well really existed!

Bebop looked at Justin and they leaned over to look in the well, but they couldn't see the bottom. Then they carefully backed up shaking and holding hands as big tears began streaming down Bebop's face. Reality had sat in on just how close they had come to death.

With their knees weakening, they sat on the ground underneath the bell until they heard two deputies' cars come barreling up. In the back seats were coon hunter Henry, Al and Herman. They had been caught trying to flag a car down on the highway. The car happened to be another deputy.

Two ambulances arrived, and the attendants ran for the woods with stretchers. Gene was leading them. Gene had made his way through the woods and found Mr. Cane, Able, Pete and Patrolman Campbell soon after all the gunfire started.

The call that Mrs. Lucy had made to the sheriff signaled the ambulances to come. She had told them she could hear gunfire and to come quickly because she knew somebody was going to wind up dead.

In a few minutes, the medics appeared again, bringing Mr. Cane and Able out of the woods. Both were alive. Both were covered with blankets. Pete was carrying one end of Mr. Cane's stretcher, and Gene was helping with Able's. Justin and Bebop darted for their dads.

By now, Lizzy and Mrs. Kate had made it around to the Fletcher site along with a group of neighbors who had heard the bell. Thanks again to Mrs. Lucy. Mrs. Kate held Mr. Cane's hand, kissing it as they wheeled him towards the ambulance, and Lizzy was doing the same with Able.

As they lifted Mr. Cane and Able in the ambulances, Mr. Cane looked over at Able and said, "You sure know your scripture... thanks."

Able smiled, "It pays off, don't it, Mr. Cane?"

Justin jumped in the back of the ambulance with his dad, and Bebop jumped in with Able.

As they pulled off, Justin said, "Dad, there's something I need to tell to you about the hay truck."

"Not now, son, that hay truck will be alright right where it is. We'll worry about that another day." Justin was thinking if his dad only knew where it really was. He knew even Abe won't be able to get him out of this one. Then he put his hand on his daddy's shoulder and rubbed his thumb back and forth over his dad's birthmark looking at it closely remembering what Able had said.

Inside Able's ambulance, Bebop had mustered the courage to tell his dad. "Pop, I's need to talk to you about the hay truck."

"Oh, Bebop, not now son," Able coughed closing his eyes fighting back the pain. Then he summons the strength to continue, "Yes, son, you sho' gonna have to help me drive that hay truck to feed them cows now. Sho' is." Able reached for Bebop's hand and squeezed it. "Don't you worry, son. You can do all the driving." With those words Bebop could feel the whipping coming already. He knew there was going to be a bad day ahead.

The ambulance sirens were blaring as they headed for the Delta hospital. The two deputy cars were in the lead. One was carrying prisoners, and the other carrying Patrolman Campbell.

As things settled, Lizzy walked over to Pete and said, "I had the strangest phone call before we left. Some woman named Naomi.

Pete, looked up and shook his head, "Lizzy you and Mrs. Kate wouldn't believe me even if I told you. Right now, let's go to the hospital and check on Cane and Able."

* * * * *

Stephen Cheek

INDEX

INDEX (continued)

Stephen Cheek